TOMAHAWK REVENGE

As the mounted Indian raced toward him with a lance, Nate instinctively raised the Hawken and went to fire, but in a flash of insight he realized the sound of the shot would carry to the Blackfeet and might lead them to his location. Instead of squeezing the trigger he darted to the right and dived for the ground. In his ears drummed the pounding hooves of the warrior's mount, and a second later something brushed his right shoulder and thudded into the earth at his side.

A heavy body slammed onto his back, stunning him, and as knees gouged him in the spine and strong hands looped around his chin, he dimly comprehended the man was trying to break his neck....

BLACK POWDER JUSTICE

Winona, who had moved over to the window, announced in Shoshone, "The snow is stopping, husband. I will go feed the horses more grass."

Nate didn't like the idea of her going out alone, but he decided against making an issue of it in front of Kennedy. "Okay, but be on your guard."

"Where is she going?" Kennedy inquired.

Nate faced him. "To feed our horses."

Kennedy, who had his eyes on the entrance, blurted, "Oh, my!"

Rising, Nate spun to see a tall man in a brown coat standing just outside the cabin with a rifle trained on his wife.

Other *Wilderness* Double Editions:
KING OF THE MOUNTAIN/
  LURE OF THE WILD
SAVAGE RENDEZVOUS/
  BLOOD FURY

WILDERNESS

TOMAHAWK REVENGE/
BLACK POWDER JUSTICE

DAVID THOMPSON

LEISURE BOOKS NEW YORK CITY

A LEISURE BOOK®
May 1997
Published by

Dorchester Publishing Co., Inc.
276 Fifth Avenue
New York, NY 10001

TOMAHAWK REVENGE

Dedicated to...
Judy, Joshua, and Shane.

Chapter One

The sharp retort carried for miles.

Those eagles and hawks soaring high above the nearby massive mountains heard it, as did the elk, deer, and buffaloes inhabiting the sea of verdant forest covering the slopes and valleys in all directions. Chipmunks ceased scampering, squirrels stopped chattering, and even bears paused to listen intently. All the song birds within hearing range fell silent. So alien a sound could only mean one thing. The most dangerous predator of all was abroad: man.

Borne by the stiff breeze, the sound echoed and reverberated, diminishing with the distance traveled, until finally another pair of ears heard it.

Up went a square chin as the listener cocked his head to one side. His broad shoulders straightened under his buckskins and his green eyes crinkled in concentration. A mane of black hair framed his rugged features. Tied at the back, suspended with the quill jutting upward, was an eagle feather. A powder horn and a bullet pouch were slanted across his muscular chest. Wedged under his brown leather belt were two flintlock pistols, one on either side of the buckle. A butcher knife in a beaded sheath dangled from his left hip. Held in his left hand was a Hawken rifle obtained months before in St. Louis.

The brawny nineteen-year-old lowered his head when the sound died away and beat a hasty path to the northeast, crossing a low ridge and descending to a wide stream meandering through a scenic valley. He turned upstream and scoured both banks until he spied another figure ahead. "Shakespeare!"

The object of the young man's attention glanced around. He also wore fringed buckskins, while on his head rested a brown beaver hat that scarcely contained his bushy gray hair. A beard and mustache of the same color gave his weathered face a grizzled aspect. Eyes the hue of a clear alpine lake regarded the younger man expectantly. A bullet pouch and powder horn adorned his person, as did a single flint-lock and a butcher knife. Held in the crook of his right arm was a rifle.

"Did you hear that shot?" asked the youthful mountaineer as he approached.

"I might be getting on in years, but my ears still work just fine," responded Shakespeare. "Is that what has you so excited?"

"It could be Indians."

"It could, Nate," Shakespeare admitted. "It could also be another trapper hunting game for his supper, like you're supposed to be doing."

"I saw an elk and was following its tracks when I heard the shot and figured I'd better get back to you."

"Afraid I can't handle myself?"

"Of course not. There isn't a white man alive who knows these Rocky Mountains better than you do. But we are in Ute country, and we both know they hate all trappers. If they cut our trail they'll go out of their way to hunt us down and kill us."

"Whoever did the shooting is miles from here. Even if it is a band of Utes, I doubt we have anything to worry about."

Nathaniel King gazed to the west at a snow-crowned peak and hoped his mentor was right. The last thing he wanted was another run-in with hostile Indians. Since venturing into the Great American Desert, as the land west of the Mississippi River was known back in the States, he'd tangled with the Kiowas, the Blackfeet, the Bloods, and others. Each time he'd been fortunate to escape with his scalp, and he wasn't eager to test his luck again.

Not that anyone would think to call him a coward. He'd proven his courage time and again, and in the process had acquired the Indian name of Grizzly Killer. Although he was tender in years, his exploits were already making the rounds of campfires in the Rockies and the Plains. If the stories continued to circulate, he reflected, one day he'd become as well known as Jim Bridger, Jed Smith, or his illustrious companion, the hardy mountain man called Shakespeare McNair.

"I've found plenty of beaver sign," that worthy man said. "We'll start setting out our traps tomorrow morning."

Nate squinted at the sun hovering an hour above the far horizon. "There's enough daylight left for us to set out a few before supper."

"Wisely and slow; they stumble that run fast."

"What?"

"I was quoting old William S.," Shakespeare disclosed.

"Oh," Nate said. He should have known. McNair's passion for the Bard of Avon was legendary among the trappers, and accounted for the mountain man's unusual sobriquet. Decades ago a fellow frontiersman had bestowed the title in jest, and it had stuck.

Now no one knew Shakespeare's true first name, and there wasn't a soul in the Rockies foolish enough to pry.

"Those who are tender in years are always in a great hurry to do this or that," Shakespeare commented. "The fire of youth hasn't yet turned to the ice of old age."

"Shakespeare again?"

"No, my own observation." Shakespeare turned to the southeast. "Let's go set up camp."

"Do you want me to go back after the elk?"

"No. It'll be miles away by now. We'll catch a few fish or shoot small game for our meal."

Nate followed dutifully. He still felt uneasy about the shot, but arguing with Shakespeare would be as productive as arguing with a rock. Surveying the landscape, he saw nothing out of the ordinary, and convinced himself he was letting his imagination get the better of him.

"Too bad we didn't bring Winona along," Shakespeare remarked. "That woman of yours sure can cook."

"You don't need to convince me," Nate said, and patted his stomach. His darling wife, a beautiful Shoshone, knew ways of preparing fabulous dishes from such common fare as buffalo, venison, and rabbit. Trained from childhood in the arts every Indian woman was required to know, Winona could sew expertly, do marvelous beadwork, ride a horse as competently as a warrior, and dress and tan buffalo and other hides. In his estimation, she was the perfect wife.

Once, he had considered marrying another. The thought unleashed a torrent of memories. Was it really only six months ago that he'd left New York City to join his Uncle Zeke on the frontier? At the time, forsaking his family, friends, and a promising job as an accountant had been an unnerving proposition, but nowhere near as hard to do as leaving behind the woman he'd loved, Adeline Van Buren.

But had he actually cared for Adeline in the depths of his heart, or only believed he did? Her beauty, wit, and wealth were enough to sway any man, and he'd fallen for her charms the first time they'd met. Few things in life had ever astonished him as much as when she reciprocated his affection. To tell the truth, he'd never felt worthy of her love. She was a goddess; he a lowly commoner. In recent days when he mused on their relationship, he consoled himself with the fact their marriage would never have worked out. She would have enslaved him to obey her every whim, and his resentment would eventually have boiled over and served to separate them.

Why did he bother thinking about Adeline anymore? Nate wondered. Now he had a wonderful wife, a woman he could treat as an equal, a woman he related to as a person instead of placing her on a pedestal, and he was blissfully, almost indecently happy. Why dwell on Adeline when he had Winona?

Was it because he felt so guilty about running off and leaving her without bothering to discuss his plans? Was it because he'd written letters promising to return to New York and wed her once he made his fortune?

His fortune!

Nate chuckled and shook his head at the foolish notions he'd once entertained. When Uncle Zeke had sent a letter promising to share "the greatest treasure in the world," Nate had naively assumed Zeke referred to gold or riches accumulated in the lucrative fur trade. He'd envisioned becoming as wealthy as Adeline's father and being able to support her in the extravagant manner to which she was accustomed. So off he'd gone to join Zeke.

Only later, as Ezekiel King lay dying, had Nate learned the nature of the treasure, a gift more precious than glittering ore or bags of money, the greatest gift a person could know: genuine freedom. The freedom to live as he pleased without having to account to others who considered themselves his betters. The freedom to let his conscience, his own inner light, be the sole determiner of his actions instead of the laws, rules, and regulations imposed by those who pompously sat in artificial positions of authority.

Freedom. Nate mentally savored the word, thinking of how much he had learned about the kind of life the Good Lord meant for people to live since coming to the wilderness. Ironic, wasn't it, that only by casting off the shackles of civilization and returning to the natural roots of humanity had he discovered the true meaning of existence?

"Is it a private joke or one you can share?"

The unexpected question brought Nate out of his reverie. "What?" he blurted out, and realized the frontiersman had stopped and was regarding him in obvious amusement. Nate likewise halted.

"What's so funny?"

"Oh. I was thinking about my past."

"Anyone under twenty hasn't had enough experience to have a past," Shakespeare said, moving on. "All they have are a few dozen memories."

"You're in a critical mood today," Nate remarked, trailing the older man.

"I get this way when I have the itch."

"You were bitten by a mosquito?"

"No," Shakespeare laughed. "I mean the itch to travel, to go off roaming by myself."

Shocked by the revelation, Nate nearly tripped over his own feet. "You plan to leave?"

"I've been thinking about it."

"What's your rush?"

"Rush? Here it is the first week in September already. We've been together pretty near two months. I wouldn't want to wear out my welcome."

"Nonsense. You're welcome to stay with us as long as you want," Nate said calmly, although secretly the prospect of his friend leaving filled him with dread. He'd grown to rely on the frontiersman's seasoned wisdom and flawless knowledge of the wildlife and people inhabiting the savage realm stretching between the Mississippi and the Pacific Ocean.

"I'd like to go see if my own cabin is still standing," Shakespeare mentioned.

"We can go together."

"You don't understand, Nate. Except for the rendezvous and an occasional trip to St. Louis, I'm not a great one for human company. Oh, I'll join up with a few friends from time to time to trap or hunt or whatever, but basically I like to be by my lonesome. Why do you think I was one of the very first white men to settle in the Rockies?"

Nate said nothing.

"Because I like my privacy. Out here a man can live without feeling crowded. I can walk for days without encountering another living soul, which certainly isn't the case back East. Too much of anything can be harmful, and that holds true for folks as well as food."

"Winona and I enjoy your company," Nate said gloomily.

"And I've liked staying with the two of you. I'm right fond of you both. But it's almost time for me to pull up stakes and get on with my life."

"We'll miss you."

"I haven't left yet," Shakespeare said, and smiled. "First I'll keep my promise to teach you all about trapping beaver, then I'll be on my way."

Nate stared out over the well-nigh limitless expanse of forest and mountains. "I don't know if we're ready to fend for ourselves yet."

"You are."

"How do you know?"

"Because I know both of you so well. Winona is a Shoshone; she can live off the land better than any white woman and most white men. You were a greenhorn when you first came out here with your uncle, but you've learned a lot since. I believe you have the makings of a man who will be remembered for years to come, just like Joe Walker."

"I'll never be as good as Walker," Nate responded, although he appreciated the compliment. Joseph Reddeford Walker, like Bridger, Smith, and McNair, was widely considered to be one of the best mountain men. Many rated him as *the* ablest mountaineer.

"Don't sell yourself short. No man can predict his destiny. We never know from one minute to another what the next moment will bring, especially out here where a man's life is at the mercy of circumstances he can't control."

They hiked onward in contemplative quiet until they arrived at a clearing bordered on the west by a bubbling spring and on the south by a large log. Tied to that log were their four horses.

"Since we'll be working along the stream anyway, why didn't we make camp there instead of a quarter of a mile away?" Nate absently inquired as he walked to his mare.

"Because waterways are a lot like roads. Everyone sticks near water when they're traveling in the wild. Indians and whites alike prefer to travel along the banks of streams and rivers where the going is easier and they can easily slake their thirst. If we camped near the stream we'd increase the likelihood of being discovered by Utes or Blackfeet," Shakespeare said, and gestured at the spring. "We're safer at this hideaway. I doubt whether even any Indians know about it, yet we're within easy walking distance of the stream. We can conduct our trapping operations in secrecy and not have to worry too much about being attacked."

Nate reached the mare and patted her neck. "Too much?"

"There's always that one in a million chance of Indians finding us, so don't let your guard down for an instant."

"I won't," Nate promised, propping his rifle between his legs while thinking of their arrival at the clearing an hour ago. They had immediately proceeded to the stream to check for beaver, not even bothering to remove their saddles. Shakespeare had once trapped the general area, five years ago, and knew the lay of the land well. Isolated and abundant with wildlife, the spot seemed ideal for the frontiersman to instruct Nate in the techniques of trapping. Nate began to unfasten the cinch.

"The reason so many trappers get killed is through sheer carelessness," Shakespeare went on in a talkative vein. "They forget to keep an eye on their surroundings and don't discover there are Indians about until it's too late. Study the ways of Nature. Animals are always wary, and we should be the same. You'll never see a squirrel lay down on the ground to take a nap since the critter knows it wouldn't last five minutes. Deer don't sleep out in the open, birds spend more time in trees than they do on the ground, and big fish stay in the deeper pools for the same reason. They're naturally wary."

Nate finished undoing the cinch and glanced at his grizzled teacher. "Don't fret about me. I have no intention of making Winona a widow so soon after we were married.''

Shakespeare grinned, and had opened his mouth to reply when a deep growl rumbled from the surrounding forest.

Chapter Two

In a flash Nate pressed the Hawken to his shoulder and pivoted, spying the source of the growl at the edge of the trees to the north. He'd expected to see one of the fierce lords of the mountains, a beast capable of crushing a man's skull with a single swipe of its mighty paw, a mighty grizzly. Instead, to his relief, he saw a large black bear. The black variety seldom bothered humans; more often than not they fled at the sight of a trapper. He started to lower the rifle.

Shakespeare had spun at the sound, and now stood with his rifle held at waist height, staring at the bear.

"For a second there I thought we were in trouble," Nate commented, wondering why the bear didn't flee. The brute looked from one to the other as if perplexed. "Get out of here!" he shouted to drive it off.

The big black charged, dirt flying from under its claws, gaining speed with every stride, its powerful muscles rippling under its inky fur, its teeth exposed as it snarled.

Shocked, Nate instinctively raised the Hawken and fired. He heard the frontiersman's rifle discharge a heartbeat later, and the black bear reacted as if struck in the head with a heavy club. The beast sagged in midstride, its chin dropping to its chest, and collapsed, sliding a yard before lying motionless on the grass within six feet of Shakespeare.

"You won't need to go hunting for our supper after all."

Blood oozed from a pair of holes in the bear's head. Nate approached the beast cautiously in case a spark of life remained, his right hand resting on a flintlock. "Why did it come after us? I thought black bears usually leave people alone."

"Usually, but not always. This proves my point about staying alert. And never, ever, take anything for granted."

"You've convinced me," Nate said, tentatively prodding the bear with his left toe. Blood smeared onto the tip of his moccasin. He set to work reloading the Hawken.

"Tell you what. If you'll tend to the horses, I'll skin the bear and carve us a couple of juicy steaks. What do you say?"

"Sounds fair to me," Nate said, and finished reloading. He was amazed at how the frontiersman took every incident in stride. No matter how unexpected, or how violent, Shakespeare seldom became rattled. The man's composure was superb, and Nate wished he could be the same way.

For the next half hour few words were spoken as each man attended to his chores. Nate unsaddled the mare and Shakespeare's white horse, then removed the packs from their pack animals. He led all four to the spring to drink, and hobbled them so they could graze without straying off. One of the first sayings Nate learned after arriving in the mountains was the basic creed of horse tending: "It's better to count ribs than tracks." Which meant it was wiser to tie a horse at night and have the animal be hungry in the morning than let it wander off to gorge itself and be taken by an Indian. Many tribes were notorious horses stealers.

Next Nate went about gathering wood for the fire, carrying armloads of broken branches to the center of the clearing and forming convenient piles for later use. He got the blaze going, arranged his blanket near the fire so it would be warm when he retired, and went to help his companion.

Shakespeare was kneeling next to the carcass, artfully employing his twelve-inch butcher knife in removing the second choice cut of meat. "About done," he said.

Twilight had descended. The last, lingering rays of sunlights streaked the western sky. All around were birds singing their farewell chorus to the expiring day. Off in the distance a coyote howled.

Nate breathed deeply and smiled. Moments like this filled him with a joy at being alive, a joy he'd never experienced back in New York City.

"After we eat we'll cut up the rest of this bear and hang the meat to dry," Shakespeare said. "We don't want it lying around overnight. Wolves and such might get the notion to pay us a visit."

"Wolves don't bother humans very often."

"There you go again. What did I just tell you about taking things for granted? True, wolves ordinarily leave us alone. But if you run into a starving pack in the middle of winter, you'll find they're just like any other animal. They'll eat whatever they can catch."

"Have you ever given any thought to writing down all you've learned over the years?"

The frontiersman laughed. "Whatever for?"

"The people in the States have a great interest in anything written about the frontier. A factual book about your experiences would sell extremely well and make you a lot of money."

"I don't need a lot of money, and I'm not about to let others exploit my life to make their own easier."

"I don't understand."

Shakespeare looked up. "Everything I know I've learned the hard way. I didn't get these gray hairs by taking it easy and living in the lap of luxury. The way I see it, life is intended to be an education. Year by year we learn certain lessons and add to our knowledge, or else we don't learn a blessed thing and blunder on making the same mistakes over and over again. If I was to put down all I've learned on paper, I'd be depriving a lot of folks of the opportunity to learn life for themselves."

"I never thought of it that way," Nate said.

Standing, Shakespeare extended a dripping slab of meat. "I'm hungry. How about you?"

They walked to the fire and the frontiersman prepared their steaks. He prided himself on his cooking ability, and hovered over the simmering slabs until they were roasted to perfection.

Nate's mouth was watering by the time his steak was placed on the end of a sharpened stick and handed over. He used his knife both to cut off succulent strips and to cram the meat in his mouth. Grease dribbled over his lower lip and down his chin, but he didn't care. He savored every bite, relishing the tangy taste and the warm sensation in his stomach. The finest steak in New York couldn't begin to compare to a slice of buffalo, bear, or deer meat prepared over an open fire high in the Rocky Mountains. There was an indescribable quality about such crude fare that satisfied the appetite like no other food.

"Tomorrow we begin educating you on the ways of the beaver," Shakespeare said between chomps.

"I'm looking forward to it," Nate said. "Was my Uncle Zeke a good trapper?"

"Your uncle was talented in everything he tried. The man had a knack, and I've seen evidence of the same trait in you."

Nate started to take another bite, then paused. "I just realized I've never written my dad to tell him Zeke died. He'd want to know."

"Were they close?"

"When they were younger. But they drifted apart after Zeke decided to leave for the frontier. My dad could never understand why Zeke wanted to go."

"How did he feel about you leaving?"

"I imagine he felt the same way."

Shakespeare lowered his steak. "Didn't you talk it over with him before you left?"

"I wrote him a letter."

"Were you afraid he'd try to stop you?"

"Yes," Nate confessed. "None of my family would have accepted the idea. They'd have badgered me mercilessly until I changed my mind. As it is, they probably despise me now."

"Never underestimate the love of your kin."

"I know my family better than you do. Why, my father forbade us from ever mentioning Zeke's name in the house. His own brother!"

"Pride is a bitter pill to swallow."

"What do you mean?"

"Your father probably knows he made a mistake and he's too proud to admit it. He won't let anyone talk about Zeke because he doesn't want to be reminded of . . ." Shakespeare paused, cocking his head.

"What is it?"

"Listen."

Nate did, but heard only the sounds of wildlife and the whisper of the breeze.

"Do you hear it?"

"Hear what?"

"The horse."

Again Nate strained his ears, and this time he detected the faint drumming of pounding hooves. He stood, swiveling in the direction of the sound, to the southwest, and gazed into the gloomy woods.

"Whoever it is must be a fool or bent on committing suicide," Shakespeare said, standing. "It's too dark to be riding a horse at a full gallop in the forest."

"I've done it," Nate commented, recalling his recent encounter with a Ute war party. He suddenly realized he was still holding the steak, and placed the meat on the grass so he could grab his rifle.

The pounding became louder and louder, and it was obvious the rider would pass very close to their camp.

"Don't shoot until we see who it is."

"I won't," Nate said. He heard the crack of a limb and the crunching of underbrush, and leaned forward to peer intently into the darkness. At the limit of his vision he perceived movement and distinguished the outline of a horse and rider heading eastward.

In a matter of seconds the newcomer was 20 yards south of the camp and still galloping recklessly when the man happened to glance to his left and spied the fire. His head snapped up and he hauled on the reins.

"It's a white man," Shakespeare said.

How could he tell? Nate wondered. *He* couldn't perceive any of the rider's features beyond noting the man wore buckskins.

"Hello!" the newcomer cried, and rode toward them. "Please don't fire. I mean you no harm."

Nate kept the Hawken handy just in case. He glanced at Shakespeare, who had also taken the precaution of grabbing his rifle, and placed his thumb on the hammer.

"Come closer, stranger," the frontiersman announced.

"Thank you." The man came to the edge of the clearing and stopped. He wore the typical attire of a mountaineer: buckskins, moccasins, and a wool cap. The inevitable bullet pouch and powder horn crisscrossed his chest. A shock of blond hair rimmed a rugged face dominated by blue eyes. "I didn't think there was another trapper within a hundred miles of here," he remarked happily.

"Do you have a name?" Shakespeare asked.

"Thaddeus Baxter at your service, sir. And who might you be?"

"Shakespeare McNair, and this here is Nate King," the frontiersman said with a nod of his head.

Baxter focused on Nate. "Aren't you the one they call Grizzly Killer? The same one who killed the rogue Canadian known as the Giant during the rendezvous?"

"I am."

"I thought I recognized the two of you," Baxter said, grinning. "The Good Lord has smiled on me."

"How is it you know us?" Shakespeare asked.

"I was at the rendezvous. Both of you were pointed out to me by an acquaintance, but we were never introduced."

"Why don't you climb on down? You're welcome to share our supper if you're hungry," Shakespeare said.

"Thank you," Baxter replied, riding closer before he dismounted and stepped to the fire. "I couldn't eat a bite right now, not after what I've been through."

"Mind telling us why you were riding your horse into the ground?"

"Blackfeet," Baxter said.

"This far south?"

"I couldn't believe it myself," Baxter stated. "I imagine it's a war party down here to raid the Utes."

"What happened?" Nate prompted.

"My own camp is about four miles from here. An hour or so before sunset I was skinning a couple of beaver I'd caught, whistling to myself without a care in the world, when my pack animal whinnied and I looked up to find a dozen or more Blackfeet creeping toward me."

"That was your shot we heard earlier," Shakespeare deduced.

"Must have been. I grabbed my rifle and fired once, killing one of the bastards, but then the rest swarmed on me and it was all I could do to fight them off using my rifle like a club," Baxter replied. "I think they were trying to take me alive. Otherwise I'd be dead right now."

"But you got away," the frontiersman said.

"Barely. My rifle was torn from my hands just as I broke loose and ran into the forest. They chased me, but I hid, then circled back to my camp. There was one warrior guarding my horses, so I knocked him on the head and cut out. Unfortunately, several others showed up and I had to leave without my pack animal and all my supplies."

"And here you are," Nate stated.

Baxter laughed lightly. "By pure chance. I might have kept going all the way to St. Louis if I hadn't spotted your camp. Without traps and a rifle, there's no sense in trapping beaver."

"We can go after your belongings in the morning," Shakespeare offered.

"And get youselves killed on my account? No, sir.

There's too many of them."

Nate gazed at the foreboding forest. "Were they after you?"

"No. They fired a few arrows but didn't give chase."

"Strange," Shakespeare said. "Blackfeet are the most persistent devils I know."

"I was surprised too," Baxter said. "Even on foot they'll go after a mounted man."

"They didn't have any horses?" Nate asked.

"Just my pack animal."

Shakespeare turned to his protégé. "Quite often the Blackfeet send out war parties on foot. They believe they can move quieter in enemy territory. I've also heard tell the warriors are expected to steal the mounts they need to ride back to their village."

"And they are some of the best horse thieves around," Baxter added.

Again Nate surveyed the woods. "What if they sent a warrior after you on your pack animal?"

"He would never catch me. My pack animal is the slowest critter this side of the Divide." Baxter chuckled. "Besides, no one in their right mind would ride as fast as I did."

"Then we should be safe here," Nate concluded.

"I didn't lead the Blackfeet to you, if that's what you're thinking," Baxter said.

Shakespeare took his seat and picked up his bear steak. "You're welcome to spend the night with us, Thaddeus."

"I'd be in your debt."

"Nonsense. It's the least we can do for a fellow trapper. There are few enough of us living in the wilderness as it is. We must help each other out when the need arises or we're no better than the animals we contend with every day."

Baxter smiled gratefully. "Thank you."

Retrieving his steak, Nate sat down and took a bite of the warm meat. While he shared Shakespeare's sentiments on helping someone in need, he entertained grave reservations about staying to trap the stream. The Blackfeet were too close for comfort, but he wasn't about to question Shakespeare's judgment. He'd see their labors through to the end, and just pray the end wasn't his own.

Chapter Three

Bright morning sunshine and invigorating, crisp mountain air served to dispel Nate's doubts of the night before. He was eager to learn the life of a free trapper, and although a slight uneasiness gnawed at the back of his mind, he was the first one done eating breakfast and raring to go. "Ready when you are," he announced after consuming several strips of dried buffalo meat.

"Hold your horses," Shakespeare said with a grin. "I'll be done in a minute." He looked at their new acquaintance, who was chewing hungrily on a piece of raw bear meat. "You can cook as much as you like."

"This is fine," Baxter said. "I usually eat light in the morning."

Shakespeare stared at the makeshift rack they'd constructed before retiring, using stout branches and rope, and noted with satisfaction the thin slices of flesh aligned side by side, well out of the reach of most predators. "By this afternoon we'll have more jerked meat than we can possibly use. If you're still keen on going, take whatever you need."

"I haven't quite made up my mind about leaving."

Nate placed his rifle stock on the ground and idly leaned on the barrel, reviewing what they'd learned of Baxter's past while sitting around the fire and conversing until after midnight.

Thaddeus Baxter hailed from Ohio. Thirty-one years old, he had a wife and two children eagerly awaiting his return. Eighteen months ago he'd left his home to travel beyond the mighty Mississippi, his head filled with notions of making it rich in the fur trade. There were many tales of those who had, most prominent of them all being John Jacob Astor.

Astor emmigrated to America from Germany at the age of twenty, went into the fur business shortly thereafter, had the audacity born of firm conviction to start his own company, and wound up earning the newspaper-bestowed title of "the richest man in the country." Many a young man, on reading of Astor's phenomenal success, bid his loved ones a hopefully temporary good-bye and headed for the prime beaver grounds in the Rocky Mountains. For every one hundred who went, perhaps a dozen were lucky enough to live to see the States again, and of that dozen none acquired great wealth.

Nate felt sympathy for the Ohioan, based on his own former dream of becoming incredibly rich. The thought of Baxter's family, though, troubled him. What would happen to them if the man died? Baxter had sent back letters with men heading homeward, but letters were no substitute for the loving presence of a husband and a father. And eighteen months was a long separation. In Nate's estimation, leaving a wife and children was far worse than leaving parents and siblings.

"I have a proposal to make," Baxter said.

"Let's hear it," Shakespeare responded.

"After a year and a half of one mishap after

another, I'm beginning to think I made a mistake. My first season trapping I collected over two hundred pelts—"

"Not bad," Shakespeare said, interrupting.

"And lost them all when I tried to cross a flooded river and the canoe capsized," Baxter went on. "My second season I fared better and took in three hundred and fifty pelts. Half the money I sent to my family, and the rest I used to outfit myself and two good men with enough traps and supplies to guarantee success." He frowned. "We'd taken over eight hundred pelts when we were attacked by Bloods. My friends were killed and I barely escaped with my life."

Nate listened intently. He'd heard similar stories of woe before. The harsh economic realities of trapping had ruined many a trapper.

For an initial investment of several hundred dollars, including the expenses of a mount, rifle, ammunition, pistols, a knife and hatchet, clothing, and provisions, a trapper stood to make a hefty profit. There were two trapping seasons each year in which the trapper could ply his trade, the spring and fall seasons. The first began when winter's ice started to break up and went on until early summer, when the quality of beaver fur declined due to the heat. The hotter it became, the thinner the fur. Then came the second season in late August or early September, lasting until the ponds and streams iced over. During each season a skilled trapper could accumulate hundreds of pelts. By rendezvous time, this translated into an average of two thousand dollars, a huge sum by any standard. After several years, a prudent trapper could save quite a hoard.

Or so it seemed on paper to men back East who had no idea of the realities of the trapping trade. They didn't know, for instance, that the Rocky Mountain Fur Company enjoyed a virtual monopoly of the trading activities in the Rockies. The Company paid two to four dollars for beaver pelts at the rendezvous, then resold them for eight dollars in St. Louis. And since the rendezvous was the only market for the trappers' furs, there was nothing that could be done to change the situation.

To make matters worse, the suppliers at the rendezvous were invariably in cahoots with the Fur Company. They overpriced their goods by as much as 2000 percent, and the trappers were forced to buy such inflated supplies or go without. In effect, the heads of the company and the suppliers grew rich at the trappers' expense.

Then why am I here? Nate asked himself. Undoubtedly because even with all the financial drawbacks and the hardships of living off the land, the life of a mountaineer offered a consolation few other ways of living could: genuine freedom. He could do as he pleased when he pleased. No one was standing over his shoulder, goading him to work harder or faster. No one could impose on him in any respect. He was the master of his own destiny, and he loved it.

"I'm tired of wasting my time and energy," Baxter was saying. "And I've been away from my family so long that my own children might not recognize me." He paused. "I was hoping you'd see fit to let me trap with you for a month. Then I'll take my fair share of the pelts and head for St. Louis. I should be able to find a buyer there who will offer a bit more than the Rocky Mountain Fur Company representatives. If I'm lucky, I'll head for Ohio with four or five hundred dollars in my pocket. What do you say?"

Shakespeare pursed his lips and stroked his beard, then looked at Nate. "What do you think?"

"I don't mind if you don't."

Baxter anxiously leaned toward the fontiersman. "Please, McNair. Your kindness would mean so much to me. I don't want to go home with empty pockets. I don't want to let my loved ones down entirely." He sighed. "I feel as if I'm a monumental failure, and this is my chance to redeem myself."

"No man is a failure if he's still breathing," Shakespeare said solemnly.

"Will you let me stay?"

"Nate has already said he has no objections, and it's his decision that counts. I'm here to teach him how to trap, nothing more. I have no intention of trapping for myself, and there's more than enough beaver hereabouts to satisfy the needs of two men."

"Then I can stay?" Baxter inquired eagerly.

"So long as you uphold your end of the work."

Baxter stood, stepped over to the frontiersman, and vigorously pumped Shakespeare's right hand. "I can never thank you enough for your Christian generosity."

"Actually, I have an ulterior motive."

"You do?"

"Yes. You're an experienced trapper, so you can help me teach Nate the tricks of the trade. With both of us instructing him, he'll learn that much quicker and I can leave that much sooner."

Nate pretended to be interested in a hawk circling to the north so neither of them would see his crest-fallen expression. Shakespeare was inordinately excited about departing. After all they had been through, nearly losing their lives time and again, after traveling so many miles together and growing so close, he was upset that Shakespeare wanted to abruptly sever their ties.

"Where are you going?" Baxter asked.

"Wherever the wind takes me."

"Will you ever visit Ohio?"

A spontaneous laugh burst from the mountain man's lips. "Never. I've had my full of civilization. The farthest east I'll ever go is St. Louis. Why do you ask?"

"I'd like to repay you some day for your kindness."

"You can repay me by watching your hair on the way east. A lone white man is at the mercy of Fate out here."

Baxter squared his shoulders. "I'll trust in the Lord to see me safely through."

For a moment Shakespeare sat perfectly still. He stared off into the distance, then pried a fingernail between two teeth to remove a wad of food. "I take it you're a Christian?"

"A Presbyterian," Baxter stated proudly.

"Is that a fact?" Shakespeare responded. "Most trappers are an irreligious lot. In all my years of living in the mountains, I've only known two Christians, and they are as different as night and day."

"Who might they be?"

"One is Jed Smith. He's the best trapper alive and the most consistent Christian I've ever met. Of course, he's also a bit inflexible at times. Always believes he knows the best way to do things and won't listen to anyone else. But he'll go out of his way to help a person in trouble."

"And who is the other man?"

"Old Bill Williams. He totes a bible everywhere he goes and claims the Lord speaks to him personally every night. Lives by himself way back in the Rockies and likes it that way. Can't stand the company of others and wouldn't go out of his way to save a dying baby."

"Aren't you being unfair?"

"No. I know Williams as well as anyone. And I suspect the rumors about him are true."

"What rumors?"

"Old Bill is partial to eating human flesh."

Baxter grimaced. "Not another one."

"You've heard about Crazy George?"

"He was the talk of the rendezvous. I understand

one of you killed him."

"I did."

"Wasn't he a friend of yours?"

"One of the best I ever had."

Nate glanced at Shakespeare, memories of that terrible night etched indelibly in his mind. Crazy George had joined a band of cutthroats and taken to murdering trappers while they slept to steal their money. Eventually Shakespeare had confronted the maniac and been forced to kill him. "We should head on out," Nate suggested.

"I agree," Shakespeare declared, rising abruptly. "Grab your equipment and let's go find us some beaver."

Five minutes later they were hiking toward the stream. Nate and Baxter carried sacks containing six traps apiece and wooden boxes containing the bait they would need. Once at the water they marched upstream until they discovered a beaver dam, where they halted on the west bank.

"Now pay close attention," Shakespeare directed Nate. "If you hope to make a living as a free trapper, this is how you will do it." He took Nate's sack and removed one of the Newhouse traps, so named for the man who manufactured them in New York. "Find us a nice, long stick."

Eagerly Nate complied, his sorrow at soon being left to fend for himself replaced by unrestrained zeal of learning the intricate details of his desired craft. He used his knife to chop off a branch three feet long. "Will this do?" he asked as he returned.

"It will do nicely. Did you bring your hatchet?"

Nate's mouth dropped at his oversight. "No. I forgot."

"You can use mine," Baxter said, and produced one from behind his back.

"First rule," Shakespeare said. "Always take all the equipment you will need."

"I'll remember next time," Nate promised.

"Okay. Now follow me." The frontiersman waded slowly into the water.

Tentatively placing his left foot in, Nate shivered when the ice-cold water immediately soaked his moccasins and enveloped his lower leg in its frigid grip.

Shakespeare noticed and chuckled. "If you can't tolerate a little cold, this is no business for you. The water in these mountain streams is never warm, not even in the summer, because most of it is snow runoff."

"I'm fine," Nate said.

"Good. Now let's attend to business." Shakespeare extended the trap. "Haven't you forgotten something?"

"No," Nate replied uncertainly.

"Second rule. Always cock your trap before you enter the water."

Only then did Nate realize the trap wasn't set. "Why didn't you have me do it sooner?"

"We learn best when we learn from our mistakes. This way you'll remember the next time," Shakespeare said, and moved closer to the bank. "Baxter, would you do the honors?"

"Gladly." The Ohioan took the Newhouse, placed it on the ground, and proceeded to stand on the leaf springs so the jaws would fall flat. He carefully adjusted the trigger and the disk until the proper tension existed, then quickly lifted first one foot, then the other. Lifting the trap by the edge of a leaf spring, he gave it to the frontiersman.

"Rule number three. Never stick your fingers or thumbs between the jaws unless you no longer have any use for them."

"I knew a man who once lost two fingers in a trap," Baxter mentioned.

"Now comes the hard part," Shakespeare said,

studying the water near the bank. He moved a few feet and pointed at a flat spot six inches below the surface. "You want to set the trap in place without disturbing the trigger. It's important that the surface be no higher than a hand width above the disk."

"Why?" Nate inquired.

"Because beavers aren't storks. They have short, stubby legs, and the trap works best if they step right on the disk. If you place it lower, they'll probably swim right over it. Here. You put it down."

Nate complied, doing so gingerly, wary of the trap accidentally snapping shut. "Now what?"

"Take the stick and insert it through the loop at the end of the chain, then pound it into the stream bed."

Again Nate obeyed, but as he went to swing the hatchet an admonition stopped him.

"Not yet. Pull the chain as far as it will go. The purpose is to drown the beaver before it can gnaw off its foot."

"They do that?"

"Every now and then. Even beaver like to live."

The disclosure bothered Nate. He envisioned a helpless beaver caught in his trap, its lungs on fire, furiously chewing on its own leg to gain freedom.

"What are you waiting for?"

"Nothing," Nate said, and did as he'd been told. Straightening, he saw the frontiersman clambering onto the bank and walked toward him. "What's next?"

"Climb on out."

Happy to quit the water, Nate joined his companions. He leaned down and wrung water from his pants.

Shakespeare pointed at the spot where Nate had deposited the rifle and bait box. "Grab your box, then get a twig six to eight inches long. Make certain the twig has leaves on one end."

Once again Nate obeyed. The small wooden box contained the musky secretion taken from several dead beavers. He'd purchased it at the rendezvous from an elderly trapper.

"Now dip the leaves in the medicine," Shakespeare said.

Nate nodded. "Medicine" was the word trappers used to describe the musk because it possessed medicinal properties. A salve made of beaver oil and castoreum, the gummy, yellow musk, worked wonders on open wounds, easing the pain and drawing out the swelling. Nate had never used the salve himself, but he'd heard many mountaineers swear by its curative properties. He opened the box and dabbed the leaves in the gum.

"That's enough. Now stick the bottom of the twig in the bank so that the leaves hang about six inches above the trap."

Dropping to one knee, Nate bent over and inserted the twig into the soft earth until he was satisfied the twig would hold fast. He stood and waited further instructions.

"Congratulations," Shakespeare said with a grin. "You've set your first beaver trap. Any beaver coming within two or three hundred yards of the medicine will smell the odor and swim over to emit some of its own musk on the spot. When the critter goes to climb out, its leg will get caught in the trap. Then it's only a matter of time before the animal drowns."

"Or chews its leg off," Nate said distastefully.

The corners of the frontiersman's eyes crinkled. "If you check your traps twice a day, as you should, any beavers you catch won't have time to gnaw off their legs. Most trappers are too lazy for their own good and only check their traps at sunup, so it's not surprising they lose a goodly number of animals."

"I'll check mine twice a day," Nate promised. The

last thing he wanted was to inflict needless suffering on poor animals whose only offense against man
was the fact they were covered with prime fur.

Shakespeare rubbed his hands together. "Let's set
up the rest of these traps. We can be done by noon
and head back to camp for some more of that bear
meat."

"Sounds good to me," Baxter said.

Along the stream they went, choosing spots to
place traps with deliberate care, traveling several
miles to the north before the last of the Newhouses
waited under the water for an unsuspecting beaver.

Nate enjoyed laying the traps. He became
accustomed to the cold water, at least to the point
that the temperature didn't bother him. He saw many
big fish swimming unconcernedly past as he labored,
and resolved to try his hand at catching several for
supper. Birds chirped in the deciduous trees and the
pines, and small creatures such as squirrels, rabbits,
and chipmunks were everywhere. The vibrant pulse
of Nature stirred his soul, and he savored the
experience of being alive.

When they turned their steps toward their camp,
Baxter gave Nate a friendly clap on the back.
"Thanks again for letting me stay. I can tell this
valley is prime beaver territory, and I should take
back enough furs to reap a tidy profit."

"I'm glad I could help."

They retraced their route eagerly, spurred by
healthy appetites, and conversed about the trapping
trade in general. Engrossed in their discussion, none
of them paid much attention to their surroundings
until they were almost to the edge of the clearing.

Nate was the first to look up and discover their
meat being pilfered from the rack, and his breath
caught in his throat at sight of the culprit.

For there, its wicked mouth crammed with strips
of flesh, stood a monster grizzly.

Chapter Four

If no one had uttered a sound, the bear might have kept on eating and peaceably departed after consuming its full. But such wasn't to be the case.

"A grizzly!" Baxter blurted out.

At the sound of a human voice the monster growled and spun toward them, twelve hundred pounds of muscle and sinew poised to hurtle forward. A yellowish-brown coat distinguished by individual white-tipped hairs gave the giant its grizzled aspect. Bulging above the beast's massive shoulders was the breed's distinctive hump. Brutish, concave features that could inspire terror in whites and Indians alike were twisted in primal hatred.

"Don't say another word," Shakespeare whispered. "Stand perfectly still and maybe it won't attack. They have pitiful eyesight and the wind is blowing in our faces."

Nate gripped his Hawken until his knuckles turned white. By some strange quirk of Fate, he seemed to have a knack for encountering grizzlies. Twice since crossing the Mississippi he'd been attacked by the terrible beasts, and twice he'd barely escaped with his life.

The grizzly raised its head and sniffed loudly, then took a lumbering stride forward.

"Don't move," Shakespeare reiterated.

The temptation to flee was hard to resist. Nate knew a grizzly could lope as rapidly as a horse when the need arose, and he naturally wanted to get as far from the monster as swiftly as he could. With unblinking eyes he watched the giant, waiting for the animal to make up its mind whether to attack or not. He didn't have long to wait.

A tremendous, rumbling challenge erupted from the grizzly's throat, and suddenly it charged.

"Scatter!" Shakespeare shouted, and ran to the left.

Nate needed no urging. He sprinted to the right, weaving among the trees, while looking over his shoulder to ascertain the fate of his fellows. Shakespeare covered the ground at a remarkably spry pace, but Baxter wasn't faring so well.

The Ohioan traveled ten yards to the east, then realized the bear was coming after him. Panicked, he slanted toward an oak tree and grasped desperately at a low-hanging limb.

Maintaining a consistent, moderate speed, not bothering to go all out, the bear closed on the blond trapper.

Nate slowed, staring at the tableau. If Baxter reached the sanctuary of the higher branches, the bear would never be able to get him. Adult grizzlies, due to their great weight, were incapable of climbing trees. And since the brute was not running as fast as it could, he gathered it merely meant to drive them from the meat and wasn't motivated by bestial bloodlust. Once the trapper was in the clear, the bear would probably return to the rack. It was comforting to know that not all encounters with grizzlies had to end in violence.

Thaddeux Baxter unexpectedly slipped. He had managed to climb onto the bottom limb, and was trying to pull himself up onto a higher one when his left hand gave way, and the next moment he fell onto the ground on his back. There was no time to try again.

The grizzly had only 20 feet to cover. Whether it originally intended to slay them or not, such easy prey aroused all of its predatory instincts and it snarled to freeze its prey in place.

Instantly Nate whirled and dashed to Baxter's aid. The man didn't stand a prayer without help. He saw Shakespeare doing the same, and shouted to draw the grizzly's attention. "Bear! Try me, you flea-ridden brute!"

Halting, the grizzly wheeled in the direction of the shout and snorted.

Baxter was clawing at his pistol.

Whipping the rifle to his shoulder, Nate hoped the bear would flee before he squeezed the trigger. Single shots seldom dispatched a grizzly; the ball only served to drive them into an insane rage. Once he fired, the battle would be joined.

The bear took a few steps toward the onrushing human, then stopped as if confused.

"Run, damn you!" Nate yelled, and saw Baxter level the flintlock.

A heartbeat later the pistol discharged.

Struck near the ear, the grizzly lurched to the left, shaking its enormous head vigorously. It recovered in seconds, spun, and bore down on the trapper.

Baxter, still on his back, scrambled on his elbows in a frantic effort to get behind the trunk.

Nate had to shoot on the run. The bear was almost upon the trapper when Nate took a hasty bead on its left eye, cocked the hammer, and squeezed the trigger. The booming of the rifle seemed to have no effect on the carnivore except to provide it with a new outlet for its fury.

Spinning with astonishing agility, the grizzly opened its mouth wide and made straight for the presumptuous human.

Reloading or running was out of the question. Nate perceived the bear would be on him before he could do either, so he let the rifle fall and drew both pistols. Extending both arms, he pointed both barrels at the creature's head, waited until 15 feet separated them, and fired both guns.

The twin balls smacked into the grizzly's forehead and jerked the huge head backwards. Its front legs buckled and it sprawled forward, sliding several feet and stopping.

Elated, Nate believed he'd slain the brute, until it abruptly heaved erect and stood swaying from side to side, blood pouring from a wound over its right eye. He backpedaled, debating whether to try to reload or seek the safety of a tree.

Growling horribly, the grizzly shuffled in for the kill.

Nate bumped into a trunk, frantically stuck both pistols under his belt, and leaped for a limb overhead.

The bear bounded the final ten feet.

His body tingling in anticipation of being torn to shreds, Nate's hands closed on the limb and he wrenched his body upward in a tight arc, his legs sailing over a higher branch at the apex of his swing. Bending his knees, he looped his calves over the branch and snapped his body upward. An intense stinging sensation lanced across his left shoulder blade, and then he was perched on the limb, momentarily safe. A glance below showed him the grizzly in the act of standing. He spied another limb above him and to his left, and he vaulted from his perch. Something tugged at his right moccasin, throwing him off balance, and even as his hand wrapped around the limb his body fell sideways. Fear rippled through every fiber of his being in that terrible moment of dismaying comprehension that he would plummet to the earth. The bear! his mind shrieked. The bear will get you!

Nate smacked into a lower branch and inadvertently somersaulted onto the ground with a bone-jarring crash. Dazed, he struggled to rise, aware of a snarling form towering above him. Vaguely he heard a shot, and then something hit his head with enough force to shatter a boulder and his consciousness swirled madly before being sucked into an inky, ethereal void.

Somewhere, someone groaned.

Belatedly, Nate realized he was the one doing the groaning, and felt his awareness returning, felt life flow along his arms and legs, and felt the most awful, painful headache he'd ever known. His thoughts shifted and danced, and for a few minutes he couldn't concentrate.

"He's coming around," someone said.

"At last," stated someone else.

Both voices were familiar, and Nate knew he should be able to identify them, but his sluggish mind refused to cooperate. He blinked, and promptly regretted the movement. Dazzling, hurting light made him wince and recoil in agony.

"Take it easy, Nate. Lie still."

A gentle hand touched his shoulder, and suddenly Nate recognized the speaker. "Shakespeare?" he croaked.

"One and the same."

"I'm here too," added the first man.

"Baxter?" Nate blinked again, then squinted, his head throbbing. He licked his dry lips, peering at a bright blue sky, and saw the heads of both men materialize above him.

"Don't try to sit up," Shakespeare warned.

"What happened?" Nate asked, gradually regaining mental control. "The bear—"

"Is dead," Shakespeare finished. "You don't need to worry about him."

"I can't remember what happened," Nate said. "Did you kill it?"

"I shot last, but the thing was already dead on its feet," Shakespeare disclosed.

"Then what hit me?"

"The grizzly. It fell on top of you."

Baxter nodded. "We had to use the horses to haul the body off of you. We were afraid we'd find you dead, crushed or suffocated."

"You were fortunate, son," Shakespeare said.

Bewildered, trying to recall the events, Nate saw the sun out of the corner of his left eye. The golden orb hung low over the horizon. "I must have been out eight or nine hours. The sun is setting."

"The sun is rising," Shakespeare corrected him.

"What?"

Again Baxter nodded. "You were unconscious yesterday afternoon and all of last night. We took turns watching over you. McNair wasn't able to sleep a wink."

"It's morning?" Nate declared, incredulous at the news. He lifted his right hand and touched his forehead. "How bad is the wound?"

"You were cut on the shoulder blade and nicked on the foot, but you haven't lost much blood," the frontiersman responded.

"Why does my head ache so badly?"

"You were trying to get up when the bear went

down. Your head took the brunt of its weight,"
Shakespeare said, and grinned. "Your head must be
as hard as iron."

"It doesn't feel like iron," Nate said. "It feels like
mush."

"Which is why you will lie under your blankets for
another day, at least."

Lowering his chin, Nate saw his blankets were
indeed draped neatly over his body almost to his
neck. "What about the beaver?"

"Thaddeus and I will take care of them," Shakespeare said. "We've already caught four."

The man from Ohio placed his hand on Nate's left
arm. "I need to thank you again. If not for your inter-
vention, the grizzly would have killed me. I've never
seen anyone stand up to one of those beasts like you
did. No wonder they call you Grizzly Killer."

"I'd rather be known as Sparrow Killer," Nate said
sincerely.

Both Shakespeare and Baxter laughed.

"This makes three of those brutes you've killed,"
Shakespeare said after a bit. "Very few trappers have
killed more than you. Most have the good sense to
run like hell when they see one."

Again they laughed.

Nate tried to grin, but the simple movement
increased the agony in his head. The pounding in his
temples drowned out all other sound, and he closed
his eyes, intending to rest for a minute. To his amazement, when next his lids pried apart there were stars
dotting the firmament. "It's night," he blurted.

"Well, look who is awake," said Shakespeare, who
was still seated in the same spot.

"Where's Thaddeus?"

"Sleeping. It's my turn to keep an eye on you."

"How late is it?"

"I don't know exactly. After midnight."

A growling in Nate's stomach reminded him he

hadn't eaten in ages. "I could use some food."

"The fire is going strong. I'll make you soup or coffee or both."

"I'd like something more substantial."

"Not yet. No solid foods until tomorrow."

"Why not?"

"When someone has been severely injured, eating solid foods can make them worse. It puts a strain on the body. So if you want food, I'll prepare bear stew."

"Did the grizzly leave enough meat to last us a while?"

"No. But there was enough meat *on* the grizzly to last for weeks."

"You carved him up?"

"Can't let prime flesh go to waste, now can we? Would you care for some stew?"

Nate smiled at the notion of consuming the bear responsible for his condition. "I'd love some."

"Then try to stay awake until I'm done," Shakespeare said, and moved off.

A cool breeze caressed Nate's brow and he savored the sensation. If there was one lesson he'd learned living in the wilderness, it was to never take life for granted. A person never knew when he might be killed by a freak mishap. All it took was a single accident, a chance encounter with a bear, a panther, or hostile Indians, to send a hapless soul into eternity.

Back in the cities the situation was different. The people were spared from the harsh reality of ever-present death by having their needs supplied at the mere exchange of money. Food, clothing, and shelter were theirs for a few coins. They didn't need to worry about starving if they couldn't track game, or going naked if they couldn't make their own clothes, or sleeping on the hard ground if they couldn't build a cabin or lodge. In a sense, they were denied certain basic experiences all persons should know if they were to truly understand the value of existence.

Was that proper? Nate asked himself. If men and women were denied the realities of life, what was left? The illusions? Did some people prefer living in the cities over the country because they preferred illusions to reality? If so, what did it say about the mental state of those who shunned the truth?

Sleepiness assailed Nate's senses and he struggled to stay alert. Rumblings in his stomach gave him the resolve necessary. He was famished, and his mouth watered at the thought of the stew his friend was preparing. He heard the pad of footsteps and looked up, expecting the frontiersman.

Instead, the Ohioan appeared.

"How are you feeling?"

"As well as can be expected. I was told you were sleeping."

"I can't seem to doze off for more than a couple of hours at a time. I'm too excited about the prospect of returning to my family." Baxter took a seat at Nate's right. "McNair told me you're married."

"Yes."

"To a Shoshone?" Baxter said.

"What's wrong with that?"

"Nothing. Nothing at all. I was surprised to hear it, is all. Most trappers take an Indian woman for a few months or even a year, but very few bother to marry them. Why did you?"

"I love her."

"You weren't motivated by religious principles?"

"No."

"Do you believe, Nate King?"

"Believe what?"

"In the Lord?"

"I believe there is a God, but I have no idea whether . . ." Nate abruptly ceased speaking when a strident chorus of piercing howls erupted from the nearby forest.

Chapter Five

"Wolves," Baxter declared, rising and drawing his flintlock.

Alarmed, his heart beating faster, Nate managed to prop himself on his elbows and glanced around. The light from the campfire illuminated the horses standing near the spring, their heads up, their nostrils flaring and their ears cocked. An encircling ring of murky vegetation enclosed their island of comforting warmth.

Shakespeare was in the act of chopping bear meat into a tin pan. He promptly placed the meat on the ground and grabbed his rifle.

The howling came from the north and west, a wavering, primitive carol that rose and fell in volume, attaining a crescendo of clamorous harmony only to drop to plaintive wails seconds later.

"Will they attack?" Baxter called out.

"I don't think so," Shakespeare answered. "They smell the bear meat. If their bellies were empty, they'd sneak up on us without a sound."

Nate hoped the mountain man was correct. In his

condition he wouldn't be able to fend off an ornery mosquito, let alone a pack of wolves. The nerve-racking minutes dragged past, with phantom shadows moving about in the undergrowth and their eerie cries wafting to the heavens.

"Why won't they go?" Baxter asked nervously.

Suddenly a large wolf materialized at the very edge of the trees, its eyes reflecting the firelight and glowing an unearthly red, its teeth exposed in a seeming canine grin. After calmly gazing from one man to another, the gray wolf at last whirled and melted into the night and with his departure the howling immediately stopped.

"Thank God," Baxter said.

"That must have been the leader," Shakespeare speculated.

"Why did he stare at us?" Baxter inquired.

"Curiosity. Maybe he wanted to get a good whiff of our scent."

"Why?"

The frontiersman knelt by the fire. "Thaddeus, do I look like a wolf to you?"

"Of course not."

"Then don't expect me to be able to think exactly like a wolf. I may know the animals of the Rockies better than most, but no matter how close a man gets to Nature, he never becomes a complete part of it. There is a quality about a man that forever separates him from the animal kingdom."

"His soul."

"And his will. Never forget the human will," Shakespeare said, and launched into a quote from his favorite author. " 'Tis in ourselves that we are thus or thus. Our bodies are gardens; to the which our wills are gardeners: so that if we will plant nettles or sow lettuce, set hyssop and weed up thyme, supply it with one gender of herbs or distract it with many, either to have it sterile with idleness or manured with industry, why, the power and corrigible authority of this lies in our wills. If the balance of our lives had not one scale of reason to poise another of sensuality, the blood and baseness of our natures would conduct us to most preposterous conclusions."

"I'm not certain I understand your meaning," the Ohioan said.

"Who can be wise, amazed, temperate and furious, loyal and neutral, in a moment? No man," Shakespeare quoted again, and chuckled.

Baxter glanced at Nate. "Does he go on like this often?"

"He has his spells."

"Do *you* understand him?"

"I don't try."

Shakespeare started stirring the contents of the tin with his butcher knife and sang out loudly, "Double, double toil and trouble; fire burn and cauldron bubble." He threw back his head and cackled uproariously.

"I'm glad I'm only staying a month," Baxter said, and moved off to be by himself.

Grinning, Nate sank down and observed the celestial display. He sympathized with poor Baxter; sometimes he was at a total loss to explain his friend's occasionally quirky behavior. Perhaps the reason for Shakespeare's bizarre sense of humor lay in the life the man had led, over four decades of living in the wild in the almost exclusive company of animals and Indians. Such an existence was bound to change a person.

A meteor streaked across the sky, leaving a glowing trail in its wake.

Nate's thoughts strayed to his wife, and he prayed she was faring well by herself. He'd been sorely tempted to bring her along, but Shakespeare had warned him they were venturing into Ute territory and had graphically detailed the bitter treatment she could expect from the Utes.

Far away a panther screamed.

Drowsiness assailed Nate, and he started to doze off once more. His eyes snapped open when he heard footsteps and smelled the delicious aroma of the stew.

"Here you are," Shakespeare said, squatting.

"I'm so hungry I could eat a bear," Nate joked, and smiled merrily.

The frontiersman shook his head, then slid his left arm under Nate's shoulders. "Let me help you sit up."

"I can manage."

"I'll help," Shakespeare said.

Nate allowed himself to be propped in a sitting position, and the tin was placed on his lap. Even through the blankets he felt the heat.

"Eat it slow," Shakespeare advised. "Chew on the bits of bear meat first, then sip of broth. If you eat too fast, you'll be sick." He offered his knife.

"I'll use my own," Nate stated, and pulled it out. He began eating slowly, convinced he'd never tasted such an exquisite meal.

"If you keep the stew down, you can have all you can eat for breakfast. By tomorrow afternoon I may even let you go for a walk."

Nate looked into the older man's kindly eyes. "I'll miss you when you go."

"Don't bring that up again."

"I can't help how I feel. Why, in many respects you're closer to me than my own father."

"You father never taught you the proper way to trap beaver."

"Don't mock me."

"I'm not. I'm simply pointing out that we've shared experiences your father never could, experiences that have drawn us close together in a special bond of friendship. You're being too hard on your father." Shakespeare paused, his brow creased, deep in contemplation. "It's not my habit to give advice unless someone asks, but in your case, since I care for you as if you were my own son, I'll make an exception."

Nate waited expectantly, astounded the mountain man would admit his affection.

"You should make the effort to go back to New York City one day," Shakespeare stated. "The ghosts of your past still haunt you, and the only way you'll put them to rest is by confronting them."

"I'll never go back there."

"All I ask is that you consider the idea."

"I will, but I'll never go back."

"Stubborn mule," Shakespeare muttered, and walked to the fire.

Shrugging, Nate bent to his meal, relishing every morsel. When he was done a pleasant warmth filled his belly and made him irresistibly sleepy. He deposited the tin pan at his side, reclined on his back, and within seconds drifted into a peaceful sleep.

Bright sunlight on his eyelids awakened him and he sat up to find the sun hovering above the eastern horizon and his companions gathering their equipment to go check the trap line. His head felt much better, and without thinking he tried to stand. Dizziness brought him down again, and he pressed his palm to his forehead and groaned.

"Stubborn, stubborn, stubborn," Shakespeare chided him. "I saw that. Stay put. I've already made coffee and several cakes, so you can relax and eat while we go freeze our feet."

"You used some of the flour?" Nate asked in surprise. Normally, the frontiersman reserved their meager supply for special occasions.

"I figured you need proper food, not just salty jerky."

"Thank you."

"I'll fetch your meal," Shakespeare said, and stepped closer.

"Let me do it," Nate objected. "I can't sit here the rest of my life. The sooner I get on my feet, the better. I promise I'll go slow."

"All right, but if you don't you'll be sorry." Shakespeare wedged a hatchet under his belt, hefted his rifle, and headed eastward.

"Take care of yourself, brother," Baxter said, and hiked after the frontiersman.

Nate watched them until they were lost from view. He glanced around the clearing and suddenly felt very alone, keenly aware of being a solitary human in the midst of a sea of often savage wildlife. To dispel the feeling he shook his head lightly and slowly pushed to his feet. The dizziness renewed its onslaught, but the attack wasn't as severe. He stood still until his sense of balance was restored, then stepped to the fire.

The fragrant aroma of the coffee tantalized his nostrils, and he hurriedly poured a cup and sat haunched near the flames. Between the fire and the coffee he was warm and comfortable in no time, and consuming a couple of tasty cakes further contributed to his peace of mind.

Nate listened to the wind in the trees and the songs of various birds. He saw a large specimen with a black head and blue plumage alight in a tree to the south and eye him warily for several minutes before flying boldly into the camp and landing on the opposite side of the campfire. Such birds were quite common at higher elevations, and the trappers referred to them as mountain jays. Unlike their noisy blue cousins in the East, these jays were remarkably reticent. "Hello, bird," he said to it, grateful for the company.

The jay hopped a few feet and tilted its head to inspect him from head to toe.

Impressed by the bird's audacity, Nate tossed crumbs to the ground, and grinned as the jay greedily devoured the bits. If only all the creatures in the Rockies were so friendly! he mused, and kept feeding his visitor until all the crumbs were gone. "That's all I have for now," he said.

Digesting the information in regal silence, the jay flapped its wings and soared off over the trees.

Chuckling, Nate poured more coffee and settled down to sip to his heart's content. Such tranquil moments were rare in the life of a mountaineer, and he intended to enjoy the interlude to the fullest.

Chipmunks scampered on boulders to the north, a rabbit hopped into sight near the spring, and a pair of ravens flew past overhead.

Nate contrasted the idyllic setting with the bear attack, and marveled at the wildly different faces Nature presented. One moment serene and beautiful, the next violent and ugly, Nature's temperament seemed to change with the breeze. If Nature possessed a personality, she would be labeled as fickle. Not to mention dangerous.

He touched his head, feeling the scalp, and found no bumps or scratches. Only then did he fully appreciate the magnitude of his fortune. A cut shoulder blade and a nicked foot were nothing compared to the alternative. To escape relatively unscathed from an encounter with a grizzly was rare enough; to do so several times constituted uncommon good luck.

The great Grizzly Killer!

Nate laughed at the thought and swallowed more perfectly sweetened coffee. If only his family could see him now! They'd probably laugh themselves to death. All except his father, who would criticize him for being a consummate fool.

He recalled Shakespeare's advice about returning to settle affairs, and he toyed with the notion of doing so. But if he did travel to the States, what about Winona? Dared he take her along? She might be overwhelmed by the experience and upset beyond measure. To someone attuned to the ways of the wilderness, the ways of the white race would border on madness. He decided to consider the matter at length later.

A horse whinnied loudly.

Nate glanced at the animals, contentedly grazing north of the spring, near the woods, and took another sip. If he felt up to the task later, he'd brush the mare and spend some time in her company. In a certain respect horses were a lot like people. If neglected, they tended to become moody. His mare was a headstrong animal prone to act up if not ridden or curried daily.

The same horse whinnied once more.

Belatedly, the coffee cup pressed to his lips, Nate realized the sound came from the southwest, not from the five animals near the spring. Alarmed, he shifted and stared into the forest.

Nothing moved.

He lowered the tin cup and straightened. Perhaps he'd been mistaken, he reasoned. Noises often echoed uncannily in the mountains. Perhaps one of their own horses had whinnied and the trees had reflected the sound from a different direction.

A flicker of motion proved otherwise.

Nate crouched and moved to his blankets. He

retrieved the Hawken, slanted to the right, and hurried behind a wide maple. The exertion produced a slight nausea, forcing him to rest his forehead on the trunk for a few seconds until the queasy sensation subsided, and when he did look to the southwest again the blood in his veins seemed to run cold as he laid eyes on an approaching Indian armed with a bow and arrows.

Chapter Six

The husky warrior had his eyes on the ground, scouring for tracks, and didn't see the camp until he casually gazed straight ahead and spotted the fire and the horses. He promptly reined up and sat still, watching intently.

Breathing shallowly, Nate froze and studied the Indian, trying to identify the man's tribe. He wasn't as skilled as Shakespeare; he couldn't tell at a glance if an Indian was a Sioux, Shoshone, Crow, Kiowa, or whatever.

Black hair hung well past the warrior's shoulders. Buckskin leggings and moccasins covered him from the waist down, but otherwise he was naked. In his right hand was the bow. A full quiver hung on his back, and a slender knife adorned his right hip.

Should he fire or not? Nate debated. If the man was hostile, then prudence dictated slaying him immediately. But what if the warrior was from a friendly tribe? As remote as the possibility might be, he couldn't afford to slay an innocent man. He opted to wait and observe what happened.

The Indian didn't budge for the longest while. At last he slid to the ground and advanced using every tree, bush, and thicket for cover, affording only fleeting glimpses of his darting form.

Nate drew his head back, squatted, and braced his left shoulder on the tree. He couldn't risk being spotted. In his condition he'd be no match for the warrior. As much as it tried his patience, he must wait, give the Indian time to enter the clearing, then spring a little surprise. If the warrior resisted, then he'd slay the man without compunction.

He held the rifle upright, his finger on the trigger, his thumb on the hammer, and slowly counted to fifty, anxious to take a peek. The seconds seemed like years. At last he inched his right eye to the edge of the trunk.

The warrior was in plain sight, an arrow nocked to his bow, standing at the south edge of the clearing with his head swinging from side to side. Apparently convinced the camp was temporarily unattended, he hurried to the fire and knelt next to the stacked packs containing the supplies. He glanced at the horses, then at the spring, then placed his bow on the grass and started to unfasten the top of a pack.

Nate had a perfect shot, but he couldn't bring himself to shoot. The Indian was in profile, intent on undoing the leather ties. He slowly stood, leveled the Hawken, and stepped boldly from concealment.

So engrossed was the warrior in discovering the contents of the pack, he didn't notice.

Well aware of how quickly an Indian could lift a bow and fire, Nate advanced several strides and deliberately cocked the hammer. The click had the desired effect.

Spinning, the Indian released the pack and grabbed for his bow, his eyes widening in consternation at being taken off guard.

"Don't!" Nate barked, aiming at the man's forehead.

His fingers about to close on the handle, the warrior stared at the unwavering Hawken and froze, his consternation changing to an expression of arrogant resentment.

"Take your hand off the bow," Nate said, and when the Indian showed no sign of complying he motioned with his head. "Step back, away from your weapon."

Even if the warrior didn't understand English, the motion and the tone were unmistakable. Reluctantly, he slid backwards and stood, his arms at his sides.

"Do you speak the white man's tongue?" Nate asked.

A stony silence was his response.

Nate walked to within three yards of the Indian. He wagged the Hawken at the man's knife and pointed at the ground.

Scowling, the warrior used two fingers to pull the knife from its sheath and dropped it. He exhaled loudly and awaited further instructions.

"Move back away from the packs," Nate said, and gestured with the rifle to get his point across. When the Indian obeyed, he motioned for the man to sit. "I'll bet you're a murdering Blackfoot."

The warrior said nothing.

Nate began to relax. There was no way the man could jump him before he fired, and the Indian knew it. He cradled the rifle in the crook of his right arm and addressed the prisoner in sign language, his fingers flying. Shakespeare and Winona had spent many hours instructing him in the universal language of the tribes, and he'd become quite proficient. "Are you a Blackfoot?"

Jutting his chin out defiantly, the Indian refused to answer.

"You act like a Blackfoot," Nate said, knowing a member of any other tribe would be insulted by the comment. He almost grinned when it elicited a response.

"The Blackfeet are cowardly dogs. They deserve to be rubbed out of existence."

"Are you a Crow?"

The warrior snorted contemptuously. "You are very ignorant, white man. I am better than any Crow. They are bigger cowards than the Blackfeet and flee at the mention of my tribe."

"What is your tribe?"

Squaring his broad shoulders, the man stated proudly, "The Utes."

Nate nodded. Since they were trapping in Ute territory, the man must be speaking the truth. "I know the Utes well. They are brave fighters."

Surprise registered at the unexpected compliment. "How do you know about my people?" the warrior asked.

"I have fought them a couple of times."

"And you are still alive?"

Grinning, Nate moved a few feet to his right to put the fire between them. "I have fought the Blackfeet too, and I can tell you they are not cowards."

The warrior wasn't interested in the Blackfeet. "How many of my people have you killed?"

Nate had to think for a moment. "Thirteen, I believe."

A crimson tinge of anger flushed the Ute's cheeks and he clenched his fists for a full five seconds before responding. "You lie. No white man has ever killed so many Utes."

"I have," Nate signed calmly.

The warrior's eyes narrowed and he scrutinized the young mountain man from head to toe. "How are you known?"

'''There are no signs for my white name. Some time ago I earned an Indian name, though, and many now call me by it.''

''What is this name?''

''Grizzly Killer.''

The Ute's eyes strayed to the rack of drying bear meat. His brow creased and he seemed to be deep in thought. ''During the Thunder Moon a warrior named Buffalo Horn led a war party of thirteen men from my village. They never came back.''

''I killed twelve of them. Another time I killed one other warrior. All of them were trying to slay me when they died,'' Nate reflected.

Disbelief wrestled with acceptance on the Ute's countenance, and finally the truth prevailed. Strangely, he smiled. ''I will be honored to take your scalp one day.''

''Many have tried.''

''For one so young to have counted so many coup, you must be a brave warrior.''

''I did what I did to survive, nothing more.''

''You survive quite well.''

Nate smiled. ''What is your name?''

''I am Two Owls.''

''Did you come here looking for us?''

''No,'' the Ute replied. ''I was hunting when I came across horse tracks and followed them until I saw your fire.''

Baxter's tracks, Nate reflected. ''Did you see any sign of the Blackfeet war party?''

Two Owls stiffened. ''What war party?''

''The prints you followed were made by a companion of mine who was escaping from a band of Blackfeet.''

Tremendously upset by the news, the Ute began to rise, then caught himself. His hands and arms moved emphatically. ''The Blackfeet can be in this area for only one reason. They are planning to raid my village.

You must let me go warn my people."

Taken unawares by the request, Nate hesitated before answering. Although he agreed with the Ute's conclusion, and even though he sympathized with the warrior's fears for the village, he wasn't about to release a member of a tribe devoted to the extermination of all trappers. "I am sorry. I cannot."

Two Owl's featured clouded. When he signed, he stabbed the air. "I should have known better than to ask a white."

"I will talk it over with my friends when they return. If they agree, we will let you go."

"When will they return?"

"I do not know."

The Ute sullenly accepted the inevitable, but he cast a longing glance at the horses.

"Do you have a wife?" Nate asked.

"A wife and three sons," the warrior replied proudly. "My boys will grow up to become great fighters and their names will be feared by all their enemies."

"Is your village near here?"

Two Owls lifted his hands to respond, then paused and grinned. "You are crafty like a coyote, Grizzly Killer."

"I am?"

"You almost tricked me into revealing the location of my people. This I will not do."

"We are not here to harm your tribe."

"Why are you in this region?"

"To trap beaver."

Frowning in displeasure, Two Owls nodded. "I guessed as much. Your kind will one day wipe the beaver out."

"You are being unfair. There are many thousands of beavers in the mountains and only a few hundred trappers. We will never wipe them out."

"I would expect you to say such things. You are

white. But my eyes are the eyes of a Ute, and I know what I know. Already have the whites killed more beaver in the past few winters than all the tribes have killed since the day the Great Mystery breathed life into all creatures."

Nate chuckled at the concept. "You have an excellent imagination."

"Laugh at me if you want, but my words are true. Why do you think my people dislike the whites so much? It is because we know the whites are destroyers and we do not want your kind to destroy the land that has fed us and clothed us for more generations than there are fingers to count with," Two Owls sighed solemnly.

"I do not know what I can say to change your mind, so I will only say you are wrong. Why would my people want the beaver to die off when they depend on the beaver for their existence?"

"My people have often discussed that very question, and we have decided the whites must all be crazy."

At this Nate laughed openly.

Two Owls regarded him reflectively for a while. "This is most odd," he stated at length.

"What is?"

"I find myself liking you."

"Have you ever talked with a white man before?"

"No."

"So this is a first for both of us. You are not the rabid killer I believed all Utes to be. You are a man, nothing more, nothing less, and perhaps that is the answer to all the questions both of us have. My people and your people live differently and have different values, but they are all still people. Instead of hating each other because of our differences, we should try to understand one another and live in peace."

The Ute appeared amazed. "I never expected to

hear such words from a white man."

Sighing, Nate indicated the surrounding mountains with a sweep of his right arm. "I have made my home here. I want to raise a family and watch my sons grow into manhood, just like you do. Naturally, I would rather live in peace with all the tribes."

"No one will ever live in peace with the Blackfeet."

"I know," Nate signed. "Fortunately, their villages are far to the north and they only travel to this region for occasional raids." He saw the Ute's lips compress, and realized he'd made a tactless mistake by reminding the warrior of the danger to the Ute village. Guilt troubled his conscience. How could he detain the warrior knowing the man's wife and children were in imminent danger? If only Shakespeare would get back! The mountain man would know what to do.

"Do I just sit here until your friends return?" Two Owls inquired.

"Yes."

"Then you will want to bind me."

"Not if you give me your word of honor that you will do as I say."

"You would trust *my* word?"

"Yes."

Two Owls leaned on his palms, his mouth pursed. Then he began to sign, "Grizzly Killer, you are unlike any white man I have ever heard of. If more whites were like you, my people would not hate them so much."

"When you are among your people again, tell them about this. Perhaps many will agree with you."

"I will tell them, but most will still dislike all trappers."

Nate was about to make a comment when the distant crack of a rifle turned his gaze to the east. His pulse quickened. As far as he knew, Shakespeare was the only other man within a radius of miles who

had a rifle, and there was no logical reason for the
mountain man to be using his Hawken to slay beaver.

Another shot sounded, not quite as loud, the
distinct blast of a flintlock.

Was that Baxter? Nate took a stride eastward,
dread gripping his soul, dread that intensified a
moment later when, so faint he could barely hear
them, there arose a series of blood-curdling war
whoops.

Chapter Seven

Nate glanced at Two Owls and debated whether to simply release the warrior, wondering if the whoops were from Blackfeet or Utes. He must go find his friends, but it wouldn't be wise to force the warrior to accompany him since he couldn't effectively watch a prisoner and be alert for an ambush at the same time. A second shot from a flintlock decided the issue and he quickly signed, "You are free to go." Whirling, he grabbed his bridle from his pile of tack but didn't bother with the saddle, then sprinted toward the horses, moving as fast as he dared, still weak but determined not to buckle.

Another rifle discharged.

Please let them be alive! Nate prayed. He slowed as he neared the animals so he wouldn't spook them, and stepped to the mare to hastily remove her hobble. Sliding on the bridle took another moment. He swung onto her and hauled on the reins, breaking into a gallop immediately, and rode across the clearing, passing the fire enroute.

Two Owls was gone.

A brief dizziness assailed him as he plunged into the trees. Fortunately his head cleared and he could concentrate on avoiding low limbs and entangling thickets. The mare responded superbly, as she always did, her hooves pounding, dirt flying.

Nate covered fifty yards before he detected movement out of the corner of his right eye and glanced to the south to behold the Ute riding hard to catch up. The grin creasing the warrior's mouth served to confirm his intentions were friendly, and Nate allowed the man to draw alongside the mare. Together they raced on.

Anxiety distorted Nate's perception of time. It seemed as if only a few minutes elapsed between leaving the camp and arriving at the west bank of the stream, although the sweat lathering his skin and the mare testified to a longer duration. He halted and looked both ways.

Two Owls pointed northward and used sign language to say, "We must go that way."

Relying on the Indian's superior instincts, Nate turned and rode along the waterway, traveling two hundred yards before he spied several traps lying in the grass. Goading the mare forward, he practically vaulted from her back to crouch beside the three Newhouses. Under no circumstances whatsoever would Shakespeare or Baxter leave prized traps unattended. He scanned the forest on both sides of the stream and saw nothing out of the ordinary.

Two Owls climbed from his black stallion and bent over to inspect the ground. He grunted and his hands flew. "There has been a fight here. See how the grass is bent?" He touched a patch of crushed blades. "Many Indians and two whites fought."

"How do you know there were two whites?"

The Ute pointed at Nate's moccasins. "White men

do not walk as Indians do. Your kind carry too much of their weight on their heels and tread heavily. My people always walk lightly like the wolves and the big cats."

Nate looked at the ground, wishing he could read sign with such skill. "What else can you tell me?"

"The whites ran into the trees that way," Two Owls said, and nodded to the west.

Springing onto the mare, Nate rode off. If the Ute was right, then his friends must be hoping they could lose their pursuers in the woods and swing around to the camp. But was it Blackfeet or Utes doing the pursuing? If the latter, his temporary truce with Two Owls might well result in an arrow in the back.

The answer was discovered unexpectedly.

They had ridden for only a minute, always bearing due west, when the mare neighed and shied away from an object in her path.

Nate reined up and looked down to discover a buckskin-clad body sprawled in the weeds. Fearing the worst, he slid to the earth and stood over the corpse. Sweet relief brought an unconscious smile at recognizing the dead man was an Indian.

Dropping from the stallion, Two Owls knelt and rolled the man over. "A Blackfoot dog," he said.

A crimson-rimmed hole in the center of the warrior's forehead revealed the cause of death. A few inches from his left hand was a war club.

"We must be very careful," Two Owls advised. "The Blackfeet will return for this body."

"They must be close," Nate said, and remounted to lead the way, moving slower, his rifle across his thighs.

Not so much as a chipmunk chattered in the surrounding forest. The patterns of Nature had been disrupted, transforming the normally vibrant woodland into a silent expanse of motionless vegetation.

Where were his friends? Nate chided himself for not insisting on accompanying them. If they were dead, his guilt would be boundless. He spied a hill not far off, and scrutinized its tree-covered slope to no avail.

Two Owls fell behind a few yards.

Nate decided to go over the hill instead of skirting it. Once on top he'd have an unobstructed view of the countryside and might spot the frontiersman and the Ohioan. With that in mind he urged the mare up the gradual slope, following a game trail, and he was almost to the crest when he heard the alien sound.

Laughter.

Harsh, gloating laughter.

Jerking on the reins, Nate took the mare into a dense stand of saplings and halted. The Ute joined him.

Slowly the laughter and chuckles grew louder. Distinct voices could be heard, talking excitedly.

The language was unfamiliar to Nate, and he deduced it must be the Blackfoot tongue. Twisting, he gazed toward the top, and shortly thereafter six warriors appeared, all in good spirits as if intoxicated by the flush of victory. They made their way down the hill and to the east, apparently going to retrieve the body of their comrade.

Nate watched them in horror. If the Blackfeet were so happy, there could only be one reason. Shakespeare and Baxter must be dead. He suddenly felt weak again and sagged, holding onto the pommel for support. Dazed by the magnitude of the calamity, unable to formulate a plan of action, he sat there until Two Owls poked him in the arm. With an effort he turned.

"What is wrong with you?" the warrior inquired.

"My friends . . . " Nate began, and his hands slumped.

"Your friends are probably still alive."

"What makes you think so?"

"The Blackfeet love to torture even more than they love to kill and steal, and they are very fond of tormenting whites. They might have taken your friends alive."

Nate had raised his arms to express his pessimism when more conversation came from the other side of the hill. Tensing, he riveted his eyes on the crest until additional Blackfeet showed up and counted them as they came over. Two. Four. Five. A few seconds went by, and then the sixth person walked into view and Nate wanted to shout for joy.

Shakespeare had his arms bound behind his back. His hat was gone, his hair tousled, his weapons missing. He stepped proudly, his chin jutting defiantly.

After the mountain man came Thaddeus Baxter. His arms were also tied, his flintlock was gone, and a nasty gash marked his left cheek. His strides were unsteady and he blinked a lot.

Nate rashly gripped the reins firmly to charge for cover, his emotions getting the better of his reason, but he was jolted back to reality by the appearance of even more Blackfeet.

Three sturdy warriors brought up the rear, two armed with bows, the third with a fusee. They were clearly ready to fire if the captives made a bid to escape.

Reluctantly, Nate let them all pass. The odds were simply too great, 14 to one in favor of the Blackfeet. Fourteen to two if he counted Two Owls on his side. When the party disappeared in the forest below, he glanced at his newfound companion. "What will the Blackfeet do next?"

The Ute answered with the certainty of one who knew his lifelong enemies well. "They will bury their dead. By tomorrow they will be on their way back to their village where your friends will be put to death."

"How long will it take them to reach their village?"

"Perhaps twelve suns. Less if they travel fast."

The information gave Nate an idea. Apparently Shakespeare and Baxter were safe enough for the time being, at least until they reached the village. His wisest recourse was to shadow the war party and wait for an opportunity to effect a rescue. Twelve days was a long time. A lot could happen.

"What will you do?" Two Owls asked.

"I will follow the Blackfeet and free my friends."

"Alone?"

"If I must."

The reply caused the Ute to straighten. "This is not my fight."

"I know."

"I have a family waiting for me."

"I know."

"I cannot help you, Grizzly Killer," Two Owls said, and frowned. "I truly wish I could."

Although his hopes were dashed, Nate kept his face impassive and shrugged. "I understand."

"You are not angry?"

"Why should I be? You have been honest with me. They are my friends; I must save them."

Two Owls stared into Nate's eyes, then wheeled his horse and looked back. "I go now. I will tell my people what has happened and try to convince them to send a war party to stop the Blackfeet, but I do not know if they will come if it means helping whites."

"I can ask no more," Nate signed.

"May the Great Mystery guide your footsteps."

"And yours."

A curt nod and a wave and the Ute was gone.

The enormity of the mountains seemed to weigh down on Nate's shoulders and shook his head to dispel a gloomy premonition of disaster. He was alone. So be it. But he could accomplish what had to be done if he stayed alert and exercised single-minded determination.

He rode slowly down the hill and dismounted at its base. Taking hold of the reins he hiked eastward, proceeding with the utmost caution, until he spotted the war party. Two of the warriors were carrying their deceased fellow warrior as the band walked toward the stream. Keeping well back, Nate trailed them, stopping when they halted on the west bank of the stream.

The Blackfeet compelled Shakespeare and Baxter to sit, deposited the body near them, and set to work making a camp.

Were they planning to stay the night right there? Nate wondered. If so, it would give him time to return to the camp, load the pack animals, and return before daylight. He watched from concealment as they used their tomahawks to chop off and strip long, straight limbs that were arranged in a conical shape much like their buffalo-hide lodges. Three of these improvised forts were constructed, and when they were completed Shakespeare and the Ohioan were rudely shoved into the middle fort and two guards were posted.

A tall, lean warrior evidently was in charge. He had issued instructions to the others during the building of the forts, and now he dispatched four of his tribesmen to the north, possibly to do some hunting. His frame and his mien set him apart, as did one other factor. In addition to a bow and arrows, he carried an extraordinary weapon tucked under a slender leather cord looped about his slim waist: a gleaming sword.

Nate was too far away to note the shape of the hilt, but from the general outline he surmised the sword must be Spanish. He couldn't begin to imagine how the Blackfoot had come to possess it, unless a war party had once conducted a raid down toward Santa Fe, which was highly unlikely because of the vast distance involved. Another possibility occurred to him. Many years ago the Spanish had mined much gold of the central Rockies. If the Blackfeet had attacked a gold train or mining camp, the sword could have been taken from a halpless conquistador and bequeathed from father to son, generation to generation.

Once satisfied the Blackfeet truly intended to remain at their camp for quite some time, Nate stealthily moved to the southwest, mounted when the forts were out of sight, and headed off at a gallop.

He realized the lives of two brave men were in his hands, and formulated various plans for saving them, everything from picking the Blackfeet off one by one to setting their forts on fire in the middle of the night. No matter how he looked at the problem, there was no way to liberate Shakespeare and Baxter without running the risk of losing their lives.

Nate's stomach reminded him he needed nourishment if he was to replenish the vitality he'd lost due to his injuries. His convalescence had been cut short just when he needed to be at the peak of his strength, and a grueling journey to Blackfoot territory promised to aggravate his condition.

He stopped twice to orient himself, and had begun to doubt he'd traveled in the right direction when he spied a wisp of smoke curling above the treetops. Thank goodness the camp was far enough from the Blackfeet so they hadn't noticed it!

Nate relaxed and slowed the mare to a walk. There was no sense in overexerting her until the need arose.

He estimated a half hour would be required to load all the pack animals and string the horses in a line. In an hour or so he could be back there watching over his friends.

He thought about Two Owls, and speculated on whether the Utes would help. Given their long-standing hatred of trappers, he doubted they would lift a finger.

Soon the clearing was visible, the campfire dying down, the horses standing near the spring, the packs undisturbed.

Nate rode into the camp and hopped down. No sooner did his moccasins touch the ground then a savage shriek shattered the stillness to his rear, and pivoting he saw a mounted Indian bearing down on him with an upraised lance poised to throw.

Chapter Eight

Nate instinctively raised the Hawken to fire, but in a flash of insight he realized the sound of the shot would carry to the Blackfeet and might lead them to his location. Instead of squeezing the trigger he darted to the right and dived for the ground. In his ears drummed the pounding hooves of the warrior's mount, and a second later something brushed his right shoulder and thudded into the earth at his side.

A tremendous whoop issued from bloodthirsty lips as the Indian bore down on him.

Rolling to the left, Nate tried to push erect. A heavy body slammed onto his back, stunning him, driving him down again, and he lost his grip on the rifle. Knees gouged him in the spine and strong hands looped around his chin from behind. He dimly realized the man was trying to break his neck, and frantically flipped onto his right side while at the same instant he whipped his left elbow back and around.

The warrior grunted and was sent flying.

Nate scrambled to his knees, struggling to clear

his thoughts, keenly aware he must prevail or perish. Twisting, he saw the Indian springing at his chest, and managed to jerk aside at the last moment.

Exceptionally agile, the warrior came down on his hands and knees and almost in the same motion jumped erect, drawing a tomahawk before he straightened.

Pushing to his feet, Nate saw his attacker's face clearly for the first time, and was shocked by the unbridled hatred displayed. The tomahawk arced at his head and he skipped to the left, his hands dropping to his pistols. Again he changed his mind. He must slay the warrior quietly, and the only way to do so was by using his butcher knife. With the thought his knife leaped from its sheath.

Hissing in fury, the Indian swung the tomahawk several times in succession, relying on his weapon's greater reach.

Forced to retreat, Nate dodged the swipes and countered with his knife, striving to slash his foe's abdomen or chest. The warrior deftly deflected the blade every time, increasing the temptation to employ the pistols. Try as he might Nate couldn't break through the other's defenses. To compound his predicament, his arms grew steadily more fatigued. If he wanted to survive he must do something and do it quickly.

An idea struck heartbeats later. Since he had the shorter weapon and couldn't hope to stab the Indian in the torso, why not take advantage of the knife's lighter weight and ease of handling?

Enraged by his failure to kill, the Indian swung wildly.

Nate backpedaled further, biding his time, and when the warrior overextended a swing and exposed the arm holding the tomahawk, he was ready. The knife flicked straight out and speared into the Indian's wrist, cutting deep and causing blood to gush forth.

If Nate expected the wound would prompt the Indian to surrender or flee, he was sadly mistaken. To his surprise the warrior shifted the tomahawk to the other hand and renewed the assault more furiously than before.

Now the fight became a desperate battle of endurance. Would the Indian weaken first from the loss of so much blood or would Nate collapse from the strain to his system?

Nate sensed he couldn't hold out much longer, and gambled everything on a last-ditch effort. He deliberately let his adversary get a little closer, let the tomahawk miss his stomach by a hair, and lunged forward to plunge his knife to the hilt below the warrior's sternum.

Gasping, the Indian stiffened, staggered, and clutched at Nate's wrist. Eyes widening, the warrior attempted to raise the tomahawk for a final blow, but his limbs betrayed him. He groaned as his legs began to buckle.

With a sharp tug Nate tore the knife free and stepped back to watch the Indian sink to the grass. The man rested on his knees, his hands going limp, and released the tomahawk. Nate kicked the weapon out of reach.

Defiant eyes were turned to the youth and a string of words were barked in an unknown tongue.

"You must be a Blackfoot," Nate signed wearily.

Not a sound came from the warrior, who doubled over and pressed both hands to his midriff.

Nate wanted to put the man out of his misery, and considered plunging the knife in again. But he needed answers, and the only one who could supply them was rapidly dying. He nudged the Indian with his left foot.

Up snapped the warrior's chin, his lips curled in a snarl.

"Who are you?" Nate signed, holding the hilt of the bloody knife with just the last two fingers on his right hand. "Why did you try to kill me?"

Gritting his teeth, the Indian moved his arms awkwardly. "White dog! You have more luck than ten ordinary men."

"Who are you? What tribe are you from?"

The warrior answered with difficulty, his fingers fluttering unsteadily. "I am proud to be a Blackfoot. One day we will kill all white dogs."

"Are you part of the war party I saw a while ago?"

"You saw my brothers. I am part of White Bear's band." The Blackfoot paused, breathing raggedly, and signed his spite. "I pray the maggots eat your intestines before another moon passes. May the vultures feast on your rotten heart and the worms on your flesh. You are—" he began to sign, and gagged, his mouth slackening. His eyelids quivered, his tongue protruded, and he pitched onto his face.

For the longest time Nate simply stood there, staring at his vanquished foe. Such hatred! He'd never known anyone to express such sheer malice. The Blackfoot had cursed him with his dying breath. And why? Just because of the color of his skin.

What had the man meant about his brothers? Was the remark meant literally, or in the sense that all men in a tribe were considered to be spiritual brothers? He realized the man had not bothered to give his name, but at least he now knew the name of the tall Indian with the sword. White Bear.

A low whinny brought Nate out of his reflection to stare at the Blackfoot's horse. It wore a leather bridle, not the rope war bridle usually used by Indians on a raid. He remembered Baxter telling how his pack animal was stolen, and deduced this must be the same animal. But why was a lone Blackfoot riding it so far from the rest of the band? Had this man been sent to scout for the Ute village and found the camp instead, then decided to wait and ambush whoever showed up?

Feeling extremely fatigued, Nate stepped to the fading fire and sat down to rest. He could afford five minutes, no more. And more than anything else he needed food. He wiped the knife clean on the grass, slid the blade back into the sheath, and walked to the rack of drying grizzly meat. Most of the strips would have to be left behind. What a waste. He grabbed a handful and returned to the fire to eat.

What was he going to do about the horses? Not counting his mare, there were five animals to lead. Would he jeopardize his chances to rescuing Shakespeare and Baxter if he took all of them along? They were bound to make noise. But if he stayed far enough from the war party the odds of being heard or seen were quite slim. Since horses were one of a man's most valuable commodities in the wild, along with a good rifle, he elected to take them.

The bear meat tasted tangy and made him thirsty. After eating he ventured to the spring and drank his fill, gulping the cold water and letting it spill over his lips and chin. With his meal out of the way, he prepared for the pursuit.

First he buried the Blackfoot. Not that he felt any obligation to treat the warrior in a civilized manner, but he didn't want any buzzards to circle overhead and draw attention to the campsite.

Next he loaded the supplies onto the horses, distributing the packs evenly on his pack animal, Shakespeare's pack animal, Baxter's pack animal, and Baxter's horse. This way the horses carried lighter loads and could move faster. He didn't put any packs on the mountain man's white horse. Like the mare, it was one of the family, so to speak, and deserved better treatment.

He crammed as much bear meat into several packs

as he could, knowing the opportunities to hunt on the trail would be few and far between. Then he extinguished the fire and scattered the ashes with his foot. The horses were permitted to slake their thirst, and in short order he was mounted and leading the string in the direction of the Blackfoot forts.

Was there anything he'd forgotten? Both pistols were loaded and wedged under his belt and the Hawken was across his thighs. He'd tossed the warrior's lance into the trees, but kept the tomahawk; it now nestled in a pack beside a different tomahawk he'd taken from another Blackfoot months ago.

All the way back he worried the Blackfeet would be gone. He grinned when he drew close enough to see the forts and saw several warriors moving about. They were three hundred yards off, which was as close as he dared get.

Nate dismounted, hid the horses in a dense stand of pines, and moved a dozen yards nearer to spy on the war party. He hoped to catch a glimpse of his friends. The guards were still posted outside the middle fort, but Shakespeare and Baxter never appeared.

The remaining hours of the day dragged past. Nate refused to leave again, no matter what, and occupied himself noting the activities of the Blackfeet. The quartet dispatched earlier returned bearing a dead deer. Two others spent their time fishing. Others gathered roots. Despite being in Ute territory, they posted no sentries.

Evening arrived. The Blackfeet entered their forts and shortly thereafter smoke poured from the tops of each. The many tales he'd heard about the fierce warriors of the northern plains and mountains were all true, as he well knew from prior experience. They were a proud people, the toughest tribe on the

frontier, the most feared of all, and they were aware
of the fact. They adopted a condescending attitude
toward other tribes and would never show fear, even
in the face of overwhelming odds.

Night settled in. Nate went to his pack animal and
took a blanket from a pack. Covering his shoulders,
he stepped to his vantage point and continued
watching.

Except for emerging to relieve themselves or to
enjoy some fresh air, the Blackfeet stayed in their
forts. Loud laughter intermittently wafted on the
breeze. Once, incredibly, the occupants of the
northernmost fort burst into song, a rhythmic chant
that went on for half an hour.

Nate ate more cold bear meat before retiring. He
curled up at the base of a tree, pulled the blanket
tight, and closed his eyes, wishing he had a cozy fire
to lie beside. In his mind's eye he reviewed the day's
events and counted himself fortunate to be alive. If
he wanted to stay that way, tomorrow he would have
to be more alert, more cautious, than ever before. One
mistake could cost him his life, not to mention the
consequences for the mountain man and the Ohioan.
He hoped he wouldn't have any difficulty in falling
asleep, and didn't.

The chattering of a squirrel in the tree above
awoke Nate with a start and he sat up, blinking and
trying to organize his thoughts. He glanced at the sun
and thought he must be dreaming. It hung well
above the eastern horizon. The morning was half
over.

Shakespeare and Baxter!

He leaped upright and stared at the forts. There
wasn't a Blackfoot anywhere. No! No! No! He
couldn't have slept so long. Stumbling in his haste,
he ran to the horses, untied them, put the blanket

in a pack, and mounted the mare. Of all the times to oversleep! Why now? Why when Shakespeare needed him the most?

Nate galloped to the forts and didn't bother to inspect them. There was no doubt the war party had departed hours ago, probably at first light. But which way? He looked in all directions and finally chose to go north. Their home territory was to the north. Hopefully, they would also stick with the stream for as far as they could.

Kneeing the mare, he gave belated chase. Since the warriors were on foot, they would leave few tracks, certainly not enough for an inexperienced tracker to follow. He kept his gaze on the land ahead, praying he would spot them before they saw him.

He traveled a mile. Two. Three. Still there was no sign of the band. Stubbornly he pressed on, refusing to give up. If, as he surmised, the war party had headed out at daylight, and if they covered four miles an hour, which was about the average over such rugged terrain, and if the current time was between nine and ten, then the Blackfeet had already gone twelve miles. Nine or ten more and he would be close on their heels.

Nate ignored everything around him. All he cared about was catching up. When the pack horses lagged he tugged brutally on the rope. He tried not to think about what would happen if he failed to find the band. If they had turned from the stream at any point, his companions were doomed.

Four more miles went by. Once he spooked a small herd of mountain buffalo, and another time a panther bounded into the underbrush at his approach.

The higher the sun climbed, the hotter it became. Sweat caked his skin, and he repeatedly moped his sleeve across his forehead. By all rights he should stop and let the animals drink, but he refused. They would drink when he did.

When he'd gone over ten miles he slowed slightly, afraid he would blunder upon the war party and ruin everything. Two more miles fell behind him and still they didn't appear. He saw a bend in the stream two hundred yards to the north, a gradual loop to the west. Trees prevented him from seeing beyond it. Slowing even more, he warily neared the bend, riding along a narrow strip of clear ground at the water's edge. With his attention exclusively focused on the curve, he neglected to scan the trees at his left elbow, and paid for his oversight when a muscular form hurtled from a limb and slammed him from the saddle.

Chapter Nine

Nate came down hard on his back, the Indian straddling him, and felt a hand clamped over his mouth. He looked up, expecting to see a knife or tomahawk spearing at his chest, and instead saw the smiling face of Two Owls. Astounded, he simply lay there as the Ute slid off and signed a greeting.

"We meet again, Grizzly Killer."

In order to communicate Nate had to push himself into a sitting posture. "What are you doing here?" he bluntly asked.

"Repaying the debt I owe you."

"What debt?" Nate inquired in confusion.

"You spared me, gave me my freedom. My life was in your hands, yet you chose not to take it. More importantly, you treated me as a human being, with respect and dignity. Now I am here to repay the debt."

Nate was about to inform the Ute it wasn't necessary when he remembered the overriding sense of obligation and duty Indians possessed. If you did

Indians a kindness they naturally expected to be able to return the favor, and were insulted if you refused.

Two Owls pointed at the bend. "If I had not stopped you, you would have ridden straight into the war party. They are resting up ahead."

"Thank you," Nate said, wondering why the warrior didn't just voice a warning.

As if he'd sensed Nate's thoughts, Two Owls related, "I would have called out to you but you do not speak the Ute tongue. And also, I did not want to be shot if you mistook me for a Blackfoot."

Nate looked around. "Did any of your people come with you?"

"No."

"Why not?"

"It was as I told you it would be. I explained all that had happened to me and advised them you are a man to be trusted, a man deserving of our help, and although some of there were of the same opinion, the majority refused to aid a white man."

"But what about the Blackfeet? Surely they wanted to send warriors to repulse the invaders."

"Some did. The others were of the opinion our tribe should devote itself to protecting the village, which at this very moment they are in the process of moving far to the south."

"They are running?"

Two Owls's lips tightened. "There are scores of women, children, and the elderly in our village. Would you have us leave all of them unprotected while the warriors go after the Blackfeet?"

"But there are only fourteen. Your tribe can easily defeat them."

"Where there are fourteen there are often fifty. The Blackfeet frequently divide their war parties into smaller bands and spread out to cover more area. My people could not be certain there is just this one small band."

"So you came back all by yourself," Nate signed, and only then fully appreciated the implications. Here was a Ute warrior, sworn enemy of all trappers and mountain men, hazarding his life to assist a white man. And why? Not because of an abiding bond of friendship; they'd hardly known each other. No, it was beause of the basic bond of shared humanity.

Two Owls grinned. "The Blackfeet should not be allowed to raid our country with impunity."

"How did your family feel about your leaving?"

"My wife was not happy but she did not object. My sons were excited and asked me to bring home the hair of many Blackfeet."

Standing, Nate brushed twigs and dirt from his buckskins and reclaimed his rifle. "Did you see my friends?"

"Yes. They are still alive. I returned to the Blackfoot camp shortly before sunrise and watched them leave, then followed. I am very surprised you did not appear. Where were you?"

Nate wasn't about to embarrass himself by disclosing he'd overslept, so he fibbed. "I was jumped by a lone Blackfoot at my camp and killed him." Before he could begin a lengthy elaboration the Ute interrupted.

"What did you do with him?"

"Buried the body. What else?"

Two Owls looked at the pack animals. "Where is his hair?"

"I let him keep it."

The warrior looked bewildered. "You did not scalp him?"

"I forgot."

Two Owls shook his head several times. "I will never understand the white man if I live a hundred and twenty winters."

For want of anything better to say, Nate signed, "One hundred and twenty winters? No one lives that long."

"Many of our people do. And I have heard of men from other tribes who lived equally as long."

One hundred and twenty years? Nate decided to check into the matter later. Right now he walked to the mare and patted her neck, thankful she hadn't spooked when the Ute jumped him.

Two Owls came over. "Do you want to see the Blackfoot camp?"

"Yes."

"Come with me."

Obediently Nate trailed after the warrior as Two Owls angled into the trees and headed northward. They crept forward until they could see the stream again. Seated or lying at ease on the bank, approximately 75 yards from the curve, were the Blackfeet. Positioned on their knees near the water, probably so they couldn't try to flee into the woods, were Shakespeare and Baxter. The Ohioan sagged, the worse for wear, but the mountain man had his shoulders squared and his eyes fixed balefully on his captors.

"They will leave soon," Two Owls disclosed. "We must be ready to follow."

Nate let the warrior lead them back to his horses. On the way Two Owls detoured a few dozen yards and retrieved his own horse.

Once back in the saddle, Nate rode slowly toward the bend. The Ute came alongside.

"Tonight I will begin to pick them off."

"What do you mean?"

Two Owls reached back and patted the bow slung in its buckskin case over his left shoulder. "I will kill them one by one."

"Is that wise?"

"We are outnumbered. We must reduce the odds."

"And the Blackfeet will know we are after them."

"So? They have a great deal distance to travel. In five suns most of them will be dead."

"And what am I supposed to do while you are picking them off?"

"Stay far back. They will not find you."

Nate reined up and the Ute did the same. "What about my friends? What will the Blackfeet do to them?"

Two Owls shrugged. "I do not know."

"The Blackfeet might kill them."

"Perhaps. But I doubt it. The Blackfeet want to take them back to their village."

"Once you start killing those warriors, who knows what will happen? I am sorry. I cannot permit you to kill any Blackfeet until I have freed my friends."

"You can not *permit* me?" Two Owls said.

"No."

"How will you stop me?"

"I will do whatever is necessary," Nate stated, leaving the rest to the Ute's imagination. He detected a flicker of resentment in the warrior's eyes and tensed. This would be a true test of how much he could rely on the man.

A minute elapsed during which Two Owls stared at the youth without blinking. Finally he nodded curtly. "As you wish. I will not slay the dogs until you have rescued your friends."

"Thank you again."

"Provided you can free them within two days," Two Owl added.

Nate frowned. Why the time constraint? What difference did it make if he took two days or ten? "Two days is not enough time."

"It is all I can spare. In three days they will be at the limit of Ute territory and I promised my wife I would go no further. Giving you two days leaves me one day to kill as many of them as I can."

"And if I do not agree?"

"In three days I start killing whether you have rescued your companions or not."

There was no doubt the Ute meant it. Nate had two choices. Push the issue and possibly have a fight on his hands or cause Two Owls to go off and stalk the war party now, or play along and try to save Shakespeare and Baxter in the alloted time. Since forty-eight hours were better than none, he chose to agree. "I will try to save them within two days."

"Good. Do not fear. Two days is more than enough."

"I hope so."

They rode to within ten feet of the bend and dismounted to check on the band. The Blackfeet were already on the march, staying close to the stream, the captives walking at the middle of the ragged line.

Nate waited until the war party was out of sight, then climbed on the mare and headed out. He went slowly, well aware a single mistake could prove fatal. Although he resented the time limitation imposed by the Ute, secretly he was glad for the warrior's company. No one knew how to fight Indians better than another Indian, and the Ute's advice could prove invaluable.

Two Owls paced his stallion to the left of the mare. "Do you mind if we talk?" he asked.

"What about?"

"I am very curious to learn about the ways of the white man. We have heard many strange stories, some of which can not possibly be true."

"What kind of stories?" Nate responded.

"My people have been told the whites believe they can own land, can buy and sell it just as they would a horse or a dog. Is this true?"

"Yes."

Two Owls chuckled. "This is foolish. The land

belongs to all. No one person has any right to own even a blade of grass. The land is ours to roam over as we please." He paused. "Is it also true the whites live in great stone villages where in the winter the air is choked with smoke from their fires?"

"This is also true."

"And most whites in these stone villages do not hunt or fish because they have others who do this work for them?"

"Yes."

"We were also told that many whites do not make their own clothes."

"In the stone villages this is often the case, but people living outside them still make much of their own clothing."

A contemptuous snort reflected the Ute's opinion of the white way of life. "Your people sound very lazy to me."

"Pampered is more like it."

Two Owls scrutinized Nate's profile. "If life in the stone villages is so easy, why did you travel to the mountains to live?"

"I was tricked."

"How?"

"An uncle claimed he would give me a great treasure if I came, so I did. As it turned out, he did not own the kind of treasure I thought he did."

"You came for money?"

"Yes."

"I know about the money whites recieve for the beaver pelts they collect. Why are your people so interested in having something you cannot eat and cannot wear? What purpose does your money serve?"

"Whites like to own money for the same reasons Indians like to own horses. The more they have, the richer they are."

"But horses have a purpose. They can be ridden or used to haul belongings or eaten when game is scarce. What can you do with money?"

"Buy clothes and food and land."

"Ah. You use money to trade for things you want, much like we trade one thing for another, such as horses for a woman."

"Yes."

"Why not trade directly? Why use money at all?"

The persistent questions began to annoy Nate. He wanted to keep his mind on the task at hand, not be distracted by idle chatter about the white man's economic system. "Because money is easier to carry in a pocket than a horse," he replied.

Two Owls chuckled. "I think I understand now, but your ways still seem strange to me."

Nate made no sign, hoping the Ute would do the same. No such luck.

"Will you go back to the stone villages to live one day?"

"Not if I can help it. I like the mountains."

"What does your guardian spirit want you to do?"

"My what?"

"Your guardian spirit. You must have gone on a vision quest and talked to the spirit being who watches over you."

"I have no idea what you are talking about."

"Guardian spirits teach us proper prayers and songs to use when addressing the spirit world. They also reveal which objects are most sacred to us and will protect us from harm. Every Ute has a guardian spirit. If your people do not, it would explain a lot of things."

Nate recalled a passage from the Bible he'd read in Sunday School when a boy. Although he couldn't quote it, he remembered the general thrust. "Now I know what you mean. My people have another word for them. They call such things guardian"—he began in sign and finished in English—"angels."

"Angels?" Two Owls said awkwardly, rolling the word on his tongue.

Nate was going to repeat the word when a harsh screech of rage arose up ahead.

Chapter Ten

Two Owls reined his stallion to the left and motioned while barking a few words in the Ute tongue.

Turning the mare, Nate hurried into the trees, leading the other horses into concealment. No sooner did the last of the pack animals reach cover than several figures appeared to the west, running along the bank. Nate was stunned to see Thaddeus Baxter out in front, pursued by two speedy Blackfeet. The Ohioan was trying to escape!

Baxter raced awkwardly, his bound arms throwing off his stride, but he maintained surprising speed nonetheless. He glanced anxiously over his shoulder again and again, desperation on his face.

For their part, the Blackfeet bounded like fleet deer. One held a war club, another a bow. They were confident of overtaking their quarry and did not exert themselves to their utmost.

Nate wanted to shout, to let Baxter know he was there, but such a move would have been foolish. The other Blackfeet were sure to appear any second.

The Ohioan didn't get very far, 50 feet at most. He was looking back one more time when his left foot snagged in a clump of weeds and down he went, pitching onto his face and upper chest. Before he could do more than rise to his knees the Blackfeet were there, each grabbing an arm and brutally yanking him erect.

Damn the bastards all to hell! Nate thought, raising the Hawken, ready to fire if they acted as if they were going to kill Baxter. Hang the consequences! He couldn't just sit there and let the man be slain.

But the warriors only wheeled and half-pulled, half-dragged the feebly struggling trapper off.

How had Baxter managed to break away from them? Nate wondered. He watched until the trio was lost to view and glanced at the Ute. "That was close."

"We will let them get a ways ahead and follow their tracks."

"I am not much of a tracker."

Two Owls grinned. "I am one of the best in my village. We will not lose them."

Nate studied the warrior for a moment. "Will you help me save my friends?" he asked.

"I came back mainly to kill Blackfeet."

"Will you help me?" Nate repeated, puzzled as to why the Ute avoided the question.

"I will do what I can," Two Owls signed enigmatically.

They fell silent and stayed hidden for ten minutes, then moved out and trailed the war party. Nate noticed a somber, thoughtful expression on the Indian, but didn't pry. He was glad for the chance to think and plan. His best bet for freeing his friends would be late at night, when most or all of the Blackfeet should be asleep. But if they made forts every night, how could he get his friends out undetected? The problem seemed unsolvable.

For over an hour the tracks led west along the stream. Two Owls raised his right hand and halted when they reached a spot where the stream narrowed and the bank was low. He leaned over the side of his mount and scanned the soft earth intently, then straightened and pointed at the opposite side. "They have crossed here."

"Lead on," Nate said.

Due north was the new direction, over a series of hills and around the base of a snow-capped peak. The sun rose ever higher and the shadows in the narrow gorges and valleys lengthened.

Nate expected the band to stop now and then to rest, but the Blackfeet kept pushing on. Why were they in such a hurry? Simply to get home? Or did they have a rendezvous with another band planned? If the latter, his problems were compounded. Fourteen Blackfeet were more than enough. Any more and a rescue became virtually impossible.

The afternoon waxed and waned and the sun dipped toward the western horizon.

"They will halt soon to make camp for the night," Two Owls said.

"I hope so."

"Once they do, we must find a suitable spot to make our camp, somewhere we can safely build a fire."

"No fire."

"If we pick carefully they will never spot it."

"No fire. I have plenty of bear meat. We do not need to cook food."

Two Owls frowned and seemed about to argue the point. Instead he faced forward and made no comment.

Only half the sun was visible when the Blackfeet

finally halted for the night. They encamped in a ravine between two mountains where they were sheltered from the elements and secure from searching eyes.

Nate would never have known they were there if not for the Ute. The two of them were following the trail and were within a quarter of a mile of the ravine when Two Owls looked up to survey the countryside and spotted a pair of Blackfeet emerging from the erosion-caused defile; he halted and gestured for Nate to do the same.

With bows in hand, apparently going to hunt meat for their supper, the two Blackfeet headed westward into dense woodland.

Two Owls moved to the left and went four hundred yards, stopping in the shelter of a barren hillock. "This is as good a spot as any to stay tonight."

"Are we safe here?"

"As safe as anywhere else."

"I mean are we too close to the Blackfeet?"

"No. They will not stray far from their camp. We should build a fort or lean-to of our own to shield us from the wind. We are at a much higher elevation than we were this morning and the temperature can drop drastically by morning," Two Owls disclosed. "We would be better off with a fire."

"No fire."

"You are a stubborn man, Grizzly Killer."

Nate set about feeding the horses. There was no water nearby, but they had slaked their thirst at the stream earlier when they were crossing and that drink would have to tide them over until the morning. He hobbled them and removed the packs, took out a handful of dried meat, then stepped over to where the Ute sat at the base of a cottonwood tree. "Would you like some bear meat?"

"Yes."

Sharing the handful equally, Nate sat down and sighed. He chewed on a strip and contemplated his predicament.

"Do you know how you will save your friends yet?"

"No. Maybe you can help me with an idea. Tell me what the Blackfeet do between evening and dawn."

"That is easy. They make their forts first. Then some go after food using only bows or lances. Fusees are never fired in enemy territory for obvious reasons, except in an emergency. The game is cleaned and cooked, and after eating they sit around talking or singing until late."

"In this case they post guards all night to watch the prisoners?"

"Of course. They probably take turns."

"At what point during the night would most of them undoubtedly be asleep?"

"Shortly before dawn everyone except the guards will be sound asleep. Do you think you will make your try then?"

"Seems to be the best time," Nate said. "But I need a distraction to draw their attention and keep them busy."

"May I make a suggestion?"

"By all means."

"Fire."

"Set the forts on fire?"

"Unless you would prefer to set the entire forest on fire."

"I have already considered torching the forts and I think it would be too dangerous. My friends could be slain before I get to them."

"They will definitely be slain if you do not do something, and this is the best idea."

Nate mentally debated the merits of the scheme in depth. He couldn't ask for a better distraction. If the Blackfeet constructed three forts each night, he'd only have to set the two not containing his friends ablaze. The cries of the warriors inside would draw the guards from the third fort, and in the confusion of the flames and the smoke he might be able to get Shakespeare and Baxter out. "I think it is the best idea."

"I thought you would."

"What will you be doing while I am crawling up to the forts to set them on fire?"

The Ute laughed. "Why must you do everything the hard way?"

"I do not understand."

"If you try crawling right up to the forts and starting the fires there, the guards are bound to hear you. Why not light two torches and carry them behind you until you are close enough to set the forts on fire? The guards will not have time to react and the forts will swiftly be engulfed in flames. You can be in and out before the Blackfeet dogs have time to piss themselves."

Another excellent suggestion. Nate signed as much.

"My people have had many years of experience battling the Blackfeet. We have learned a few tricks in that time."

"The Utes are known far and wide as powerful fighters," Nate truthfully noted. "I am surprised the Blackfeet travel such a great distance to raid your villages."

"That is why they come."

"Again I do not understand."

Leaning against the trunk, Two Owls explained patiently. "The greater the enemy, the greater the glory. Why count coup on dogs when you can count them on panthers?"

"You are telling me the Blackfeet like to raid the Utes because they know your people are tough in warfare?"

"Yes. I do not know how it is with you whites, but Indians measure the might of a tribe by the might of its enemies. Do you ever hear of the Blackfeet raiding the Otos or the Iowas?"

"No," Nate admitted.

Two Owls grunted. "Because the Blackfeet would not soil their hands fighting such pathetic adversaries. The Otos, Iowas, and others are weak, and the Blackfeet will not stoop to granting such weaklings the distinction of being their enemies."

Nate was astonished by the information. No one had ever told him about this aspect of Indian affairs. "You almost sound like you admire the Blackfeet. I thought you hated them."

"I hate them, but I am wise enough to admire their fighting skill."

"Do all tribes share this philosophy?"

"Some. Not all. Only the best."

The man's proud boasting almost made Nate chuckle, but he wisely refrained. They ate for a while. Two Owls requested more meat, which Nate gladly provided. Twilight descended.

"One last time I will urge you to agree to a fire," the Ute said.

A nip already was in the air. Nate gazed at the snow crowning the mountains and felt a slight chill. Even with blankets, by morning they would be extremely uncomfortable. He glanced at the slope of the hillock, calculating. "I doubt the Blackfeet would see our smoke."

"They will not," Two Owls said, sitting forward, sensing victory. "I will build a lean-to and we will place the fire inside. Most of the smoke will be dispersed before it rises as high as the trees."

Nate had used the same trick once himself, against the Utes. He reluctantly nodded. "All right. Build your fire."

With enthusiastic alacrity Two Owls set up a sizeable lean-to and got a small fire going underneath, in the center. When satisfied with his handiwork he sat back and rubbed his hands together over the flickering flames. "I am glad you finally agreed. I was afraid we would come to blows."

"Why?"

Two Owls looked at him. "If you had said no I was going to build a fire anyway."

Nate couldn't help but laugh. He liked the man, despite his arrogance.

"Will you try to rescue your friends tonight?"

"Since you know the ways of the Blackfeet better than I do, what would you recommend?"

"I would wait until tomorrow night. The farther they travel, the less of a chance they will be expecting pursuit. You will take them completely by surprise."

"Do you think we could lose their trail tomorrow?"

"No. I can track a snake over solid rock. And there is no bad weather to worry about."

"How do you know?"

Two Owls made a sweeping motion toward the nearest peaks. "I have lived here all my life. I can determine the weather we will have by the taste of the air."

Lord, what a braggart! Nate nodded as if he believed the statement, and stared at the forest. Having another day worked out well, gave him time to steel his nerves for the attempt. He felt confident the Blackfeet would not harm his friends until then. By the day after tomorrow the three of them would be en route to his cabin. The beaver would have to wait until another time. Next year, maybe.

"Grizzly Killer?"

"Yes?"

"How many coups have you counted?"

Nate cocked his head. Why ask such a personal question? Then he recollected that warriors from many tribes boasted of their exploits after the fact;

indeed, they were expected to relate the details to the entire tribe at special ceremonies. How many *had* he killed? He honestly could't recall. "I have lost count," he replied.

Two Owls was dumbfounded for a moment. He recovered his composure and leaned forward. "How can a man forget how many enemies he has killed?"

"My people do not keep track of such things."

"You do not count coup?"

"No."

Two Owls clucked and shook his head. "Truly you whites are a strange race. There must be a purpose for your existence, but I cannot imagine what it is. You do not seem to know anything about the right way to live. When I tell my people all I have learned, they will think I exaggerated."

"You?" Nate responded, and hid his broad grin by feeding a branch to the flames.

Chapter Eleven

The next day began with a flurry of activity.

A strong hand shaking Nate's right shoulder awoke him before the sun appeared on the eastern horizon. Stars still dominated the heavens. Blinking in momentary confusion, he looked up at Two Owls, then sat and rubbed his eyes. A nip in the air made him shiver. "What is it?"

"What do you think? We must be ready to leave by sunrise."

"But this early?"

"Would you rather they started without us?"

Nate recalled the frantic search of the day before and shook his head. "I will be ready quickly." He threw off his blanket, noticed the fire had dwindled to smoldering embers, and stretched. His first priority was relieving his bladder; then he attended to loading the packs on the horses and preparing the mare for travel. Checking all his guns came next. The Ute made no effort to help and Nate wasn't about to ask. A rosy glow painted the sky in the east by the time he finished.

"No wonder the Blackfeet got a head start on you yesterday," Two Owls joked. "You take half a day just getting ready to leave."

Grinning more out of courtesy than any keen appreciation of the Ute's sense of humor, Nate went to the fire and stomped it out. He climbed on the mare and signed, "After you."

Two Owls rode slowly around the hillock until he had a clear view of the ravine. He held up his hand and halted.

Pushing against the stirrups so he could stand in the saddle, Nate was able to see the country beyond. He involuntarily stiffened at the sight of Shakespeare and Baxter being pushed and prodded northward. Both men were ringed by Blackfeet; apparently the band had no intention of letting a repeat of yesterday's escape attempt occur. At their head walked White Bear.

Not until the war party disappeared in the distance did Two Owls goad his stallion forward.

Nate arched his spine to alleviate stiffness in his lower back, and resigned himself to another day of tedious tracking. His inner thighs ached from all the riding he'd done, which gave him a little added incentive to free his friends. In his mind's eye he reviewed his plans for the rescue, going over it again and again, plotting for contingencies.

By mid-morning the temperature had climbed into the sixties. By noon the sun shone down mercilessly on the two of them and their animals and the air hung like a sweltering, heavy robe over the landscape.

Nate wiped perspiration from his brow with the sleeve of his buckskins and longed for a drink. He hadn't realized it could get so hot at the higher elevations. They were skirting a mountain on their right. Overhead an eagle soared. He wished he had the bird's vantage point so he could scan the horizon for water.

Not much later they came to a small lake. Two Owls stopped and studied the shore, then rode boldly to the edge of the bank and slid off his horse.

Uncertain whether they should expose themselves so brazenly, Nate reluctantly rode to the lake and dismounted. His eyes roved over the shore on each side and saw no evidence of the band.

The Ute noticed and chuckled. "We are safe, Grizzly Killer. The Blackfeet passed this way much earlier."

"What if they're resting on the north shore? They could see us."

Two Owls nodded at the ground. "They rested here for a while, then hurried on. Remember, they want ot reach their village as quickly as they can so they can show off their prisoners. Their people will celebrate the capture of your friends for days."

"Not if I can help it." Nate let the mare drink and knelt to splash some refreshing moisture on his face. When she finished he dropped prone and greedily gulped until he couldn't take another drop. As he straightened he saw the warrior regarding him critically.

"You should not drink so much at one time. When going long periods without water it is better to drink in moderation when the opportunity arises."

"You concentrate on the Blackfeet and I will take care of my drinking."

"As you wish. But do not bother to complain if your stomach aches shortly."

"My stomach is fine," Nate declared testily.

A half hour later his stomach disagreed. They had ridden two miles from the lake when he felt an acute spasm and almost doubled over. Thankfully the Ute was in front and couldn't see his discomfort. The pain mystified him. He'd drunk equally as much on other occasions, so why should he have trouble now?

Before them lay a verdant meadow. A buck stood to the northwest, chewing contentedly, undisturbed by their presence. From a cluster of boulders to the east several groundhogs stood erect and studied them before one of the creatures uttered a shrill cry and they all darted into their burrows.

Nate gritted his teeth and patiently weathered his bellyache. The spasms grew progressively worse for 15 minutes, then abruptly abated. He mentally vowed never to drink so much again. Ever.

The terrain consisted of rolling hills sandwiched between regal mountains. In the distance to the north reared a bald peak that strongly resembled a human skull in its general outline. They made directly toward it, and the closer they came the more realistic the imaginary skull appeared.

"That is Dead Man's Mountain," Two Owls revealed, indicating the peak with a jerk of his thumb. "My people consider it to be bad medicine."

"Why?"

"Once three Utes went up the mountain to catch eagles and pluck their feathers. Two of the men were never seen again. The third stumbled into our village, said, 'The big hairy thing,' and died."

"The big hairy thing?"

Two Owls nodded, twisting so his gestures could be seen better. "That is what he told the man who caught him as he fell to the ground."

"What was he referring to?"

"We have no idea."

"A grizzly maybe?"

"If a grizzly had attacked him, he would have said so."

"Were there claw marks on him?" Nate asked.

"None. No marks at all. Our medicine man

believed he saw something that frightened him so badly it scared him to death."

Nate chuckled. "And you believe this story?"

"Yes. It happened in my great-grandfather's time and he saw the man who died. When I was a child he told the tale to me and swore it was true."

Lifting his right hand over his eyes to shield them away from the sunlight, Nate scrutinized the mountain. "There must be a logical explanation," he commented after a minute.

Two Owls slowed so he could ride even with the youth. "Why?"

"Because there are logical explanations for everything."

"Do all whites believe this?"

"Most do, yes."

"Then most whites are fools. There are matters men will never understand. The ways of spirit beings, for instance, are beyond our power to comprehend."

"Are these the same guardian spirits you were talking about before?"

"Those and many others," Two Owls said, and motioned at the atmosphere. "The spirit beings who live all around us. Surely you have talked to one?"

"Not recently."

"Go on a vision quest sometime. You will see what I mean."

"One day," Nate signed noncommittally, inwardly laughing at the notion of communicating with unseen spirits.

"Have you ever seen a lake monster?" the Ute unexpectedly inquired.

"There are no such things."

Two Owls adopted an exasperated expression. "There are men in my tribe who have seen them, so do not sit there and tell me such creatures do not exist."

"Can you blame me for being skeptical? I would have to see one myself before I could believe such an outrageous yarn."

"Go to Bear Lake. A monster lives in the water and is seen often."

"I have been there. The last rendezvous was held on the south shore, and not one person reported seeing any monster," Nate signed with all the patience he could muster.

"No wonder. There were too many people there and the monster stayed in hiding at the bottom of the lake."

"How convenient."

"If you do not believe me, ask the Shoshones."

Nate straightened and studied the warrior's features. Two Owls had no way of knowing he was married to a Shoshone so the remark had been made innocently. "Why them?"

"They live in the vicinity of Bear Lake and they know all about the monster. A woman we captured told us all about it. The beast is like a great serpent but has short legs and sometimes crawls out onto the land. She also told us the monster sprays water out of its mouth."

"Was she suffering from a blow on the head at the time?"

Hissing in anger, Two Owls rode several yards in front of the mare.

Nate grinned and shook his head in amazement. How could any sane person believe such nonsense. When he returned to his cabin he would ask Winona about the so-called monster, and he felt certain she would laugh and agree with him that the woman had concocted the entire story. Lake monster indeed!

They continued tracking the Blackfeet in strained silence. Two Owls did not ask another question the remainder of the day. Only when the sun completed its transit of the sky and evening was almost upon them did he deign to look at Nate.

"We should make camp soon."

"Pick a spot. I trust your judgment," Nate responded, and realized he'd made a mistake when the Ute's lips compressed.

They had been rising steadily for the better part of an hour, and above them loomed a ragged ridge. Two Owls rode to just below it and slid from his horse. He stepped higher and peered at whatever lay above, then motioned for Nate to join him.

Gripping the Hawken in his left hand, Nate moved next to the warrior and gazed out over a plateau stretching for three or four miles. In the foreground was a level, grassy field covering 20 to 30 acres. Across the field lay a pond, then dense forest. And erecting their forts on the north side of the pond were the Blackfeet.

"They have selected their campsite wisely," Two Owls noted. "To get close enough to hurl your torches will require great stealth."

Nate said nothing. He'd already perceived as much and was plotting his approach.

"I could do it for you."

Surprised, Nate turned. "The job is mine. They are my friends."

"True, but I can move quieter than any white ever born. My chances of success are better than yours."

"Thank you, but no. I will do the task myself."

"As you wish."

They walked to their horses and led them lower into a stand of pine trees.

"Tonight we will not use a fire," Two Owls stated.

Nodding absently, Nate started to remove a pack from his pack horse.

"What are you doing?" Two Owls asked.

"Unloading the . . ." Nate lowered his arms as

comprehension dawned. They might need to make a swift escape, in which case there wouldn't be time to strap all the packs on the animals. Although the horses were tired and deserved their rest, he had to leave them fully burdened until the rescue of his friends was achieved. He tightened the pack and reclined against a nearby tree.

Two Owls strolled over. "You should use what light is left to spy on the Blackfeet and plan your strategy."

"I will soon. Thanks."

The Ute squatted and scratched his chest. "Do you have a wife, Grizzly Killer?"

"Yes," Nate replied, wondering why the warrior asked such a question.

"Do you have children?"

"Not yet."

"Have as many as you can. Children are the sweetest blessings of the Great Mystery."

"I had no idea the Utes were such devoted parents," Nate signed. The Ute glowered and began to rise, so he quickly added, "I was complimenting your people, not insulting them."

Two Owls eased down again. "Children are the legacy we leave for future generations. They are more precious than the finest hides." He paused. "I was told once that whites hit their children to punish them. Is this true?"

Nate thought of the beatings his own father had administered when he was younger. "Yes."

Revulsion rippled over the Ute's countenance. "How disgusting. We never hit our children. There are better methods to use when instructing them in proper behavior. When you hit a child, you hurt the child's soul."

"I will try to remember that when I have my own children."

"Since you do not pray to your guardian spirit, how do you contact the spirit world?"

What was all this leading up to? Nate wondered. He signed, "Whites usually pray directly to the Great Mystery."

"Then I will do the same for you."

"I do not understand."

"Even though you are a white, I like you, Grizzly Killer. If you are killed tonight, I will pray to the Great Mystery on your behalf and ask that the passage of your soul from this world to the next be swift and safe."

"Thank you," Nate signed, and meant it.

Chapter Twelve

Sleeping was impossible. Nate tried to get some rest, but couldn't. He lay on his back on a patch of soft grass and covered himself with a blanket, then spent about an hour tossing and turning and staring at the stars. Finally he gave the notion up as a lost cause, replaced the blanket in a pack, and sat down close to the Ute, who still sat under the tree. Without a fire they could barely see one another, so he had to pay particular attention when the warrior used sign language.

"Are you ready?"

"Yes. I want to get it over with."

"Be patient. Do not try to rush or you will be killed. As much as I despise the Blackfeet, I must admit they are excellent fighters."

"I plan to sneak past them into the woods north of the pond, make a small fire where it cannot be seen, and light two torches. Then I will set the forts ablaze. The rest will be in the Great Mystery's hands."

Two Owls grunted. "Your plan is a good one. I will

take cover in the field of grass and kill any Blackfeet who try to stop you."

"Just be certain you do not shoot my friends or me by mistake."

The Ute grinned. "When I shoot someone, Grizzly Killer, it is never by mistake."

They engaged in small talk to pass the time. Nate was surprised to learn the Utes had not always been noted for their warlike tendencies. Many years ago, before the coming of the Spaniards, the Utes lived in small family groups. They spent most of their time in the high mountain valleys seeking fish, berries, and game. When the weather turned cold they would follow the buffalo and antelope to the south and stay there until spring.

But the advent of the Spanish changed Ute life forever. The simple hunters and seed gatherers obtained horses and became expert horsemen. The family groups banded together and began conducting raids on Spanish settlements and other tribes. In short order the Utes were expert marauders, ranging far and wide to count coup, steal more horses, and plunder at will.

Soon the Utes were in contention with other powerful tribes: the Cheyenne, Arapaho, Comanche, and Kiowa. They held their own against all of them. Only one other tribe successfully conducted raids into Ute territory on a regular basis. The Blackfeet.

Nate found it hard to conceive of the Utes as seed gatherers and peaceful hunters, and he marveled at the fact that possession of horses should make such a big difference in their lives. Granted, horses gave the tribes greater mobility than ever before and enabled those who possessed mounts to have an unfair advantage in battle, but he couldn't understand the drastic change.

Two Owls plied Nate with questions about life in

the white man's world. How many whites were there? How many stone villages? How many horses did the Great Chief of all the whites own? How many coups had the Great Chief counted?

Nate answered honestly, and was annoyed when many of his answers were greeted with smiles. The Utes found it incredible that there were ten million people in the United States, and that in one village alone, New York City, there were over 125,000. He found it humorous Nate didn't know the number of horses owned by the President. And he laughed at learning the Great Chief did not count coup after the Indian fashion.

Midnight came and went. The night grew progressively cooler. Wolves howled and panthers screamed. A strong breeze from the northwest rattled the trees.

Despite the late hour, Nate felt no fatigue. Nervousness assailed him, and he had to force his arms and legs to stay still. He glanced time and again at the sky, especially the eastern horizon, gauging the passage of the stars, and tried not to dwell on the job he must do.

They had settled into a mutually reflective silence for a long while when Two Owls gazed overhead, cleared his throat, and signed, "It is time."

Nate stood and hefted the Hawken. "Then I will be on my way."

"Do you have what is necessary to start the fire?"

"In my pouch," Nate assured him, and looked into the warrior's eyes. "Be careful."

"You too."

They climbed to the summit of the plateau and headed due north, moving quietly through the tall grass. Once a large animal, possibly a deer, snorted and ran off. They crouched and waited a suitable interval before resuming their approach, reaching the south shore of the pond safely.

Nate knelt and parted the grass to stare across the oval body of water. He estimated it to be 60 feet in diameter. The three forts were easy to distinguish due to their unnatural conical shape. Not a glimmer of light showed inside any of them. He glanced at the Ute, gave a wave, and bore to the right, swinging wide around the pond until he attained the sanctuary of the woods.

In order to avoid being heard or seen, Nate traveled a good 30 yards before he stumbled on a narrow gully that would suit his purposes ideally. He gathered limbs from under several trees, piled them at the bottom of the gully, and opened his pouch to remove his flint and steel. Next he broke a few twigs into small pieces to use as kindling and added three pinches of coarse black powder from his powder horn to serve as tinder.

On only the fifth strike to the flint on the steel did the sparks ignite the powder, which flashed and sparked and in turn ignited the kindling. A few strategically placed puffs and the kindling caught, the flames growing rapidly, and soon the limbs were burning and crackling.

Now Nate had to hurry. He scoured his immediate vicinity for a pair of suitable makeshift torches, and found two stout broken pine limbs that would suffice. Cradling the rifle under his left arm, he used his butcher knife to strip off the shoots and seized each limb by its thin end. Rising, he held the thick ends in the flames until both caught.

Clambering from the gully with two makeshift torches in his hands proved difficult, but he managed. Bending at the waist, he ran sideways while keeping the torches low to the ground. When he had gone two thirds of the way to the pond he turned with his back to the south and moved backwards, his body hopefully screening the torches from

enemy eyes. Not that he expected many of the
Blackfeet to be awake. Perhaps those guarding his
friends were, but the rest should be sound asleep.

He tripped and corrected his balance in the nick
of time. One of the limbs sputtered as if on the verge
of going out. With bated breath he waited until the
flames burned brightly, then hastened onward, his
head twisted so he could see any obstacles.

The forts had been erected in a row, from west to
east, spaced ten feet apart. As before, the Blackfeet
had placed Shakespeare and Baxter in the middle
structure. Earlier, Nate had watched as his friends
were shoved inside and followed by a pair of
Blackfeet.

Please let there be only two in the fort still! he
prayed as he drew within 20 feet of the inky shapes
and paused to gird himself. He must not slow down
for even a second once he burst from cover. To stand
still would be to die.

So far no sound at all issued from the forts.

Nate clamped his arm down harder on the
Hawken, gripped the limbs more securely, whirled,
and charged, his moccasins smacking on the pine
needles and soft earth underfoot. Go! he goaded
himself. Go! Go!

He sped from the forest and reached the wester-
most fort. Instantly he propped the torch against it,
letting the flames lick at the poles, and dashed to the
fort to the east, repeating the procedure. He stood
back to watch the structure catch, then ran around
to the front, gripping the rifle in both hands.

Not a sound issued from the structures. All the
Blackfeet were evidently still slumbering.

Nate ran to the middle fort and stood to the right
of the doorway, waiting. His body tingled in expectation. Soon. They had to notice the flames soon.

They did. Loud screeches arose in the west fort,

followed moments later by shouts in the east one. A warrior in the middle fort shouted something in the Blackfeet language.

Bracing his legs, Nate gripped the Hawken by the barrel and focused on the waist-high doorway. What's taking them so long? he wondered in amazement. They should be bolting out of there like frightened rabbits. He detected motion out of the corner of his eye and looked up.

A Blackfoot was emerging from the west fort, a war club clutched in his right hand. He glanced around, spied the youth, and vented a war whoop as he sprang erect. No sooner did he stand, however, than an arrow flashed out of the night and thudded into his chest, the impact spinning him to the left. He blinked, stared mutely at the feathers jutting from his body, and pitched over.

Distracted by the man's death, Nate didn't realize someone was scrambling from the fort at his very feet until he heard a feral hiss and glanced down in consternation to see a burly Blackfoot about to bury a tomahawk in his legs. He threw himself backward, barely evading the blow, then swung the heavy Hawken like a club and clipped the Indian on the jaw.

The Blackfoot sagged, still conscious but dazed.

Nate kicked him, delivering the tip of his right moccasin to the point of the warrior's chin. Teeth crunched and the Blackfoot collapsed. Bending forward, Nate grabbed the man by the shoulders and heaved, pulling the warrior all the way out.

More and more yells of alarm were voiced as the rest of the war party awakened. A second Blackfoot exited the fort to the west, and promptly received a shaft in his jugular for the effort.

From Nate's rear arose a ghastly shriek, and he twisted to observe yet another warrior who had just stepped outside and been greeted by the lethal flight of an arrow into his left eye. The Blackfoot grabbed at the shaft, sagged against the poles, and toppled over.

Grayish-white smoke billowed upward from the pair of burning forts. Already poles were ablaze.

Another warrior started to crawl from the middle fort.

Nate looked down, intending to club this one as he had the other, saving his balls for when they would really be needed. He found himself staring down the barrel of a fusee angled awkwardly in the direction of his head, and his immediate reaction was to jerk to the right, diving for the ground.

The fusee went off, booming like a cannon, narrowly missing him. Fusees were trade guns distributed by the Hudson's Bay Company and others, inferior smooth-bored flintlocks that were no match for the rifled arms of the trappers at long range but were decidedly deadly close up.

Nate returned the favor the moment his shoulder struck the earth, leveling the Hawken at the warrior's enraged face and sending a ball boring into the man's brain. He pushed to his feet and quickly dragged the Indian aside, then dropped to one knee and peered into the gloomy interior. "Shakespeare?"

"We're here, son. Hurry. Our arms and legs are tied."

Hastening inside, Nate dimly perceived the prone forms of his friends. He drew his butcher knife and set to work while listening to the bellows of the Blackfeet as they communicated back and forth. Had any more tried to escape the burning forts and been transfixed by arrows?

"Thank God you've come!" Baxter declared. "I'd about given us up for dead."

"Don't dawdle," Shakespeare advised. "I speak a little of the Blackfoot tongue. They're frantic because every warrior who has stepped outside has been killed, and they're getting set to pour out all at once before it's too late."

Nate appreciated the warning. Two Owls could not possibly cover both forts simultaneously and prevent all the Blackfeet from reaching cover. He sliced off the leather strips binding Shakespeare's wrists and ankles, then turned to Baxter.

"Please hurry," the Ohioan pleaded.

"Who is out there doing the killing?" Shakespeare asked, moving to the doorway. "Did you meet another trapper?"

"No. It's a friend of mine. A Ute."

"A Ute!" Baxter exclaimed. "They're as bad as the Blackfeet."

"I'll be damned," Shakespeare said, and chuckled.

Baxter went on in a rush. "Where did you meet a Ute? How do we know he can be trusted? They're heathen like all the rest."

With a final slash of his knife Nate freed the Ohioan and slid the knife in its sheath. He ignored the questions and moved to the doorway. "This is no time for talking. Stay close to me and we'll get out of this alive." He gave each of them one of his flint-locks even though his rifle was unloaded.

"The Blackfeet are awful quiet all of a sudden," Shakespeare noted.

Nate realized the band had stopped shouting. They must be about to make their bid, he deduced, and gambled on beating them to the high grass. "Follow me!" he cried, and darted through the doorway. He angled to the right, planning to skirt the pond and plunge into the field. He had to go past the west fort to do so, which was now fully ablaze on the side nearest the forest. As he came abreast of the doorway he glanced down.

Suddenly Blackfeet poured from the fort, four all

told, one after the other in a mad scramble to flee the flames. The first one saw Nate, voiced a fierce roar, and lunged.

The warrior's fingers just touched Nate's right leg as he went by and spurred him to go faster. Nate cast a hasty glance over his shoulder and saw Baxter fire at close range into the warrior's head. Then all three of them were past the forts and racing for their lives.

More Blackfeet emerged from the east fort. One of them was hit squarely in the neck by an arrow, but the rest were on their feet in a heartbeat and gave chase, uttering savage whoops.

Where was Two Owls? Nate wondered, his legs pumping. Only ten feet separated him from the tall grass, ten feet to possible safety, when a Blackfoot arrow struck him.

Chapter Thirteen

The shaft caught Nate in the back, in the right side just below the ribs, lancing his body with sheer torment and causing him to stumble and almost fall. If Shakespeare and Baxter hadn't paused to assist him, he would have gone down and been at the mercy of the Blackfeet. But sturdy hands seized him by the upper arms and propelled him the remaining distance to the field.

Shock made Nate dizzy and he nearly dropped his rifle. Only vaguely was he conscious of doing his best to keep up, running mechanically, struggling to recover his composure. If he didn't, he'd die. Think! Use your brain and think!

"Keep going, son," Shakespeare said.

"We won't let go of you," Baxter added.

But Nate knew they must. The Blackfeet would overtake them easily otherwise. He lowered his right hand and felt the bloody stone tip of the arrow protruding two or three inches from his flesh. Had it punctured a vital organ? He couldn't tell, and he

couldn't stop to examine the wound until the three
of them eluded the Blackfeet.

"They're gaining," Baxter said.

Clarity abruptly returned. Nate was conscious of
his driving legs and his thudding heart. He
suppressed the pain and declared, "Let go."

"Not yet," the mountain man replied.

"Let go of me," Nate insisted. "I can manage. I'm
only slowing you down."

"No," Shakespeare said.

"Are you sure?" Baxter asked.

"Let go," Nate reiterated, and twisted to wrench
himself from their grasp. His brashness threw all
three of them off stride, but they stayed erect and
sprinted on into the night in a weaving pattern.
Gritting his teeth, he looked back once more and
spotted the warriors fanning out, the nearest 20 feet
away.

"Which way?" Baxter asked.

"South," Nate answered in a raspy tone. "Our
horses are below the rim."

For another minute the marathon of death
continued. Nate fell a few feet behind his
companions. His buckskin shirt became drenched
with his blood, and the rubbing motion of the shaft
inside his body produced intense nausea. It felt as
if someone had their finger inside of him, poking
around carelessly, and he wanted so badly to scream
in anguish. But he couldn't. Not now. He must be
strong. He must have the stamina of a bull or be
slaughtered like a cow.

"They're still gaining," Baxter said anxiously.

Again Nate glanced at their pursuers and made an
impulsive decision. Perhaps they would have a better
chance if they didn't stay together. If each one of
them only had two or three Blackfeet after them, the
odds were better they would escape. In his agony the

idea seemed logical and he told the others, "Split up!"

"No!" Shakespeare responded.

But Nate had already slanted to the right, his right hand grasping the arrow to hold it steady, the grass swishing as the blades parted before him. His right side hurt terribly and grew worse the farther he fled. In his excruciating torment he lost all sense of direction, all sense of the distance he traveled. He simply ran and weaved, ran and weaved, and when he finally drew up short it was to gape in astonishment at a wall of trees blocking his path.

The forest?

It couldn't be the forest! He should be at the southern rim with the horses waiting below. Unless —and the insight chilled his soul—unless he had gone the wrong way.

He looked to the east and, sure enough, there were the blazing forts. He was 40 yards from them, confounded by his own stupidity. Turning, grimacing as he did, he spied a bounding figure 30 feet off.

A Blackfoot!

In a panic he spun and dashed among the trees, afraid of crashing into a trunk and aggravating his wound. He ran until his breath came in ragged gasps and the pain in his side had spread to his chest and abdomen. He ran until he could run no more, and then he collapsed onto his knees and doubled over, biting his lips to suppress a groan.

Lord, he hurt!

Nate tried to quiet his breathing and listened, hearing nothing to indicate the Blackfeet were still after him. Sweat caked his skin from head to toe. Even his hair was soaked. He gingerly felt the arrow, and pushed a finger through the tear in his buckskin shirt to gingerly touch the surprisingly neat edge of the hole. To his immense relief the blood flow seemed to have ceased. Perhaps he wouldn't bleed to death after all.

He straightened with much difficulty and pondered his next move. First and foremost the arrow must come out. If he kept running with the shaft inside, the friction might tear open a crucial vein or rupture an untouched organ. But how could he remove it without assistance?

A means occurred to him, but he balked at attempting so grueling a task. Successive waves of agony convinced him to try, and he placed his Hawken at his side and reached his right arm behind his back. His fingers contacted the smooth feathers and he closed his hand around the thin shaft. Did he dare go through with it? Taking a deep breath, he steeled his sinews, then snapped his arm upward, trying to break the arrow.

Exquisite torture racked his entire being. His spine arched and he opened his mouth to scream, choking the cry in his throat, venting a gurgling whine. He thought for a moment he might pass out, but didn't. Don't give up! he chided himself. Try again.

Nate tightened his grip, tensed, fought off a brief attack of vertigo, and duplicated the snapping motion, putting all of his strength into the act. Through pounding waves of soul-wrenching misery he distinctly heard the crack, and his hand came around holding the broken section. He stared at the feathers, waiting for his head to clear, marveling that he had succeeded halfway. The worst was yet to come.

Tossing the piece to the ground, Nate clutched the front of the arrow just below the point with both hands and girded himself for the second phase. Please let me make it, he prayed. Slowly, so as not to tear his insides more than they already were, he pulled on the shaft, drawing it from the hole, the sickening sensation making him shudder violently. He had to pause and catch his breath, composing his nerves, then tried again. A revolting squishing noise accompanied the extraction, and it took all of his self-control to keep going. When at last the shaft came clear, he closed his eyes and doubled over.

Now what should he do? Think, Nate! Think. The wisest course seemed to be to head back to the rim and find his friends. They would treat the wound and bandage him. He was cetainly in no condition to take care of himself, and he didn't want to wander around in the forest with bloodthirsty Blackfeet hunting his scalp.

Nate waited for his strength to return, breathing shallowly, leery of passing out. He envisioned Winona's beautiful features, and recalled the gentle feel of her loving hands on his naked body. More than anything else in the world he wanted to see her again, to hold her in his arms and taste her lips on his own. Thinking about her soothed him, made him appreciate the fact he was still alive, still able to fight, to escape.

At length he roused from his reflection and shoved to his feet. His sides protested the movement, and he pressed his right elbow on the hole as he shuffled back toward the field. He must be careful. The Blackfeet were around somewhere.

Perhaps he should find a hiding place and stay there until daylight? The idea appealed to him, but his desire to rejoin Shakespeare and Baxter overrode his common sense.

Nate walked unsteadily toward the field. He could see the forts over a hundred yards away, burning so brightly they were undoubtedly visible for many miles. With them to orient him, he had no difficulty determining in which direction to travel. Unfortunately, his legs were endowed with a mind of their own. They longed to rest. For that matter, his entire body wanted to curl into a ball and not move for a year. Annoyed at his weakness, he branded his body a traitor and willed it to keep going.

He checked the wound as he walked. The exit hole exuded a trickle of blood but the entry hole wasn't bleeding at all. Perhaps he wouldn't need to cauterize.

Off in the distance a shot sounded.

Nate halted, listening for additional discharges. Had that been a rifle, a flintlock, or a fusee? He guessed it came from the end of the plateau. Maybe the Blackfeet were trying to take the horses! He hurried, or attempted to, but his body stubbornly refused to obey his mental commands. He mopped his brow with his left hand, and stopped in mid-stride when his negligence dawned.

He'd forgotten the Hawken!

Stunned by his stupidity, Nate turned and headed back. How could he forget the most essential piece of equipment a mountaineer owned? Sure, he was hurting, but pain was no excuse for being recklessly careless.

He came to the spot where he thought he'd extracted the arrow but saw no sign of the pieces or his rifle. Confused, he searched in an ever-widening circle. Every second of delay made him increasingly impatient.

After a minute Nate decided he was wrong, that he'd pulled out the arrow farther north, and trudged a dozen yards to search again. Still nothing. Exasperated, he went another dozen yards, and another, and each time he failed to locate the Hawken.

Fatigue and the stress to his system caused him to trip twice. He became intermittently dizzy, and worried he would pass out. His right foot bumped into a log. Sighing, he sat down and clutched his side.

Another shot cracked to the south.

Nate looked up. The damn Blackfeet must still be after his companions or Two Owls. He longed desperately to help them, and the motivation sufficed to bring him to his feet. To give up while breath remained was inconceivable. He'd continue on until he dropped from exhaustion.

Five minutes later he had yet to locate the rifle. His resolve evaporated like dew under the morning sun. Doubt plagued him. Doubt he could recover the Hawken. Doubt he would see Shakespeare again. Doubt he would ever again experience Winona's tender caress. His mental and emotional states fluctuated as rapidly as the breeze.

On the verge of collapsing, moving each foot with supreme effort, his eyes downcast, Nate was stepping over the rifle before he realized it was indeed there. Grinning, he grunted and bent down to reclaim his weapon. Vertigo assailed him and he sank to his knees.

A minute or so and he'd be fine. Just a minute. His chin sagged and he licked his exceptionally dry lips.

Somewhere nearby a twig snapped.

Nate's head snapped up and he froze, his ears straining to their limit, expecting to hear the muffled tread of moccasin-covered feet or a whispered phrase in the Blackfoot tongue. He shifted position quietly to grab the rifle. The gun was empty but he could still employ it as a club, and if Fate granted him the time he could reload.

A heavy silence hung over the forest.

Were there Blackfeet close at hand or were his frayed nerves playing a trick on him? Nate surveyed the woods and saw nothing to alarm him. He had begun to believe he was exaggerating the danger when the soft crunch of a footstep off to his left confirmed he wasn't alone.

Nate eased down on his left side, wincing at the discomfort, and glued his unblinking eyes on the forest. He instinctively knew it wasn't his friends come looking for him. The Blackfeet, true to their persistent natures, had not stopped searching for him.

Something moved, a shadow among shadows.

He perceived the outline of a man, an Indian, 15 yards off and heading cautiously northward. Whether the warrior carried a bow, lance, club, or fusee was irrelevant. In his state Nate was no match for an infant let alone a robust scalper of white men.

Nate scarcely breathed, watching the Blackfoot cross his line of vision and disappear in the trees. He halfheartedly wished he had not given his pistols to the others. Several times the warrior glanced in his direction but failed to spot him.

Full comprehension of his predicament hit him with the force of an avalanche. Although he'd always known in the back of his mind that he could die at any time, he was now closer to death than he'd ever been. If the wound didn't kill him, the Blackfeet would. The reality sank into the core of his being and chilled his blood.

Nate listened for the longest time, wanting to make certain the Indian had departed before trying to flee. To rise required a herculean exertion. He tottered, mulling whether to reload the rifle, and realized the chore would take more time than he could afford to spare. Using the Hawken as a crutch to prevent him from falling, he turned and hiked toward the field.

Luck might be on his side, he consoled himself. If most of the Blackfeet were off after Shakespeare and Baxter, and the one after him had missed him in the dark, he should be able to get to the horses without difficulty. All he had to do was stay on his feet.

Was that all?

He opened his mouth to laugh aloud, but checked himself in time. The indiscretion startled him. Was he so befuddled that he would betray his presence so foolishly?

Perspiration coated his brow as he channeled all of his concentration into reaching the field. Take it easy, he admonished himself. Take it one step at a time. That was all. One measly step. The field wasn't all that far. In minutes the single steps would add up to the distance he needed to cover. Just keep going no matter what the cost.

No matter what.

An eternity seemed to pass before all those steps ultimately did bring him to the edge of the forest, and he crouched behind a tree to catch his breath. To the east, 30 yards distant, burned the forts. Somehow, probably from sparks, the middle fort had been touched off and was burning furiously. Combined, the forts radiated light over the tall grass and into the adjacent forest.

Nate surmised he might see a few Blackfeet moving about, but there were none. His gaze raked the field repeatedly. Not so much as a single blade moved unnaturally. Even so, he hesitated, preferring to stay right where he was for the time being. He was temporarily safe. Why increase the odds of being spotted by leaving the sanctuary of the forest?

His fluttering eyelids answered the question. If he keeled over he would be at the mercy of the Blackfeet, other predators, and the weather. As long as he kept moving, he'd be all right. Which was easier said than accomplished.

Nate used tree limbs to pull himself up and stood stiffly, then hobbled into the grass that bordered the very edge of the trunks. Despite the anguish he stayed hunched over, ignoring the pain in his lower back. What was one more pain to a man trapped in a living nightmare, a hell worse than the Inferno?

His guardian angel must have been watching over him because he crossed the field without being attacked. The sight of the rim expanded his heart with joy and he walked the final five yards without the aid of the rifle. Soon he would be with his companions!

Nate stepped to the edge and halted, scanning the trees below, beaming in triumph that proved to be premature the very next instant when onrushing footsteps sounded to his rear and he twisted in horror to see a Blackfoot holding a war club aloft, a club that smashed into his right temple and sent him sailing from the plateau. The last coherent thought he had was inanely sublime; he hoped there were no Blackfeet in the hereafter.

Chapter Fourteen

Why did he feel as if he was in a boat being rocked violently by huge waves?

The sensation surprised him. He'd thought the afterlife would be different; at the very least it wouldn't be so dark. He couldn't see a blessed thing. Then he became aware of a hand on his left shoulder, shaking him rudely, and realized he wasn't dead after all but alive and simply had his eyes closed. Alive! The word echoed in his brain like the joyous peals of church bells.

The pain engulfed him a second later and brought him back to reality. Groaning, he opened his eyes, and he knew he might have been better off being dead because staring balefully down at him was a tall Blackfoot, the one who carried the Spanish sword, the warrior named White Bear.

Other Blackfeet materialized above and around him, most with malevolent expressions.

Nate didn't move or speak. Anything he did might provoke them. He scanned their painted faces and

saw one of the warriors holding his rifle and wearing
his bullet pouch and powder horn. If his hazy
memory served, it was the same Blackfoot who had
struck him with the war club.

White Bear growled a string of words in his
language.

Still Nate stayed immobile.

Lashing out angrily, White Bear hit him across the
face and barked more Blackfoot words.

The blow stung wickedly. Nate suppressed his rage
and shook his head to signify he did not understand.

White Bear turned and addressed one of the
warriors. They conversed for a bit, then White Bear
looked at Nate and his hands signed a question: "Do
you know sign language, white man?"

Nate hesitated. Should he admit his knowledge of
not? A second slap prompted him to reveal he could
use sign, if only to buy time, to delay his eventual
torture. "Yes, White Bear."

Astonishment lined the Blackfoot's visage. "How
do you know my name?"

Instead of telling the truth, Nate responded,
"Every trapper has heard of the mighty Blackfoot
warrior who wears a sword."

The false claim sparked a brief debate among the
Blackfeet until White Bear silenced them with a wave
of his arm.

"How are you known?"

"I am Grizzly Killer."

Several of the warriors laughed.

"How did one so young earn such a name?" White
Bear asked, smirking.

"By killing grizzlies."

More mirth greeted the assertion.

White Bear did not appreciate the humor. "Where
are your friends?" he demanded gruffly.

"I do not know," Nate replied, elated to learn the

frontiersman, the Ohioan, and the Ute were safe.

"Lie to me and I will cut out your tongue," White Bear vowed.

"I have no idea," Nate insisted, refusing to be cowed. "We were separated last night during the fight."

"The fight was two suns ago."

Shock brought Nate to a sitting posture, his right side on fire, to gaze around in bewilderment. There was no sign of the forts. To the left ran a creek, to the right was a hill.

"We have carried you," White Bear revealed. "We do not want you to die yet."

Two days! Nate blinked and pressed his hand to the wound. No wonder the pain wasn't quite as bad as before. And no wonder he was starved.

"You and your friends killed many of my people. You will suffer for each one who died."

Nate looked at his captors again and was pleased to count only nine.

"In another day we will join a war party of our brothers," White Bear disclosed. "Then we shall decide what to do with you."

So he had at least another day of life. Nate glanced at the wound and discovered his shirt had been cut and a gummy substance of some sort applied to the hole. "What is this?"

"An herbal poultice to stop the bleeding and prevent infection," White Bear signed, and saw the incredulity on the youth's countenance.

The illogical practice of patching up a wounded enemy just to kill him later made a perverse sort of sense. Nate knew the Blackfeet delighted in torturing captured enemies, employing the most devious and cruel means imaginable, and since they intended to give him a taste of their savage cruelty, they wouldn't want him to die on them before the event.

A young warrior stepped forward. "I am Red Elk, the one who tended you."

Nate automatically signed, "Thank you." He was surprised when the warrior's mouth creased in an apparently genuine smile.

White Bear scowled and glanced at Red Elk, and perhaps because he had just been using sign language and felt no need to resort to his own tongue, or perhaps because he wanted Nate to know what he said, he addressed Red Elk in the same manner. "Remember he is our enemy and must be slain. All whites are our enemies."

"Even the white who saved my life?"

Some of the others growled in agreement.

"A white saved your life?" Nate inquired.

"Two winters ago," Red Elk related. "I was out hunting by myself far south of our village and tried to cross a frozen river. The ice broke. Try as I might, I could not climb out. I thought the cold would kill me or I would drown. But after a time a lone white trapper came by. He used a rope to pull me out and then made a fire so I could get warm." Red Elk paused. "That trapper saved my life. The next morning he left and I never saw him again."

White Bear snorted. "The only reason he saved you was because he did not know you were a Blackfoot. Had he known he would have left you in the freezing water."

"I do not know that."

"Why else did he save you?" White Bear asked.

Nate saw Red Elk's troubled expression, and realized he really owed his herbal treatment to the unknown trapper who had saved the warrior's life. Red Elk had tended to him out of a sense of obligation to whites in general. Whatever the case, he was glad. And he was surprised to discover not all Blackfeet viewed trappers as implacable foes.

White Bear stood and barked directions. He looked at Red Elk and spoke scornfully for a bit, then moved off to lead the band northward.

"You must get on your feet," Red Elk told Nate.

Using his palms to push erect, Nate swayed and almost pitched onto his face. He righted himself with a supreme effort and took a tentative stride. "I am weak," he informed the Blackfoot. "I do not know if I can keep up."

"If you do not, White Bear will chop off a few of your fingers."

The added incentive sufficed to compel Nate forward. He gained strength with every step. Loud growling in his stomach reminded him of his hunger. "I am starving. When can I eat?"

"When we do," Red Elk answered. He gazed at the backs of his fellow tribesmen, who were all hastening off at a brisk clip. "I am sorry, Grizzly Killer. I would not treat you like this, but I am not the leader of the war party."

"I understand."

"White Bear has placed me in charge of you. If you try to escape, I will be forced to kill you."

"One way or the other I will die," Nate said.

"Yes."

They hiked in silence for half an hour, Nate doing his best to keep up. The Blackfoot apparently weren't concerned about him fleeing; they hardly paid any attention to him except to glance over their shoulders every so often and sneer. He desperately craved food and drink and longed to stop, but he took the threat of losing his fingers seriously and plodded onward, a dull ache in his side, his stomach berating him in a marvelous imitation of an enraged grizzly.

"Are you well enough to converse?" Red Elk inquired as they trudged over the crest of a ridge.

"Yes," Nate replied, eager to do anything to take

his mind off his suffering.

"I imagine you know that most of my people hate whites."

"I got that impression."

"Do you know why?"

"I was told it is because when the first party of whites to ever visit your territory passed through, they killed a Blackfoot," Nate answered, referring to the incident involving the famed Lewis and Clark expedition.

Lewis had separated from his companion to explore land in the vicinity of Maria's River, taking six men along, and his party ran into a small band of Blackfeet. A fight broke out when the Indians attempted to steal some guns. One Blackfoot was stabbed to death, another shot in the stomach, and the rest fled. Ever since the Blackfeet had killed whites indiscriminately.

"They were not the first party," Red Elk said. "Other whites had visited our people and we always treated them with kindness and fairness." He frowned. "Those warriors who tried to steal guns shamed our tribe."

Nate glanced at him. "Do other Blackfeet feel the same way you do?"

"Yes."

"Then why do your people go out of their way to kill my people?"

"The white-haters are the ones who kill so many trappers. The rest of us will not attack whites unless we are attacked first."

"It is sad your leaders do not feel as you do."

"Some of our leaders do. Some do not."

"White Bear is obviously one who does."

"No one hates whites more than he does. It took me much talk to persuade him to let me put a poultice on your wounds, and I was surprised when he finally agreed."

"He wants me alive for whatever torture he has planned," Nate signed.

"I am afraid you are right." Red Elk looked into Nate's eyes. "I pity you, Grizzly Killer. The last trapper White Bear captured died a horrible death. He was staked out on a grizzly trail and eaten alive by the next bear that came by."

Nate envisioned such a fate and involuntarily shuddered.

"There is one good thing," Red Elk said.

"What is that?"

"White Bear never kills an enemy the same way twice. He will come up with a new means of killing you."

They lapsed into silence, and for several more hours Nate endured constant torment. He gritted his teeth to keep from crying out and showing any weakness. When White Bear finally called a halt near a spring, Nate sank to the ground in relief. Another warrior brought over three strips of dried deer meat, which Nate consumed in less than a minute. He ate so fast, he felt sick. A drink of cold mountain water settled his stomach and revived him considerably. Still, he moved with difficulty when White Bear instructed the band to resume their trek.

The rest of the day was more of the same. When the sun sank to the west they stopped on the south bank of a narrow stream. Red Elk and a second warrior stood guard while the rest constructed two forts. Hunters were sent out to secure meat. Another caught a few fish.

Nate was prodded at lance point into one of the forts, and he sat there alone until Red Elk carried a makeshift bark plate containing roasted deer meat and fish. Nate ate hungrily even though the food practically burned his tongue.

Red Elk stayed and watched him eat. When the final morsel was consumed, he gestured at the doorway. "You can drink from the stream if you wish. I would advise you to do so. You will get no more food or drink until morning."

"There is something else I must also do."

"What?"

"You know."

Red Elk's forehead creased in perplexity. "I have no idea what you are talking about."

"I need to relieve myself."

This elicited a laugh from the young Blackfoot. "You can go, but I am required to watch you the whole time."

"If you must, you must," Nate said. It would be pointless to argue. He had to make the best of the situation until an opportunity to escape presented itself. If one did. So he let the Blackfoot escort him to the spring and drank until he couldn't drink another sip, then walked behind a tree and did his private business.

Red Elk discreetly stayed a few yards away and pretended to be fascinated by a nearby boulder.

Once Nate was back in the fort, Red Elk sat near the doorway. He seemed preoccupied and signed nothing.

Nate was appalled when two warriors came in and bound his wrists and ankles, just like the Blackfeet had done with Shakespeare and Baxter. One of them shoved him onto his left side, then both laughed as they departed. Now he was deprived of his sole means of communication.

Not until twilight draped the landscape did several Blackfeet enter and build a fire, making themselves as comfortable as they could.

What a night! Nate had to endure the agony of his wound and the taunts and barbs of the trio, who constantly mocked him and poked him with a lance. Red Elk did not participate. All four Blackfeet eventually fell asleep, and snored loud enough to rouse a hibernating black bear.

Nate attempted to sleep, but couldn't at first. He tried to free his hands and failed.

Wolves howled not far off, yet not one Indian stirred.

An owl hooted close by.

Nate listened to the sounds, his soul dominated by despair, and tried to refrain from thinking about the fate in store for him. Think about Shakespeare, he told himself. Think about his best friend in all creation being safe and sound. Think about his parents and family back in New York, who would, thankfully, be spared the knowledge of his grisly demise. And think about Winona, his darling Winona, who would mourn him and sing an ancient Shoshone chant in honor of his passing.

What a terrible way to end a life!

He wanted to rant and rave, to have a tantrum of epic proportions to protest his unjust fortune. Was this his just reward for a life lived decently, for always doing unto others as he would have them do unto him? Granted, he hadn't attended church as regularly as he should, but he'd never taken the Lord's name in vain, never killed wantonly or abused a woman or child. So why should he end his earthly days in the clutches of a murderous savage? It wasn't *fair*!

Nate twisted his head to stare at the smoke drifting out the opening at the top of the fort. A few stars were visible. He longed to be on his mare, riding at a gallop across a verdant plain, the breeze on his face and joy in his heart. He didn't want to die, not when he had his whole life ahead of him. Somehow, some way, he *must* get loose.

His eyelids drooped and his left cheek sagged to the ground. An earthy scent filled his nostrils. Earth. The natural cloak for a corpse. Would the Blackfeet bury him or leave his body for the scavengers? What a stupid question. They would leave his remains for the buzzards to peck at and the maggots to gorge on. With this ghastly image in his troubled mind, he drifted into a fitful sleep.

Chapter Fifteen

Nate awoke to the sensation of someone poking him in the ribs, and opened his eyes to stare up in befuddled confusion at a smirking Blackfoot warrior. For a few seconds he forgot where he was and what had happened, until his harrowing ordeal came back in a rush and prompted him to sit up and glare at his tormentor.

The warrior laughed and exited the fort.

With a start, Nate realized he was alone. His wound ached dully and his buckskins felt clammy. He lifted his arms and inspected the cord binding his wrists, thinking he would tear into it with his teeth. Before he could, in came Red Elk.

"Hello, Grizzly Killer. I will untie you," the young Blackfoot said, and quickly did as he promised. "Does that feel better?"

"Yes," Nate signed awkwardly, his hands and feet tingling. He flexed his fingers and rotated his ankles in an attempt to restore his constricted circulation.

"We are leaving soon. Would you like dried buffalo meat for breakfast?"

"I would be grateful."

Red Elk nodded and departed to fetch the food.

Another day in the hands of the Blackfeet! Nate frowned at the prospect. Perhaps, though, an opportunity might arise for him to flee. If so, the Blackfeet wouldn't find him as easy to recapture as Baxter. He was fleet of foot and knew it; few of his childhood companions had ever matched his speed and he'd won practically every race he ever entered. He'd always liked to run, and had often done it for exercise. If the chance came up he'd be off like a shot.

A minute later Red Elk entered and gave him a half-dozen pieces of meat.

"Thank you," Nate signed. He bit off a mouthful and chewed heartily.

"Today we will join up with another war party," Red Elk mentioned. "The man who leads it is Chief Medicine Bottle. He is a wise and decent warrior, and I will ask him in private to spare your life."

Nate stopped chewing. "Do you really think he will?"

"I do not know. Even if Medicine Bottle should want to let you go, White Bear will oppose the idea and he has much influence in our councils."

Against his better judgment Nate let his hopes climb. "Who will make the final decision?"

"They might let the warriors take a vote."

"Then I am doomed."

Red Elk's lips compressed. "Do not give up hope as long as there is breath in your body. The Great Mystery works in mysterious ways, a man never knows from one minute to the next what his destiny will be."

"You have great wisdom for one so young," Nate said as a compliment.

"My father, Curly Hair, was known far and wide as a man of outstanding intelligence and his voice always carried exceptional weight in our councils. He taught me well before he was ambushed and killed by lowly Crows."

"I am sorry to hear that."

"Do not be. My father has passed on to a better world where there is always plenty of game and no white men," Red Elk signed, and grinned.

Suddenly a gruff voice bellowed outside.

"White Bears wants you," Red Elk translated.

Clutching the dried meat in his left hand, Nate went out the doorway on his hands and knees and rose. The cool air refreshed him. To the east a rosy glow emanated from below the eastern horizon.

White Bear and the other warriors were conversing. They all fell silent and the tall Blackfoot turned to Nate.

"We must make haste today if we are to reach the rendezvous point with our brothers. You will keep up or I will slice off your ears. Do you understand?"

"Yes," Nate responded, gesturing defiantly.

A wicked sneer curled the hateful warrior's countenance. "I hope you cannot keep up, white dung. Your ears would look nice on the wall of my lodge."

Nate clenched his fists, his blood boiling, but maintained his self-control.

"We go," White Bear stated, and then spoke loudly in his own tongue. Off he strode, taking the lead, and the rest dutifully followed.

The morning hours went by quickly. Nate felt better the farther he walked. Apparently he had not lost enough blood to pose a threat to his life and his organs were all intact. The buffalo meat barely filled his stomach, but they stopped once to drink at a stream and simply quenching his thirst did wonders for his constitution. Several times he tried to draw Red Elk into sign conversation. The warrior was polite but unresponsive and Nate gave up the attempt.

White Bear led them along valleys, over hills, and around jagged peaks. By noon they were descending a slope into a wide valley distinguished by a lake in the center.

"We will meet Medicine Bottle there," Red Elk signed, and nodded at the simmering body of water.

Anxiety surged anew in Nate. Soon his fate would be decided. All morning he had waited for the perfect opportunity to run, but although he was at the rear of the line, there were always Blackfeet gazing over their shoulders and watching him. Then too, he didn't know how much trust he could safely bestow on Red Elk. If he ran, would the warrior be compelled to plant an arrow between his shoulder blades? Obligations were one thing and tribal loyalties quite another, and he was unsure which would win out in the warrior's heart if he put them to the test.

They were still half a mile from the lake when figures were spotted moving about and smoke from several fires began rising skyward. White Bear called a halt. Although he believed it was Medicine Bottle's party, he decided to be on the safe side and sent a warrior ahead to check. Soon the man returned with news that Medicine Bottle was indeed there, having just arrived, and a freshly killed buck was being butchered for a feast.

All these facts Red Elk relayed for Nate's benefit. Nate chided himself for being an idiot and not trying to escape anyway, because now it was too late. He counted 20 warriors near the lake. The odds against him had increased drastically.

White Bear hailed those setting up the camp, and soon the two war parties were mingling and talking excitedly, recounting their exploits since they'd separated to raid the Utes.

Nate saw a short, stocky, elderly Indian in earnest discussion with White Bear.

"That is Chief Medicine Bottle," Red Elk revealed. Many were the narrowed eyes cast in Nate's direction. He read loathing and enmity in many faces. But in one visage there was only curiosity tinged with a trace of sadness. Chief Medicine Bottle stared at him for a full minute. Nate smiled in return and moved his hands to say, "I have heard you are a fair man. I am happy to meet you."

The chief displayed no reaction and did not answer, but his discussion with White Bear became more animated.

"The other war party did not locate a Ute village either," Red Elk disclosed. "They found a spot where many lodges had been camped, but the Utes had gone. If not for your capture, this raid would shame us all."

"What else are they saying?"

"Some of them are very mad we lost six warriors. One man over there wants to cut off your head. Another says your privates should be hacked off and forced down your throat—"

"That is enough," Nate signed, interrupting. "As I said before, I am doomed."

Red Elk motioned at a nearby fire. "Why not rest until the matter is decided."

Gladly Nate complied. Sitting close to the flames, his chin on his knees, he focused on the tips of his moccasins and closed his mind to contemplation of his fate. Or tried to. There was no doubt the Blackfeet would elect to torture him. Once he knew for certain, once they came to grab him, he would fight to the death. If he could grab a weapon they would be forced to kill him on the spot instead of carrying out their fiendish designs, and a speedy end was vastly preferable to slow, lingering torment.

Footsteps crunched on the ground behind him.

Twisting, Nate discovered Chief Medicine Bottle. The older man's eyes seemed to probe into the depths of his being.

"I am told you are known as Grizzly Killer."

"Yes. The name was given to me by a Cheyenne."

"And have you killed many grizzlies?" Medicine Bottle signed.

"Only three."

"That is more than most men, Indian or white. You must be brave, and you will shortly need all of your bravery. In a while a meeting will be called and we will decide what to do with you. A few want to take you to our village. Many others are incensed at the deaths of their brothers and want to kill you now."

"Where do you stand?"

"I will do as the Great Mystery guides me to do." So signing, the stately warrior turned and started to walk off. Red Elk addressed him and they exchanged words. Medicine Bottle glanced down at Nate and grunted, then left.

"What did the two of you talk about?" Nate inquired.

Red Elk walked to the other side of the campfire and sat down. "I asked him to spare your life as I said I would. He told me he will do his best to help. I must guard you while the council is in progress. Would you like to talk or be alone with your thoughts?"

"Talk," Nate responded gratefully. He watched the rest of the warriors gather 20 feet away, to the west. The feast seemed to be momentarily forgotten.

"You do not show any fear. That is good," Red Elk said.

"Perhaps I do not show it outside, but inside I am very afraid," Nate admitted.

"How is your wound?"

"It is the least of my concerns."

Red Elk laughed. "I like you, Grizzly Killer. It is most unfortunate we have met under these circumstances and that I am a Blackfoot and you are just a white. You have the spirit of an Indian, I think."

"I wish I *was* an Indian right about now. A Blackfoot."

The rejoinder brought more laughter from the warrior. "Are all whites like you?"

"No," Nate confessed. "Not at all. There are many different kinds of whites, good and bad, wise and foolish, kind and savage, just like there are different kinds of Blackfeet."

"Yet you and the only other white I ever met are honorable men. If I had the power I would order the hostilities between our people to cease."

How I wish you did, Nate though morosely. He looked at the council again, and saw the Blackfeet seated in a wide circle with Chief Medicine Bottle and White Bear on the north side next to one another. He also spied the warrior who had his Hawken, pouch, and powder horn, and was strongly tempted to race over and try to rip the gun from the man's grasp.

"Would you like food?" Red Elk asked.

"Thank you, no. I could not eat anything."

"Later then."

Nate absently nodded. If there was a later. To occupy himself with something other than morbid feelings of death, he examined the arrow's exit hole, and was relieved to see no trace of blood or infection. Indian herbal remedies were amazing. They possessed curative properties unknown to white doctors and were remarkably effective. He mentally filed the notion to learn as many as he could if he survived.

White Bear stood and discoursed at length with repeated jabs of his finger at Nate. Many cries of acclamation were interjected by the aroused warriors. Lances were rattled against shields, war clubs and tomahawks waved in the air.

"Do you want to know his words?" Red Elk asked.

Why not? "Yes," Nate responded.

"White Bear is telling them you deserve the most horrible death imaginable. Skinning alive is too good for you. He thinks you should be held down while a young rattlesnake is forced down your throat."

"I bet he pulled legs off spiders when he was a child," Nate said.

Chief Medicine Bottle now rose and spoke in slow, measured words, his tone as soothing as a gentle summer's breeze. He also pointed frequently at Nate. Not once did anyone shout. None of the warriors became agitated. They listened attentively and respectfully.

"He is saying you should not be blamed for attacking White Bear's party," Red Elk revealed. "Your friends had been taken and you were only doing as any man would do. He deeply regrets the loss of our brothers, but says killing you will not bring them back or honor their deaths. He believes we should let you go so that you may tell all whites the Blackfeet are an honorable race who do not take base revenge unjustly."

Nate could have hugged the chief. He didn't know the man, and yet here Medicine Bottle was opposing another popular leader to save him. From this day forth he would never again think of the Blackfeet as brutal savages bent only on slaughter. There was dignity to be found in all races of men if one only looked.

After a bit Chief Medicine Bottle took his seat, and then commenced a general debate with most of the warriors voicing their opinions in turn.

"Some agree with Medicine Bottle," Red Elk

explained. "Others side with White Bear."

It was most unfortunate, Nate reflected, that Indian chiefs didn't have the same degree of authority vested in white leaders. While chiefs could try to influence tribal decisions and were considered final arbiters in many matters, they could not dictate policy. Even on raids, individual warriors were permitted to do as they pleased. Indian society enjoyed a level of democracy yet to be attained by the so-called civilized nation existing east of the Mississippi.

The debate went on and on.

Nate saw Red Elk frown at one point and asked, "What is wrong?"

Shaking his head sadly, the warrior responded with, "You will know soon enough."

"Have they decided?"

"No. They are about to vote."

"Then why are you upset?"

"Even honorable people do dishonorable acts when they lose sight of their humanity."

"What?"

"I was quoting my father," Red Elk stated, and would sign no more. He sat with his head bowed, contemplating.

Troubled, Nate glanced at the circle. Chief Medicine Bottle was on his feet again, evidently appealing to each of the warriors one by one to voice their opinion. He went completely around the circle, then closed his eyes.

White Bear did not appear particularly pleased. He frowned and muttered something under his breath when the last of the warriors spoke.

What was happening? Nate wondered, his hopes rising yet again. If White Bear was unhappy, then surely their decision must be good news. Perhaps he would be spared. He saw Medicine Bottle open his eyes and speak, and all the Blackfeet rose and came toward him. Standing, he saw Red Elk coming around the fire and looking very sad. Why?

Chief Medicine Bottle led the Blackfeet, White Bear a stride behind. They halted a yard away and the elderly warrior's kindly eyes regarded Nate with a tinge of regret.

"Grizzly Killer, we have reached a decision," he signed.

"What is it?"

"We have decided you shall not be put to death immediately. Nor will you be tortured."

Nate smiled in partial relief. What did he mean by not put to death *immediately*?

"Instead," Medicine Bottle went on, "you shall run the gauntlet."

Chapter Sixteen

The gauntlet. Two rows of ten warriors, the lines six feet apart, each man armed with a war club, tomahawk, or eyedagg. In this instance the rows extended from north to south, from the shore of the lake into a field. Near the water stood Chief Medicine Bottle, White Bear, and the remaining Blackfeet.

Nate faced the lines and gulped. Every warrior except one grinned at him, eager to smash his skull or rip open his body. He glanced to his right at the chief.

"We are a fair people, Grizzly Killer, despite what you may now believe. You have slain some of our brothers and the warriors of our village demand that you pay a price, but instead of shooting and scalping you on the spot we have voted on a reasonable alternative."

"You call this reasonable?" Nate responded, nodding at the two rows.

"It is more reasonable than tying you to stakes and skinning you alive."

Nate had no argument there.

"You are about to engage in a test of your mettle. Should you prevail, you will be permitted to live. If not, we will take it as an indication you were a cold-hearted murderer and took our brothers' lives out of sheer hatred."

"What must I do?" Nate said, although he knew very well what he must do.

"You will run from this end of the gauntlet to the far end," Medicine Bottle directed. "If you try to break out of the lines you will be shot."

"May I fight back?"

"You may defend yourself as you see fit."

"And once I make it to the far end I am free to go in peace?"

White Bear laughed.

"If you are still alive at the end of the rows you will have completed the first half of your trial," Medicine Bottle patiently answered.

Almost afraid to ask, Nate forced his hands to move and frame the question. "What is the second half?"

"You may run in any direction as fast as you can. Three of our warriors will chase you. If you are caught, they will slay you on the spot. If you elude them you are free."

A snort of contempt came from White Bear. "You will not elude us, white dog. I am one of the three who will give chase, along with Buffalo Horn and Crooked Nose." He indicated two warriors on his right.

Nate looked at their hostile faces and discovered one of his pursuers was to be the warrior who had appropriated the Hawken. "How much of a head start will I be given?"

"None," White Bear signed. "Once you are clear of the lines we will come after you."

Medicine Bottle looked at the tall warrior. "What harm can a slight lead do? Think of the sport he will give you."

Raising his right arm over his eyes to shield them from the bright sun, White Bear scanned the stretch of land past the rows and grinned. "Very well. Do you see the short pine tree, white dog?"

Nate spied a stunted pine approximately one hundred yards distant. "Yes."

"It will be the marker. The moment you pass it, we will give chase."

Of what benefit was a measily one-hundred-yard lead? Nate fumed, and decided to be grateful for the slight advantage Medicine Bottle had manipulated the pugnacious White Bear into giving him. The way things stood, he doubted he would ever reach that tree anyway.

"Now you must take off your clothes," White Bear signed.

"What?" Nate responded in disbelief.

Chief Medicine Bottle nodded. "It is our custom. Any man who runs the gauntlet must do so naked."

"I refuse!" Nate replied angrily.

"Why?" Medicine Bottle queried.

"It is against the customs of my people to go anywhere without clothes on. We consider such behavior a great shame."

White Bear laughed harshly. "Your customs are of no concern to us. You will take off your clothes or we will kill you now." He paused, his lips curled in a mask of wickedness. "Please keep them on."

What should I do? Nate frantically asked himself. Traipsing around naked went against every principle he believed in, every moral precept he'd ever been taught. But if he didn't do as they wanted, he would surely die. If he stripped he would live a while longer. Viewed in such light, he didn't have any choice. "Do I get to keep my moccasins on?" he asked, stalling.

"Nothing," White Bear stated.

All eyes were on Nate as he began removing his garb. He untied his moccasins first and tugged them off, then raised his buckskin shirt. The strain of reaching his arms over his head speared agony through his body but couldn't be helped.

"Hurry, white dog," White Bear declared, using his favorite expression again.

Nate gripped the top of his pants, then paused to glance at the chief. "Must I wait for a signal to begin?"

"You may begin whenever you like," Medicine Bottle revealed.

Good, Nate thought, and bent at the waist as he peeled the buckskin pants from his pale legs, first the right, then the left, deliberately moving slowly, letting them think he was embarrassed or cowed or scared to death or whatever they wanted. Just so they didn't suspect his ulterior motive. They'd expect him to hesitate, to be afraid to enter the gauntlet, and they would be off their guard.

Nate extended his right arm, let the pants fall, and suddenly took off in full stride, his arms and legs flying, staying stooped over to present a smaller target, his eyes darting right and left. The ruse worked. He was past the first two men on each side before the rest awoke to the deception with bellows of rage. From behind him came White Bear's roar. He ignored the noise and concentrated on the warriors. If his attention lapsed for a heartbeat he was dead.

A lean Blackfoot stood on the right, a war club in the hand that he now raised overhead.

Nate saw the man's shoulder muscles tighten and knew the swing was coming. He dodged to the left, nearer the other row, and the club descended, nicking his arm. Ignoring the pain, he pressed on.

On the left was another warrior, this one wielding a tomahawk and grinning in anticipation.

In two bounds Nate was there, twisting to confront his foe as the tomahawk arced down toward his forehead. He leaped in closer, using his left forearm to block the descending swipe, and planted his right fist on the tip of the warrior's nose, flattening him.

Onward he went, never slowing for an instant because to slow down meant he would never see Winona again, never know the joy of a majestic high-country morning once more or witness the radiant hues coloring the heavens as the sun rose and set.

The next Blackfoot had a war club.

Nate ran directly at the man. Part of the rules, if such there were, seemed to entail that the Blackfeet could not stray into the middle of the gauntlet; they must attack from their appointed spots on the sides. Most runners probably stayed in the center and were easily cut down, but he had no intention of doing the same. The Blackfeet weren't going to get him without a battle they would long recall.

Whooping loudly, the next warrior hefted his club and carefully gauged the distance before swinging. Nate didn't bother trying to deflect the Blackfoot's arm this time. He went for the war club, his hands rising to meet it and grasping the wooden handle just below the pointed stone attached to the top. The tip of the stone came within an inch of his left eye before he checked its momentum. He wrenched on the weapon, striving to disarm his foe, but the warrior held on with all his might and hissed, delaying him when he must not be delayed, so instead of continuing to pull he simply let go.

Taken unawares, the warrior's own strength and stance worked against him and he stumbled backward away from the line.

Keep going! Nate's mind screamed, and he did, cognizant of a pain in his side but suppressing the sensation as he closed on another warrior on the left, a skinny man with a long-handled tomahawk.

The man drew the weapon back, his teeth exposed in an animal snarl.

This time Nate knew he must do something different. That long handle ruled out the direct approach, so he tried a clever ploy, waiting until the warrior started his swing and then diving at the man's legs, diving under the sweeping tomahawk and tackling the skinny Blackfoot. They both went down, Nate winding up on top, and he drove his fists in a furious flurry, pounding the warrior's jaw and stunning him. Lunging, Nate grabbed the tomahawk from the man's limp fingers, rose, and raced toward the end of the rows.

The remaining Blackfeet appeared disconcerted by the unique maneuver.

Nate wasn't going to give them the chance to gather their wits. He swung the tomahawk wildly, screeching like a madman, darting at each man in turn, and in turn the first three ducked aside rather than engage him. The rest held their ground and swung their weapons, but they were hampered by having to stay on the side and the fact most of them carried shorter clubs or tomahawks, which put them at a costly disadvantage. Stone and metal and wood clashed, clanged, and smacked together, and in a swirling rush of motion Nate swept past all but the last pair.

They were braced, these two, the man on the left with an eyedagg, a weapon incorporating a wooden handle and an angled metal spike at the end, while the man on the right held a war club.

The man on the right was Red Elk.

Nate had seen White Bear badger the younger warrior, goading the youth into taking a position in the line. Although he hadn't understood the words, he'd guessed that White Bear had called Red Elk's manhood and loyalty to the tribe into question. Under the probing stares of his fellow warriors, Red Elk had had no choice but to take a spot.

And now here he was, ready to attack.

For an instant their eyes met, and Nate registered commingled hurt and anger befor Red Elk's club descended toward his brow. He blocked the blow with the tomahawk and instantly pivoted to face the other Blackfoot, who surprised him by leaping forward and employing the eyedagg with both hands in an overhand strike.

Nate ducked to the left, evading the spike, and at the moment he shifted he saw Red Elk materialize in the very spot he'd just vacated. He tried to shout a warning, but he could do nothing more than gape in shocked horror as the eyedagg struck Red Elk between the eyes and bored several inches into the warrior's flesh and bone.

Red Elk's eyes widened, his arms went limp, and his entire body quivered violently.

The other Blackfoot, aghast at his mistake, gaped at his tribesman in an appalled daze.

Enraged at Red Elk's senseless death, Nate buried the edge of his tomahawk in the Blackfoot's neck, severing a vein or artery, causing blood to gush out. He yanked the blade out and dashed past the sputtering Blackfoot, into the open, wondering if he would get an arrow or a ball in the back before he covered ten yards. Incredibly, he didn't, and he focused on the stunted pine, running all out.

The reality of his achievement sank in. He'd done it! Survived the gauntlet! But he still had to outrun three fleet Blackfeet when he was already in pain and winded. The naked soles of his feet padded on the grass and weeds. Occasionally he stepped on a sharp stone or twig and flinched. No matter how much it hurt, he determined he wasn't stopping for hell or high water.

Harsh shouts arose to his rear.

Nate was tempted to look back and see if White Bear and the others had violated the agreement, but he didn't want to break his stride. Twenty yards beyond the stunted pine grew a verdant expanse of woodland. If he could reach those trees, he might be able to shake the trio of avenging furies.

He glanced at a snow-crowned peak to the south and succumbed to momentary despair. Even if he should, by some miracle, elude White Bear, Crooked Nose, and Buffalo Horn, how was he going to survive alone and naked in the wilderness, his sole weapon a tomahawk? If he encountered a grizzly the outcome would be a foregone conclusion.

Nate drew nearer to the pine. His left foot came down hard on a sharp stone and he stumbled, almost going down. He reestablished his running rhythm and sped on, feeling moist drops on his left sole. The stone had cut him. He hoped the laceration wasn't serious because he couldn't stop to check.

Each second became an eternity as he ran, ran, ran. Nate was still five yards from the stunted pine when tremendous cheers from the vicinity of the lake heralded the unleashing of the undoubtedly eager pursuers. He didn't bother to look until he reached the forest and paused to gulp in air.

The three incensed Blackfeet were bounding in pursuit, White Bear in the lead.

Spinning, Nate dashed into the woods and immediately angled to the east, weaving among the trees, thickets, and boulders. Broken limbs and shattered branches lay in profusion on the ground, any one of which could tear open his feet and legs, and he was kept busy avoiding such normally harmless obstacles.

After traveling 20 yards Nate slanted to the south again, opting for a zigzag course to make tracking him more difficult, hopefully slowing down the warriors. Despite his best efforts he was repeatedly jabbed and speared by the vegetation he passed, crisscrossing his skin with tiny red slash marks.

Nate glanced over his shoulder time and again, but saw no sign of the Blackfeet. As the minutes went by and the trio still didn't appear, he became mystified. Blackfeet warriors, like most Indians, were fast runners. A lifetime spent in the wilderness, of hunting and raiding and living on the raw edge of existence, hardened Indian men and endowed them with extraordinary speed and stamina. He should have seen them by now. Why hadn't he?

Think!

He tried to reason as they would, plan as they would. Since they had seen him race to the woods, White Bear and the other two were aware of his own capability. Perhaps they had reasoned they couldn't hope to overtake him, which seemed a ridiculous notion but was the only explanation he could think of.

What would they do then?

Think!

They must know the lay of the land better than he did since they had selected the lake as a rendezvous point. Was it possible for them to get ahead of him? Was there a shortcut? He grinned at his stupidity. Here he was, fleeing due south along the verdant basin of a valley. There was no way they could take any shortcut that would bring them in front of him.

Still puzzled, Nate raced deeper into the woods, farther from the war party. Every stride he took raised his confidence a notch higher. Once he escaped, he could devote his attention to securing clothing and food.

A twig snapped off to the right.

Gazing in that direction, Nate gasped in astonishment at spying one of the Blackfeet 40 feet away, parallel with his position, effortlessly keeping pace. Bewildered, he glanced to the left and saw the warrior who had taken the Hawken an equal distance away. The Blackfeet weren't trying to overtake him; they already had! Now they were playing with him before moving in for the kill!

Chapter Seventeen

Nate instantly increased his pace, his sinews straining, his feet thudding on the ground.

Both Indians did likewise, each grinning wickedly.

Ahead appeared a low knoll.

Nate slowed a bit and saw them do the same. The chilling realization that he was at their mercy aroused a spark of self-recriminatin. What a fool he'd been! White Bear must have selected the fastest runners in the war party, warriors who could easily overtake him, who didn't need to stick to his exact trail. For that matter, they'd undoubtedly surmised he would be heading back into the heart of Ute country, which meant going south.

Damn his idiocy!

The recrimination changed to indignation. He resolved to fight to the last. Since he couldn't hope to outrun them, he must resort to strategy. But what to do? He gazed at the knoll and an idea blossomed.

Both warriors were still staying abreast of him. Good. If they continued to do so, they would each skirt the knoll, one passing by on the right, the other the left, leaving him to go up and over. For a few seconds as he neared the top he would be out of their sight.

Nate gripped the tomahawk handle tighter and steeled his body. He made the knoll and started up, keeping his eyes fixed straight ahead so he wouldn't give away his intentions. When only three yards from the top he quickly looked to both sides and watched the warriors spring past the sides of the low hillock. Abruptly halting, he wheeled to the left, bent at the waist, and ran toward the bottom, not stopping until he came to a wide tree and crouched in the shelter of the trunk.

He envisioned the two Blackfeet stopping and gazing in confusion at the crest of the knoll when he failed to appear. They would naturally hasten back to investigate his disappearance. If the Great Mystery smiled on him, they would simply retrace their steps. The warrior carrying his rifle would pass within a few feet of his position. The rest would be up to Nate.

He peeked around the trunk and tingled at the sight of the warrior already heading back and staring in perplexity up at the knoll. Since the man's nose bore no evidence of a break, he deduced this one must be Buffalo Horn.

The Blackfoot trotted slowly, the Hawken in his left hand. He wore only buckskin pants and moccasins. On his left hip hung a knife in a beaded sheath.

Keep coming! Nate thought.

Clearly confused, Buffalo Horn raised his right arm and waved.

Nate looked and saw Crooked Nose, an arrow notched to the bow he held, rounding the opposite side of the knoll, similarly searching. Crooked Nose returned the wave and shook his head. Nate glanced

A SPECIAL OFFER FOR LEISURE WESTERN READERS ONLY!

Get FOUR FREE Western Novels

Travel to the Old West in all its glory and drama—without leaving your home!

Plus, you'll save between $3.00 and $6.00 every time you buy!

GET YOUR 4 FREE BOOKS NOW— A VALUE BETWEEN $16 AND $20

Mail the Free Book Certificate Today!

FREE BOOKS CERTIFICATE!

YES! I want to subscribe to the Leisure Western Book Club. Please send my 4 FREE BOOKS. Then, each month, I'll receive the four newest Leisure Western Selections to preview FREE for 10 days. If I decide to keep them, I will pay the Special Members Only discounted price of just $3.36 each, a total of $13.44. This saves me between $3 and $6 off the bookstore price. There are no shipping, handling or other charges. There is no minimum number of books I must buy and I may cancel the program at any time. In any case, the 4 FREE BOOKS are mine to keep—at a value of between $17 and $20! Offer valid only in the USA.

Name_____

Address_____

City_____ State_____

Zip_____ Phone_____

Biggest Savings Offer!

For those of you who would like to pay us in advance by check or credit card—we've got an even bigger savings in mind. Interested? Check here. ☐

If under 18, parent or guardian must sign.
Terms, prices and conditions subject to change. Subscription subject to acceptance. Leisure Books reserves the right to reject any order or cancel any subscription.

GET FOUR BOOKS TOTALLY
FREE—A VALUE BETWEEN
$16 AND $20

▼ Tear here and mail your FREE book card today! ▼

PLEASE RUSH
MY FOUR FREE
BOOKS TO ME
RIGHT AWAY!

Leisure Western Book Club
P.O. Box 6613
Edison, NJ 08818-6613

at Buffalo Horn.

The Blackfoot was ten feet away, eyes roving over the slope, probing every shadow, every nook and cranny. He rotated slowly to the left, gazing to the south, his back to the tree.

Nate might never have a better chance. He launched himself from concealment and charged, the tomahawk uplifted, and heard Crooked Nose shout a warning.

Buffalo Horn whirled and started to level the rifle, amazement lining his features.

I'm not going to make it! Nate thought. He still had six feet to go and the Hawken was almost even with his stomach, so he did the only thing he could think of; he threw the tomahawk at the Blackfoot's head. Having never thrown a tomahawk before, he expected to do no more than force the warrior to duck and buy himself the seconds he needed to reach the Blackfoot. He certainly never expected to score a hit. But he did.

The tomahawk flew end over end and the razor-sharp blade caught Buffalo Horn full on the nose, splitting both nostrils and eliciting a scream from the terrified man. The tomahawk stuck fast, and Buffalo Horn let go of the rifle and grabbed the handle to yank the weapon out. Blood flowed copiously.

Nate dove, landing on his right shoulder and rolling the final yard to rise to his knees at Buffalo Horn's feet, his fingers closing on the Hawken.

The warrior staggered backward and wrenched the tomahawk free, the suction producing a bubbling sucking sound. His eyes fluttered and his knees buckled. Groaning, he sank down and fell onto his left side.

Nate started to rise as an arrow streaked from his right and missed his head by a hair. He twisted to find Crooked Nose racing toward him.

His face betraying rabid rage, the Blackfoot was notching a second arrow on the bowstring.

Up came the Hawken in a practiced, fluid motion. Nate sighted squarely on the warrior's chest, cocked the hammer, and fired. The booming blast was sweeter to his ears than the most melodious music ever created by mortal man.

The ball took the Blackfoot dead center, the impact lifting him from his feet to crash onto his back. Crooked Nose tried to rise, staring down at the neat, bloody hole in the middle of his chest, then collapsed without a sound.

Silence gripped the forest.

Nate looked from one to the other, thinking they might still rise, that he couldn't possibly have defeated them both. After a minute he stood and walked over to Buffalo Horn, convinced he had triumphed. Two down and one to go.

One to go!

White Bear was out there somewhere.

With a start Nate scanned the woods on all sides but saw nothing. Chiding himself for his negligence, he knelt and stripped his powder horn and ammo pouch from Buffalo Horn. He slung both across his chest and hurriedly reloaded, breathing a sigh of relief when the ball and patch were finally shoved home down the barrel. He replaced the rod and scoured the forest again.

Where was White Bear?

He took a step, and his glance fell on the pants and moccasins the dead man wore. Crooked Nose was slightly smaller, but the clothes might fit. He crouched and removed them, then slid into the pants. They were tight but serviceable. In moments the moccasins covered his sore, bleeding, blistering feet. The knife and tomahawk were around his waist. He headed south.

Nervously fingering the trigger, Nate constantly scoured the vegetation for some sign of his enemy. Why hadn't White Bear been with the others? Or had White Bear been out there somewhere and witnessed the whole incident? If so, why hadn't the Blackfoot tried to aid his fellows? The many questions were an annoying distraction, so he shook his head to clear his mind and devoted his full attention to simply staying alive.

Nate covered a quarter of a mile without seeing White Bear. He entertained the idea that the warrior had taken a different course from the others and must be far away.

A mile later he climbed to the top of a rise and stared down at the valley. He could see the lake and smoke curling up from the campfires, but there were no Blackfeet on his heels. Allowing himself the luxury of a victory smile, Nate turned and continued over the rise into the next valley. He had to descend a boulder-strewn slope, moving among giant rocks ten and 12 feet in height. The warm air felt nice on his skin. He touched the arrow wound and found it to be sore.

Halfway down the slope he was compelled to pass between two huge boulders with barely enough space between them for him to squeeze through. He lowered the rifle to his side and eased into the notch, the rough stone scraping his back and chest, then stepped into the clear.

Nate hefted the Hawken and took a pace. A scraping noise to his right made him start to rotate, but a heavy object smashed into the back of his head before he could complete the move. Brilliant points of lights danced in front of his face, dazzling him, and his legs went weak. He tottered and dropped to his right knee, pressing the rifle on the ground for support.

A gleaming streak of light seemed to come out of

nowhere and something struck the rifle barrel a
jarring blow, severely stinging his hand and knocking
the gun loose. He blinked frantically, trying to regain
control, and stiffened when the hard point of a
slender weapon touched his neck.

A few gruff words were spoken mockingly.

Nate recognized the cold voice and tensed. His
vision cleared. He flicked his eyes to the left and
looked up at the malevolent face of White Bear.

The Blackfoot addressed him scornfully, then
stepped back, withdrawing the tip of his sword. He
motioned for Nate to stand.

Slowly, his arms at his sides, Nate rose and glared
at the warrior. He'd been outfoxed, plain and simple,
by that smirking bastard. An urge to clamp his hands
around the Blackfoot's throat seized him, and it was
all he could do to stay still as White Bear wagged the
sword and laughed.

Again the warrior motioned, this time indicating
Nate should walk lower down the slope.

Reluctantly Nate complied, halting when the
Blackfoot barked a word in the tribal tongue, then
turned.

White Bear had not budged. He was 12 feet away,
grinning, and he now did a most surprising thing; he
slid his sword under the cord around his waist.

Nate waited, suspecting a trick.

"At last it is just the two of us, white dog, man to
man," the Blackfoot signed.

Nate didn't bother to respond.

"You are more resourceful than I gave you credit
for being," White Bear went on. "Only two men out
of ten survive the gauntlet."

The Hawken was lying near the Blackfoot's feet.
Nate glanced at it, wishing it was closer.

"Your friend Red Elk did not survive," White Bear
taunted him. "He received the fate he deserved."

The slur against the young warrior prompted Nate to reply. "Why did he deserve to die? Because he felt whites and Blackfeet can live together in peace?"

"Yes. He was a fool."

"He was an honorable man, which is more than I can say for you."

White Bear placed his right hand on the sword's hilt. "I have enjoyed slaying few men as much as I will enjoy slaying you."

"My people have a saying," Nate related, and was about to go into detail about unborn chickens when he realized the warrior had probably never seen one. He adjusted the axiom accordingly. "Never count your birds before they are hatched."

"What birds?"

"Ravens. Jays. Sparrows. Any kind you want."

White Bear nodded. "As I suspected. All whites are crazy." He drew the sword. "Soon there will be one less crazy white in the mountains, one less white to destroy the beaver and kill all the buffalo."

Nate drew the tomahawk.

"I could have killed you at any time, dog," White Bear signed, and pointed at his bow and quiver lying beside a boulder eight feet away. "But that would have been the easy way, the way of a coward. No, I want to kill you in man-to-man combat. I want to see the fear in your eyes and feel my sword cut through your body. When you are dead I will chop your body into pieces for the vultures and the coyotes. All except your hair. Your scalp will hang on my lodge for all my brothers to see."

"First you must take it," Nate countered, "and it will take more than words to do that."

Raising the sword, White Bear sprang to the attack.

Nate barely got the tomahawk up in time to deflect a vicious swipe that would have split his skull like an overripe melon. He quickly backpedaled, blocking blow after blow, the sword biting into the tomahawk's wooden handle again and again, sending chips flying.

White Bear vented a roar of rage and redoubled his efforts.

Dodging to the right, Nate swung at the Blackfoot's legs, only to have the swing expertly countered. The sword point arced at his throat, and he skipped rearward to avoid being impaled. More strikes rained down on him and he staved off each one, but his right arm was rapidly tiring. After all he had been through his body couldn't sustain such a brutal pace indefinitely. He needed to win soon or he would tire and fall easy prey to the gloating warrior.

The Blackfoot sneered as he fought, his face conveying unmitigated contempt, and wielded the sword with remarkable agility. His glittering sword was constantly in motion, slashing and stabbing, a blur of golden light.

Nate was forced to retreat down the slope. He worried about tripping over an unseen obstacle and exposing himself to his enemy. Once he almost did go down when his left heel bumped into a rock and he lost his balance and nearly fell.

White Bear took instant advantage, lancing the point at Nate's throat.

Only by jerking his head to the right did Nate evade the tip. He batted the blade aside with the tomahawk and righted himself, his mind racing, seeking to somehow achieve victory before another such inadvertent blunder cost him his life.

The warrior seemed angered by the miss. He swung with berserk abandon.

Under the savage onslaught Nate felt his arm tiring even faster. Fingernail-sized bits of wood had been hacked from the tomahawk's handle. All other factors being equal, a tomahawk was simply no match for a sword; it was shorter and possessed a smaller cutting edge. The best he could hope to do was block all the Blackfoot's blows.

White Bear evidently realized the tomahawk was all that stood between him and triumph. He concentrated on the handle, repeatedly slicing into the wood in an attempt to chip the tomahawk in half.

Nate knew it was only a matter of time before the Blackfoot would succeed. Once the tomahawk was rendered useless, what did he have left to fight with? The knife?

The knife!

The new surge of vigor coursed through Nate's veins as inspiration provided him with a means of prevailing over his adversary. The hunting knife still hung in its beaded sheath on his left hip. Ever so slowly, his left hand moving at a snail's pace, he inched toward the hilt. He suddenly turned sideways and swung the tomahawk furiously. If he could keep the Blackfoot's attention exclusively on the light axe, his plan would succeed.

Displaying surprise at the unexpected, renewed resistance, White Bear backed up a yard, then held his ground. For the first time since their fight began he was on the defensive.

Nate maintained the pressure, his right arm flashing while his left crept to the knife. His hand wrapped around the hilt. Now all he had to do was find an opening.

White Bear parried yet another blow and speared the sword at the youth's abdomen.

Sliding to the left, Nate stumbled when his foot encountered a shallow depression. He fell onto his left knee, the tomahawk upraised to deflect the sword.

The warrior delivered a terrific blow backed by all

the power in his body, and the keen edge bit clear through the wooden handle and swept downward.

There was no time to react. Nate felt the Spanish sword bite into his right shoulder and threw himself to the rear, landing on his back. A moist sensation indicated the Blackfoot had drawn blood. Nate placed his right palm on the grass and tried to shove erect, but already the tall Blackfoot towered above him with the sword held high for the killing stroke.

White Bear grinned and swung.

Chapter Eighteen

In desperation Nate twisted to the left and the sword struck the ground, missing his ear by a hair. For a moment White Bear's face was close to his and he stared into the warrior's hate-filled eyes. Then he whipped the hunting knife out and around, driving the blade up and into the Blackfoot's chest, all the way in, and twisting.

White Bear's mouth slackened and he uttered a gurgling wheeze. He blinked rapidly and grimaced, then tore himself loose and staggered a few feet, the sword dangling from his right hand.

Nate surged erect and crouched, ready to resist another attack, blood dripping from his knife.

The Blackfoot tried to lift the sword again, but his arm refused to cooperate. He looked down at the blood pumping from the hole in his chest and groaned. His eyes closed for a second and he swallowed hard, then he glanced around and shuffled unsteadily to the right until he collided with a waist-high boulder. The sword fell. He sank to the ground with his back to the boulder and looked at Nate. "You have won, white dog," he signed sluggishly.

Nate lowered the knife.

"I am bleeding badly inside. I can feel it," White Bear said.

Squatting, Nate wiped the hunting knife clean on a small bush.

"Finish me off."

Nate replaced the knife in its sheath and straightened.

"Finish me off."

"Why should I?" Nate asked, walking over to pick up the sword.

"I am too weak to fight, to even stand. All I can do is sit here and bleed to death. This is no way for a warrior to die. Kill me so I can go to the next world with dignity."

"No."

White Bear attempted to lift his arms. Suddenly he coughed and blood trickled from the left corner of his mouth. "See? This is a horrible way to die. Kill me, now, or I will curse you. I will call on the spirits of the air and the land to destroy you."

Nate started to turn.

The warrior scowled and lightly smacked the earth at his side. "White dog! I knew you had no honor the first time I laid eyes on you. All whites are the same. None of you know anything about the ways of the Great Mystery, about the proper ways to live and die. You do not treat your enemies with respect because you do not know how to respect yourselves. You are cowards, all of you. You do not deserve to be called men!" Further weakened by moving his arms and hands, White Bear sagged, a crimson streak now issuing from the right side of his mouth also.

Pivoting, Nate studied the warrior's countenance, studied the almost palpable animosity, and came to a decision.

White Bear grinned and raised his hands one last time. "Do you have any honor, white dog? If so, prove it."

Nate did.

The sun hung an hour above the western horizon when he emerged from a stretch of forest and began hiking across a wide meadow. His entire body ached, and many lacerations stung terribly, and both the arrow and sword wounds hurt intensely. He suppressed the pain and marched onward.

A pair of elk were grazing to the east. They calmly watched him approach, their gums rising and falling as they chewed.

Nate gazed at them, debating whether to shoot one for his supper, then glanced to the south and halted.

A large body of riders was heading directly toward him. They were Indians.

Since they would be on him before he could hope to reach the shelter of the trees, and suspecting they would turn out to be hostile, he raised the Hawken and took a bead on one of those in the lead, realizing as he did that two of those riders were white men. He lowered the rifle and waited.

One of the white men waved.

Amazement washed over Nate as he recognized Shakespeare and Baxter. Sweet relief flooded his soul and he returned the wave.

The mountain man was astride his white horse and leading Nate's mare. Baxter had their other animals on a string.

Not until the riders were 30 yards off did Nate recognize the warrior riding on Baxter's right as Two Owls. He placed the stock of his rifle on the grass and leaned on the barrel, grinning happily.

There were over 50 Indians in all, and they formed into a semicircle around him as they drew to a halt.

"Nate!" Shakespeare bellowed, and vaulted from

his mount to dash up and embrace the younger man. He stopped with his arms outstretched, gazing at the wounds, cuts, and bruises, and snorted. "Lord, son, you're a mess. Have you been playing in the briar patch again?"

Chuckling, Nate gave his mentor a hug, then stepped back and asked in a suddenly raspy voice, "Are you all right? I was worried sick about you."

"Never felt better." Shakespeare looked to the north. "Where are the Blackfeet? We saw them take you, but there wasn't a thing we could do about it."

"The war party met up with another one at a lake north of here. They might still be there."

"They just upped and let you go, did they?"

"I escaped," Nate said, and left it at that. He glanced at Two Owls and signed, "It is good to see you again."

"I am glad you still live, Grizzly Killer," the Ute replied. He gestured proudly at the other warriors. "My people came to help us after the village was safely moved."

"Did you know Two Owls is their chief?" Shakespeare mentioned.

Nate's surprise showed. "Why did you keep it a secret?" he asked the Ute.

"What difference does it make? Chiefs are only ordinary men. When they start thinking they are special they deserve to be smeared with buffalo manure and made to eat grass." Two Owls stared northward. "We are going to punish the Blackfeet for trying to raid our village. Would you like to come?"

"Another time," Nate answered. He walked to the mare, stroked her neck, and swung into the saddle.

"I guess now we can tend to our beaver trapping," Shakespeare said. "We recovered all the traps so we can start whenever you want."

"Next month, maybe."

"What?"

"You wanted some time to yourself, as I recall. Well, you can have it. If you're of a mind, swing by my cabin in a month and you can teach me more about trapping then."

"You're going home?"

"As fast as I can." Nate glanced at Baxter. "Would you be so kind as to remove my two pack animals from the string."

"Sure. Glad to." The Ohioan climbed down to do as he was requested.

"What happened to you?" Shakespeare inquired.

"Nothing."

"Then why are you in such an all-fired hurry to get home?"

Nate touched the hole in his side. "The best woman in the world is back there anxiously waiting for me to return. I don't want to keep her waiting."

"What harm would another few weeks do?"

Nate looked at the mountain man. "Didn't you once tell me that a long time ago you were deeply in love with a Flathead woman?"

"Yes," Shakespeare said softly.

"And I know you have almost met your Maker a time or two."

"I have," Shakespeare conceded.

"Then you should be able to understand," Nate said, and moved over to take the leads to his pack animals from Baxter. "Thank you."

"Sorry to see you go. Take care of yourself."

"You too. Don't keep your family waiting," Nate said, and turned to the Ute chief. "May the Great Mystery guide your every footstep."

"And yours, Grizzly Killer."

Finally Nate stared at the mountain man, his eyes conveying the depth of his affection. "Do you understand now?"

"I believe I do."

"No hard feelings?"

"You know better."

Smiling gratefully, Nate faced eastward and galloped off.

For a minute no one spoke or signed a word.

Baxter broke the silence. "Now what was all that about?" he wondered aloud.

The frontiersman sighed. "Would you like some advice, Thaddeus?" he asked while watching the youth recede in the distance.

"I'm always open to reasonable suggestions."

"Good. Then do that wife of yours a favor and either go back to Ohio or divorce her."

"I don't believe in divorce."

Shakespeare glanced at him and beamed. "Then you shouldn't have any trouble making up your mind."

Epilogue

She was seated on a log near the cabin, her head bowed, her long, raven hair hanging down past her knees. A sleeveless leather dress clung to her slender figure and moccasins adorned her small feet. Leaning down, she used a finger to draw the likeness of a cradleboard in the dirt, humming as she etched the lines.

Intuition made her stiffen and stand. She sensed the presence of someone else and spun in alarm, her incipient fear changing to dominating joy when she spied the man on horseback and the pair of pack animals he led. Her eyes brightened and she ran to meet him, voicing one of the few English words she knew. "Nate! Nate!"

He galloped the rest of the way and jumped from the mare before the animal had stopped. In a rush he swept her into his arms and held her tight, savoring the feel of her and the scent of her hair and never wanting to let her go. "Winona," he said, nearly choking on the word.

After a time she pushed back and stared in shock at his battered body. "What happened?" she signed. "Where is Shakespeare?"

"We ran into some Blackfeet," Nate revealed, and quickly added, "Shakespeare is fine. He will stop to see us during the next moon."

"Where is your shirt?" Winona asked, and looked at his legs. "And where are the pants you wore when you left?"

"It is a long story and I will tell you the details later," Nate pledged. He tenderly kissed her. "I have ridden hard to get here, and now all I want to do is lie in bed with you for a week."

Winona grinned. "What do you have in mind?"

"We can try to make that baby you have been talking about?"

"There is no need."

"Why?" Nate asked.

As she placed her hands on her abdomen, Winona's grin widened. Then she signed, "Because we have already made our baby."

"We have?" Nate responded, and her meaning sank home. "We have!" he repeated, joyously, impulsively taking her in his arms and whirling her about. Suddenly he stopped and set her down. "Sorry. I should not be so rough," he signed.

"I will not break."

"So you say. But until the baby is born I will handle all the difficult chores. You just take it easy."

Winona giggled. "Perhaps I should be with child more often."

Nate embraced her, and for that sweet moment in time and eternity they shared a supreme bliss and their souls soared on the uplifting currents of mutual abiding love.

BLACK POWDER JUSTICE

Dedicated to
Judy, Joshua, and Shane.
And to
Melinda, Michelle, and Jennifer,
who could all give Annie Oakley a run
for her money.
"Ride until you drop."

Chapter One

Winter in the Rocky Mountains.

A white blanket of snow two feet deep covered the majestic peaks that reared thousands of feet into the crisp air. Ominous gray clouds drifted sluggishly from the northwest to the southeast, threatening to litter the primeval landscape with even more snow. High in the sky over one remote valley sailed a solitary eagle, sliding just below the clouds, its wings outspread as it gracefully soared on the uplifting currents.

In the valley, clustered near a narrow stream, browsed a small herd of mountain buffalo. Their shaggy coats insulated them from the sub-zero temperatures and their stringy beards were caked with snow and ice formed by their dripping saliva. Unlike their plains brethren, mountain buffalo stayed in the forested higher elevations the year round. They were as massive as their bovid kin, with males in their prime attaining a height of six feet at the shoulders, and weighing close to two thousand pounds. Their massive heads sported horns with a spread of three feet.

Many of the mighty beasts were using their powerful hoofs to clear snow from the underlying vegetation. Some simply stood and chewed their cuds. A young bull detached itself from the herd and moved a dozen yards to the treeline to the north. It selected a suitably stout tree and commenced rubbing its horns against the bark, doing so again and again until the bark began to wear away.

The breeze suddenly shifted, now coming from the north.

A second later the young bull stopped rubbing and loudly sniffed the air. It backed up several strides, tilting its huge head upward, its nostrils flaring.

Several others in the herd looked up and tested the breeze for scent. One of the animals abruptly bolted to the south, pounding through the stream to the opposite bank and throwing up a spray of snow as it ran toward the forest. In short order the rest did the same.

Spinning around, displaying remarkable agility for so enormous a beast, the young bull managed to take two strides before the sharp blast of a rifle shattered the stillness of the woodland. It dashed another three yards, then its front legs gave out and it crashed to the ground, rolling over and coming to rest on its right side.

The shot spurred the herd to greater speed. They gained the forest and plowed deep into the sheltering trees. In less than a minute the breaking of branches and the smashing of underbrush died down and only the whispering whistle of the wind remained. That, and the wheezing of the young bull.

A figure appeared to the north of the dying bison, a broad-shouldered, bearded man who advanced toward the brute with a Hawken rifle clenched firmly in his brawny hands. He wore a heavy red and black Mackinaw coat over beaded buckskins. Sturdy moccasins constructed from dressed elk skins protected his feet from the elements. A dark handcrafted hat fashioned from beaver pelts crowned his youthful head, scarcely containing his mane of long black hair.

In addition to the rifle he was armed with a pair of flintlock pistols which were positioned on both sides of the large silver buckle on the brown leather belt that encircled his Mackinaw at the waist. A butcher knife dangled from a beaded sheath on his left hip. Tucked under the belt and slanted over his left hip was a tomahawk. Crisscrossing his muscular chest were two indispensable items no mountaineer could do without—a powder-horn and a bullet-pouch.

Nineteen year old Nathaniel King stepped cautiously up to the young bull. His green eyes narrowed and his steely body tensed, ready for action should the beast suddenly rise. Buffalos were the most unpredictable critters on God's green earth, and when provoked they exhibited a fierce temperament that rivaled that of grizzly bears. They were tough, hardy animals, extremely difficult to kill. He'd heard of bison being shot over two-dozen times and still eluding the hapless hunters after them. Given the buffalos' reputation and disposition, he wasn't about to take reckless chances.

Nate stood over the brute and placed the Hawken barrel near its head. The bull still breathed, although laboriously, wheezing like a steam engine. Its eyes were wide. Blood flecked its mouth, dribbling from one corner, and the tip of its succulent tongue protruded. He pressed the rifle stock to his right shoulder and sighted on a point a few inches above the animal's left eye. Killing meat for the table was one thing; letting any creature suffer needlessly was another. His thumb pulled the hammer back until it clicked, then his trigger finger began to curl around the cool metal.

The bull then went into violent convulsions, lifting its head and snorting as its legs thrashed about wildly.

To avoid being gored Nate jumped back and waited for the fit to subside. In seconds the buffalo ceased moving entirely, its great head sagged onto the soft cushion of snow, and it expired with a protracted exhalation that stirred the settled flakes near its mouth.

Nate prodded the beast to make certain it was dead, then gazed skyward at the gray clouds. Soon it would snow, and unless he wanted to be caught in a blizzard he'd better hurry. Accordingly, he drew his keen edged butcher knife and set to work dressing the bull.

As he sliced open the abdominal cavity and warmed his hands in the beast's intestines, Nate thought about his beloved wife who eagerly awaited his return back at their cabin. He also thought of the new life taking form within her—the baby now five and a half months into the making in her womb.

He found it hard to accept that it was the middle of January. Only last April—April 1, 1828 to be exact—he'd left his father and mother, his job, his friends, and another woman he'd mistakenly believed he loved, back in New York City and ventured west to make his fortune. He'd given up his dreams of becoming an accountant in a prominent metropolitan firm to join his Uncle Zeke, the black sheep of the King family, who had gone into the wilderness many years before and never returned. Zeke had written to him, promising to share 'the greatest treasure in the world' if Nate would only join him beyond the frontier.

"What a fool I was!" Nate reflected, then immediately changed his mind. True, he'd envisioned becoming partners with Zeke in a lucrative fur trading enterprise, or perhaps in mining some of the fabulous veins of gold or silver rumored to exist in the Rockies. And true, Zeke's underlying intent had been to introduce Nate to the life of a *mountain man*, as some had taken to calling those rugged trappers and hunters who lived as the Indians did by eaking an existence from an invariably hostile land. The true treasure Zeke had wanted his nephew to possess was the gift of genuine freedom, of a life where a man's worth was measured by his character, strength, and endurance, and where the only constraints were those imposed by Nature and the will of the Almighty.

How ironic, Nate mused. If he hadn't entertained those foolish notions of attaining great wealth he never would have wound up enjoying that true freedom Zeke had prized above all else. And now he felt the same way! He'd grown to appreciate the value of the life his late uncle had extolled. He had grown to realize that God had never meant for humanity to be cooped up in filthy cities of stone and brick where men and women suffered through lives of quiet desperation.

Such a horrible existence was no longer for him!

He inhaled the frigid air and caught a whiff of the tangy scent of the bull's blood. *This* was the life. This was the way the Good Lord meant for men to live. He called no one master, had no obligations to anyone other than his wife and himself. There were no pompous politicians trying to dictate his behavior, no bosses looking over his shoulder.

In every sense of the word, he was a free man.

Nate chuckled, then paused in his busy work when a snowflake fell within an inch of his nose and landed on the ground near his knees. He stared upward and frowned, seeing many more such flakes descending. The snowfall had begun. Soon it would intensify to the point where he wouldn't be able to see his hands in front of his face.

He had a choice to make. Skinning and dressing the entire buffalo before the brunt of the storm hit would be impossible. Either he made a lean-to in the trees and waited for the snow to stop, which could take hours, or he removed enough meat to feed Winona and himself for a week or so and returned home. He'd wandered less than two miles from the cabin since he began hunting, so the latter prospect was infinitely more appealing.

Nate hurriedly removed a sizeable strip of hide and carved off a thigh section of meat. He placed them to one side, then went about gathering limbs with which to cover the bull. Concealing it wouldn't do much good where wolves or panthers were concerned, since both could smell fresh blood half a mile off if the wind was right. But the neatly arranged limbs might prevent the kill from being spotted by other animals or by Indians who might be in the area.

The snow was falling steadily by the time Nate finished and wrapped the meat in the hide. He straightened, grabbed his Hawken, and headed to the northeast. The nearest peaks were obscured by the gradually building storm, depriving him of the landmarks he ordinarily relied on to guide his steps. Consequently, he moved slower than he normally would, selecting his route with care to avoid blundering into a ravine or over a cliff.

He made relatively good progress for the first twenty minutes or so. Then the rate of falling snow dramatically increased and he could barely distinguish trees twenty feet ahead.

The Hawken in his right hand, the bundle of meat under his left arm, Nate trudged onward, determined to get through no matter what. Several more minutes elapsed.

He felt something moist drip onto his left hand, first one drop, then others, and looking down he discovered that blood had seeped through the hide and onto his forearm. He'd removed the deerskin gloves Winona had sewn for him at the onset of cold weather in order to shoot at the bull, and he now paused to take them from the pockets of his Mackinaw and gratefully eased his chilled fingers into the soft material.

Taking the rifle and bundle again in hand, Nate resumed hiking through the sea of white and traveled a hundred yards before he heard the first of the howls. He halted, listening to the distant wail, wondering if the sound might be the wind. A second howl, slightly closer, dispelled his wishful thinking.

There were wolves abroad.

He hastened off. Normally wolves posed no problems for solitary humans. The stealthy and wily carnivores would run at the sight of man. There were exceptions to the rule, however. If a single wolf or a pack had gone long without food, they would tempt fate. And in the winter, when game was scarce and bringing prey such as deer and elk down became extremely difficult even for skilled stalkers, the wolves would hunt anything that moved.

Nate had heard a story once about a trapper who lost a leg to a pack of ravenous wolves and he had no intention of suffering a similar or worse fortune. He forged diligently northeastward until he ascended a rise located less than a mile from the lake near which his cabin stood.

At that moment more howls erupted to his rear and they were much, much closer.

Hefting the Hawken, Nate increased his pace. The wolves were on his trail. They must be following the scent of the dripping blood. He considered abandoning the meat, of simply leaving the bundle for them to find and buying the time he would need to make his escape, but the thought of Winona going hungry firmed his resolve. His wife needed the food. She was eating for two and she depended on him to provide the nourishment she required. He wasn't about to let her down.

The slope was slick and Nate nearly lost his footing several times en route to the bottom. He estimated he had another thirty feet to go when a strident howl, sounding as if it were at the top of the rise, caused him to glance over his shoulder in alarm. The snow screened the crest from his view. He derived some small comfort from the fact that since he couldn't see the wolves, they couldn't see him. Or so he hoped.

As Nate faced front his left foot hit a slippery spot and swept out from under him. He frantically tried to regain his balance, to no avail. Gravity brought him down onto his backside and he started to slide, gathering momentum with every yard. A small boulder loomed in his path and he threw himself to the left, hoping to roll out of harm's way. He wasn't completely successful.

A searing pain lanced his right leg as his shin struck the boulder with a jarring impact. Nate grit his teeth to keep from crying out. He spun, out of control, and tumbled the rest of the distance to the bottom, landing hard on his shoulders in a mound of snow.

Dazed, Nate struggled into a sitting position and took stock. He'd instinctively retained his grip on the rifle and the meat. Grunting, he tried to rise, his right leg in torment. From his rear came a low growl and he twisted to behold several dark four-legged forms gliding down the slope.

The wolves had found him.

Chapter Two

His pulse quickening, Nate surged to his feet and swung around to face the onrushing shadows. All three timber wolves halted, the nearest approximately fifteen feet off, their features shrouded by the driving snow. He could distinguish the general outline of their sleek bodies, but nothing more.

One of the beasts snarled.

Nate waited expectantly, his every nerve tingling, for the wolves to charge. He didn't dare fire while holding the buffalo meat. Shooting a powerful Hawken accurately one-handed was next to impossible and might well result in a busted limb. But he wasn't about to let go of the meat except as a last resort since he knew full well the wolves would be on it in a flash.

A minute went by. Two minutes. And still the

wolves only stood there, silently regarding him, perhaps taking his measure in their bestial way.

What now? Nate asked himself. The longer he stayed put, the colder he'd become. His reflexes would be dulled, even sluggish. The wolves would have a distinct advantage. He couldn't allow that to happen.

Taking a deep breath, Nate slowly backed away from the animals, ignoring the acute discomfort in his right leg. His eyes darted from wolf to wolf in anticipation of being attacked but the threesome were as still as statues. After going a dozen feet he warily wheeled and resumed his trek.

The storm intensified again, the falling snow becoming a virtual swirling white wall, obliterating the landscape in all directions. Nate lost sight of the wolves, and he paused to listen for their footfalls, but heard only the swishing snow and gusting wind. Lowering his head into the flake laden air, he made for home, vowing not to stop again until he held Winona in his arms.

Repeatedly Nate bumped into obstacles; logs, trees, rocks, and boulders were impossible to see. His right leg pained him less with every step, leading him to believe it was only badly bruised or sprained but not broken.

If the wolves were out there, they made no sound. Once, briefly, a shadowy form materialized on the right, then just as promptly vanished.

Nate couldn't find any points of reference and had no idea where he was. He guessed he was moving in the right direction and stubbornly forged onward, not daunted in the least at the prospect of being lost. There were trees all around him and it would be an easy task to construct a temporary shelter that would keep him relatively comfortable and safe until the snow abated.

Knowing he must only have three-quarters of a

mile to cover inspired him with hope that he would find the cabin before too long. Granted, spying a lone structure in the midst of a raging snowstorm wouldn't be easy, but he should be able to locate the lake without too much difficulty, and once he did finding the cabin would be a simple task.

Nate trudged through the forest for an indefinite period, losing all track of time. His exertion made him sweat, and the sweat in turn cooled and caused him to shiver. Oh, what he wouldn't give for a roaring fire and a hot cup of coffee!

He skirted a huge pine tree blocking his path and stopped to rest for a moment. The instant he did, something plowed into his legs from the rear and bowled him over. Caught off-guard, he felt teeth tear into his left calf as he fell onto his back. And then whatever had attacked him was gone, evaporating like a specter into the mist of white particles.

The wolves!

Nate rolled onto his right elbow and shoved upright. A scan of the area showed only snow. He bent down to look at his calf and found blood staining his legging and moccasin.

What were they up to? Why nip at him and run?

He hastened into the storm, hoping he wouldn't lose too much blood. If so, he might as well dig a hole in the ground and bury himself because he'd never reach the cabin alive.

Another streaking figure hurtled out of the snow and struck him in the lower legs.

Again Nate went down and was bitten, only this time on the opposite leg. The wolf disappeared into the storm. He swiftly rose, his other leg bleeding, and tried in vain to spot the beasts.

Somewhere to his rear one of the predators howled.

Nate turned and ran blindly, seeking to elude them and not paying much attention to the terrain. When a pine loomed in front of him he slowed, then dropped to his knees and scooted under its overhanging branches. He placed his back to the trunk, deposited the meat at his side, and gripped the rifle in both hands.

Now let them come!

Their tactics abruptly made complete sense. He'd once witnessed a pack of seven wolves kill a young moose by continually harassing it—taking turns running in and biting its flanks until eventually the moose collapsed and was easy prey for their raking teeth. These crafty wolves were trying the same devious ploy on him.

Thanks to the long tree limbs Nate could see for a few yards in all directions. The wolves wouldn't be able to get at him without being spotted. He cocked the Hawken and impatiently awaited the next assault.

His mind strayed to thoughts of Winona. He imagined her sitting by the fireplace in their cabin, probably worried half to death about him. Just so she stayed in there and didn't come looking for him.

What was that?

Something moved in the snow, a fleeting flicker that gave no hint of its cause.

The wolves had him boxed in. If he could only slay one of them the rest might leave. But how to accomplish the deed? He pondered the problem until an idea occured to him that brought a grin to his lips.

Taking the bundle of meat, he slid it out until the hide sat just at the edge of the sheltering tree limbs. Then he put his back to the trunk and trained the rifle barrel on the bait. The range was only eight feet. If he stayed alert, he couldn't miss.

Although the wolves had to know the buffalo meat was there, they made no attempt to claim it for their own.

Nate wondered if the animals were trying to wait

him out. Sooner or later he'd grow drowsy, perhaps doze off. Stealing the bundle would then be child's play. He reminded himself not to underestimate the intelligence of the three creatures.

Sure enough, lethargy set in and his eyelids fluttered and drooped. He forced himself awake and examined his wounds. Both were bleeding profusely, which must be weakening him considerably.

Nate shook his head and went to yawn. A vague shadow popped into sight near the buffalo meat and he froze, his finger touching the trigger.

Ever so cautiously the wolf came forward.

He could see its head now, its mouth curved back in a feral snarl and a hungry gleam in its eyes. The wolf was lean, nearly gaunt, and had long been without food. Under different circumstances he might have been moved to pity the animal, but his wife's need took precedence over the wolf's.

Nate sighted along the barrel, fixing a bead on the beast's sloping forehead. He resisted the temptation to fire until the wolf stood right beside the bundle, about to bite into the hide, and then he squeezed the trigger.

The sharp retort was amplified by the limbs overhead. At the sound the wolf sprang backwards, or tried to, but got only a foot before crumbling in the snow, a neat hole smack dab between its eyes.

Nate lost no time. He hastily reloaded, placing the rifle butt on the ground and pouring sufficient black powder from his powder-horn into the palm of his left hand. He fed the grains down the muzzle, wrapped a ball in a patch, then used the ramrod to shove the ball down on top of the powder. Replacing the ramrod under the barrel, he scoured the vicinity for the remaining wolves.

Given the well known fact that wolves, like most animals in the Rockies, were notoriously gun shy,

Nate concluded that the pair had fled. A nagging doubt, however, rooted him in place for five minutes. Finally he moved to the dead wolf, debating whether to take its skin, and decided his first priority was to reach Winona.

Clasping the bundle under his left arm, Nate slid out from under the pine tree and tramped into the storm. Both legs were stiff and sore. After walking a bit they loosened up but hurt terribly. His eagerness to reach the cabin mounted with each stride he took.

So intent was he on finding his home, he failed to watch his back trail, so the first inkling he had of impending danger was the throaty growl of a charging wolf to his rear. Whirling, he dropped the meat and attempted to level the Hawken, but the barrel was still slanted toward the ground when the two wolves hurtled through the air and slammed into his chest.

Nate was knocked down hard onto his shoulders with a pair of snapping jaws within inches of his face. He released the Hawken and grabbed a hairy throat in each hand, digging his fingers into their flesh, striving to hold them at bay.

The wolves were in a primal fury. They clawed at his coat and bit at his head, their combined weight and strength formidable.

It was all Nate could do to hold on. One of the wolves snared the tip of his chin, its tapered teeth digging in deep. In dread of having one of them bite into his neck, Nate frantically threw himself to the right and heaved, then tried to regain his footing.

Both wolves recovered instantaneously and scrambled to their feet. The larger of the duo sprang.

In a virtual blur Nate drew his right flintlock and snapped off a shot, the tip of the pistol barrel almost touching the wolf's nose when it discharged a small cloud of smoke and lethal lead. The ball bored into the animal's skull, the impact flipping it onto its back. The last wolf never even paused. Growling, the beast leaped and chomped down on the extended arm.

Nate almost screamed from the agony. The flintlock fell from his grasp and he arched his spine, then dropped his left hand to the butcher knife. His fingers closed around the hilt and he swept the razor-edged blade up and in, sinking it into the wolf's exposed chest.

Snarling savagely, the wolf opened its jaws, darted to the left, and closed in again.

Swinging the butcher knife in an arc, Nate cut a furrow in the wolf's face, nearly taking out an eye. The beast bounded out of his reach and crouched, its teeth exposed. He lunged, swinging recklessly, and drove the animal farther back.

For a moment the two adversaries eyed one another.

Then the wolf came in fast and low, going for the legs.

Nate twisted to the left and speared the knife at the wolf's back. He scored, slicing its fur open. In a twinkling the animal pivoted and pounced, burying its teeth into his left leg.

The *pain*! Never had Nate known such excrutiating torture. He cried out, dropping the knife, and endeavored to jerk his leg lose. The wolf held firm, however, and in desperation he drew his other flintlock, pressed the barrel to the top of the animal's cranium, cocked the hammer, and fired.

Its body going limp, the wolf collapsed on the spot, blood and bits of gray matter spurting from the hole in its head. But even in death the beast's jaws stayed locked on Nate's leg.

Squatting, Nate stuck the flintlock under his belt and gripped the wolf's jaws, trying to pry them apart. He strained for all he was worth, his face becoming red, his veins bulging. With a supreme effort he managed to wrench the teeth from his flesh and sank back on the snow, exhausted.

But Nate realized this ordeal was far from over. He grit his teeth and sat up to inspect his wounds. The amount of blood he was losing appalled him. He couldn't waste precious time in recuperating. He had to get on his feet and get to the cabin or he would surely die.

Spurred by the realization of his own mortality, Nate collected his weapons, tucked the prized meat under his left arm, and hastened in what he hoped was the direction of the cabin and the lake. He felt blood trickling down his arm and legs and tried not to dwell on it. Keep going, he prodded himself. Just keep going. You'll reach the cabin.

Countless snow flakes swirled around him and caked his hat, coat, and moccasins. He trudged ever forward, his shoulders hunched, shivering more and more as time wore on. His legs became progressively weaker. He bumped into objects, recovered his balance, and pressed on.

I'm coming, Winona! he wanted to shout.

Nate's senses swam. He had no idea how far he traveled or how much time had elapsed. It took all of his concentration merely to move one foot ahead of the other. Left. Right. Left. Right. With single-minded purpose he plowed toward the woman he loved.

I'm coming, Winona!

Numbness set in, creeping up his legs to his thighs, an odd tingling compounded by his now constant shivering. He wished he could lie down and rest. A few hours sleep might restore his vitality.

What was he thinking? Nate chided himself for his momentary weakness and walked on. His vision blurred and he was startled when he smacked into a tree and fell to his knees. Grimacing, he willed his legs to straighten so he could continue but they refused to obey his mental command. He tried again with the same result.

This couldn't be happening.

He couldn't die now, not when he'd found the greatest happiness any man had ever known.

Nate swallowed and felt nauseous. He tried a third time to stand. Instead, a strange wave of black emptiness engulfed his consciousness and he began to pitch onto his face. In that final second before the void claimed him, he raised his head and called out the name of the woman who meant more to him than life itself, shouting at the top of his lungs in defiance to the wilderness that had bested him: "WWWIIINNNOOONNNAAA!"

Then he struck the ground. The last sensation he experienced was the soft snow against his skin.

Chapter Three

He seemed to be at the bottom of a murky pool. Far above him lay the shimmering surface. He pushed off from the bottom and swam with even, strong strokes toward the beckoning light. Oddly, for every stroke he took the surface receded the same distance. He made no headway. His lungs began to ache.

With a start he realized that he wasn't in a pool. Water didn't envelope him; a heavy, moist air did, a palpable substance unlike any he'd ever known or heard about. He stroked harder, kicking his legs but still he made no progress. His lungs began to ache.

Somewhere someone shouted, a muffled cry he barely heard. He flailed his arms and pumped his legs with all his might, yet the surface mocked him by receding farther. Something materialized above him, a huge mass that swept down toward him and blocked out the light. He opened his mouth to scream and felt his wind cut off.

"Nate! Nate! It's me!"

The urgent voice, so intimately familiar, penetrated to the core of his being, stirring his very soul, and Nate became instantly wide awake. His eyes snapped open and he looked around him in confusion, fearing he'd dreamed hearing her. "Winona?" he blurted, then saw her seated beside him on the right. They were both on the bed in their cabin.

"I am here, husband," his wife stated, using her native tongue, the musical language of the Shoshone tribe.

"Thank the Lord," Nate breathed in English, his eyes drinking in her beauty. He knew she would understand him. They each spoke the other's language with a fair degree of fluency, although he would be the first to admit that she spoke more English than he did Shoshone. Frequently they conducted conversations in both tongues, as much to keep in practice as anything else.

Like most women in her tribe, Winona possessed high, prominent cheekbones that served to accent her natural loveliness. Hip-length, luxurious black hair and lively brown eyes imbued her with an aura of innate vitality. A beaded buckskin dress, bulging at the abdomen, covered her otherwise supple figure.

"The Great Mystery was indeed watching over you," Winona said softly, reaching over to tenderly stroke his brow. "If I hadn't heard you yell, you would have died in the blizzard."

The blizzard! Nate's memory of shooting the young bull and the attack by the wolves returned in a rush and he went to sit up. Searing pain in his right arm made him wince and look down at himself. All he had on were his leggins and they had been slit from their bottom edges to his thighs to afford access to his wounds.

"Please stay still," Winona urged. "The wolves you fought tore you very badly and you're weak. I put herbs on the bites to help them heal."

"Thank you," Nate said gratefully. He frowned as he studied the ragged gashes in his body; there were two on his left leg, one on his right, a nasty laceration on his right arm several inches above the wrist, and the injury to his chin. Small wonder he ached from his head to his toes. "How did you know it was wolves?"

"You talked in your sleep," Winona said.

Nate looked at the window, at the narrow space between the sill and the flap, and saw snow still falling outside. From the amount of subdued light it must be daytime. "How long was I unconscious?"

"Most of yesterday and all night. It's morning now."

"What?" Nate said in surprise. To him it was as if mere minutes had elapsed. He keenly appreciated owing his life to her. Had she not found him, he'd be in the spirit world, as the Indians liked to say. "You heard me call your name?"

Winona nodded. "You were only twenty steps from the rear of the cabin when you collapsed."

"And you carried me inside by yourself?" Nate asked in alarm.

"No," Winona said, and grinned. "A black bear helped me."

"This is no joking matter," Nate said. "You shouldn't be lifting something as heavy as I am in your condition." He touched her bulging belly. "You took a great risk."

"Don't be silly. I couldn't leave you there to die."

Nate gazed affectionately into her eyes. "I'm sorry for the trouble I caused you."

"Yes, you were a lot of trouble," Winona stated in mock seriousness. "I can't wait to tell my people how the mighty Grizzly Killer let himself be beaten by a few hungry wolves."

Her cheery laughter a second later prompted him to join in. He could readily imagine the mirth her story would provoke in the Shoshones, who possessed a keen sense of humor.

The mighty Grizzly Killer! Nate recalled the Cheyenne Warrior called White Eagle who had bestowed the name on him months ago after he'd tangled with his first brown bear, as some of the mountaineers referred to that most savage denizen of the Rockies. Somehow, the title had stuck. Perhaps the fact he'd been compelled to slay three of the fierce brutes since leaving the States had something to do with it, for now the Cheyennes, the Shoshones, the dreaded Blackfeet, the Bannocks, Utes, Nez Perces, and Flatheads all knew him by his Indian name.

To Nate's amazement, tales of his presumed exploits were being told around many a campfire from the Mississippi to the mountains. He could partially understand being a topic of conversation for the trappers, who spent every evening enjoying fireside chats about the latest news and gossip. But he'd been stunned to learn that word of his exploits had passed among the various Indian tribes gathered for the rendezvous last year at Bear Lake, or Sweet Lake as some called it.

Winona herself had told him that her people were boasting to all who would listen of their friendship with the famous Grizzly Killer. The white man who could kill a Grizzly with a mere knife, the free trapper who had saved their tribe from the Blackfeet had married one of their prettiest maidens.

Nate often found his spreading notoriety embarrassing. If he wasn't careful, he'd soon be nearly as famous as Jed Smith, Jim Bridger, or Joseph Walker.

Or Shakespeare McNair.

Thinking of the wise old mountain man who had been his mentor after the death of his Uncle Zeke, Nate smiled and wished Shakespeare was still staying at the cabin. He missed his friend's companionship, missed Shakespeare's wit and insights. If he lived only half as long and acquired only half as much wisdom as McNair, he'd be two times as smart as the average person.

"Would you care for some buffalo stew, husband?" Winona inquired.

Nate stared at the corner of the cabin where the pots and pans were kept, then at the stone fireplace he'd built shortly before winter set in. A heavy pot purchased at the rendezvous hung over low flames. "You brought in the bundle I was carrying too?"

"I couldn't pry your fingers off it," Winona revealed. "And after all the trouble you went to in bringing the meat back, I had no intention of leaving it to rot."

The prospect of food caused Nate's stomach to growl loudly. "Yes, I'd like some stew very much. Even better, I could eat a thick, juicy steak."

"You've been without food for too long to eat steak now," Winona cautioned him. "A few days of soup and herbs will restore your strength. Then you can have steak."

Nate pretended to pout. "I had no idea wives could be so much like mothers."

Rising, Winona placed a hand on her stomach. "Motherhood comes naturally to women." She stepped around the end of the bed and walked toward the fireplace.

Settling back, Nate fondly watched her stir the contents of the pot. Despite his wounds and the attendant pain, he was supremely content. Simply being alive made him thankful. Having the most wonderful wife on the North American continent was an added gift. To think, if he'd stayed back in New York he might have wound up married to Adeline!

Adeline Van Buren was the exquisitely cultured—some would say exquisitely *spoiled*—daughter of an extremely wealthy man in New York City. Because Nate's father had known her father, they'd become acquainted. Her charm and radiant good looks had mesmerized Nate and he'd fallen head over heels for her. To his utter astonishment, Adeline had reciprocated. They'd even discussed marriage. Acutely aware of his financial shortcomings, Nate had eagerly jumped at the chance to share in his uncle's wealth in an effort to provide Adeline with the many luxuries to which she'd grown accustomed.

How strange fate could be, Nate reflected. He'd left New York with every intention of returning to Adeline a rich man. Now he didn't care if he ever went East or saw her again, although infrequently a twinge of guilt bothered him. One day, maybe, he would take a trip back and explain everything to her. He owed her that much, at least.

"I dried and salted most of the meat," Winona announced, interrupting his contemplation. "We have enough to last until the new moon."

"The cold should preserve the rest of the kill," Nate mentioned. "In two or three days I'll go get more."

"You will not go anywhere until you are healed."

Nate chuckled. "I thought Indian wives always go along with whatever their husbands want."

A spontaneous laugh erupted from Winona's lips. "Where did you ever hear such a crazy thing?"

"Here and there."

"Indian women are taught to always obey their husbands, yes. But we also speak our minds when the need arises. If our husbands behave like idiots, we tell them so," Winona said, and smirked. "Although not in public."

Nate thought of all the newspaper stories he'd read about Indians back in New York and frowned. Most had contained dreadful inaccuracies and exaggerations. Many editorialists had claimed that all Indians were savages who deserved to be forced off their lands to make room for the whites. And no less a personage than Andrew Jackson, the hero of the Battle of New Orleans who was running for President of the United States, had gone so far as to state the Indians were an inferior race.

The fools. What did they know about Indians, about Indian values and the Indian way of life? Nate would like to line up every one of the bigots and personally put a ball between their eyes. He wondered if Jackson had won the election and reminded himself to ask the next trappers he encountered. If so, it did not bode well for Indians everywhere.

"Nate?"

He looked up to find her regarding him solemnly. "Yes?"

"May I ask you a question?"

"Since when does an Indian woman need her husband's permission to ask a question?" Nate quipped.

"Do you ever regret marrying me?"

Shocked, Nate forgot himself and rose onto his elbows. "Why do you ask?"

"Do you?"

"Of course not. I love you with all my heart."

"But would you be happier married to a white woman?"

Nate's brow knit as he tried to ascertain the reason for her concern. He'd never mentioned a word to her about Adeline. "No, I wouldn't," he stated firmly. "I couldn't possibly be happier than I am right at this moment. I'm insulted, Winona, that you would even think to ask."

"I don't mean to offend you."

"Then why bring it up?"

Winona stopped stirring and faced him. "Who is Adeline?"

If the roof had collapsed onto his head, Nate wouldn't have been more flabbergasted than he was. "Where did you hear her name?"

"From you. While you were unconscious."

Nate detected hurt in her eyes and struggled to keep his voice calm, his face composed. "What did I say about her?"

"Nothing. You only called her name. Four times."

"I see," Nate said, stalling, debating whether to reveal the whole truth. He didn't want to upset Winona more than she already had been. "Adeline Van Buren is a woman I knew in New York City. We were friends."

"Only friends?"

"More than friends," Nate admitted. "We were thinking about getting married."

"Oh," Winona said, the word barely audible. She turned to the pot again.

"Come here," Nate said.

Winona didn't budge.

"Please."

Her slender shoulders slumping, Winona let go of the ladle and came over to the edge of the bed.

"Sit down. Please."

Winona complied reluctantly, averting her gaze.

Grunting, Nate sat up and placed his hands on her shoulders. "Look at me."

She did so, moisture rimming her eyes.

"You're all upset for no reason," Nate assured her. "Adeline Van Buren means nothing to me. I have no regrets over leaving her." He paused, pulled Winona forward, and gently kissed her. "I married you, dearest, because I love you more than any woman

I've ever known. More than I could ever care for Adeline. I want to spend the rest of my life with you, raising a family and growing old together. And, God willing, I want to be buried at your side when we both go to meet our Maker." He paused again. "Do you understand? I would *not* be happier married to a white woman. I would be miserable without you."

Winona suddenly threw her arms around him and pressed her face to his neck. "Thank you, husband," she said quietly.

Nate felt her tears on his skin and a lump formed in his throat. He stroked her hair, chiding himself for not telling her about Adeline sooner. Causing her misery was the last thing he ever wanted to do. He opened his mouth to tell her as much when from outside the cabin came a sound that inevitably heralded trouble.

The crack of a shot.

Chapter Four

Nate let his arms drop and Winona promptly stood, their mutual anxiety forgotten.

Nate put his palms on the bed and swung his legs over the side.

"What do you think you are doing?"

Nate ignored the question, touched his soles to the rough wooden floor, and shoved. He succeeded in rising although his legs shrieked in protest. Swaying precariously, he might have fallen had not Winona quickly stepped to his side and looped an arm around his waist.

"You should stay in bed," she scolded him.

"Help me to the window," Nate said, and moved stiffly when she reluctantly complied. They stood next to the deerskin flap that his Uncle Zeke had tacked to the top of the window years ago when the cabin was built. Winona had rolled up the bottom edge half an inch and tied it at that height for ventilation. "How far off do you think that shot was?"

"The other side of the lake."

Nate nodded. "I'd guess the same." He bent at the waist and peered out the crack. All he saw was snow and more snow. "Who would be out in weather like this?" he asked absently.

"Utes."

Incipient apprehension flared in Nate's breast. He was in no condition to do battle with a band of bloodthirsty Utes. The cabin was located in their territory and his uncle had fought off marauding warriors on several occasions. "I hope you're wrong," he said.

"Even if there is a war party in the area, I doubt they can find our cabin."

Nate liked the way she referred to their home as "our." He listened for a minute, then began to straighten.

From the distance came a second shot, muffled by the heavy snow and echoing off the high peaks that rimmed the valley in which the cabin was situated.

"That one was a little closer," Nate commented, at a loss to explain the gunfire. Certainly no one would be hunting in such inclement weather; seeing the game would be impossible. Perhaps the shots were signals of some sort.

"You should lie down," Winona proposed. "I will keep watch out the window."

"That's my job," Nate disagreed. "Get me a chair and I'll be fine."

Hesitating, Winona frowned to emphasize her displeasure, then went to a nearby chair he'd constructed with his own hands and set it in front of the sill. "Here."

"Thank you," Nate said gratefully, sinking down. He didn't know how much longer he could have stayed on his feet. Uncharacteristic weakness pervaded him and he longed to curl up on the bed and sleep for a week.

"Would you like your stew?"

"Yes. And my guns and my other set of buckskins."

Winona wisely brought the Hawken and both flintlocks over first. None were loaded. He frowned at his oversight. No matter how badly he'd been hurt, reloading should have been his first priority. Nate requested the powder-horn and the ammunition-pouch and prepared all three guns in case there should be uninvited visitors. Next he put on the clothes, wedged the pistols under his belt, then started in on the stew. Never had buffalo meat and broth tasted so delicious. He chewed each morsel and savored every drop.

Carting over the other chair, Winona took a seat on his left and watched him finish off the meal. "Would you like more?"

"Not now," Nate said, rubbing his stomach. "Another drop and I'll be too drowsy to stay awake." He gave her the bowl and positioned the Hawken on his lap. The meal had invigorated him and he felt ready to wrestle a bear. A *small* bear. He was close enough to the window that a slight, cool breeze touched his face and made him feel chilly, a convincing reminder he mustn't push himself too hard or he'd be back in bed in no time.

Winona moved off, and when next she stepped into view she had a heavy buffalo robe draped over her shoulders. She walked to the front door and gripped the wooden latch.

"Where are you heading?" Nate inquired.

"One of us must check on the horses."

"I'll do it," Nate said, rising.

"Please, husband. You must stay inside and stay warm. I will be back soon."

Nate stood. Their four animals were in a pen he'd constructed on the south side of the cabin. Verifying the horses were all right would take only a minute, but he didn't like the notion of Winona venturing out in the blizzard when there might be Utes in the vicinity. "I'll go."

"You're being stubborn. I will be fine."

Moving over to where his patched Mackinaw hung on a hook on the wall, Nate propped the rifle against his left leg, took the red coat down, and slipped his arms into the sleeves. "Thank you for sewing the rips."

"Don't change the subject," Winona said stiffly. "You shouldn't go out and you know it."

"If it will make you feel any better," Nate offered to appease her, "why don't we both go?"

"If you insist. But stay close to me."

Nate found his moccasins, put them on, and retrieved the Hawken. "I'll go first," he offered.

A blast of icy wind tore into their cozy home the moment he opened the stout door. Tucking his chin to his chest, Nate steeled himself and walked outside. The whipping snow obscured everything beyond a range of fifteen feet. Moist flakes lashed his cheeks.

Winona closed the door behind them.

To their left, stacked against the cabin, was the immense stack of firewood Nate had cut for the winter. Since their home faced due east, he turned right, staying close to the wall as he walked to the corner and peered around the edge. The snow prevented him from seeing the entire pen. He reasoned that the animals would instinctively congregate at the west side of the fence where the forest beyond was thickest and would act as a windbreak.

Nate walked to the pen and began to follow the fence around. He glanced at his wife, who was to his left, and smiled. She gave him a stare every bit as frosty as the blizzard. Annoyed that she didn't appreciate his selfless gesture in not wanting to expose her to potential danger, he trudged around the south end of the pen and halted when he finally spied the four horses.

The animals had indeed gathered to the west and were huddled together. They gazed at him longingly, as if in the expectation he would make them warm again.

Winona stepped to a pile of grass they had collected to use as feed and dumped several arm loads over the top rail, in reality a long limb like all the rest Nate had employed to fashion the fence.

None of the horses moved.

Taking his wife's elbow, Nate started to retrace their route. The cold was causing him to shiver and he was eager to get inside where the fire would warm him. He entertained the idea of eating another bowl of stew, and thus preoccupied he hiked to within a yard of the entrance when he stopped in midstride.

The front door hung open.

Stunned, Nate exchanged an alarmed glance with Winona. He leveled the Hawkin and eased cautiously to the jamb. Had someone been watching the cabin and seen them depart? He rejected that idea because of the limited field of visibility, but then a shadow flitted across the doorway.

Any doubt that there was someone inside evaporated and Nate's features hardened. It must be Utes, he deduced. If so, they'd pay dearly for violating his home. He cocked the hammer, being careful not to let it click loudly, and peeked into the cabin. His anger gave way to baffled amusement.

A portly white man attired in buckskins stood at the fireplace ladling stew into his fleshy mouth as swiftly as he could dip the implement. He sported a scruffy beard and a thin moustache. On his head

perched a cap made from an otter skin. A Kentucky
rifle leaned against the wall nearby.

Nate slid into the room and advanced halfway to
the fireplace before speaking. "That's my stew you're
helping yourself to, stranger."

At the sound of Nate's voice the man started,
dropped the ladle, and spun, some of the broth
dripping down over his fat jowls. He blinked a few
times, then glanced at the Kentucky rifle.

"You'll be dead before you touch it," Nate warned
gravely.

The man looked past him as Winona entered, then
swallowed and licked his lips.

"Do you have a name?" Nate asked.

"Kennedy, sir," the man responded in a high,
whining voice. "Isaac Kennedy at your service."

"And what are you doing helping yourself to our
stew?"

"I'm sorry," Kennedy said, and went on in a rush
of words as if anxious to explain before he was shot.
"I truly am. But I was cold and starving and when I
stumbled on your cabin and no one answered my
knock I just opened the door and saw the stew and
couldn't resist the temptation."

Unable to suppress a grin, Nate let the Hawken
barrel droop. He shifted and glanced at Winona, then
nodded at the door. She scanned the area outside
before closing it.

"I didn't mean no harm, sir," Kennedy said. "But I
was so hungry. I haven't eaten for over twenty-four
hours."

"That long, eh?" Nate responded with a straight
face. He studied the stranger, trying to ascertain the
man's character. One fact was obvious; Isaac Kennedy had no place being in the wilderness. The man
clearly was no mountaineer.

"And it's so cold out there," Kennedy said, shuddering. "I swear I nearly froze to death a dozen times."

Nate had a thought. "Was that you doing the shooting earlier?"

"No, sir. That must have been my two partners," Kennedy said. "We became separated and they were probably searching for me. I heard them shoot but I couldn't answer them."

"Why not?"

"I snagged my powder-horn on a tree limb and it was torn off. I tried to find it, but couldn't."

Nate stared at the Kentucky rifle. "Your gun isn't loaded?"

"No, sir. I forgot to load it after I shot at a rabbit the day before yesterday."

"It's not very smart to wander around the mountains with an empty rifle."

"I know. Newton and Lambert are always reminding me to reload right after I fire, but I keep forgetting."

"I take it that Newton and Lambert are your partners?"

"Yes, sir."

"Stop calling me sir. My name is Nate King," Nate revealed, and motioned at Winona. "This is Winona, my wife."

"Pleased to make your acquaintance," Kennedy said, wiping his left sleeve across his chin. He looked at the Hawken and gulped. "You're not fixing to shoot me, are you?"

"No," Nate said. He gave the rifle to Winona, who hung it on a rack on the north wall next to the bed. Removing the Mackinaw, he exposed the two flint-locks and saw the man's eyes widen. "What are you and your partners doing in this neck of the woods?" he asked as he hung the coat up.

"We're trappers, sir."

"Is that a fact?" Nate remarked, concealing his disbelief. Why the man should lie, he didn't know. But if Isaac Kennedy was a trapper, then Nate was the Queen of England. "I'm a free trapper myself. Do you work for one of the fur companies?"

"No," Kennedy answered quickly, a bit too quickly. "We're free trappers also."

"Have you been at it long?"

"Newton and Lambert have. This is my first trip into the Rockies."

"I never would have guessed," Nate said. He gestured at one of the chairs. "Why don't you take a seat, Isaac, and we'll give you a bowl of stew."

"I don't want to impose."

"Nonsense. We wouldn't be good Samaritans if we didn't feed those in need."

Rubbing his thick hands together in anticipation, Kennedy grinned and walked over to sit down. "Thank you. I'll never forget your hospitality. I can't get over how friendly folks are west of the Mississippi. The people in Independence, Missouri, were courteous and helpful to a fault."

Nate idly scratched the left side of his beard, carefully avoiding the bite mark. Independence, located on the very edge of the frontier, had been founded two years ago and served as the start-off point for many traveling into these vast uncharted lands. "I gather you're from the East."

"Ohio," Kennedy answered, watching as Winona moved to the pot with a bowl in her hand.

"Did you come all this way on foot?"

"No sir. My horse ran away when I fell off it."

Nate wasn't certain he'd heard correctly. "You fell off your horse?"

"Right after I snagged my ammo-pouch on that tree," Kennedy said, unable to take his eyes off the stew being ladled into the bowl.

"Tell me, Isaac. What did you do before you decided to become a trapper?"

"I was a merchant. Owned my own store," Kennedy said, almost drooling as Winona approached him with the steaming stew.

"And where do you and your partners plan to do your trapping?"

Kennedy gazed at Nate and replied in all innocence: "In Ute country."

Chapter Five

The tall man stood beside his horse in the sheltering midst of a stand of high pines and peered skyward at the diminishing snowfall. He patted his mount, then swung lithely into the saddle. Buckskins and a brown wool coat covered his thin frame. His angular face was surrounded by a black beard at the bottom and a tangled mop of dark hair at the top. Eyes the color of a high country lake but colder than the snow regarded his surroundings with the alert air of a seasoned mountaineer. A perpetual sneer curled his thin lips. In his right hand he clutched a rifle. Snug under the black belt girding his coat was a flintlock.

He goaded his horse out of the pines and across a tract of clear land toward a jumble of boulders at the base of the mountains bordering the valley on the east side. His body swayed slightly with the stride of his animal, as if the horse and him were one entity.

As he neared the boulders he surveyed the area until he saw a spiral of smoke rising from behind several monoliths positioned close together. Urging his horse to go faster he soon arrived at the site and passed between a pair of boulders each the size of a house to find a campfire blazing and another man squatting by the flames who looked up at his advent on the scene.

The second man also wore buckskins and a black coat. He possessed a stockier build and wore a cap constructed from a wolf pelt with the tail dangling down his back. His hair was brown, as were his eyes. A short, trimmed beard lent his face a squarish profile. Leaning on a rock near his left hand was a modified .60 caliber Kentucky rifle, its barrel having been trimmed by several inches and a larger than normal stock added.

A dozen yards behind the man, tethered in a string, were seven pack animals all bearing heavy loads consisting of long wooden crates. Close-by stood a saddle horse.

"Any luck, Lambert?" the man at the fire asked.

"None," the rider responded, reining up and sliding to the ground. He walked over to the fire, tucked his rifle under his left arm, and extended his fingers toward the welcome warmth. "That damn fool probably got himself killed."

"I hope not."

Lambert snorted. "We don't need that idiot, Newton. I say good riddance to the stupid son of a bitch. In all my born days I've never met anyone so incompetent."

Taking a seat, the man called Newton regarded his companion critically. "You're not using your head, partner. We do need Kennedy."

"Why do we need that simpleton?"

"Because he has the money and the business contacts. We don't."

"What's to stop us from making them *our* contacts?" Lambert asked.

Newton sighed. "We've been all through this already. Kennedy was in business for over ten years. He knows all the right people and has a reputation as an honest businessman. The ones who sell the goods to him wouldn't give us the time of day."

"I hate having to rely on him," Lambert groused.

"And you think I like it?"

Lambert gazed upward. The snow had tapered to a trickle. "I suppose we should continue searching for him," he said reluctantly.

"The sooner we find Isaac, the sooner we can reach the Utes," Newton mentioned.

"And the sooner we get our pelts," Lambert added, grinning. "Then we'll have more money than either of us could make in a lifetime of trapping lousy beaver. We won't know what to do with it all."

The stocky Newton grabbed his rifle and stood. "I know what I'm going to do with my share."

"Let me guess. You're going to St. Louis and bed a different whore every night."

"St. Louis, hell. I'm going to New York City. Whores there have class."

"A whore is a whore, Newton, and it doesn't make a difference whether she's in St. Louis or New York. Pay her price and she'll spread her legs."

"Shows how much you know. The whores in New York City wear nicer, fancier clothes with a lot of frills and lace and such. And they smell a hell of a lot better. Why, some of them take a bath every single day."

Lambert cackled. "Now I know you're pulling my leg. There's isn't a person alive who takes a bath every day. Once a year is more than enough. Take them too often and you wind up sickly."

"Have it your way," Newton said testily, adjusting

his hat. "But I've been to New York and I know what I'm talking about." He began kicking snow onto the fire and white smoke billowed heavenward.

"I didn't mean to get you riled."

"I'm not."

"I know better. I know that temper of yours."

"Drop it," Newton stated, kicking furiously. In a minute he had the flames extinguished and the smoldering embers soaked under a layer of snow.

Lambert walked to his horse and swung up. "Want me to take the north side of the valley and you can take the south?"

"We'll stick together," Newton said. "We're in Ute country now and we can't take any chances."

"They won't harm us."

"Only a fool would trust a savage," Newton stated. "If you're not careful you'll get your throat slit and your hair taken."

"Their chief gave his word."

"*One* of their chiefs made the deal with us," Newton corrected him. "The chiefs of the other villages would just as soon skin us alive."

"I'm not worried," Lambert declared. "We talked our way out of a scalping once and we can do it again."

"We were lucky, is all," Newton said. "Two Owls could have had us rubbed out any time he wanted." He paused. "I'm still not convinced he won't anyway once he gets what he wants."

"Are you saying we should turn around and head for the States after coming all this distance?"

"Of course not. We'd be crazier than loons to give up now."

"Let's go, then."

Newton went to the pack animals and took the reins in his left hand, then mounted his saddle horse. He took the lead, riding between the boulders and pausing once he was in the clear. The snow had practically stopped. His gaze drifted westward to a tranquil lake and the country on the far side. Suddenly he stiffened and asked, "Do you see what I see over yonder?"

Halting, Lambert took one look and smirked. "I'll be tarred and feathered. Who the hell would have a cabin way out here?"

"Let's find out."

Nate waited until Isaac Kennedy had greedily finished the bowl before broaching the subject of trapping again. He spent the time observing the greenhorn while Winona bustled about the cabin.

"A truly marvelous repast," Kennedy said at last, smacking his lips and staring at Winona. "My compliments to the lady of the house."

"My wife is an excellent cook," Nate commented. "But then, most Indian women are. They have to be."

"Why is that?"

"Because an Indian man doesn't want to take for his wife a woman who hasn't mastered the art of keeping a home. Cooking, sewing, the working of hides, the care of a teepee, all these are the responsibilities of the women."

"It sounds terribly boring."

"Someone who doesn't know any better would likely think so," Nate said testily, "but Indian women take pride in their work. In some tribes the women belong to special societies just like the warriors. They compete to see who can weave the prettiest patterns or who can cure the most number of hides. It's quite an honor for a woman to be considered the best at any task."

"But isn't it demeaning that the men get to go out and do the hunting and make war while the women do all the petty chores?"

"There's nothing petty about the work they do. The welfare and comfort of their families depends on them," Nate disclosed, annoyed at the man's attitude. "Besides, warriors never look down their noses at the women. They treat women with the respect they deserve."

Kennedy shrugged. "I guess I would make a terrible Indian."

"Do tell."

The portly man glanced at Nate's face and in the strained silence that ensued squirmed uncomfortably in his chair. "I didn't mean to offend you," he said at length. "And I didn't intend to insult the Indians, either. The good Lord knows I'm in no position to judge or speak badly of anyone."

"Oh?"

Kennedy abruptly rose and carried the bowl to the table. "Should I put this here?"

"Be my guest," Nate said, wondering what to make of the man's behavior. When Kennedy sat down he brought up the subject that most interested him. "You say that you plan to trap in Ute country?"

"Yes, indeed. Newton and Lambert know the way. I came along simply to watch over my investment."

"I don't understand. Did you foot the bill for the supplies?"

"The supplies? Oh, yes," Kennedy said. "I paid for everything."

"What kind of traps did you purchase? Newhouses?"

"I don't remember."

"How many pounds of powder and lead did you bring?"

"I'm not certain."

"What about flour and coffee?"

"We brought some."

"How much?"

"I don't know."

Nate's brow furrowed. For somehow who had fit out the trapping expedition, Kennedy knew precious little about the gear and goods purchased. "Well, I hope you know what you're doing."

"Why?"

"Because venturing into the heart of Ute country to trap beaver is about as dangerous as sticking your head in a grizzly's mouth to examine its teeth."

"I'm not worried. Newton and Lambert know what they're doing."

"Have they told you about the Utes?"

"Yes."

"Then you know that the Utes hate all whites? You know that they exterminate every trapper foolish enough to enter their territory? You know that next to the Blackfeet, the Utes are probably the most feared tribe in the northern half of the Rockies?"

Anxiety crept into Kennedy's expression. "Newton and Lambert never told me all those details."

"If I was you I'd think twice about carrying out your original plan. Head north a ways. There's plenty of prime beaver country and you won't need to worry so much about the Utes."

"I appreciate your concern, Nate, but we'll be all right. My friends know a Ute chief."

"Do you know this chief's name?"

"Two Owls."

A flood of memories washed over Nate. He'd met Two Owls himself several months ago and they had formed a temporary, uneasy alliance against the dreaded Blackfeet. Eventually they'd parted on friendly terms but he couldn't guarantee the Ute warrior would be so kindly disposed the next time they encountered one another. "How is it your friends know him?"

"They ran into Two Owls when they were trapping out here a few seasons ago."

"And they're still alive?"

"They talked him out of killing them."

It occurred to Nate that Newton and Lambert might be the biggest liars ever to don a pair of britches. There wasn't a trapper alive who could dissuade hostile warriors from taking their hair. The only reason he'd been able to hook up with Two Owls had been because he'd gotten the drop on the chief and refused to take his life. Out of a sense of gratitude or obligation, Two Owls had then helped Nate fight the Blackfeet.

Winona, who had moved over to the window, announced in Shoshone, "The snow is stopping, husband. I will go feed the horses more grass."

Twisting, Nate saw a few flakes trickling down and the sky beginning to brighten as the cloud cover moved eastward. "I will go."

"You should stay with our guest," Winona said, putting on her buffalo robe.

Nate hesitated. He didn't like the idea of her going out alone, but he decided against making an issue of it in front of Kennedy. "Okay. But be on your guard."

"Always," Winona said, smiling, and stepped to the door.

"Where is she going?" Kennedy inquired.

Nate faced him. "To feed our horses."

"You have horses? Is there any chance I could borrow one to go find Newton and Lambert?"

"We'll go together in a while," Nate proposed, unwilling to lend a precious horse to someone who had lost his own. He heard the latch slide open as Winona prepared to depart, then tensed when she gasped loudly.

Kennedy, who had his eyes on the entrance, blurted, "Oh, my!"

Rising, Nate spun to see a tall man in a brown coat standing just outside the cabin with a rifle trained on his wife.

Chapter Six

Nate instantly made a grab for one of his flintlocks but the newcomer's sharp warning prevented him from drawing.

"Try it and the squaw dies!"

Furious, Nate froze with his fingers almost touching the pistol. He watched the man motion Winona to move back and he followed her inside.

Isaac Kennedy jumped from his chair. "Lambert, what is the meaning of this outrage? These people saved my life!"

Another, stockier, man appeared in the doorway. This one wore a black coat and had a modified rifle in his right hand. He surveyed the interior briefly, then focused on Nate.

"What do you want?" Nate snapped, almost unable to resist the temptation to bring his flintlocks into play. If only he could distract the one called Lambert! The other man, he deduced, must be Newton.

"We were crouched below your window," Newton said, pointing at the crack between the sill and the flap. "We couldn't help but overhear parts of your conversation with our partner, Mr. Kennedy."

"So?"

"So our partner talks too much."

Kennedy took several steps toward the two men. "I don't understand. Why are you doing this?"

"Because you shot off your big mouth, jackass," Lambert stated.

"I told them nothing."

"Nothing and everything," Newton said, moving over to the table to inspect the empty bowl put there by Kennedy. "Is that buffalo stew I smell?"

No one said anything.

Newton glanced at Winona. "Take off the robe and fetch me a bowl, woman, and be quick about it."

Instead of obeying, Winona defiantly stayed where she was and glared at him.

"Do it or my friend here will shoot your man," Newton said.

Lambert looked at Nate and smirked.

Without hesitation Winona let the robe fall to the floor, got a clean bowl from the cupboard, and walked to the pot.

"I like a woman who knows how to listen," Newton said. He chuckled and took a seat at the table, then gazed at Kennedy. "I'm disappointed in you, Isaac. I thought you had more brains than you do."

"But I didn't tell them a *thing*!" the portly merchant protested.

"You only think you didn't," Newton said. "But we heard some of the questions this trapper was asking you. You made him suspicious."

"I did? How?"

Newton sighed and rested his elbows on the table top. "Isaac, what are we going to do with you? Sometimes you are more trouble than you're worth."

"Sometimes?" Lambert echoed, and snorted contemptuously.

Nate's eyes flicked from one to the other as he impatiently waited for them to let down their guard. They both impressed him as being hard men, sinister sorts capable of slaying Winona and him without any provocation. Lambert, in particular, had the air of a wolverine eager to tear into its prey.

"Now then," Newton said, aligning his rifle on the table so the barrel pointed directly at Nate, "be so kind as to put those pistols of yours on the floor. And do it slowly or your woman will be seeking a new man."

Hesitating, Nate debated the wisdom of making a reckless attempt to cut both men down. He was certain he could drill a ball through one of them but the second would then send a ball into him. Winona would be on her own.

Lambert swung his rifle to cover Nate. "You heard my friend. Do it now, trapper."

Reluctantly, rage making his blood race, Nate slowly drew the right flintlock, then the left, and eased them to the wooden floor.

"Step away from the guns," Newton instructed.

Again Nate complied, his resentment knowing no bounds. His rifle was on the wall, his knife and tomahawk by the bed. Completely unarmed, he was at the mercy of the intruders.

Lambert came forward and took the pistols to the table, prudently keeping out of the line of fire. "Do we do it now?" he asked Newton.

"What's your hurry? We've just spent weeks trekking across the plains and into these mountains, trying our best to stay warm every foot of the way. We wasted over a day searching for Isaac while trying to

survive one of the worst blizzards I've seen in ages,"
Newton said. "I reckon we owe ourselves a treat. It's
warm in here and there's hot food. I say we stay a
while."

"And what about him?" Lambert inquired, nodding at Nate.

Newton drummed his fingers on the table. "What's
your name, trapper?"

"King. Nate King."

"King," Newton repeated, pondering. "Why do I
have the feeling I should know that name?"

At that moment Winona approached the table
bearing a bowl of stew and a wooden spoon. She kept
her features composed, betraying no trace of fear.

Newton stared at her protruding belly. "Your mis-
sus will be having her litter of half-breeds in four or
five months if I'm not mistaken, King," he said
sarcastically.

The insult cut Nate to the quick. He clenched his
fists and took a step but Lambert promptly covered
him.

"Hmmmmm," Newton said, deep in contemplation. He took the bowl and eagerly began eating.

"Hey, what about me?" Lambert asked.

"After I'm done I'll watch them and you can fill
your stomach," Newton proposed.

Winona returned to the fireplace and stood beside
the pot with the ladle in her hand, her gaze resting on
her husband.

For over a minute not a word was uttered. The only
sounds were the crackling of the flames and the
slurping noises Newton made as he ate.

Isaac Kennedy wore a bewildered countenance.
He stared at his partners, looking from one to the
other repeatedly. Several times he opened his mouth
as if to speak but changed his mind.

The man in the brown coat finally broke the
silence. He glanced at the south wall, where a dozen

traps hung, and wagged his Kentucky rifle at Nate. "Nice traps you've got there, King. Newhouses, aren't they?"

Nate simply glowered.

"Newhouses are the best around," Lambert went on mockingly. "If we were fixing to trap our pelts we'd take yours along."

Kennedy found his voice. "I don't want these kind people harmed," he said softly.

Lambert laughed.

"Did you hear me?" Kennedy addressed Newton. "We should up and leave now. This has gone far enough."

Belching, Newton pushed the bowl aside and beamed at the merchant. "Isaac, leave this to us. We've lived in these mountains off and on for the better part of ten years. We know what we're doing."

"If you hurt them our deal is off," Kennedy blustered nervously.

Newton leaned back and laced his hands behind his neck. "We haven't traveled this far to call it off now, Isaac. Not when we're days away from becoming rich men."

"I'll take the pack animals and go back to Missouri."

"I'm sorry, Isaac, but we can't allow you to do that."

"How will you stop me?"

Lambert chortled.

"Need you really ask?" Newton responded.

Total horror etched itself in Kennedy's face. He swallowed hard and exclaimed, "Dear Lord in heaven."

"I want you to understand," Newton said. "A chance like this comes along once in a lifetime for men like Lambert and me. We can't let it pass us by. If we called this off, you could always go back to owning a store and making a comfortable living. But Lambert and me would have to go back to trapping or whatever other backbreaking jobs we could find." He paused and frowned. "You can see my point, can't you?"

"I can see we're in the wrong here."

"City types!" Lambert declared bitterly. "It just proves that you can educate a fool but it doesn't mean he can think."

"I know I don't want to be party to a killing," Kennedy stated.

Newton stood and went over to the portly man. He placed his right hand on Kennedy's shoulder. "If there was any other way, I'd do it. But what if someone starts to ask questions later? What if the Army gets involved? If word should reach Fort Leavenworth there might be an investigation. Then suppose an officer was to show up here and this trapper was to tell him about these three men who came by in the dead of winter heading for the middle of Ute country. How long do you figure it would be before the Army put two and two together and was on our trail?"

Gnawing on his lower lip, Kennedy looked at Nate and Winona. "I didn't realize—."

"Of course you didn't. You let us handle this situation our way," Newton said.

Nate had listened to the exchange with an intense curiosity in the hope of learning the exact nature of their business with the Utes. Clearly they weren't planning to trap beaver. He well recognized the fate Newton and Lambert had in store for Winona and him. Outnumbered and covered, there wasn't much he could do. But he wasn't about to roll over and be murdered without a fight. If he had to, he'd charge Lambert and try to grab the pistols from the table.

Kennedy placed his right hand over his eyes and bowed his head. "What have I gotten myself into?"

"Don't fret yourself," Newton said. "You were all

for the enterprise back in Ohio when I first brought the idea up. You like the idea of having ten thousand dollars or more just as much as we do. Why don't you take a stroll outside? Maybe walk down to the lake?"

Nodding, Kennedy lowered his hand and moved toward the door.

Suddenly Nate saw an opportunity to turn the tables. The portly merchant inadvertently walked between Lambert and him, momentarily screening him from Lambert's view. Newton was staring at Winona. In that split-second Nate hurled himself forward, sweeping Kennedy aside with a powerful thrust of his arm and barreling into Lambert, grabbing the rifle barrel in one hand and Lambert's throat in the other.

Nate's momentum carried both of them into the table. Lambert recovered from his shock swiftly and tried to wrench the Kentucky free. They rolled to the right, off the table, and crashed onto the floor with Lambert on the bottom. Nate drove his right knee into the man's groin and Lambert screeched and tried to double over.

"Nate! Behind you!"

Winona's warning impelled Nate to let go of Lambert and roll again, to the right once more. It was well he did. The heavy stock of Newton's rifle swished through the very space his head had occupied a heartbeat before. Twisting, he saw Newton towering above him and swept his legs into the bastard's shins, knocking Newton backwards.

Newton stumbled against the table, waving his arms in an effort to retain his balance.

Surging erect, Nate felt a fleeting weakness induced by his many wounds but he disregarded the sensation and planted his left fist on the tip of Newton's chin. His foe swayed and Nate followed through with a right that buckled Newton's legs.

For a moment Nate had the upper hand.

Then Lambert rose, his face a beet red, and slammed his rifle barrel across the back of Nate's head.

Propelled forward, staggered by the cowardly strike, his senses swimming, Nate tripped over Newton and fell onto the table. He felt Newton's arms wrap around his legs and start to pull him down. Vigorously shaking his head to clear it, he glimpsed someone moving past him and shifted to find his wife brashly rushing Lambert with the ladle upraised to hit him in the face.

Snarling, Lambert struck her across the forehead with the rifle and Winona dropped on the spot.

"No!" Nate bellowed, his wife's plight fanning his fury. He pushed off the table and tried to kick loose from Newton even as he twisted and swung wildly at Lambert.

Shuffling aside, still in pain from Nate's kick, Lambert evaded the blow.

A fist rammed into Nate's gut and he bent over to flail at Newton. He rained three punches before the stocky cutthroat yanked him off his feet and he fell face down.

Isaac Kennedy was prancing about frantically in the background yelling, "No! No! No!"

Nate tried to rise again but Lambert stepped in close and delivered a kick to his ribs. Excruciating agony flared in his chest. He sputtered, still game, and put both hands on the floor. Another kick sapped all of his strength. He went limp and barely heard Newton growl two words.

"Do it."

Rough hands seized Nate's shoulders and he was flipped onto his back to gaze up at Lambert's feral features. The Kentucky rifle materialized above his face. He could see the barrel pointing at his forehead,

- could see the dark muzzle opening mere inches away, and he desperately jerked his head to the left at the very instant a tremendous explosion occurred, searing fire scorched his skin, and everything abruptly went black.

Chapter Seven

The bone numbing cold awakened him.

Nate opened his eyes and promptly wished he hadn't. His head throbbed with waves of pain, his chest ached terribly, and the bites itched unbearably. He gazed at the ceiling, commingled relief and astonishment at being alive sweeping through him. Suddenly he thought about Winona and impulsively attempted to push off the floor.

A veritable avalanche of anguish rocked his head.

Involuntarily crying out, Nate lay still and waited for the agonizing pulsations to cease. He took stock. The dim light in the cabin convinced him the time must be close to evening. Either that, or he'd been unconscious for who knew how long. His mouth and throat were as dry as a desert.

Of all his discomforts the pervading cold became the most bothersome. His skin broke out in goose bumps and he shivered uncontrollably. What had happened to the fire?

Nate slowly twisted his head to gaze at the fireplace. Sure enough, the blaze had long since gone out. He looked toward the entrance and discovered the door hung wide open. No one else was in the cabin.

The sons of bitches had taken Winona!

Grunting, he tried once more to sit up. The pain overwhelmed him. He closed his eyes and waited it out. When he could think straight again he tentatively raised his right hand to his face. His skin was sore to the touch and his fingertips became smudged with black powder. He realized he'd sustained powder burns when the rifle went off.

Girding himself, Nate lightly ran his fingers over his forehead and temples. On his right side, level with his eye, he found the start of a quarter-inch deep furrow that ran the length of his head. Merely touching it made him flinch. Apparently the ball had gouged him severely, then passed into the floorboards. A fraction deeper and he wouldn't have survived.

Nate slowly endeavored to sit yet again. His head rose several inches but jerked up short, his long hair seeming to be caught on something. He reached behind him and his palm pressed onto a sticky puddle. Blood, no doubt. His blood. Tracing its outline, he found a wide pool that had nearly dried.

Exercising care, he grasped his hair and proceeded to tug it loose. The movement aggravated his gunshot wound but couldn't be helped. Gradually the strands came free and he could sit upright.

Vertigo attacked him as he straightened. He rested, gazing right and left, enraged at seeing the pantry had been ransacked. Scanning the interior, he made another distressing discovery.

The Hawken was gone.

Nate scowled and got onto his knees, his head shrieking in protest the entire time. Taking a few deep breaths, he then stood, reaching out to the table for support.

Both flintlocks were also gone.

He stayed put for several minutes, noting all the items missing besides the guns and food. The powder he normally kept in a far corner had been stolen, as had his supply of lead. Several spare blankets stored on a shelf not far from the bed were gone. His traps still hung on the wall and the pots and pans he'd purchased for Winona hadn't appealed to the killers.

Nate took a cautious step, then a second. Snail-like, he crossed to the fireplace and picked up the wooden stick that substituted as a poker. Jabbing an end into the embers, he probed and poked until he located a hot spot. He took a handful of tinder from the small pile Winona stockpiled to the left of the fireplace and dropped the dry twigs in. Leaning down, his left arm braced on the wall, he huffed and puffed until the tinder caught. Adding a few small logs, he soon had the fire going again.

He admired his accomplishment for a minute, enjoying the warmth the flames radiated. Dizziness struck him once more and he moved haltingly to a chair to sit down until the uncomfortable feeling dissipated. How long would the attacks persist? he wondered. He couldn't afford any delays, not when Winona was in the clutches of hardened killers.

Or was she?

A shocking thought occurred to him. What if Newton and Lambert hadn't abducted her? What if—and a ripple of stark fear flowed along his spine— she was lying outside in the snow, dead?

Nate straightened and walked to the entrance. A gust of wind chilled him as he surveyed the ground and a fine spray of white mist hit his face. Practically everything was white; the trees, the boulders, the logs, the undergrowth, and the ground. The mantle of snow was two and a half feet deep and made finding tracks ridiculously easy.

There they were, right in front of him. Nate readily distinguished Winona's slender moccasin prints from those of the men. All four sets bore to the right. He did the same, neglecting to take his coat in his anxiety.

The trail led to the pen, which was empty. Nate found where Winona had mounted her brown mare and where his other animals had been added to a string the cutthroats possessed, bringing the grand total of animals being led to ten.

Why so many?

Deciding he didn't have the time to waste in idle speculation, Nate went into the cabin and closed the door. He scoured the room for weapons, finding only his knife and tomahawk lying under the bed. Either Winona had hidden them there or the killers had not needed them. Probably the latter, he figured, since Winona must have believed he was dead.

Nate strapped the knife around his waist and tucked the tomahawk handle under the belt. He slipped into his Mackinaw, found his hat, and moved to the door. Common sense told him to wait until he'd recovered his strength, but every minute he took to recuperate meant Winona got that much further away.

He reached for the latch when a peculiar thing happened. The door began swirling around him, going faster and faster, and his body started tingling all over. He tottered rearward, swinging his arms about to find support of any sort.

A veil of darkness abruptly enveloped him and he felt himself crashing to the floor.

* * *

"I don't see why you had to bring her along," Isaac Kennedy groused for the umpteenth time since leaving the King homestead.

Newton, riding ahead of the portly merchant and the Indian woman, glanced back in irritation. "Would you rather we shot her?"

"No."

"Then shut your trap," Newton advised, and gazed past the woman to where Lambert led the pack string. He faced due west, seeking the easiest passage through the forest, avoiding dense thickets and clusters of boulders.

"What do you plan to do with her, Ike?" Kennedy inquired.

"I'm fixing to make a present of her."

"Who would—," Kennedy began, then blurted out, "you wouldn't!"

"Why not? Two Owls will be right pleased."

"Damn you, man, she's pregnant."

"Noticed, did you?" Newton responded, grinning. "That only makes it better."

"How do you figure?"

"First of all, she's a Shoshone. The Utes are always raiding the Shoshones to steal horses and women. They think highly of Shoshone bitches," Newton detailed.

Kennedy frowned.

"Second of all, even if Two Owls doesn't want to keep her for himself he can always swap her for a few horses or other goods. She's the perfect gift."

"It's not civilized, I tell you."

Newton gestured at the rugged countryside. "This isn't civilization, storekeeper. Out here a man does what he has to do to get by."

His cheeks flushing with anger, Kennedy dropped back to ride alongside their prisoner. He stared at her, admiring her beautiful features and the manner in which she nobly held her chin high. "I'm truly sorry," he said.

Winona gazed straight ahead.

"If I'd known this was going to happen, I never would have stopped at your cabin," Kennedy assured her.

She didn't answer.

"I know you can speak English," Kennedy said. "I heard you call out to your husband. Why won't you talk to me?"

Deigning to cast a reproachful glance at him, Winona stated curtly, "Your heart is small."

Confused, Kennedy did a double take. "As far as I know my heart is perfectly normal."

Winona gave him a look that left no doubt she equated him with horse dung. She wrapped her robe tighter around her body and rode a shade faster to get ahead of him.

Undeterred, Kennedy caught up with her mare. "What do you mean by my heart is small?"

From Newton came a contemptuous translation. "She means you're a coward, Isaac. Shoshones, and most other Indians for that matter, look down their noses at cowards."

Lambert, overhearing, laughed heartily.

Kennedy bowed his head in shame and rode in silence for a while. Every breath he expelled formed a small white cloud before him and his lungs tingled from the frigid air. The tips of his fingers, although well covered by thick gloves, became cold. He glanced at the Shoshone woman, marveling at the fact she wasn't in the least bothered by the inclement weather even though her face and hands were fully exposed to the elements.

Their party crossed a rise and wound into a narrow valley below.

"I guess I can't blame you for thinking poorly of me," Kennedy said softly, trying to come to grips with his conscience. "I would too if I was in your shoes."

"She doesn't care how you feel, Isaac," Newton interjected without bothering to look around. "If she had the chance she'd gut you wide open."

"Would you?" Kennedy bluntly asked.

Winona looked at him, her spiteful expression confirming Newton's statement.

"I've never had anyone hate me before," Kennedy commented, hurt by her eloquent rebuke.

"You'll grow accustomed to it out here," Newton declared. "Folks hate Lambert and me all the time."

"I can't imagine why," Kennedy said.

Twisting, Newton's eyes narrowed as he regarded the merchant. "Watch it, partner. No man insults me and lives to brag of the deed.

"I meant no offense," Kennedy replied quickly.

"No, you never do," Newton taunted him, swinging about again.

Isaac Kennedy clenched his left hand and almost made a remark he would surely regret. He checked his temper and gazed at the woman again. Newton was undoubtedly correct. She had no interest in anything he wanted to say, but say it he must if only to make her understand that he deeply regretted her husband's death. He'd never been party to a killing before and the guilt weighed heavily on his soul. "Winona?"

Predictably, she ignored him.

"Fine, then. Suit yourself. But I'm going to speak my piece whether you like it or not," Kennedy stated, and paused. "I had no idea what I was getting myself into when I agreed to Newton's proposal. You see, I'm not a man of violence. I've made my living as a merchant, which is about as peaceful a life as one can find. All I wanted out of this venture was to make a sizeable profit. Do you understand?"

Winona rode onward, her lips compressed.

"I was tending my store and minding my own business back in Ohio when Newton came in one day. He was on his way from New York City, where he'd just visited his sister, back to the frontier. He saw the beaver hats I was selling and happened to mention that he knew a way to become rich off beaver pelts if he could only find a financial backer for the goods he needed. Well, I decided to provide the money."

A clump of snow fell from a nearby tree with a swish and a thud.

"You see, I'd been working for years in the mercantile profession and never really gotten ahead. Oh, I had a thousand squirreled away for a rainy day or old age, but like any man I wanted more. Newton's proposal intrigued me. Here was a way to reap a thirty thousand dollar profit from one trip into the Rockies. That's ten thousand apiece. And if this trip is successful, there's a chance we can do the same thing next year."

"You're wasting your breath, Isaac," Newton stated, sounding annoyed.

"She deserves to know."

"Like hell she does. She speaks English, savvy?"

"What?"

"If you tell her everything, we'll have to do the same to her as we did to her husband."

"Oh," Kennedy said. He hadn't considered that.

On all sides lay a great quiet, as if every creature in the mountains had found a convenient shelter during the blizzard and was still deep in slumber. Half the sky had cleared of clouds and bright sunlight lent the snow a brilliant luster.

Newton abruptly halted, staring to the southwest.

"Why have you stopped?" Kennedy asked as he reined up. "Do you see some game we can shoot for our supper?"

"All you ever think about is food," Newton said.

Kennedy gazed to the southwest in casual curiosity and immediately stiffened in alarm. Perhaps a quarter of a mile away, on a hill, were two riders. "Are those Indians?"

"They sure are," Newton answered.

"Do you know what kind?"

"Utes."

Chapter Eight

Nate awoke with a start and sat up, the movement racking his head with torment. He seemed to be making a habit of this. He gazed at the window, shocked to see evening was descending. Rising, he glanced at the fire. Tiny flames were all that remained of the blaze he'd started earlier.

Now what should he do?

Perturbed, he opened the door and gazed out over the hoary landscape. Already long shadows criss-crossed the snow. In another hour darkness would claim the Rockies.

Damn.

Nate slammed the door. Sudden pounding in his right temple emphasized his foolishness. He staggered to a chair and sat down. As much as the very thought upset him, leaving now was out of the question. Tracking Winona's captors at night would be difficult, even with the tracks in the snow to aid him. The bitter cold alone would severely aggravate his condition.

He realized he had no choice. He must stay overnight at the cabin and begin the pursuit at first light. In a way, perhaps, the delay would be a blessing. A night of sleep would do wonders to invigorate him for the ordeal he must face in the morning.

Nate's stomach growled, reminding him he needed food. Since the pantry had been emptied, he must find it elsewhere. But he was in no condition to do any hunting.

Wait a second.

What about the buffalo stew?

He rose and hurried to the pot hanging above the embers, a smile his reaction at finding the pot a third full. The rotten cutthroats hadn't been as thorough as they figured. He stirred the contents with the ladle, finding the stew almost hard. But that was okay. Once he got the fire roaring and added handfuls of snow, the stew would be fit for a king.

Nate set about preparing his meal. In due course he had the fire crackling, the snow in the pot, the Mackinaw hanging on a hook, and he was standing next to the fireplace inhaling the delicious aroma of the boiling meat and vegetables.

Although he tried not to dwell on Winona, she filled his mind every second. He knew there were men vile enough to force themselves on even a pregnant woman, and he frequently shuddered as his imagination conjured the most horrible scenes conceivable. Each time he got a grip on himself and attempted to carry on, but a profound sorrow gripped his soul.

Snug and warm by the fire, he ate three bowls of stew, ate to the point where his stomach seemed ready to burst at the seams. He sat afterwards for hours staring morosely into the flickering red and yellow fingers, reviewing all the joyous experiences he'd shared with Winona. She'd brought him more happiness than he'd ever expected to know. If anything happened to her, he'd track those three bastards down to the far ends of the earth if need be to satisfy his thirst for vengeance.

He thought about tracking them, about the monumental difficulties entailed, and frowned. On foot he stood little chance of overtaking them any time soon. Somehow, he must acquire a mount.

The weather would help him, though, by slowing their party down. Horses tended to move much slower than otherwise in two to three feet of snow and the severe cold would hamper the animals as well.

Nate sagged in the chair, his chin dropping to his chest. His eyelids fluttered as sleep tried to claim him. Rising, he shuffled to the bed and collapsed on his back with a relieved sigh.

Soon slumber overcame him, and his last mental image before drifting off was of Winona.

"If only those Utes had bothered to speak to us," Isaac Kennedy mentioned while hunkered beside the campfire and rubbing his hands together near the flames.

"I told you before," Newton mentioned from where he sat on Kennedy's right, "we were lucky they up and vanished into the forest. For all we know, they might not have been from Two Owls' village."

"Is that bad?"

"How many times must I tell you the same thing?" Newton snapped. "Our deal is with Two Owls. If Utes from any other village catch us, they'll stake us out for the buzzards."

"How can we avoid these other Indians?"

"We can't."

"Can't one of you ride ahead, find Two Owls,

and bring him here? That would solve all our problems."

From the other side of the fire Lambert vented an oath, then said angrily, "The only problem around here is you, storekeeper. You flap your gums more than a bird flaps its wings."

Kennedy glared at the tall man. "I don't like it when you talk to me like that."

"And I don't give a damn what you like," Lambert growled.

"That's enough out of both of you," Newton declared. "I'm sick and tired of listening to all this bellyaching."

"It's not my fault," Kennedy said.

"You should never have come along," Newton responded. "In these mountains you're like a fish out of water. We could have handled the trade just fine without you."

"I couldn't stay in Ohio after all I invested in this enterprise."

"You would have been a lot more comfortable right now, and a hell of a lot safer, if you had."

Kennedy couldn't argue the point. Despite the roaring fire his backside and shoulders were chilly and the jerky they'd consumed for supper had barely whetted his appetite. Staying in Ohio would have been the smart thing to do. He didn't want to tell his partners, but the main reason he came along was because he didn't trust them as far as he could throw them.

He glanced to his left at the Shoshone woman, admiring her profile. She hadn't taken a bite to eat and refused a cup of coffee. Now she sat over a yard from the flames, her buffalo robe draped loosely over her slender shoulders, apparently unaffected by the freezing temperature.

"Hey, quit making cow eyes at that woman," Newton said jokingly. "She has no interest in you."

"I beg your pardon," Kennedy replied indignantly. "I wasn't making cow eyes."

"Sure you weren't. Hell, man, you've been eyeing her ever since we left the cabin. But if you even so much as touch her, she'll kill you."

Embarrassed by the accusation, Kennedy looked at the fire, feeling his cheeks flush crimson. "Why must you always be so crude?"

"You call it crude. I call it telling the truth. You're smitten with her, Isaac. It's as plain as the nose on your face. Don't feel bad about it, though. Happens to a lot of whites. They take one look at an Indian gal, at all that long, dark hair and those full lips, and they can't wait to dip their pork in the barrel."

Lambert cackled.

"Please. Stop," Kennedy said. "You'll hurt her feelings."

"She's a lousy squaw," Newton said. "She doesn't have feelings, not like white folks do. Indians aren't quite human."

"I don't believe that."

"Of course not. You have mush for brains."

Both Newton and Lambert laughed merrily.

Kennedy waited until they were done before commenting. "Nate King didn't believe Indians are less than human."

"Nate King was a jack—," Newton began, then abruptly tensed and snapped his fingers. "Son of a bitch! I remember now."

"Remember what?" Lambert asked.

"Don't you recollect when we were in St. Louis? We went to a tavern while Isaac tucked himself in early at the hotel."

"Yeah. So?"

"So we got to chatting with that old fart, that trapper who had been to the rendezvous last year."

"I remember," Lambert said.

"Then *think*, stupid. What did he tell us?"

Lambert shrugged. "Oh, he went on about all the drinking and whoring he did. And he bragged about the money he made from his furs."

"What else?"

After pondering for a bit, Lambert continued, "He told us about a fight that took place between that *voyageur* from Canada called the Giant and some guy the Indians called Grizzly Killer, a free trapper named—." He stopped, then blurted, "Son of a bitch! That was him!"

"Must of been," Newton said, nodding. "Geez, from all we heard, we were lucky to get the jump on him or we'd be pushing up flowers come Spring."

"He was a tough bastard," Lambert begrudgingly admitted.

"Was King someone famous?" Kennedy inquired.

"In these mountains he was," Newton answered. "That old-timer claimed King killed a grizzly bear with just a knife."

"Is such a feat possible?"

"No," Lambert said. "That old trapper was just spouting his mouth off."

At that moment all three men were surprised when their prisoner spoke up.

"My husband did kill a grizzly with a knife," Winona stated softly.

Newton glanced at her and chuckled. "Well, look who decided to join the conversation. I take it you don't much appreciate us speaking poorly of your husband?"

"Since all of you will soon be dead, your words don't matter."

Kennedy arched his back. "Why will we all soon be dead?"

"Because my husband will catch you and kill you."

Her statement provoked laughter from Lambert and a nervous titter from Kennedy, but Newton studied her face closely.

"Your husband is dead, squaw."

"Not true. You only think he is. But neither of you bothered to examine him. I did while you were busy stealing our food and guns. He was still alive."

"You're lying," Lambert said.

"Believe what you want," Winona said, her gaze on the fire. "You will learn the truth soon enough."

Kennedy saw his partners exchange startled looks and realized they both believed her. Inexplicably, a tingle ran down his spine.

"Even if you are telling the truth, woman," Lambert said, "your husband was on his last legs. He'll never come after us."

"He will."

"How can you be so damn certain?"

"Because he is my husband. Because he is Grizzly Killer," Winona said proudly, her eyes sparkling.

Newton suddenly stood and stalked over to her. He grabbed the front of her robe and peered into her eyes as if trying to see into the depths of her being. Finally he gave her a hard shove and shook a fist in her face. "Damn you, squaw. Damn you all to hell."

Winona sat perfectly still and composed.

Now Lambert also rose and stared along their back trail. "You really reckon he'll come?"

"If he's as good as they say he is, he will," Newton stated. "And our tracks in the snow will lead him right to us."

"But he's on foot."

"For how long? What if he had other horses loose somewhere, out foraging?"

Moving around the fire, Lambert glowered at Winona. "Were there other horses?"

She didn't respond.

"Answer me, bitch!" Lambert barked, and raised his right hand to slap her.

"No!" Kennedy cried, rising. "Don't hurt her."

"Give me one good reason why I shouldn't bust her head," Lambert said.

"Would Two Owls like your gift if she's all battered and bruised?"

Hesitating, Lambert hissed and reluctantly lowered his arm. "Smart, storekeeper. Real smart. You said the one thing that will keep her in one piece."

Kennedy sighed in relief.

"What do we do, Ike?" Lambert queried his stocky friend. "Let it pass and hope he doesn't show?"

"You know we can't," Newton said solemnly. He scratched his chin while stepping to the east, the breeze whipping his wolf tail. "We got a late start today and only traveled about seven miles, I figure. One of us could ride back to that cabin at dawn, check on Grizzly Killer, and catch up with the string by tomorrow night."

"It's the only way," Lambert said, nodding.

"I'll go," Kennedy volunteered.

"Will you put a ball in King when you see him?" Newton asked scornfully.

"No."

"Then don't be dumb. One of us has to take care of him." Newton walked to where his bedroll lay and rummaged in the blanket. "Low card goes?"

"Fine by me," Lambert said.

"Here are the cards," Newton announced, rising with a worn deck in his right hand. He placed them on top of the bedroll, backs up, and made a fan of the deck. "Do you want to pick first?"

"You can."

Without hesitation Newton scooped a card up and held it out for all to see.

"The ten of spades," Lambert said, and grinned. "Hell, that should be easy to beat." He stepped to the bedroll and leaned down, his hand poised to pick, then paused uncertainly.

"We don't have all night," Newton prompted.

Lambert selected a card and turned it over. The dancing flames revealed it to be a two of clubs. "You always did have all the luck," he muttered, dropping the card on the blanket.

"Look at the bright side," Newton said. "You're the one who gets to kill King if he's still kicking."

"Yeah," Lambert said. He chuckled. "And this time I'll do the job right."

Chapter Nine

The rosy rim of the sun had just risen above the eastern horizon when Nate emerged from the cabin, shut the door behind him, and began his pursuit. The frigid air pierced deep into his lungs, invigorating him. With the snow halfway up his thighs, every step required extra effort, aggravating the bites and the temple wound. He'd bandaged the nasty furrow using strips of cloth from an old store-bought shirt he'd brought from New York City. His beaver hat helped keep the bandage in place.

A pair of ravens glided overhead, one of them uttering a raucous cry. Sparrows flitted in a nearby tree chirping contentedly.

· Nate walked to one side of the trail left by the vermin who'd taken Winona. His entire body ached and he could have used another week in bed to heal.

But now he had no intention of resting for more than a few hours at a stretch until his beloved wife was safe in his arms again. A grim smile touched his lips at the thought of what he would do when he found the men.

He rounded the cabin and pressed westward. Thankfully, the wind had died down as it often did in the morning. He wouldn't need to worry too much about frostbite.

Nate always liked the aftermath of a heavy snow, when the mighty Rockies were transformed into a strange, pillowy landscape straight out of a fairy tale. The sagging trees, laden with snow on every branch, resembled white mushrooms. Boulders normally stark and angular became smooth white mounds. And the hard ground, draped in its soft covering of white fluff, appeared inviting enough to dive into.

He touched the hilt of the knife and the tomahawk handle, wishing he had a gun. Perhaps, if he had the time later, he would make a lance or even a bow. Anything to even the odds.

The golden orb in the east climbed steadily higher as Nate trudged onward. The bright glare reflected by the snow caused him to constantly squint to prevent snow blindness. He went half a mile. A mile. The farther he went, the better he felt as his muscles limbered up. The exercise did wonders for his constitution.

Nate kept his hands in his pockets and his chin low, concentrating on the clearly defined tracks. Knowing Newton and company had quite a head start, he only occasionally glanced up at the trail ahead. So it was with considerable surprise that at one such point he spied a solitary rider approaching from the opposite direction.

He halted in astonishment and automatically moved to the north behind a tree. Had they sent someone back? Why? He shielded his eyes with his left hand so he could see better and studied the oncoming figure, who was several hundred yards off. With a start he realized the man was an Indian.

A Ute.

Nate flattened against the trunk and peeked at the warrior, who rode parallel with the tracks in the snow. For some reason the Ute was following the backtrail, his eyes on the prints and not the terrain surrounding him. That's what comes from overconfidence, Nate reflected. Since the Utes tended to view this territory as their own, they could be a mite careless at times.

He slowly drew the tomahawk and eased from sight. If he could get the Ute's horse, he could rescue Winona before the sun set. But taking the mount would be next to impossible. The Ute wouldn't relinquish the animal without a fight, and Nate had observed a bow in the man's hand and a quiver slung over the warrior's back. Together they gave the Ute a nearly insurmountable advantage. A tomahawk was no match for a bow and arrows.

Nate knew Indian youths were taught at an early age how to properly use a bow, and by the time they were full grown they could hit a target the size of a pumpkin ten times out of ten while firing from the back of a galloping horse.

The trail lay only ten feet away, but in the time it would take Nate to reach the warrior with the tomahawk, the Ute would be able to unleash two or three arrows. The trick, then, was to attack the warrior before the man nocked a shaft.

Nate racked his brain for a way of prevailing and finally an idea struck him that promised success if he was lucky. Squatting, he held the tomahawk under his left arm while he packed together a large snowball. The simplistic trick he would employ was as old as the hills, yet sometimes the old ways were the best.

Straightening, he pressed his back to the trunk and waited. He wouldn't throw until the Ute was abreast of the tree, and then he must move like lightning to bring the warrior down.

An upsetting thought suddenly occurred to him.

The Ute was bound to spot the tracks he'd made moving from the trail to the tree. The warrior would instantly put two and two together and perceive there was someone behind the trunk. As soon as he popped out, he'd be changed into a porcupine with feathers jutting out of his body every which way.

That wouldn't do.

Nate had to launch his snowball well before the Ute spotted his tracks. Yet to do so increased the risk of being seen. He risked a look-see and found the warrior approximately two hundred yards away.

There wasn't much time.

The seconds seemed to crawl by.

At last Nate heard the soft thud of hooves as the Indian's stallion approached. He gripped the snowball tightly. Now came the moment of truth. Should he kill the warrior or try to take the man alive?

An unbidden thought abruptly bothered him.

What if the Ute was a member of Two Owls' village? He owed a lot to the chief, after all, and didn't want to do anything to antagonize him. But when he weighed Winona's life in the balance, his obligation to Two Owls must rate as secondary.

The warrior's stallion snorted.

Nate tensed. Had the horse detected his scent? No, there wasn't a sufficient breeze. Taking a deep breath, he eased his eyes to the edge of the trunk.

Riding casually along fifty yards distant, humming softly, clad in buckskins and moccasins, the Ute was alternately gazing at the trail and surveying the forest. The bow rested on his thighs. On his left hip was a knife. He held the reins loosely in his left hand.

Nate's nerves vibrated as he waited for the warrior to draw closer. Forty yards separated them. Then thirty. At twenty he hefted the snowball. At fifteen he saw the Ute suddenly look straight ahead and feared the man had seen his tracks.

The Ute unexpectedly whipped an arrow from his quiver even as he elevated the bow, and a fraction of a second later the string twanged and the shaft leaped through the air.

Only the arrow wasn't aimed at Nate.

Mystified, Nate glimpsed the streaking shaft as it sped in a beeline along the trail, passing his tree by a wide margin. He heard a thud attended by a peculiar squeal, and shifting to the other side of the tree he looked out to discover a jack rabbit smack dab in the center of the tracks, thrashing and convulsing with the arrow transfixing its wiry form.

Concentrating on his kill, the Ute rode past the point where Nate had veered off to the tree and dismounted. The warrior placed the bow on the snow as he knelt beside the rabbit and drew his knife.

Not one to waste a singular opportunity, Nate burst from concealment, his legs kicking up snow in a fine spray, the snowball in his right hand and the toma-hawk in his left. He covered only a yard before the Ute looked up and saw him.

Instantly the warrior's cat-like reflexes came into play. In a smooth motion the man let go of the knife and scooped up the bow, his left hand darting for the arrows perched in his deer hide quiver.

Nate covered five of the ten feet. He saw the arrow pulled clear of the quiver and he flashed his right arm back, then out again. The snowball flew from his chilled fingers, right on target.

In the act of nocking the arrow to his bow, the Ute was unable to evade the projectile. With a sticky splat the snowball struck him full in the face, the snow getting into his eyes and nostrils, and he instinctively wiped at his face to clear his vision.

No you don't! Nate thought, and reached the warrior, the tomahawk upraised. He swung with all his might, using the flat side of the weapon instead of the razor edge, striking the warrior on the head above the ear.

Stunned, the Ute crumpled.

Nate yanked the man's knife from its sheath and tossed it a few yards away. He stripped off the quiver, placed it on his own back, and picked up the bow. With the tomahawk in his right hand in case the Ute tried to interfere, he backed up to the Indian's mount.

The stallion shied nervously at Nate's approach, its nostrils flaring.

He spun and grabbed the reins in the same hand that held the bow. The powerful animal nearly tore them loose. He held on, though, and spoke in a soft, soothing voice. Gradually the stallion calmed down to the point where he swung onto its back without mishap. Tucking the tomahawk under his belt, he glanced at the warrior and nocked an arrow to the bow string.

The Ute was just sitting up, his hand clasped to his bruised head. He blinked, saw Nate, and surged to his feet.

Nate trained the arrow on the man but didn't pull the string back. He motioned with his head, indicating the warrior should move farther from the horse. The Ute reluctantly complied, glaring his animosity. When Nate was satisfied the man couldn't possibly reach him before he could wheel and ride off, he lowered the bow.

A string of harsh Ute words burst from the man's mouth.

Not knowing the Ute tongue, Nate shook his head

and employed his hands in making sign language. No one knew exactly which tribe had originated the practice of signing. Indian legends had it that sign language had existed since the dawn of time. Winona had taught him well. He could converse as readily now in sign as he could in English. "I have no wish to kill you. Stand where you are and you will not be hurt."

The Ute's response was short and to the point. "Horse thief."

"I am called Grizzly Killer. You have heard of me?"

Stiffening, the warrior studied Nate for a moment. "Yes. You have killed many of my people."

"They were trying to kill me!"

"Why are you stealing my horse?"

"I need it. Bad white men have taken my wife and stolen my horses. I must find these men and kill them."

The Ute pondered the revelation for a bit before moving his arms again. "How many men are there?"

"Three," Nate answered, then thought to ask, "What are you called?"

"Barking Dog."

Nate would have grinned if not for the fact he was well aware of the special significance Indians attached to names. An Indian child received its name soon after birth. The name selected might be that of a favorite animal of the parent, a noteworthy event that took place on the day the baby was born, or perhaps a name honoring a valorous deed the parent had once performed. While Indian women invariably kept the names bestowed on them at birth, the men often changed theirs to reflect a brave deed they personally accomplished, to commemorate their encounter with an unusual animal, or in observance of a special dream. There were exceptions, however. Any Indian born with a physical deformity was usually known more by a name that signified the deformity, such as Short Leg or Hump Back. Very few Indian children, though, were born deformed. "Do you know the mountain with twin peaks south of here?" Nate asked.

"Yes," Barking Dog responded. "We call them the Breasts of Life."

"Good. In two weeks I will deliver your horse at the small lake on the north side of that mountain. I will tie it to a tree on the north shore and you may get it then."

The Ute's brow knit. "You will not keep it?"

"No."

"And what is to stop me from waiting with many men from my village?"

"Nothing. But a man of honor would not commit such a wicked deed."

Barking Dog smiled. "For a white man you are very wise."

"My wife is Shoshone. Maybe her ways have rubbed off on me," Nate signed with a grin. "I am sorry I must take your horse. I threw your knife in the snow," he disclosed, pointing at the spot. "So you can make a lance for your walk back to your village."

The Ute glanced at the spot and saw the knife hilt jutting in the air. "You are very strange, Grizzly Killer. Most whites would kill me and be done with it."

"Which village are you from?"

Surprised by the question, Barking Dog cocked his head. "The village of Chief Eagle Horse. Why?"

"I was curious," Nate said, and started to turn the stallion.

"Wait," the Ute signed urgently.

"What?"

"Though you are stealing my horse, you spared my life. I owe you my life, and I can not take such an obligation lightly. I will repay you now so I can kill you if we meet again after you return my stallion."

Now it was Nate's turn to grin. "How?"

"I have seen your wife."

A lightning bolt coursed through Nate's body. "Where? When?"

"Yesterday. Spotted Wolf and I saw three white men and an Indian woman. They must be the bad whites and your wife. They are not more than half a day's ride from here."

"The woman was unharmed?"

"Yes. We watched them for a while, then Spotted Wolf went to our village to get more warriors while I followed their backtrail to see if there were more whites around."

"How long before Spotted Wolf returns?"

"Four sleeps at the most."

Nate looked into the warrior's dark eyes, silently conveying his gratitude, then whipped the stallion around and rode hard to the west. By nightfall Winona would be safe or else.

Chapter Ten

Lambert had gone over a mile when he found the tracks of a large horse emerging from the trees on the south. Since the hooves weren't shod it had to be an Indian mount. He reined up and looked over his shoulder, trying to spot Newton and the others, but they had long since vanished into the forest.

He had a decision to make. Should he continue to the King cabin or go warn his friend that savages were shadowing them? He decided to press onward. It was only one lousy Indian, after all, and he was going in the same direction. With luck, he'd slay the savage *and* finish off Grizzly Killer.

Gripping his Kentucky rifle firmly, he moved toward the valley where the King cabin was situated. Fear of an ambush prompted him to be extra alert. He constantly surveyed the woods ahead but saw only wildlife.

A few black-tailed deer regarded him from a hill to the north before fleeing into the trees. At one point a golden eagle soared overhead. And once a lynx bounded across the trail less than forty yards away.

Lambert covered two more miles. His mind started to stray as he thought about the unbelievable wealth that would soon be his. Ten thousand dollars! Maybe more depending on how good a bargain they struck with that crafty Two Owls. Never in his wildest dreams had he expected to possess such an incredible fortune. To him, or to anyone who barely eked out a living year after year, such a sum was a godsend.

To think that he owed his good fortune to the worst mishap that could befall any trapper; being captured by hostile Indians. If Newton and he hadn't taken a chance a year ago and ventured deep into Ute country to do their trapping, they never would have been captured by a war party of Utes. Then they would never have been taken to Two Owls' village and Newton would never have had the opportunity to make his desperate pitch to the chief.

Lambert chuckled. The most amazing moment in his life had been when Two Owls agreed to the deal. Of course, Newton had no intention of making good. His friend had made the proposal simply as a last-ditch means of saving their lives. In fact, one of the other Utes had been sharpening his knife to take Lambert's hair when the inspiration struck Newton.

Good old Newton.

They'd joked about their narrow escape all the way back to St. Louis, vowing never again to go anywhere near Ute country. Then Newton had taken it into his head to visit his kin in New York City, and on the way back had met Isaac Kennedy.

Now look at them.

Soon they would have more money than they could earn in nine or ten seasons of trapping. Soon they—.

What was that?

Lambert abruptly reined up as he spied a horse-
man far off to the east. The rider was moving at a
reckless pace, his horse throwing up a wide wake of
white spray. He hunched low over the pommel and
moved into the trees on the right side of the trail.
Dismounting, he looped the reins around a branch,
cradled the Kentucky in his arms, and walked to the
tree nearest the tracks. Concealed there, he peered
out and studied the man, anticipating it would be the
Indian who had been shadowing them.

His first observation was that the man rode a
stallion. The sheer size of the horse precluded it
being a mare. An Indian horse, he guessed, and
gleefully anticipated putting a ball into the bastard's
head.

Then he saw the hint of red in the man's coat.

Red?

As in a Mackinaw?

Lambert tensed, recalling the Mackinaw in the
King cabin, hanging on the wall.

No, it couldn't be!

Even if the rotten squaw was right about her
husband being alive, there was no way that King
could be in pursuit so soon after being shot.

Lambert nervously licked his lips, his eyes narrow-
ing. If that was indeed Grizzly Killer, then the man
wasn't human. Lambert had seen the wound caused
by his ball. He'd leaned down and laughed into
King's face after shooting him. Blood had been
pouring onto the floor.

That couldn't be Nate King!

Uneasy, Lambert watched the rider come ever
closer. He saw the Mackinaw clearly, saw the big man
astride the stallion, and swallowed a lump that
formed in his throat. It *was* King.

He shook his head, dispelling his anxiety. So what
if Grizzly Killer had survived? Another ball would do

the trick, and this time Lambert intended to make doubly certain that the son of a bitch breathed his last before bearing the good news to Newton.

He checked the Kentucky, even going so far as to tamp the ramrod down the barrel to verify the ball and patch were properly placed at the bottom and ready to fire. Satisfied, he replaced the ramrod and cocked the hammer.

Let the Grizzly Killer come.

Lambert was ready.

He cradled the Kentucky again and leaned against the trunk, studying the lay of the land to determine how close he should let King get. Since he didn't want to miss, the closer, the better. Twenty to twenty-five yards should be about right. He noticed a tree on the north side of the trail that appeared to be about that distance off. Fine. When King came abreast of the tree, he'd shoot.

Hell, it would be easy.

Lambert grinned and idly observed King's rapid progress. The man was pushing the stallion to its limits, evidently in a hurry to reach his squaw. Lambert snickered contemptuously. He despised Indian lovers. To him, every buck and squaw in the West deserved the same treatment; extermination. No trapper or mountaineer would be safe as long as the Indians were allowed to exist. One day, he reasoned, the Indians west of the Mississippi would suffer the same fate as the Indians east of the Mississippi. They would either be killed off or driven from their lands. It couldn't happen soon enough to suit him.

King was now a quarter of a mile distant.

Crouching, Lambert braced the rifle barrel against the tree. He trained the sight on the approximate spot Grizzly Killer would be when he pulled trigger.

The cold air tingled his nose and made him want to sneeze. He pinched the tip of his nose together to nip the sneeze in the bud. Even the faintest of sounds sometimes carried far in the Rockies and he was taking no chances on alerting King.

He recalled the stories that old fart had related about Grizzly Killer. No less a personage than Shakespeare McNair, one of the premiere mountain men, had taken King under his wing and educated him in the ways of the wilderness. King was supposed to be a crack shot and utterly fearless. The Shoshones and the Cheyennes in particular held him in great respect. And the Blackfeet, it was rumored, wanted King's hair more than any other white man's because Grizzly Killer had been instrumental in helping a band of Shoshones defeat a war party led by a noted Blackfoot warrior.

King rounded a stand of small pines and came directly toward Lambert's position. Grinning, he held the Kentucky steady and lightly touched his finger to the trigger.

Any moment now.

Nate held his body close to the stallion, squinting to compensate for the bright glare of sunlight reflecting off the mantle of snow. He heard the arrows bouncing slightly in the quiver and hoped none would fall out. When he overtook the cutthroats he might need every single shaft.

His body pained him terribly but he ignored it. Every now and then his head took to throbbing. The agony would subside after a spell, though.

He scanned the trail ahead as he rode, seeing the line of tracks made by Barking Dog near those made by the party bearing westward. Then he noticed another set. Straightening, perplexed, he saw where a second set of prints had paralleled the trail for a considerable distance stretching back in the direction the killers had gone.

What did it mean?

As he drew nearer he discerned that this second set had angled away from the trail and into the trees to the south. Had Barking Dog lied? Had the other Ute accompanied Barking Dog this far and then headed for their village?

He glanced at the treeline, mystified, observing the sunlight glint off the tip of a thin horizontal branch. Simultaneously came the chilling realization that branches were incapable of reflecting sunshine.

Rifle barrels, on the other hand, could.

So superbly coordinated were Nate's reflexes that the very instant he saw the glinting object and perceived it to be a rifle, he threw himself from the stallion, diving to the right, and he was scarcely out of the saddle when the booming of the ambusher's weapon proved his instincts correct. Landing on his right shoulder, he rolled upright and sprinted toward the woods. Two arrows fell out as he rolled but the rest stayed in the quiver.

The stallion continued galloping westward, spooked by the rifle blast.

Nate reached a tree in five bounds and darted behind its bole. He crouched, slid an arrow out, and nocked it. Who was out there? he reflected, catching his breath and letting his racing blood slow down. Very few Indians owned rifles, and most of those who did were dwellers of the plains. Not more than a dozen Utes all told, he estimated, owned a firearm, which made the likelihood of his attacker being an Ute warrior extremely remote.

There was only one logical conclusion: Either Newton or Lambert had backtracked.

He peered out, searching the vegetation opposite for his adversary. A hint of motion prompted him to jerk his head back a fraction of a second before a rifle cracked and the ball smacked into the tree.

Whoever it was, the man could reload quickly.

Nate glanced over his shoulder, debating whether to seek sanctuary in the forest and make the killer come after him. If he had a rifle instead of a bow, he would naturally stand firm. But he'd not wielded a bow regularly since he was much younger and felt at a grave disadvantage. He stared at the shroud of smoke hovering beside the tree where the killer was concealed, wishing it would dissipate on the wind so he could see his enemy. Then it occured to him: If he couldn't spot the ambusher, neither could the man spot him.

Suddenly dashing to the right, staying bent at the waist, Nate ran from tree to tree, expecting to hear the boom of the rifle at any second. Traveling a dozen yards, he stopped behind a pine tree and knelt to study the forest on the other side of the trail.

There lingered enough smoke to partially obscure the trunk, but the left leg of the man bearing the rifle was in full view.

Nate raised the bow and sighted on the killer's limb. He breathed shallowly so the tip of the arrow would hold steady, then pulled the string back to his cheek, straining his arm to its limit. About to fire, he hesitated.

What if he missed? He would alert the ambusher to the fact he'd moved. Since he couldn't guarantee he could hit the leg, perhaps he should try to work his way around the man and come up on the killer from the rear.

He lowered the bow and continued running to the west. After twenty yards he halted and from the shelter of an oak tree checked on the ambusher. Beyond discerning an outline of the man's body, he couldn't identify who it was. The killer appeared to be concentrating on the tree Nate had vacated.

Now came the difficult part. He braced his legs,

tensed, and focused on a tree across the way. Once committed, he would be in the open for a good thirty feet. If Newton or Lambert spied him, there would be plenty of time for whichever one was trying to kill him to place a perfect shot.

Nate bolted, sprinting as quickly as humanly possible through the high snow, his progress retarded by the clinging white fluff. He didn't bother glancing toward the killer. Any distraction, however brief, slowed him marginally. Run! he mentally shouted at himself. Run like you've never run before.

To his utter amazement, Nate reached the sheltering woods without being shot. He squatted beside a pine and beamed at the prospect of gaining the upper hand. Exercising extreme caution, he advanced slowly toward the tree screening his foe. He moved in a crouch, waddling through the snow at times, always making certain there was undergrowth or a tree between him and the ambusher. Knowing the snap of a single twig would give him away, he was especially careful not to brush against any branches.

At last he drew within twenty feet of his quarry, pausing behind a waist-high boulder to tighten his grip on the arrow and the bow. All he had to do was jump up, aim, and let the shaft fly.

Nate straightened, the bow sweeping up, the arrow level. There stood the tree in question. There were the tracks in the snow leading from the woods to the tree, and the packed snow at the base of the tree that indicated the man had indeed been at that spot. But there were no tracks leading away and the killer himself was nowhere in sight.

Mystified, Nate moved around the boulder. Where could the ambusher have gone? Was the man employing the same tactic he'd just executed and now their positions were reversed? He scanned the forest but saw nothing.

Damn.

Nate stepped toward the tree, intending to search the area where he'd first gone to ground. He took several strides when he heard a distinct click to his rear and a mocking voice declared triumphantly:

"Make one move and you're a dead man!"

Chapter Eleven

Nate became a statue. The voice sounded close enough to convince him that if he tried going to the right or left, a ball would pierce his back before he could hope to whirl and fire.

"Wise man," the voice taunted. "Now drop that bow and put your arms in the air."

Frowning, Nate complied. He recognized the speaker as Lambert before he pivoted. The killer smirked and pointed the Kentucky at his chest.

"So we meet again. Fancy that," Lambert joked, coming to within six feet and halting. "I've heard of being hard to kill, but you're worse than any grizzly that ever lived. No wonder they call you Grizzly Killer."

"You know who I am?" Nate said to keep the killer chatting. Why hadn't Lambert simply shot him and been done with it?

"We figured it out," Lambert answered. "Actually, Newton did. Then that squaw of yours got to bragging about how you'd be after us before long and we decided one of us should come back and plant you in your grave real personal like."

"Have you harmed my wife?"

"Your squaw is fine, Indian lover. We're not about to lay a finger on her since we plan to give her to the Utes."

Anger made Nate clench his fists. "Put down that gun and we'll settle this man to man."

"That head shot must have addled your brains," Lambert said, and snorted. "I've got the drop on you and I intend to keep it until I'm ready to send you to meet your Maker." He wagged the Kentucky. "How does it feel knowing your life is in my hands?"

Nate didn't bother to answer.

"I could have killed you when you were trying to sneak up on me but I didn't want to spoil my fun," Lambert went on. "I'm fixing to take my time, make you suffer a little first."

"You're mighty brave when you're up against an unarmed man," Nate commented.

Lambert's gaze dropped to Nate's waist. "You're not exactly unarmed, are you? Use one hand and drop that knife and the tomahawk. And no sudden moves unless you want a ball in your head."

Easing his right arm downward, Nate tugged the tomahawk free and let it fall into the snow. He used two fingers and pulled the knife from its sheath.

Adopting a cocky attitude, Lambert nodded at the trail of tracks leading from the forest to the tree. "Pretty clever of me to walk backwards in my own footprints so you couldn't figure out where I'd gone, huh?"

"You're brilliant," Nate said, and started to lower the knife toward the ground, his eyes riveted to Lambert's. The killer laughed and blinked. It wasn't much of an opening, but it was all Nate was likely to get. Even as Lambert's eyes closed, he gripped the knife firmly and flipped it straight at the killer's face while hurling himself to the right.

Lambert fired, but he squeezed the trigger while ducking to the left to avoid the knife and the movement threw his aim off.

Nate felt the ball tear at the edge of his Mackinaw sleeve as it streaked past, and then he was bounding forward, taking the offensive, his arms extended. He slammed into Lambert, wrapping his arms around the man's waist, and they both went down, the Kentucky pinned between them.

Hissing like an enraged rattler, Lambert drove his knee into Nate's groin. The blow landed squarely and Nate almost released his hold to try and roll away. Sheer grit sparked him to swing his right fist into Lambert's jaw instead, rocking the man's head back. He planted a left, the combination sufficient to cause Lambert to sag, stunned.

Nate heaved to his feet, grabbing the Kentucky as he did and wrenching the rifle from Lambert's grasp. He tossed it aside. No sooner had he done so, however, than Lambert kicked him in the stomach, doubling him over.

"Damn you!" the cutthroat roared, and kicked again, sweeping his left foot into Nate's neck.

Staggered, Nate stumbled rearward.

Lambert swept upright, his right hand clawing for the flintlock adorning his waist. "I'll finish you off proper," he barked.

Ignoring his pain, Nate sprang just as the pistol swept clear of the belt. He batted the barrel away with his left forearm and rammed his right fist into his enemy's mouth, knocking Lambert backwards.

Again the trapper tried to bring the flintlock into play.

Nate pressed his initiative to keep Lambert off

balance, raining a flurry of blows to the man's face, battering him without let up. He pummeled Lambert to his knees, then slammed his own knee into Lambert's face.

Down the tall man went, still gripping the flintlock.

Pouncing on Lambert's arm to pin it to the ground, Nate tore the pistol from the man's grasp. No sooner had he done so, however, than Lambert desperately punched him on the throat. Had the swing been delivered with all of Lambert's strength, it might have crushed Nate's windpipe. As it was, Nate fell onto his right side, releasing the flintlock to clasp his neck, his features contorted in acute anguish, wheezing as he tried to breathe.

Lambert scrambled to his knees, then jumped on Nate and tried to clamp both hands around the younger man's neck.

Although short of breath Nate resisted furiously, blocking Lambert's hands and trying to return the favor by seizing the killer's neck. They grappled and rolled, their faces inches from one another, with Lambert's teeth exposed in an almost bestial snarl. They were evenly matched and the battle raged on for over a minute with neither one gaining an edge.

Nate hurt everywhere. Try as he might he couldn't prevail, and to make matters worse they rolled into a large tree, his spine absorbing most of the impact. He had to let go, gasping for air.

Pushing erect, Lambert back-pedaled and began scouring the snow for the flintlock.

Nate wasn't about to let him find it. Gritting his teeth, he shoved to his feet and charged. Lambert turned to meet him and tried to connect with a punch, but Nate evaded the man's flashing arm. They warily circled each other, seeking an opening they could exploit.

Blood seeped from Lambert's crushed lips. He licked them and spat, his gaze never leaving Nate's face. "I'm going to skin you alive," he stated, the words slightly distorted.

"First you have to beat me," Nate retorted.

In a savage onslaught Lambert attempted to do just that, making up in brute strength what he lacked in finesse. He flailed away, trying to beat Nate into the ground, but most of his blows were countered.

Blocking the strikes made Nate's arms ache horribly. He cast about for a stout limb he could employ as a club or *anything* that would serve as a weapon. A few feet to the left was a narrow, tapered hole in the snow where a heavy object had been tossed and sank down. Was it the flintlock? Praying such was the case, he summoned a reservoir of stamina and punched. One of his uppercuts scored, tottering Lambert rearward.

Whirling, Nate dived at the hole and thrust his eager hands into the frigid snow, his fingers exploring for the flintlock. Instead, he touched slender cold steel and his right hand drew forth his butcher knife.

Lambert shouted out in victory.

Twisting, Nate saw the killer raising the flintlock from the snow. The man's thumb curled around the hammer and started to pull it back. "No!" Nate cried, bounding at his adversary, the knife hilt clutched in his right hand.

Elevating the flintlock, Lambert grinned.

Nate was still a foot away when the tall man squeezed the trigger and they both heard the loud ticking sound of the flint as the firestone struck the steel pan. But there was no loud retort; the black powder didn't ignite. It was a misfire, undoubtedly caused by wet snow fouling the piece.

Because Nate was already moving at top speed, including his right arm which was spearing toward Lambert even as the killer pulled trigger, there was no time for Nate to alter the sweep of his hand, even if he wanted to. A heartbeat after the flintlock misfired, his knife sank to the hilt into Lambert's chest with a muted thud.

Lambert stiffened and jerked backwards, the useless pistol falling from his trembling hand, his eyes widening, shock transforming his face into a pallid mask.

Nate released the knife and stood still, watching his enemy carefully.

"Damn you," Lambert exclaimed, taking the jutting hilt in both hands. He braced and heaved, extracting the blade cleanly, but in doing so he permitted his life's blood to gush forth like a geyser, the crimson fluid spraying out from his chest and splattering his clothing and the snow at his feet.

There were no words for Nate to say. He clenched his fists and waited for the inevitable.

"Dear Lord," Lambert breathed, flinging the knife down. He pressed his palms to the slit, vainly endeavoring to staunch the pumping blood. Gripped by sudden dizziness, he fell to his knees. "I'm dying," he wailed. "I'm dying."

Nate's features hardened.

"Help me!" Lambert blurted frantically. "Please help me!" He made as if to reach for Nate, but the action only allowed the blood to gush faster. "Please!"

"Good riddance."

Lambert was too terrified of the Grim Reaper to be mad. He coughed, red spittle rimming his lips, and doubled in half. "This can't be!" he stated. "I'm not ready to die."

"Few ever are," Nate said, retrieving both the flintlock and his knife.

Lambert coughed again, violently, and leaned down until his forehead rested in the snow. "I feel so weak, so cold."

Satisfied the man no longer posed a threat, Nate

went about collecting all their weapons. He held the Kentucky and smiled. It wasn't a Hawken, but it would suffice for the job at hand. He went back to Lambert and listened to the killer's labored breathing.

"Grizzly Killer?"

"Yes?"

"My head is all fuzzy. I can't seem to think straight."

"It won't be long now."

Lambert twisted to look up. Blood was trickling from both corners of his mouth. "Will you do me a favor?"

"Depends."

"I—I have a sister in Ohio. Cincinnati. Her name is Christine Lambert. Will—will you get word back to her?"

Frowning, Nate hesitated. Why should he do a favor for someone who had tried to kill him and stolen his wife?

"Please, King. Write her a note, a line, anything," Lambert pleaded, his voice quavering, his words barely audible. "She's the only kin I have. I don't want her worrying on my no-good account."

About to say no, Nate saw tears rimming the mountaineer's eyes. A pool of blood soaked snow had formed under Lambert's chest. "All right," he said, and sighed. "I'll send a line back East with the first person I meet who is heading to the States."

Lambert smiled wanly. "Thank you," he said sincerely, and stiffened, uttering gurgling noises, his tongue protruding as he tried to suck in air. He attempted to speak one last time but produced an inarticulate grunt. His body sagged, his eyes locked wide open, and he ceased breathing.

Nate waited a moment before stepping forward to verify the man had died. He wasted no time removing

Lambert's ammo-pouch and powder-horn. Rising, he scoured the forest for the killer's mount and spied the horse screened in the timber. He took several strides, then halted and glanced over his shoulder. Should he bury Lambert or simply leave him? Shrugging, he continued to the horse.

The Almighty had made carrion eaters for a reason.

Ike Newton had abruptly reined up and stared thoughtfully eastward. "Did you hear that?"

"Hear what?" Isaac Kennedy asked, stopping. He was in the lead. Behind him came the Shoshone woman, then Newton with the string.

"I thought I heard a shot."

"I heard nothing."

"You wouldn't," Newton snapped. He glanced at Winona. "Did you?"

"My husband has killed your friend."

Newton rode forward until he was beside her. "You don't know that. You're just trying to rattle me."

"I know," Winona said softly.

"Bull," Newton declared, moving ahead of both of them, sick to death of Kennedy's company and wishing he'd never decided to take the squaw along as a gift for Two Owls. He looked back once more, wondering if the bitch was right. Naw. She couldn't be. Lambert had killed a couple of dozen Indians and whites in his time. He felt certain his friend had taken care of Grizzly Killer.

They were moving slowly up a steep slope toward a narrow pass between two snow covered mountains. Once beyond the pass they would be in a valley where Two Owls wintered.

Newton idly scanned the shimmering peaks around them and spied a soaring hawk far off. He thought about the Ute chief and wondered whether the savage would double-cross them. If so, there wasn't a damn thing they could do about it. They'd simply have to take Two Owls at his word and hope for the best.

He glanced at the Shoshone, pondering her devotion to the man called Grizzly Killer. She was a squaw, but she also possessed the kind of traits he most admired in a woman. What would it be like to be loved by someone like her? How did some men rate such sterling wives while others wound up with shrews? Secretly, he envied Nate King. If a fine woman had ever loved him, he might have amounted to something. A good woman's love, he'd once heard a traveler at a tavern say, could make the difference between a happy life and damnation.

Sighing, Newton cradled his Kentucky and focused on the pass. The depth of the snow increased the higher they went, and their horses were finding the going difficult.

"Ike?" Kennedy spoke up.

"What now?"

"Suppose she's right. Suppose Lambert is dead."

"He's not."

"But just suppose he is. Maybe we should release her."

"Don't you ever give up?" Newton stated testily.

"Hear me out. If King *is* after us, we serve our own best interests by letting her go. Once he has his wife back safe and sound, he'll leave us alone."

"No, he won't."

"Why not?"

"Because men like Nate King aren't the kind to overlook a little thing like being shot and left for dead and having their wives taken. If it takes Grizzly Killer the rest of his born days, he'll track us down."

They lapsed into an uncomfortable silence until they attained the pass, a gap no more than eight feet wide. There the snow lay only nine or ten inches in depth, thanks to the sheltering influence of the two mountains. On both slopes were huge boulders caked with snow.

Newton reined up and waited for the others to join him. The squaw came up on his left, Kennedy the right. He gazed eastward and was surprised to spot a lone horse far in the distance galloping in their direction. "What the hell!" he blurted.

Stopping, Kennedy twisted in his saddle and looked. "Is that's Lambert's horse?"

"It's impossible to tell at this range," Newton said, although he believed the animal to be larger.

Kennedy's eyes narrowed. "There's no rider."

"I noticed."

"What does it mean?"

"I don't know," Newton said, watching the horse plow steadily onward.

"Should one of us go catch it?"

"Isaac, you ask too doggoned many questions," Newton barked. He hesitated uncertainly, and at that moment a chilling sound emanated from the left-hand slope, a sound every mountaineer dreaded.

It was a low, guttural growl.

Shifting, Newton glanced at the white slope and felt his blood turn to ice at beholding an enormous panther perched on top of a boulder a mere twelve feet away. Even as he laid eyes on the big cat it snarled and leaped at the Shoshone woman.

Chapter Twelve

Mounted on Lambert's horse, Nate continued his pursuit. He had the bow and the quiver rolled up in a blanket behind the saddle. The reloaded Kentucky was in the crook of his right arm. And the flintlock had been added to the knife and tomahawk adorning his waist.

The fight had taken a lot out of him. He felt alternately weak and strong, clear-headed and slightly dizzy. As much as he longed to rescue Winona, he must not push himself excessively hard for fear of passing out again. He concentrated on staying with the trail, holding the horse to a steady but not rapid pace.

The tracks left by Barking Dog's fleeing stallion were freshly defined in the snow, and from the length of its gait it appeared the animal had no intention of slowing any time soon.

Nate forged ahead, alert for more Indians or his quarry. The trail was winding toward a pair of mountains miles off. From the extensive trapping he had done in the area during the fall, he knew a pass existed between those peaks and beyond it lay a valley where game was plentiful.

The thought of game reminded him about food and made his stomach rumble. He debated whether to stop and decided not to waste precious time hunting. There would be ample opportunity to eat after he rescued Winona.

As he rode his mind drifted. He speculated as to whether he'd made a blunder by settling in a cabin situated so remotely. If he took Winona to St. Louis, for instance, they'd be a lot safer during the winter months. But the trips back and forth would be extremely taxing, and they'd be compelled to deal with the ugly specter of bigotry. There were plenty of whites who despised Indians, no matter which tribe they belonged to. And if something should happen to him while there, Winona might find herself alone in a strange city and forced to rely on the kindness of total strangers.

He'd previously given serious consideration to wintering with Winona's tribe. The Shoshones would be delighted to have them in their village during the colder months. Except for the ongoing raids by the Blackfeet and the Utes, there would be little danger.

However, he had to confess that he preferred to stay right where he was, in their cabin. Yes, they were at the mercy of the elements. Yes, they were in constant danger of attack. And yes, they could well starve. But the cabin was their *home*, and he'd rather take his chances there than anywhere else.

The time passed slowly. The brightness of the snow hurt his eyes and made them water.

What if he went snow blind? A chronic ailment of trappers who spent winters in the Rockies, snow blindness often came on suddenly and sometimes took up to a week to go away. The only cure was resting and staying indoors in subdued light. Even then, those who recovered complained for a long time afterward that everything they looked at was enveloped in a reddish haze.

To go snow blind now would doom Winona to captivity among the Utes and force him to try and return to the cabin. He squinted, making his eyes thin slits. The less light that struck them, the lower the risk of injury.

The time seemed to crawl by.

He still had a couple of miles to go before reaching the two mountains when a faint retort reached his ears from the vicinity of the pass. His pulse quickened. Newton and the others must be in trouble, which did not bode well for Winona. He goaded Lambert's horse to go faster and forgot about keeping his eyes narrowed against the glare.

Rarely seen by Indians and mountaineers, the largest cats in the Rockies were known for their reclusive nature. Often over seven and a half feet long from the tip of their nose to the end of their tail, they sport a tawny coat with small dark patches on the backs of their tapered ears and accenting their whisker patches. These cats were referred to as panthers by the majority of the trappers. A few called them catamounts. Others used the French word for such felines, calling them *couguars*, while some had taken to speaking of the huge cats as mountain lions.

By any name they were trouble when aroused or hungry, and no one knew this fact better than Ike Newton. Seven years ago, while trapping near Sweet Lake, he'd tangled with a panther that had tried to take a beaver caught in one of his traps. He'd managed to scare the critter off with a shot from his pistol. But this time he couldn't afford to miss.

At the moment the panther launched itself into the air, Newton was bringing the Kentucky up while thumbing back the hammer. With the squaw between the cat and him, he didn't have much of a shot. He simply elevated the barrel in the general direction of the hurtling beast, pulled trigger, and hoped for the best.

The panther's tapered claws were within a foot of Winona's face when the heavy lead smacked into the cat's brow. The hit fell right between its slanted eyes and flipped the animal rearward in a tight loop. Its two hundred and fifty pound body crashed down into the snow head first and it lay perfectly still.

A few of the pack horses shied, compelling Newton to grip the lead tightly.

Winona hadn't so much as budged. She simply stared at the dead cat, her features stone-like.

"I say!" Kennedy blurted. "That was remarkable shooting, Ike."

"I was lucky," Newton responded gruffly, annoyed at how close he'd come to losing his gift for Two Owls.

The storekeeper edged his mount nearer to the cat. "I didn't know panthers attacked people."

"Ordinarily they don't," Newton confirmed. "I figure it was going for her horse and she was just in the way." He snickered. "Which is a break for me."

Kennedy glanced at him. "I don't understand."

"Now I don't need to worry about the squaw sticking a knife in my ribs while I'm sleeping. She won't do a damn thing to me."

"Why not?"

"Because I just saved her life, you idiot, and Indians are real particular about such things. Save a buck or a squaw and they owe you for life. And if they happen to be your enemy in the first place, then they can't kill you until they repay the favor," Newton

said, and laughed merrily. "I could hand her a gun
and she wouldn't even shoot me."

"An excellent suggestion," Kennedy declared.
"Considering the dangers in this wilderness, she
should have the means to protect herself."

"Isaac."

"Yes?"

"I'm not *really* fixing to hand a gun over to her."

"But you just said—."

"Move out," Newton barked, and did just that,
taking the lead. He would have been better off
shooting Kennedy, he irately reflected. Newton had
traveled almost to the end of the pass before remem-
bering that his Kentucky was empty. Stopping, he
moved back to the first pack horse and removed Nate
King's loaded Hawken from the blanket in which
he'd rolled it before departing the King cabin. He
stuck the Kentucky in the pack and examined the
Hawken.

He'd heard generally favorable reports about
Hawkens. Manufactured by Jacob and Samuel
Hawken of St. Louis, they were reputed to be highly
reliable and extremely accurate in competent hands.
Their only drawback was their weight. A few trappers
who had purchased Hawkens later sold the rifles
because they were too heavy to be toting all over the
Rockies. This despite the fact that Hawkens were
much shorter than conventional long rifles, the typical Hawken having a thirty-four inch barrel while the
average Kentucky sported a barrel of forty-four
inches.

There was one other advantage Hawkens possessed
over the Kentucky and Harper's Ferry rifles.
Hawkens used the newfangled percussion system of
firing instead of relying on the spark of a flint on steel
to ignite the black powder.

He hefted the rifle, liking its sturdy feel, then

realized the Shoshone was glaring at him. Without looking at her he wheeled his horse and resumed their journey.

It took them a while to work their way down from the pass to the valley below. The going was slippery and several of the pack animals nearly lost their balance. Once on level ground they rode rapidly toward a stream and followed the winding ribbon of water into a dense forest.

Newton felt on edge. He had no guarantee that Two Owls' warriors wouldn't shoot on sight and there was always the risk of running into Utes from another village since their hunting ranges tended to broadly overlap. To compound the danger, Blackfeet war parties frequently invaded Ute territory. Running into those devils would decidedly ruin all of his well laid plans.

He glanced up at the sky and glimpsed the afternoon sun through the canopy of limbs overhead. If Lambert didn't return by nightfall, then he would be inclined to believe the squaw; his friend truly had been rubbed out. If so, *he* could expect Grizzly Killer to show up sooner or later, probably sooner. A man whose wife had been abducted seldom dallied when seeking vengeance.

For the next several hours they walked deeper into the long, sinuous valley, heading toward the far end some twenty miles distant where they might find Two Owls' encampment. The snow under the trees lay to a depth of two feet or more and the pack horses at times had to struggle through higher drifts up to their chests. No one bothered to speak during all this time. Each of them was immersed in thought. Winona rode with her back straight, her chin jutting defiantly. Kennedy frequently gazed at her when he felt certain she wouldn't notice. Occasionally he would cast a dark look at his partner.

The sun hung just above the western horizon when Newton finally raised his right hand to call a halt as they were entering a wide clearing on the south side of the stream. "This is where we'll camp," he announced.

"At last," Kennedy breathed, sliding to the ground near the water. He surveyed the vast, wild domain of Indians and wildlife and sighed. "When will we find Two Owls?"

"How should I know?" Newton responded, waiting for the squaw to dismount before doing the same. "We'll find him when we find him."

"Someone who didn't know better might swear you don't have the foggiest idea where to locate him."

Newton took an angry stride toward the storekeeper, then drew up short in disgust. "This isn't the civilized East, Isaac. It's not like New York City or Ohio where you can make a business appointment, then sit down at the appointed time to discuss selling or swapping your goods. I told Two Owls I'd look him up after I got the items he wants. For all he knows, I'm not even coming." He paused. "Frankly, I was shocked when he agreed to let us go. He must really want the merchandise."

"Of course he does," Kennedy said. "He'll have more than all the other tribes combined. Why, he could even prevent the Blackfeet from invading his territory."

"Prevent them, hell. He can march on up to Blackfoot country and drive the bastards clear into Canada."

Winona, who had been listening with interest to the discussion, glanced at the wooden crates. There were four on each pack animal, bringing the grand total to twenty-eight. "What are in those?" she inquired.

Newton snorted. "Well, look who's decided to be

civil." He jabbed a thumb toward the crates. "It's none of your damn business what's inside those crates, and if I find you poking around where you shouldn't be, I'll slit your throat. Savvy?"

"Yes."

"You wouldn't slit her pretty throat, would you?" Kennedy asked apprehensively.

"I sure as hell would. Killing squaws and bucks is the same as killing any animal."

"But Indians are people, the same as us."

"Indians are nothing like us, idiot," Newton stated harshly. "They're heathens, plain and simple. Didn't you hear what President Jackson said? He called Indians an inferior race who should be pushed aside to make room for us whites."

"I read an account in the newspaper," Kennedy said.

"There you have it. When the President of the United States, no less a man than Old Hickory, calls Indians inferior, then they're damn well inferior," Newton snapped. "It's our duty as white men to rub every last one out."

Kennedy stared at the crates. "Is that one of the reasons you're trading with Two Owls?"

"Hell yes. He'll use these to wipe out every enemy he has, and those enemies are mostly other tribes. We're doing our part to reduce the Indian population."

"You said 'mostly'," Kennedy noted. "Won't Two Owls use them against trappers also?"

"Probably," Newton said with a shrug. "But it will serve any trapper right for being stupid enough to be caught by the Utes."

"But you were caught by the Utes once."

"Don't quibble, Isaac. Why, if President Jackson knew what we were up to, he'd likely give us a medal."

"Then why are you worried about the Army finding out?"

Newton hefted the Hawken and scowled. "You ask too damn many questions. A man has got to learn when to keep his mouth shut out here or he'll wind up eating lead." He nodded at the horses. "Get busy watering and feeding our critters."

"Why don't you do it?" Kennedy responded indignantly.

"Because one of us must keep an eye on the squaw to see she doesn't try and slip away," Newton said. "And since I couldn't trust you to watch a tree stump, I get the job."

Scowling, Isaac Kennedy sullenly proceeded. But as he worked he cast many a side-long glance at Ike Newton, the sparks of ripening hatred blazing to life in his eyes.

Chapter Thirteen

The sun hung above the western horizon when Nate's vision first blurred briefly, causing him to rein up and blink rapidly as tears of discomfort washed over his pupils. He had just made it safely through the high pass and down the slippery slope. The sight of the dead panther had brought immense relief; the dead cat explained the shot he'd heard earlier and tended to indicate Winona was still safe.

Now he wiped the back of his left hand across his eyes and gazed at a narrow stream in front of him. The landscape came into sharp focus again, prompting a sigh of relief. For a second there he'd figured he was coming down with snow blindness.

He urged Lambert's horse onward, sticking to the trail left by Winona and her abductors. Soon the sun would set and he'd be unable to track them. As much as he despised the very idea, he would need to halt for the night. Knowing that his precious wife was somewhere in the tract of forest just ahead made him all the more eager to overtake the scoundrels and save her.

Nate paralleled the stream and entered the trees. A hint of movement drew his attention to the northwest. There, grazing on a thin strip of brown grass he exposed, was Barking Dog's stallion. Evidently the animal had followed the scent of the other horses until hunger compelled it to eat. Recalling his promise to return it if possible, Nate approached the big animal cautiously, fearing it would bolt.

The stallion simply munched and scarcely paid attention to his presence.

Sliding to the ground, Nate walked over and gripped the stallion's Indian-style bridle. A length of rope had been looped twice in the middle around the horse's lower jaw to form a lark's-head knot that served as the bit, leaving the ends free for use as the reins. He patted the animal's neck and uttered soft words, then undid the knot and removed the bridle. Making a single loop at one end, he slipped the loop over the stallion's head, clasped the other end, and climbed back into the saddle.

Turning Lambert's horse, Nate resumed his pursuit. He realized he must find a suitable spot to camp soon or darkness would catch him stranded in the trees. There was plenty of water but he had to find ample food for both animals before he could rest for the night.

The upper rim of the sun was barely visible when he finally found a small open space bordering the stream and called it quits for the day. He guessed Newton and company to have at least a five mile lead, probably more. If not for the deep snow he would have caught up with them by now.

Nate let the horses drink a little, then went into the forest and searched for vegetation. He kicked the snow aside at various points, exposing the ground underneath, until he found an area overgrown with weeds and brown grass. Clearing off a ten-foot circle, he stood by and idly watched the animals eat. As he stood there his vision blurred for the second time.

Panicked, he barely breathed until once again everything became crystal clear. Why did it keep happening? he wondered. He was glad night would soon descend, giving his eyes relief from the shimmering snow cover.

A loud rumbling in his stomach reminded him of his own need for food. After all the wounds he'd sustained, he couldn't afford to go for long without eating. Yet if he waited for the horses to get their fill, it would be too dark for him to shoot accurately. Accordingly, he tied both animals to tree limbs bordering the cleared space and walked into the undergrowth to find game.

Only then did the difficulty of his task become apparent. The heavy snow had driven the majority of wild animals into their dens, burrows, or heavy brush. Few creatures other than birds were abroad. He walked hundreds of yards and saw only a few sparrows.

His stomach growled again. Nate halted beside a towering pine tree to scan the landscape. The sun had disappeared and already the amount of light had diminished by a third. To compound the situation, the air was rapidly becoming colder. He cradled the Kentucky in his elbows and began to make a loop back toward the horses. As he passed a thicket he registered movement out of the corner of his left eye and peered into the tangle of thin, barren branches to discover a white rabbit moving slowly out the far side.

Instantly Nate snapped the rifle to his shoulder,

cocked the hammer, and took a bead on his potential supper. He steadied his arms before squeezing the trigger. At the booming retort the rabbit flipped into the air and landed on its side, then thrashed about on the snow, staining the cover crimson, before it expired.

Elated, Nate barged through the thicket and scooped the mammal up. He couldn't wait to sink his teeth into a roasted piece of meat. Spinning, he hastened back to the horses. The darkness intensified more every minute. Verifying the animals were all right, he decided to let them continue grazing and went to the small clearing beside the stream. He bustled about gathering limbs and soon had a roaring fire going. The welcome warmth brought a smile to his lips.

Skinning and preparing the rabbit took less than five minutes. Next he erected a makeshift spit over the fire. After finding two forked branches, he imbedded the bottom end of each into the ground, one on either side of the flames. He used his knife to smooth down and sharpen a long, slender, straight branch and inserted the tip through several chunks of rabbit meat. Then, after suspending the straight piece between the forks, he squatted and watched in anticipation as the crackling fingers of red and orange licked at the meat.

The delicious aroma made his mouth water. He greedily licked his lips and turned the spit occasionally to prevent the meat from burning. All the while his stomach did its best to imitate an enraged grizzly bear. When finally satisfied that the meat had been roasted long enough, he deposited the Kentucky at his side and lifted the long branch.

His nose tingled and his lips quivered as he raised the meat to his mouth. The rabbit was hot to the touch, but he took a bite anyway. Slowly, savoring the taste, he chewed the mouthful and swallowed. He inadvertently looked into the fire, thinking to himself that he'd never eaten such flavorful rabbit, and unexpectedly his vision blurred for the third time.

Nate immediately closed his eyes and swung his head away from the bright flames. Both of his temples pounded painfully as he waited for the sensation to subside. Dear Lord! What would he do? He'd be at the complete mercy of the elements and any wild animal that came along without his sight. Not to mention poor Winona's certain fate if he failed to save her.

After a bit he tentatively cracked his eyelids and felt monumental relief at being able to see perfectly once again. Keeping his back to the fire, he proceeded to polish off the rest of the meat on the spit. It barely whetted his appetite. Accordingly, he slid several more chunks onto the sharpened branch and carefully aligned it on the forked limbs while keeping his gaze averted from the flames.

Feeling renewed, his insides wonderfully warm, Nate started to stretch when he heard a sound that turned his blood cold.

Both Lambert's horse and Barking Dog's stallion started neighing in terror.

Isaac Kennedy was furious, both at himself and his recently acquired business associate. He was mad at himself for going along with such a hare-brained, get-rich-quick scheme when he should have known better. And he was mad at Newton for a variety of reasons, not the least of which was the trapper's condescending attitude and demeaning remarks.

Back in Ohio, when Newton had first proposed the idea, the mountaineer had behaved like a proper gentleman. But after they journeyed to St. Louis and were joined by Lambert, Newton's attitude changed, becoming one of open sarcasm. Lambert had only aggravated the situated and fueled Newton's underlying contempt. Now Isaac knew that both men had despised him. They saw him as a blithering incompetent.

How dare they!

He was the one who had put up the capital for their venture. *He* was the one who had obtained the merchandise needed to conduct trade with the Utes. *He* was the one who had dropped everything and left the comfortable life to ensure their success.

The ungrateful sons of bitches.

As Kennedy sat on the east side of the fire contemplating the injustice done him, his gaze strayed to the lovely Shoshone woman off to his left. He'd never known an Indian woman before, never realized how truly beautiful they were. The mere sight of her stimulated him in a way he hadn't been stimulated in ages. He secretly watched her, his gaze lingering on her exquisite face. Every now and then he would look lower and frown.

Seated on the west side of the campfire, absently gnawing on jerked venison, Ike Newton was also staring at the Shoshone, only he did so openly and with malice etching his expression. "It appears you were right, squaw," he declared bitterly. "If Lambert was still alive, he'd have caught up with us by now. Which means your husband likely killed him."

Winona said nothing, her eyes fixed on the inky wall of vegetation bordering the clearing.

"Lambert was the best friend I ever had," Newton went on. "I'm not about to take this lying down." He touched the Hawken lying across his lap. "I aim to pay Grizzly Killer back."

"You would be wise to let me go and leave this country as fast as your legs will carry you," Winona said. "If you don't, my husband will hunt you down."

"Let him come, bitch."

Kennedy stiffened. "That's no way to talk to a lady."

"Lady?" Newton repeated, and chuckled. "Indian women are little better than whores, Isaac."

"They are not."

"What the hell do you know? Have you ever lived with a squaw?"

"No."

"Ever bedded one, even once?"

"Of course not."

"Then don't go getting on your high horse unless you've been in the saddle. I bet you don't know that trappers at the rendezvous can practically buy any Indian woman they want."

"What do you mean 'buy' them?"

Newton laughed. "You're a storekeeper. You're supposed to know all about buying and selling and stuff like that." He paused. "I'm telling you that trappers can buy Indian girls for a day, a month, hell, even a year if they want. A few yacks, like King, marry them."

"I don't believe you."

Leaning forward, Newton clenched his fists and glowered. "No man calls me a liar and gets away with it."

"I'm sorry. I didn't mean to say you weren't telling the truth."

"It sure sounded like that to me."

Kennedy deliberately refrained from meeting the trapper's stare. He glanced down at his right side where his rifle lay propped on his bedroll. "I've been meaning to ask you, Ike. Would you do me a favor?"

"What?" Newton responded in surprise.

"I still don't have the hang of loading my gun. Either I don't add enough powder or I forget to wrap a patch around the ball. Would you load it for me? If we run into hostile Indians I want to be prepared."

Newton muttered a sentence under his breath, only a few words of which were audible, something to the effect of "waste of manhood." Then he sighed and nodded. "Sure. I'll load your piece for you. Bring it here."

Grabbing his rifle, Kennedy rose and walked around behind Winona to hand the gun to his partner. "Sorry I'm so scatterbrained, Ike."

"We can't all be Daniel Boone," Newton said, referring to the Pennsylvania-born frontiersman who had died only eight years before yet whose exploits were already legendary. He stood and methodically commenced reloading the storekeeper's rifle using his own powder-horn and taking a ball from his own ammo-pouch.

Kennedy stood patiently to one side, observing. His eyes darted to the Shoshone woman twice. He clasped his hands at his waist and nervously twined and untwined his fingers.

"The trouble with you and most Easterners," Newton said as he worked, "is that none of you were ever taught how to fend for yourselves. You've grown so accustomed to buying whatever you need to live, you can't even provide the necessities. Why, if you ever found yourself stranded in the Rockies, you wouldn't last two days."

"I suppose not," Kennedy said, gnawing on his lower lip.

"It's not your fault," Newton said, removing the ramrod from the portly man's gun so he could shove the ball and patch down the barrel. "I blame your parents. Any father who doesn't teach his kids how to live off the land, find water and kill game, isn't much of a father in my book."

"You're absolutely right, Ike," Kennedy said, glancing to his left at the sizeable pile of broken branches he'd gathered earlier for use as firewood during the night.

"I doubt anyone in New York City even knows how to skin a deer," Newton rambled on while sliding the ramrod down the Kentucky. "At the rate things are going, in fifty years no one will be able to make do for themselves."

"Deplorable," Kennedy stated. He tentatively stepped toward the pile. "I think I'll add another limb to the fire."

"Just one," Newton advised. "If we use too many now, you'll have to go out in the middle of the night and collect more."

"I wouldn't want that to happen," Kennedy replied, and leaned down to select the stoutest branch he could find. Holding it in both hands, he stared at his partner's back and gave the branch a practice swing.

"Your rifle is loaded," Newton announced, replacing the ramrod. "Try not to blow your foot off."

"I won't," Kennedy said, sliding up behind the trapper and raising the branch on high. Then, ever so politely, he said, "Ike?"

"Yeah?" Newton responded, pivoting.

The storekeeper swung the branch with all his strength, putting his entire weight into it. His blow caught Newton squarely on the forehead and spun the man around. Newton fell where he stood, the Kentucky slipping from his limp fingers, his hair within inches of the flames.

Quickly Kennedy discarded the club and scooped up the Kentucky rifle. As fast as he was, though, the Shoshone almost beat him to the punch. The instant Newton fell, Winona made a move toward the Hawken lying near his feet. Kennedy swung the Kentucky toward her and shook his head. "Stop!"

She paused, her arm outstretched toward the rifle.

"The last thing in the world I want to do is hurt you," Kennedy told her, "but I will if you force me.

Until you prove that you can be trusted, I can't let you get your hands on a weapon."

Winona frowned, her gaze lingering on her husband's gun.

Not taking a chance, Kennedy kicked the Hawken aside. "All right. I want you to get the horses ready. We're moving out."

"You want to travel at night?"

"Yes. I plan to deliver the merchandise to Two Owls myself, and the sooner we get going, the sooner we'll reach his village. Once I have the beaver furs he promised, I can head back to the States a rich man."

"Why take me along? You can do it yourself."

"I'm afraid not. I need someone who can interpret for me."

"But I don't speak the Ute tongue."

"Newton told me all about Indian sign language. So get cracking with the horses."

Straightening, Winona gazed westward. "You are taking a great risk. Two Owls agreed to trade with Newton and Lambert, not you. He might take your crates and have you scalped. And it is certain the Utes will never let me leave their village."

"You let me worry about Two Owls," Kennedy said. "Don't fret yourself about the Utes keeping you hostage, either. I have a plan that will keep you out of their clutches."

"And then what? Will you take me back to my husband?"

Kennedy hesitated before answering. The corners of his mouth tilted upward when he spoke. "You have my word that once we're done with the Utes, I'll take you back."

Ike Newton unexpectedly groaned.

"What about him?" Winona asked.

"What indeed?" Kennedy rejoined. He stepped to the Hawken, tucked the Kentucky under his left arm, and bent over to retrieve the shorter rifle. Cocking the hammer, he moved to the trapper's side and pointed the barrel at Newton's head.

"You would shoot a man who can't defend himself?" Winona inquired.

Kennedy had never killed anyone in his life. But he thought of the thirty thousand dollars he stood to gain and the bonus besides if he played his cards right, and he had no trouble at all pulling the trigger. The recoil made the Hawken jerk in his hands. He looked down through the gunsmoke and grimaced at the mess the ball had made of Newton's face.

Winona was silent, her expression grim.

"Put this rifle on one of the pack animals," Kennedy directed, and tossed the Hawken to her. She caught it and walked toward the tethered string.

Far in the distance a wolf howled.

Grinning, Kennedy gazed up at the stars and inhaled the crisp air. Instead of feeling remorse over killing Newton, he felt invigorated. So this was what it felt like to stand on one's own feet! For perhaps the first time in his life he'd taken his destiny into his own hands and he felt marvelous. Glancing at Winona, who was moving among the pack animals, he hefted the Kentucky and chuckled. Ike had been right all along.

Fending for one's self was the only way to live.

Chapter Fourteen

Nate raced through the gloomy forest toward the horses, the rifle in his right hand. Both animals were still whinnying in fright. He had ten yards to cover when a feral snarl reached his ears. Increasing his pace, he crashed through the brush and burst from the woods into the clearing.

Both horses were trying to pull free, their great hooves stamping the ground, their ears pricked and their eyes wide.

The source of their fear was crouched on the east side of the open space. A large lynx, a cat not half the size of a mountain lion but equally savage if cornered, hissed at Nate the second he appeared, then wheeled and bounded into the undergrowth.

Nate let it go. He watched the thickly furred body and stubby tail disappear in the darkness before going to the horses to calm them. Since it would be virtually impossible for a lynx to bring down a full grown horse, he assumed the cat had merely been curious. From accounts related by other trappers, he knew that lynxes typically subsisted on birds, rodents, and the remains of dead deer or moose. Occasionally they would bring down a starving or sickly deer, but for the most part the larger mammals were beyond their capability to subdue.

He calmed both horses and led them back to the campfire. Halfway there he stopped short at the faint sound of a shot coming from much farther up the valley. He cocked his head, waiting for a second retort, but heard none.

Logic dictated that Newton or Kennedy must be responsible. Why had they fired? He doubted they were hunting game so late. Could they possibly mean the shot as a signal for Lambert? If so, they were doomed to be terribly disappointed.

He secured both animals and sat down to finish eating the rabbit. The chunks he'd placed on the spit were quite well cooked. He dug into them relishing the meal, and only when the last edible portion of the rabbit was sliding down his throat did he lean back, smack his lips, and wipe his greasy hands on his buckskins. For good measure he belched.

Nate was careful not to stare at the fire, even indirectly. His eyes seemed to have recovered. Now all he needed was a good night's rest and he'd be after those bastards in the morning.

He reluctantly rose and gathered spare wood to be used before dawn. After accumulating a sufficient quantity, he scooped out the snow down to the ground within a foot of the flames. Taking the blanket Lambert had carried in a roll tied behind his saddle, he spread it in the hole, then settled down on his back and nestled the rifle against his right side.

Nate closed his eyes and listened to the crackling of the fire and the whispering of the wind. As fatigued as he was, he expected to fall sound asleep within minutes. But this wasn't the case. His mind raced of its own volition, reviewing the incident at the cabin and the subsequent events with startling clarity.

He rolled onto his side, thinking the change of position would enable him to finally doze off. Try as he might, though, he couldn't get the image of Winona in Newton's clutches out of his mind. Surely even a scoundrel like Newton wouldn't lay a finger on a pregnant woman, he assured himself. But the assurance rang false.

Opening his eyes, he gazed up at the stars. Deep down he blamed himself for Winona's predicament. Had he been more vigilant back at the cabin, had he not accepted Kennedy with open arms and thus allowed himself to be distracted, she wouldn't be in their hands.

He'd completely forgotten two rules of thumb passed on by his mentor, Shakespeare McNair. As one who had spent the greater portion of his life in the wilderness, Shakespeare knew best how to survive. The old mountaineer was a veritable fount of wisdom, and Shakespeare had said, quite somberly, "Out here a man can't afford to let his guard down for a minute. If you want to last, you must amend the golden rule a mite. Love your enemies, but always remember to keep your gun loaded."

Truer words had never been spoken, Nate reflected. Of course, sometimes the mountain man made no sense whatsoever, such as the time Shakespeare had said, "If a man hasn't made any enemies by the time he's thirty-five, then he can pretty much chalk up his life as a failure." What the hell was *that* supposed to mean?

He rolled over on his other side and shifted his weight. The idea of not even bothering to sleep occurred to him. If he saddled up right away, he might overtake Winona by morning. But he's also likely to be so tuckered out that he wouldn't be worth a hoot against Newton. The trapper was bound to be a tough customer in a pinch. Kennedy, on the other hand, didn't worry him in the least. If ever a totally harmless specimen of manhood had been born, the portly storekeeper was the one.

Gradually his mind wound down. He roused himself once to feed more branches to the fire and check on the horses, then he settled back down and, in no time flat, he was snoring away. Even in sleep, though, his anxiety made itself known. He dreamed a horrifying dream in which his beloved wife was ravaged repeatedly by a smirking Ike Newton and—surprise of all surprises—an equally lewd Isaac Kennedy. Several times he called out her name and was awakened by his own shout.

Toward morning he broke out in a sweat and woke up with a violent case of the shivers. Feeding the flames, he moved closer and let the warmth seep into his pores. Drowsiness descended again and he dozed off, fitfully stirring every now and then to glance around.

Another dream terrified him beyond belief. In it, he saw Winona tied to a burning stake while prancing Utes whooped in delight around her. Gratefully, his mind then sank into an inky realm devoid of thoughts and dreams and he slumbered quietly, oblivious to the world around him.

The neighing of the horses awoke Nate with a start and he sat up to see the sun already above the eastern horizon. Furious at himself for oversleeping, he glanced toward the trees where the animals were tied and felt the short hairs at the nape of his neck tingle.

Standing twenty feet away, its eyes fixed balefully on the mounts, was an enormous grizzly.

Nate leaped to his feet, the Kentucky in his hands. No matter how many times he saw the brutes or tangled with them, he still couldn't get over their immense size and power.

The lords of the Rockies were awe-inspiring beasts. Standing four and a half feet high at the front shoulders when on all fours, their bulk was accented by the prominent bulge between their shoulder blades. With a length of over seven feet, grizzly bears were the undisputed masters of their domain. Not even the formidable wolverine could match a grizzly in combat. Whites and Indians alike feared them and gave them a wide berth whenever possible.

Now, as the grizzly swung its massive head to stare at Nate, his previous encounters with the fierce beasts flashed before him. The first time was when he was en route to the Rockies with his Uncle Zeke. At the Republican River a grizzly had charged him, and only by the grace of God had he survived. Weeks later, on the way to the rendezvous, another one had attacked him. Finally, while trapping beaver with Shakespeare, a third grizzly had charged him with the combined ferocity of all three.

He curled his thumb around the hammer and hoped this time would be different. Shakespeare had advised him to always stand completely still when confronted by a grizzly. Any movement might draw the mighty beast closer, and running was an engraved invitation to attack. So he stood his ground and waited for the bear to make the next move.

Nate knew that many mountaineers believed that no wild animal, no matter how savage, would dare attack the face of man. That was why most trappers, when charged by a grizzly, stood and faced the onrushing bruin with their gun at the ready. Nine times out of ten the tactic worked, the charging grizzly halting within yards of the human, only to wheel and race off. But there was always that tenth time when the grizzly didn't stop, and then the bear made short work of the trapper even if wounded first.

But Nate held little stock in this theory.

None other than Meriweather Lewis, of Lewis and Clark fame, had described the grizzly bear as extremely hard to die and the most fierce of all the wild creatures in existence. In *THE HISTORY OF THE EXPEDITION OF CAPTAINS LEWIS AND CLARK*, published in 1814, numerous spine-tingling encounters with grizzly bears were related.

The grizzly watching Nate suddenly advanced straight toward him. He held his breath, bracing for an attack, wondering if he might be able to reach the forest and clamber up a tree before being mauled to death.

Grunting, the bear halted. It cocked its head and regarded the buckskin-clad figure intently, as if trying to determine whether the man was edible.

For his part, Nate suppressed the stark terror that threatened to engulf him. He could see the bear's sides heaving as it breathed, see the brute's nose flaring as it sniffed the air for his scent. His mouth went dry and he nearly bolted.

The grizzly bear glanced at the horses for a moment, then nonchalantly turned and went into the woods, making little noise despite its bulk. Seconds later the shaggy beast was swallowed up by the forest.

Nate waited, scanning the perimeter of the clearing, dreading that the bear would circle around and come at him from another direction. After a minute he realized the grizzly had indeed departed and exhaled, only then realizing he had been holding his breath.

He walked to the horses and comforted them. Since the sun had already risen, he opted to forego breakfast and instead saddled Lambert's horse. He put out the fire by dumping a mound of snow on the flickering embers, took a long draught of ice-cold water from the stream, and mounted up.

Eager to reach Winona, Nate pushed the horses

hard, sticking to the tell-tale trail made by her abductors and their animals. His body still ached and his head still hurt, but the pain had diminished considerably. Of more concern was the bright snow. He didn't want a repeat of yesterday so he avoided staring directly at the shimmering cover when possible. By constantly looking down at the horse, then only briefly surveying the terrain ahead, he found that the glare didn't bother his eyes nearly as much as before.

He had to estimate the miles he covered. Two. Three. Five. There was still no sign of where Newton and company had camped for the night.

And then he saw the buzzards.

There were seven of the big black birds in all, swinging in wide, lazy circles hundreds of feet above the ground perhaps a quarter of a mile to the west. Their wings outspread, they soared on the uplifting air currents, their attention focused on something below.

Puzzled and not a little anxious, Nate urged his mount to go faster through the deep snow while hauling on the lead to pull the Indian stallion along. When at last he glimpsed a clearing, he slowed and held the Kentucky ready to fire. There were buzzards near the center, four of five of them clustered around a body lying in the snow.

What if it was Winona?

The unthinkable spurred Nate to lash his horse into a gallop. He burst from the trees in a spray of snow. Immediately the buzzards took to the air, noisily flapping their powerful wings, gaining altitude rapidly. He rode over to the corpse and reined up, elated to discover it was a man lying there, not a woman. Sliding down, he crouched and inspected the body.

Logic told Nate the dead man must be Ike Newton. The figure was the same size and wearing the same clothes the rogue mountaineer had worn when last Nate saw him. But identifying the man by his facial features was out of the question, simply because the face no longer existed. Judging from the powder burns on the shreds of forehead and chin remaining, the scoundrel had been shot in the face at a range of less than an inch. Then the buzzards had feasted on the exposed portions of Newton's body, pecking away at the fingers and consuming both eyes, the nose, and the soft areas of the mouth and cheeks. Between the ball and the birds there wasn't anything left but a few pieces of pinkish flesh and exposed bone.

The sight made Nate feel queasy. He stood and stepped away to catch his breath, glad that another foe had fallen but at a loss to explain the reason. Obviously the single shot he'd heard the night before had been the one that killed Newton. But who pulled the trigger? Isaac Kennedy? He grinned at the ludicrous notion. The storekeeper couldn't harm a fly, let alone kill in cold blood.

But if Kennedy hadn't committed the deed, then who? Certainly not Winona. Had she succeeded in slaying Newton, she would have headed in haste toward the cabin and he would have met her on the trail. Could it have been Indians, then? If so, the Utes were the likeliest candidates. And if his supposition was correct, it meant the Utes now had his wife and Kennedy and were taking them to a village.

He scanned the clearing, seeking signs of the Indians. If the Utes did attack the camp, there were bound to be plenty of tracks to confirm it. He saw where the string of horses had been tethered and the footprints of Newton, Kennedy, and Winona in the snow, but no others. Confused, he looked at the line of trees beyond where the pack animals had been tied and saw a sight that made him stiffen and his mouth go slack in utter bewilderment.

Chapter Fifteen

Isaac Kennedy was ready to keel over. He'd never felt so tired in all his life. It took tremendous effort to stay upright in the saddle, the Kentucky cradled in his right arm, and his eyes on the Shoshone woman riding a few feet in front of him. He yawned and glanced over his shoulder at the pack of horses he was leading, watching them plod wearily along.

Perhaps he'd made a mistake in traveling at night. Not only didn't they find Two Owls' village, but now all of them, including the animals, were exhausted. Having to contend with the cold and forging through the deep snow had taken a heavy toll.

They were nearing a point where the valley temporarily narrowed, with high hills to both the right and left. On their right the stream bubbled and gurgled over a stretch of rocks.

"Winona," Kennedy said.

She responded without looking at him. "Yes?"

"I figure we should take a break. What do you think?"

"You have the gun."

Kennedy hefted the rifle, his forehead creasing. "So? What are you trying to say?"

"You have the gun," Winona reiterated. "The decision is yours."

"But I want your opinion. What do you think we should do?"

"I think you should go back to the white man's land as fast as your horse will carry you. And I think you should let me go to find my husband."

"I'm not giving up now, not when I'm so close." Kennedy declared. "As far as your husband is concerned, you'll see him after we conclude our business with Two Owls."

"What business is that?"

"You'll know soon enough."

They rode on in a strained silence. Kennedy wished there was something he could say to dispel her resentment toward him. He sensed she despised his very presence. But her attitude would change once he took her back to the States. Once she became dependent on him for her well being and grew to appreciate the value of a dollar, she'd change her tune. Or, in this case, thirty thousand dollars. The thought made him chuckle.

Kennedy gazed to the south and saw several elk moving in the trees. He toyed with the notion of trying to shoot one, but since Winona would undoubtedly take off the second he squeezed the trigger and he would no longer have a loaded gun to keep her in line, he refrained. Besides, he knew he was a lousy shot and might well waste the ball.

Sighing, Kennedy let his eyes rove over the hills. To his joy, on the hill to the north, in a clearing halfway

up, were seven mounted Indians who were watching
Winona and him intently. Grinning, he reined up and
waved.

The warriors simply stared.

"Winona," Kennedy said excitedly. "Look! Utes!"

She halted, turning her horse sideways. Gazing in
the direction he was, she saw the seven men, her grip
on her reins tightening. "We are in trouble."

"Why? Two Owls' warriors won't hurt us."

"Those men are not Utes."

"Which tribe are they from?" Kennedy inquired,
amused by her nervousness. He felt confident he
could talk his way out of any difficulty. If not, he
could scare the seven off with a shot; surely the
Indians weren't about to go up against a white man
armed with a rifle since none of the band carried a
gun.

"Those are Arapahos," Winona disclosed. "They
live on the plains east of the mountains."

"What are they doing here?"

"Either they are hunting or on a raid," Winona
speculated. "The Utes and the Arapahos fight all the
time. We must take cover right away."

"And let them think we're afraid? Nonsense,"
Kennedy stated emphatically.

The seven warriors rode into the woods bordering
the clearing, heading toward the valley floor.

Winona looked at the storekeeper, her expression
grave. "Listen to me. We must run and find somewhere we can defend ourselves or soon you will lose
your hair and I will be on my way to an Arapaho
village."

The earnest appeal impressed Kennedy. She rarely
displayed any emotion, yet here she was genuinely
frightened. Undoubtedly she didn't fully appreciate
the change that had taken place inside him. Now that
he could stand on his own feet, now that he had
proven his manhood by slaying Ike Newton, he could

protect her from anyone and anything. Still, to humor her, he nodded and said, "All right. Lead the
way."

She expertly spun her horse and took off into the
woods to the south, her hair flying, her robe flapping.

Tugging on the pack string lead, Kennedy followed.
He was afraid she might try to pull far ahead and lose
him. A check back failed to disclose the exact where-
abouts of the seven warriors. They could be anywhere, approaching from any direction. He goaded
his mount to go faster.

Winona made for the base of the southern hill.
When she reached it, she turned to the left.

"Hold up!" Kennedy commanded, stopping.
"You're going the wrong way. We want to go west, not
east."

Halting abruptly, Winona swung toward him, her
annoyance obvious. "If we go west the Arapahos will
catch us easily."

"West is where Two Owls' village lies," Kennedy
noted. "Are you trying to pull the wool over my eyes?
Going east will only take us back toward your cabin."
He jabbed a finger westward. "We go that way. Head
out."

Hesitating, Winona gazed in the direction she
wanted to go, then toward the hill the Arapahos were
descending.

"I won't take no for an answer," Kennedy warned
her, hefting the Kentucky rifle.

"You are a fool," Winona snapped, and reined her
horse around. She rode past him without another
glance, staying close to the slope.

Chuckling to himself, Kennedy trailed her. His
newfound resolve amazed even him. To think that he
had wasted so many years being a mouse when deep
down he was a veritable tiger. For the very first time
in his life he felt in control; he was the master of his
own destiny instead of the slave of circumstances.

They rode for almost ten minutes without mishap, leaving both hills behind. All around them the forest lay deathly still. Even the birds had ceased to chirp.

Kennedy noticed the lack of wildlife and the quiet but attached no special significance to either. He noticed Winona constantly scanning the woods and grinned at her anxiety. As he had expected, those Arapahos hadn't given chase. He recalled all the gory tales Newton and Lambert had told him about Indians in general and was astonished at how gullible he'd been. Those illiterate trappers had exaggerated their stories, embellishing the yarns with outlandish claims of rampant Indian savagery. Well, now he knew better. Now he knew that he didn't have anything to be worried about so long as he kept his wits about him and didn't give in to mindless fear.

They passed through a stand of saplings, crossed a clearing, and entered a tract of tall pines.

Kennedy let his eyes dwell on the Shoshone's back. He tried to imagine her naked and tingled at the thought of lying abed with her. How unfortunate that she was heavy with child. He'd have to wait until after she delivered before he could—

Something streaked out of the vegetation on the right and thudded into the storekeeper's right calf.

Startled, lanced with pain, Kennedy glanced down and was stunned to behold the feathered end of an arrow jutting from his leg. Suddenly his horse whinnied and tried to buck him. He realized the arrow point and several inches of the thin shaft were imbedded in the animal's flesh. Clasping the reins firmly, he brought the horse under control. Only then did he look up and see Winona riding as fast as she could away from him.

"Wait!" Kennedy cried, and goaded his horse onward, retaining his grip on the string lead. The pain, surprisingly, subsided, although blood poured from the wound. He functioned mechanically, his mind unable to come to terms with the reality of being shot with an arrow. Glancing over his shoulder, he saw no sign of the war party.

With his right leg pinned to his mount's side, riding was awkward. Kennedy tried to wrench his leg loose, but couldn't. He heard a swishing sound and felt a sharp twinge in his lower left side. Peering down, he discovered the bloody tip of an arrow protruding from his abdomen.

He'd been hit again! Shot in the back, no less!

Kennedy rode harder. He didn't understand why there wasn't more pain. He'd never liked pain much and trembled at the idea of suffering intense agony. Skirting a pine, he tugged on the rope lead, listening to the muffled drumming of the many hooves to his rear. If he released the rope he could ride as fast as Winona. But doing so meant abandoning the pack animals, meant leaving the crates for the Arapahos. And he'd rather die than give up the merchandise that would bring him thirty thousand dollars or more.

A hammer seemed to strike him between the shoulder blades and his body was knocked forward over the saddle by the impact. Straightening, an odd burning sensation in his chest, Kennedy gasped at finding another crimson coated arrow tip and two inches of wooden shaft sticking from his torso.

They were skewering him at will!

He twisted, extended the Kentucky backwards, and, using just his right hand, fired. The shot had two consequences that took him unawares. First the recoil wrenched the rifle from his grip and it fell into the snow. Then the lead pack animals, frightened by the blast, the spurt of flame, and the cloud of gunpowder, went into a panicked frenzy, pulling at the lead rope in an effort to break free.

Kennedy lost his hold on the lead. He went ten more yards before he could bring the horse to a stop.

If he could retrieve the rifle, he still stood a chance. Starting to wheel his mount, he experienced a searing spasm in his left shoulder. Don't look! his mind screamed. It's just another arrow.

He brought the horse around and saw the pack animals merely standing there eight feet away, docile now. But where was the rifle? Retracing his steps, he spied the rifle stock poking out of the snow. All he had to do was reach it and he'd be fine. Dizziness hit him then, causing him to sway, and he thought for a second that he might pass out. A forceful blow hit him in the chest, then another, rocking him backwards. His vision cleared and he gaped in horror at two more arrows stuck in him.

No! This couldn't be happening!

His arms went weak and limp. A heartbeat later his legs did the same. Before he could straighten up, he fell to the right, toppling into the snow and tearing his impaled leg from the horse in the bargain. He crashed onto his right shoulder, the snow cushioning his descent.

Kennedy blinked and tried to rise. His body refused to cooperate. It occurred to him that he might be dying. Strangely, he felt no fear.

A shadow fell across him. Then another. Straining, he twisted his neck and saw a pair of buckskin clad Indians regarding him coldly. Others appeared beside them and they conversed in soft tones.

Kennedy groaned when one of the warriors stepped up and flipped him onto his back. He tried to speak, to tell them he was friendly, that he meant no harm, but his lips barely moved.

The Arapaho who had flipped him over drew a large knife from a beaded sheath on his left hip and squatted.

They were fixing to scalp him! Kennedy knew it and he braced himself for the ordeal. To his bewilderment, the warrior lowered the knife below his chin, not toward the top of his head. A peculiar stinging in his neck made him flinch. On its heels came the oddest feeling of all, as if warm water was spraying onto his throat.

The warrior raised the knife into view. Blood dripped from the keen blade.

Kennedy's pulse pounded in his temples. That was *his* blood! The savage had slit his throat. Tears filled his eyes and he could barely see the Indians move over to the pack animals. A crate smashed to the ground.

Loud, excited whoops burst from the warriors.

Tears poured down Kennedy's cheeks. The bastards had found the rifles! Now he would never be able to trade with Two Owls for all the beaver hides the Utes had caught during the past year. Now he would never reap the profit of his trip west. All that trouble, all that work, and for nothing. He should have stuck to storekeeping and told Ike Newton to go jump in a lake.

He took some small comfort from knowing Winona had eluded the war party. Hopefully, she would make it safely back to her husband. If anyone could protect her, it would be that fellow Grizzly Killer.

Another shadow hovered over him.

Kennedy peered upward. There stood the Indian who had slit his throat. He wanted to rise, to flail away, but could do nothing except watch in fascination as the warrior now produced a tomahawk. The Arapaho grinned at him, waved the tomahawk in the air, then raised it up high.

A pervailing calm had seeped into every fiber of Isaac Kennedy's being. With incredible clarity he observed the gleaming tomahawk streak straight at his face. There was a second of fleeting pain and one eye seemed to be sliding to the right while the other slid to the left. Then everything faded to black.

Chapter Sixteen

Nate ran to the trees and halted in front of a pine, not quite able to believe his eyes. There, propped against the trunk, was his Hawken. He scooped the rifle up, afraid it had been damaged somehow and that was the reason it had been left behind. To his amazement, the rifle was in perfect working order, the stock, barrel, and trigger mechanism intact. Confused, he walked to the horses.

None of this made any sense. Had Utes been responsible for slaying Ike Newton and taking Winona and the storekeeper, they would surely have taken the Hawken as well. Even if Indians weren't to blame—which he thought unlikely—no one in their right mind would ride off and leave an excellent Hawken rifle in the middle of nowhere.

No, it was as if someone had deliberately left the

Hawken there for him to find. But who? Certainly not Newton, who lay there dead. Kennedy, perhaps. The storekeeper had seemed to be the sort who would help others in need. Or could his wife have done it? Not very likely. He couldn't see any of the scoundrels letting her get her hands on a gun.

Not about to look a gift horse in the mouth, Nate reloaded his prized rifle, then slid the Kentucky into a scabbard on Lambert's horse. With two rifles, the flintlock, his tomahawk and knife at his disposal, he felt ready to take on the entire Ute nation, if need be, to rescue Winona.

Nate mounted and resumed his search. He gazed skyward and saw the buzzards still circling. The big birds would make short work of Ike Newton's remains. Between them and the varmints, in a day or two all that remained of Newton would be bleached bones.

He stayed with the tracks, pushing the horses, eager to close the gap. Then, from far ahead, came the distinct crack of a single shot. He reined in, listening, waiting for more. When none sounded, he lashed his mount into a gallop. So far luck had been on his side. As far as he knew, Winona was still alive. But the longer he took to reach her, the greater the likelihood he would find her dead.

Winona raced for a quarter of a mile before she saw signs of pursuit. Two Arapahos on sturdy, fleet horses were hot on her trail. They spied her and whooped in delight.

She grit her teeth and fled ever westward, desperately seeking a means of outsmarting the duo and escaping. The mantle of snow would thwart any attempt she made to conceal her tracks. Unless she could outrun them, a slim chance given that her horse was fatigued already, she would fall into their clutches.

In one respect she was grateful. Had the war party been composed of Kiowas or Comanches, her life would be in immediate danger; both frequently killed female captives. Arapahos, on the other hand, weren't quite as bloodthirsty and often adopted females taken in raids into their tribes. Not that living as a prisoner of the Arapahos was in itself appealing.

She wanted her Nate, wanted to see his handsome face again and hold his powerful body in her arms. He must be out of his mind with worry for her and it was all her fault. She should have checked out the window before heading outside to feed the horses. At the very least she should have taken a flintlock. If she'd had a pistol in her hand when she opened the door and saw that man pointing a rifle at her, she could have tried to shoot him. Even if she'd failed, the delay would have given Nate time to bring his weapons to bear.

Yes, she had failed her husband and she felt mightily shamed by it. Shoshone women prided themselves on being good wives. A woman who couldn't keep her lodge clean and tidy, or couldn't cook or sew or prepare hides, or who failed to anticipate her husband's needs and give him the support he needed, was regarded as a failure in Shoshone society. She would be cast out by the other women and refused membership into the various womens' societies devoted to excellence in those arts and crafts so crucial to the happiness and welfare of any family. And although Shoshone women seldom went on raids, they were expected to aid in the defense of the village and to be there when their husbands needed them.

Nate had told her conditions were quite different among the whites. Many white women no longer bothered with those responsibilities that were common expressions of a Shoshone woman's love for her family, the cleaning and washing and sewing. They hired other women to do those chores and devoted themselves to sitting around and chatting or buying new clothes or taking strolls to get 'fresh air'. She couldn't conceive of any woman spending time in such a frivolous fashion, but then the ways of the whites often mystified her. As a race they had lost touch with the Great Medicine and were no longer guided by the spirit in all things. They were too interested in things going on outside them and not enough in their inner being.

She looked back to discover the Arapahos had gained hundreds of yards. Both men were grinning. To them catching an unarmed woman constituted a pleasant game. She wished she had a gun, or a bow or a knife. She would teach them that Shoshone women were not to be taken lightly.

The chase took them over a rise and ever farther into the valley. Deer took flight at their approach. A hawk observed the proceeding from far overhead. Rabbits bounded into the brush.

Winona's horse began to flag. She felt equally weary. Since her abduction she had been unable to catch more than snatches of sleep. Her appetite had diminished, and in her condition she needed to eat for two. Traveling all night had further weakened her. But she refused to give up. She would resist the Arapahos until she collapsed from fatigue.

Suddenly nature itself conspired against her. In front of her loomed a steep hillock slick with snow. If she tried to go around she would lose much ground so she went straight up. Her horse managed to go a dozen feet before its hooves started slipping and sliding.

Winona felt the animal going down. Fearful of the consequences to the baby should the horse roll over her, she threw herself to the right onto her shoulder. The heavy buffalo robe absorbed the brunt of the plunge and she rolled upright. Her horse was on its side, sliding down to the bottom of the hillock, plowing a wide path through the snow.

She forged through the clinging white blanket and reached the animal as it went to stand. Speaking softly, she grabbed the bridle and tried to soothe its jangled nerves. Brittle laughter brought her around to confront its source.

Thirty feet out, riding slowly, were the two Arapahos. They joked and laughed, pointing at her horse and the slope.

Winona went to swing on her mount, but a sharp pain in her belly made her double over and gasp. She must be careful or she would hurt the baby. The possibility of losing the child filled her with dread. Struggling to keep her composure, she straightened and faced the Arapahos.

Both were rugged examples of their tribe, hardened by a life that brooked no flabbiness or laziness. They wore buckskins styled in the manner of their people. One wore his hair long and flowing, the other wore his braided. They both carried bows and sported full quivers on their backs.

Grinning, the warriors rode closer and halted. The man with the braided hair addressed her in his own tongue.

Winona stood impassively. She knew few words in the Arapaho language and refused to respond in sign. Then she received a shock.

"What is a Shoshone woman doing so far from her tribe?" the braided one asked in perfect Shoshone.

Instead of answering, Winona rejoined sarcastically, "Where did an Arapaho dog learn to speak the language of those who are his betters?"

The warrior laughed uproariously. He translated for the other man and they both regarded her with commingled amusement and respect.

"I am He Wolf," the braided warrior announced. "I

once had a Shoshone wife for several winters after I took her in a raid. She taught me your tongue, but otherwise she was useless. She could not cook and her feet were cold at night. I traded her for three horses." He pointed at his companion. "This is Swift Wind In The Morning. How are you called?"

"Winona."

"And what were you doing with that fat white man?"

"He stole me from my lodge, which is only a few sleeps from here. Soon my husband will come to take me back."

He Wolf translated again. Swift Wind In The Morning shifted and began to scan the surrounding woods carefully.

"You lie, woman," He Wolf declared. "There are no Shoshone lodges in this part of the mountains."

Winona allowed herself the luxury of a smirk. "I did not say it was a Shoshone lodge. My husband is a white man and we live in a house of wood. He is as strong as three men and does not know the meaning of fear. You would be wise to let me go to him before he finds you and feeds you to the buzzard and bear."

"How is this great warrior called?" He Wolf inquired sarcastically.

"He is known as Grizzly Killer."

He Wolf's eyes narrowed. "I have heard of such a white from our brothers, the Cheyennes. They say this man killed a grizzly using just a knife."

"He has killed three grizzlies," Winona boasted proudly, "and ten times that many enemies. Soon he will add your hair to the list."

After mulling her words for a bit, He Wolf turned to Swift Wind In The Morning and the two conversed in their own language. Finally He Wolf stared at her again.

"We are taking you with us. Get on your horse."

"You will not live to regret this," Winona assured him.

"There are seven of us on this raid. We are more than a match for any ten white men, let alone one," He Wolf asserted, and jerked his thumb at her animal. "Now climb on your horse."

Since there was no other choice, Winona complied, her buffalo robe falling open as she did. The pain in her abdomen had abated and she felt well enough to ride.

He Wolf leaned forward, studying her figure as she settled on the animal. "You are with child," he stated in surprise. "How many moons until the baby will be born?"

"Three."

"This is bad news," He Wolf said. "We do not want a half-breed in our village."

"My son will be a great man like his father. He will honor any tribe who befriends him."

"How do you know it is a boy?"

"I know."

Grunting, He Wolf motioned for her to precede them.

Despite Winona's display of courage and her confidence in Nate, she was extremely worried. The Arapaho warrior had a point. They were seven; Nate but one. The odds were overwhelmingly in their favor. She must find a way to aid her husband. Outsmarting those two wicked trappers and the lecher Kennedy had been relatively easy; she'd been able to hide Nate's knife and tomahawk under their bed without being detected, and later had left the Hawken propped against a tree for Nate instead of putting it on the pack animals as Kennedy had ordered. But tricking the Arapahos would not be so easy. They were naturally more alert than the white men had been, and one of them was bound to be watching every move she made. Still, as Nate's partner for life she couldn't sit idly by and do nothing. A good wife always stood by her husband's side no matter the odds.

They rode back to the pack animals.

Winona saw Isaac Kennedy lying dead in crimson stained snow, his face split wide open. The five other warriors were laughing and joking, standing near a crate that had broken apart, each man holding in his hands one of the items that had been packed inside.

Rifles!

Startled, Winona gazed at the other crates. From the comments the trappers and Kennedy had made, she now understood everything. When Newton and Lambert had been captured by Two Owls a year ago, they must have promised to bring the Ute chief guns in exchange for their lives. No doubt they had offered to trade the firearms for prime beaver pelts and other furs. But now dozens of top quality rifles were in the possession of the Arapahos, who would not hesitate to use them against other tribes and whites alike if need be.

She knew that rifles were formidable weapons. The more powerful guns could shoot farther than bows and in the hands of skilled shooters, such as Nate, they were amazingly accurate and reliable. Already she knew of instances where badly outnumbered trappers had held off determined attacking warriors using the lethal firepower of their rifles.

Most of the guns owned by Indians were inferior to those employed by the whites. Fusees, those cheap trade rifles frequently bestowed on unsuspecting warriors, had neither the range nor the accuracy of Kentucky rifles and Hawkens. Consequently, the possession of guns had not made any difference so far in deciding the outcome of the many raids and encounters between various tribes. But all that could change, she realized. If the Arapahos learned to use the rifles in those crates, they might well be able to conquer all their foes and become the dominant tribe west of the Great River.

The warriors prepared to depart. He Wolf and Swift Wind In The Morning also claimed rifles, and the rest from the broken crate were tied in a bundle on a pack horse. As the men worked they glanced repeatedly at the surrounding forest.

Winona knew they were looking for Utes. The shot fired earlier would attract any Ute warriors in the vicinity. And since this was Ute territory, the Arapahos could find themselves overwhelmed by the fierce mountain dwellers.

Soon they were on their way, bearing to the northeast. They crossed the stream and made for the hills bordering the valley. Forced to ride between He Wolf and Swift Wind in the Morning, Winona resigned herself to going along with them for the time being. She only hoped she could escape before Nate overtook the band or there would be much blood spilled —and some of it might be his.

Chapter Seventeen

Nate sat astride Lambert's horse and stared down at the grisly remains of Isaac Kennedy. Jagged flesh and a portion of the cranium had been exposed by a tomahawk blow to the head. Congealed blood coated the man's chin and neck. The buzzards had yet to discover the body and none of the carrion eaters had touched it. He felt a twinge of regret that the kindly storekeeper had been killed. The man should never have ventured into the Rocky Mountains. Kennedy had been as out of place in the wilderness as he would be now back in the city.

Turning the horse, Nate examined the snow, discovering the tracks of many Indians, as well as those of the pack animals, and the trail they'd made heading to the northeast. As near as he could tell, Kennedy and Winona had been alone when they were ambushed by warriors. He saw where a single horse had ridden on west at great speed, and then three horses had returned. By the depth of the hooves he knew all three carried riders and surmised one of them had been his darling wife. He wasn't skilled enough to tell if the footprints scattered about had been made by Utes or warriors from another tribe, but the direction of travel hinted that he wasn't dealing with Two Owls' people.

He squared his broad shoulders and rode out, squinting up at the sun. If he pushed himself he might overtake the band by nightfall. He estimated there were at least a half-dozen warriors in the war party, enough to give any sane man pause. But short of death, he wasn't about to stop.

The gleaming snow bothered his eyes again, compelling him to avert his gaze from the brilliant crust as much as possible. He was hungry and thirsty but ignored both sensations. There would be time to eat *after* Winona was safe in his arms, not before.

The trail brought him to the hills on the north side of the valley. The band had skirted the base of one, passed between it and the next hill, then turned to the east, staying in a narrow tract between the hills and a high range of mountains rearing up to the clouds.

He became convinced that the band didn't consist of Utes. Whoever these warriors were, they were trying to keep out of sight by taking the route between the foothills and the mountains, a tactic only warriors belonging to a tribe at war with the Utes would use. He mentally ticked off a list of likely candidates. There were the feared Blackfeet, the Bloods, the Crows, the Cheyennes, the Arapahos, or possibly the Kiowas or Comanches. He wouldn't know until he saw them, and even then he might not be able to identify the band because he hadn't previously encountered members from all of those tribes.

All he could do was ride and pray.

The golden orb in the azure sky arced ever higher and he drew abreast of a narrow gap in the mountains. The tracks went right into it. Stopping, he studied the opening, his suspicions aroused. Only twenty feet wide and winding in serpentine fashion, the gap was a perfect spot for an ambush. The slopes on both sides were covered with snow laden trees. There could be warriors concealed there at that very moment, watching his every move.

He hesitated, torn between common sense and devotion to Winona. To go around the gap would take him hours. Since time was of the essence, he rested the Hawken across his pommel and rode on, a swarm of butterflies fluttering in his stomach. He searched the snow for telltale tracks leading into the trees. To his surprise, there were none.

At the north end of the gap he halted once more. Before him stretched a 'hole', as most trappers and mountaineers would call it, a level valley averaging five miles in width and completely hemmed in by mountains. The trail went straight across the open ground into woods a hundred yards off.

Evidently the war party had no idea anyone was following them. He nodded in satisfaction and moved out, firmly gripping the lead rope to Barking Dog's horse. Lambert's animal diligently forged through the deep snow, cold breath puffing from its nostrils.

Somewhere a bird screeched.

Nate scanned the treeline, not really expecting trouble. Any ambush would have been sprung in the gap—or so he believed until he registered movement in the shadows. A second later a pair of mounted warriors appeared, each armed with a bow and arrow. At once they voiced their war cries and charged.

When Winona saw the two Arapahos drop back from the column she immediately knew their pur-

pose and unconsciously halted, her anxiety over
Nate's welfare eclipsing her prudence.

"Keep going," He Wolf instructed gruffly. He was
on her right and had reined in when she did.

Reluctantly Winona complied, her heart pounding
in her chest. Those men would wait for Nate and
attack him as soon as he showed up. She licked her
lips, debating whether to bolt into the trees in an
effort to escape. Only the knowledge that the Arapahos would easily catch her dissuaded her from making the attempt. That, and her concern for the new
life in her body. More strenuous riding might well
cause her to deliver prematurely, a fate she would
avoid at all costs. The baby hadn't been born yet but
already it was a part of Nate and her, as important to
them as their own lives. This was a fulfillment of
their cherished dreams and an investment in the
future of their bloodline, a full-fledged member
of the family to be carefully nurtured every
moment.

She had noticed that the two warriors staying
behind took only bows and arrows. As near as she
could determine, although the Arapahos were tremendously excited over discovering the guns there
wasn't a one of them who had ever fired a rifle and
knew how to properly load the black powder and a
ball. No doubt they would learn in time. But for now
they couldn't make use of the devastating firepower
the dozens of rifles held against Nate, which relieved
her greatly.

She rode in tense anticipation of hearing gunshots,
paying no attention to her captors until He Wolf
addressed her.

"You are worried about your precious Grizzly
Killer," he commented sarcastically.

"No," Winona lied.

"If he is all you claimed, you would have nothing to
worry about," He Wolf mocked her. "His reputation

is probably highly overrated. After all, he is only a white man.''

''But he has learned to live like us and to like our ways,'' Winona told him. ''He is not like most whites. He does not look down on us.''

''All whites should be rubbed out,'' the Arapaho stated emphatically. ''They are not worth the air they breathe.''

''Why do you hate them so?''

''Because they have no respect for the spirits,'' He Wolf declared. ''Most of them care about nothing except furs and money. They know nothing of the Great Medicine, nothing of the spirit in all things. They come to our land, kill the beaver and the buffalo, and act like they are better than us.'' He snorted. ''I say wipe them all out.''

''The whites will never go away,'' Winona said. ''From what my husband tells me, there are more whites than there are rocks in these mountains, more even than all the blades of grass on the plains.''

He Wolf laughed. ''Do you believe everything your husband tells you?''

''He does not lie.''

''Bah! All whites speak with two tongues. None of them would know the truth if it bit them on the nose.''

They rode in silence for a quarter of a mile.

''I would like to know something,'' He Wolf said. ''You make me curious.''

''About what?''

''You,'' He Wolf said. ''You seem to be a proud Shoshone woman, yet you have taken a white man for a husband. Why? What do you see in him that you could not find in any Shoshone man?''

Winona glanced at the Arapaho, wondering if he was taunting her again. His expression convinced her of his sincerity. He truly wanted to know. ''Men are

men and women are women no matter the color of
their skin and the ways of life they have known. Oh,
there are differences, but deep down we are all
people. The reason I took Grizzly Killer for my life
partner is very simple. He makes my heart sing."

For a while He Wolf didn't speak, then he responded softly. "I envy you, Winona. My heart never
sang for any woman, although my loins have hun-
gered after several. One day, perhaps, I will know the
joy of love."

"Not if you don't release me so I can return to my
husband. He will kill every one of you if you do not."

"Your foolishness grates on my nerves," He Wolf
remarked. "Do not expect any pity from me when
your husband's scalp is hanging in one of our lodges
and you are wailing your grief to the sky."

At that instant, from the direction of the gap, there
arose loud yells. War whoops.

Winona reined up in alarm.

Grinning, He Wolf paused to look back. "Now we
will have the test of your words. And soon I will hold
Grizzly Killer's hair in my hands."

Nate stopped, released the lead, and whipped the
Hawken to his right shoulder. Both warriors already
had shafts nocked to their bow strings and were
drawing those strings back, trying to hold the bows
steady as they attacked, not an easy feat when galloping through heavy snow. He cocked the hammer,
took a bead on the man on the right, held it several
seconds to be sure, then squeezed the trigger.

The Hawken boomed at the selfsame moment the
two warriors let their arrows fly.

Nate saw the man on the right throw his arms into
the air and hurtle off the rear of his onrushing mount.
Just then a pair of streaking shafts cleaved the air
within inches of his head, one on either side. He

lowered the Hawken to the saddle and tugged on th
Kentucky, sliding the rifle from its scabbard.
glance showed him the second warrior coming o
strong, another arrow nocked and ready.

The Indian loosed the shaft.

This time Nate wrenched his horse to the right, ar
it was well he did so for the arrow whizzed throug
the very space his head had occupied. He urged th
animal forward, elevating the Kentucky as he di
electing to meet his foe head-on.

Exhibiting astonishing ability, the warrior had
third shaft nocked and was taking certain aim.

Nate did likewise, struggling to keep the barr
from bobbing up and down with the rhythm of h
horse. He rushed his shot to prevent the warrior fro
getting too close, the Kentucky cracking loudly as h
stroked the trigger.

The ball took the man high in the left shoulder an
flipped him off his steed. He fell onto his right side i
the snow, the bow and arrow flying from his finger
But he was far from finished. Rolling to his feet, h
ignored the bleeding hole in his shoulder and pr
duced a war club that he waved overhead as he ra
forward.

While admiring the man's courage, Nate knew h
couldn't allow the warrior to get within strikin
range. Holding both rifles in the same hand he hel
the reins, he yanked the flintlock from under his be
and cocked the pistol while bearing down on hi
adversary.

The warrior, now twenty yards off, whooped hi
defiance.

Nate waited until only half that distance separate
them before firing. The heavy pistol blasted an
bucked his arm upward.

A hole blossomed in the Indian's forehead. H
seemed to slam into an invisible wall, his charg

checked in midstride. Slowly crumbling, he stumbled a few feet, his mouth moving soundlessly. Then he pitched onto his face with his arms out flung.

Reining up, Nate replaced the flintlock, drew his tomahawk, and slid to the ground. He stepped to the man's side and flipped him over to verify the warrior had been slain. Not that there could be much doubt. One look was all it took to confirm the Indian would never ambush another mountaineer.

Nate glanced at the first warrior he'd slain, who was prone and motionless, then devoted his energies to reloading all of his guns. As he worked, he replayed the attack in his mind. Why had the warriors confronted him head-on when they could easily have shot him from concealment? If they had waited until he was close to the trees, he would have fallen without getting off a shot. Surely they'd realized as much.

So why had they brazenly charged him in the open?

He recollected the stories his Uncle Zeke and Shakespeare had told him about Indian conflicts and recalled his own experiences. Many Indian tribes, he knew, relished warfare; the Blackfeet and the Comanches were just two examples of tribes existing in a perpetual state of war. But it was not the actual bloody fighting they relished so much as it was the chance to gain personal glory.

As a consequence of this urge, most tribes adhered to rules of conduct in warfare, rules designed to garner individual warriors the greatest possible honor. And while the rules varied slightly from tribe to tribe, they all revolved around the counting of *coup*.

The word came from a French term having to do with striking or hitting another. Warriors took great pride in engaging enemies face to face. Those who exposed themselves during a battle ranked higher than those who killed while hidden. Also, those who slew a foe using their hands, a tomahawk, a stick or a lance, were rated above those who killed from a distance using a bow or a gun.

Did that have something to do with the reason the two warriors charged him outright? Sure, they'd used bows, but probably only because they felt they had to in order to stand a fair chance against his rifles.

He gazed at the dead man near his moccasins, trying to identify the warrior's tribe of origin. The style of buckskins and the Indian's braided hair were indicative of the Cheyennes, but not quite the same. Zeke had once told him that the Arapahos and the Cheyennes were the closest of allies, and that Arapaho customs and attire strongly mimicked those of the Cheyennes. Was it possible, then, that he was up against a war party of Arapahos?

At length Nate finished reloading and remounted. He rode back to retrieve Barking Dog's stallion, which had halted the moment he released it, then headed for the forest with the Hawken clutched in his right hand. A brief pause beside the first warrior confirmed the man was dead.

Exercising supreme caution, Nate continued to the treeline. He saw no sign of more Arapahos. The rest must be farther ahead with Winona and the pack animals.

Advancing into the woods, he stopped long enough to loop the stallion's lead around a branch. He wanted his hands free when he caught up with the war party. As an added preparation, he rested the Kentucky across his thighs.

Believing himself as prepared as possible, Nate brought his horse to a steady trot. The tracks were as easy to follow as ever, and half a mile into the trees he spied fresh horse droppings in the snow, so fresh that the droppings had not yet had time to harden and freeze or be covered sinking in the snow. He realized he would overtake them soon. Girding himself, he kept on going, and as he did he thought of a psalm his mother had often read to him when he was a small child. How did it go again? Oh, yeah. He commenced quietly mouthing the words: "The Lord is my shepherd. . . ."

Chapter Eighteen

Unbridled terror overflowed Winona's heart at the sound of the first shot. Her mind filled with horrid images of Nate being transfixed by arrows. She couldn't have moved if her life depended on it, but fortunately none of the Arapahos were moving, either. They were as intently interested in the outcome of the battle as she was, each man sitting with his head cocked to listen better. He Wolf had swung his mount completely around and sat with a stern expression.

A second shot cracked, then there were more whoops, and finally a third gun discharged.

Silence ensued.

All of the Arapahos began talking at once and gesturing excitedly along their backtrail.

A twinge of relief contended with Winona's fear for

her husband's life. Nate had fired three times, indicating the two warriors hadn't taken him by surprise. And knowing how well he could shoot, she surmised there were now two less members of the war party.

He Wolf glanced at her, his countenance somber. "It seems your husband is worthy of his name."

"I told you," Winona gloated.

"He will catch us soon if he has not been wounded," He Wolf remarked, surveying the landscape ahead. "We must prepare."

"What will you do?"

"You know what we must do," He Wolf said. He shifted and barked instructions to the other warriors. Immediately they all moved on, riding swiftly, pulling the reluctant pack animals along, making for a meadow visible through the trees to the northeast.

Winona deliberately stayed alongside He Wolf. "You can let me go. I will persuade my husband to let you leave this territory in peace."

"The Arapahos are not cowards. We do not run from battle."

"All my husband wants is me," Winona said, then quickly corrected herself, "and our horses. You can take the guns back to your people. Think of what so many rifles would mean to your tribe."

"I do not need a woman to instruct me in matters that rightfully concern only warriors," He Wolf said indignantly. He looked at her sternly. "You are wasting your breath if you think you can talk us out of killing your husband. He has counted coup on us. Now we will count coup on him."

"You are a fool."

The Arapaho glared at her. "Am I? Stare into my eyes and tell me that a Shoshone warrior would do any differently than I am doing."

Winona frowned. "I cannot."

"No," He Wolf said. "I knew you could not deny the

truth. No warrior would simply ride off now. We must make a stand or we will not be able to hold our heads up again."

"Then I have a request to make."

"You are in no position to be making requests."

"Give me a weapon so I can fight by my husband's side."

The Arapaho looked at her. "You would do such a thing?"

"A wife must share her husband's fate."

The corner of He Wolf's mouth curled in a lopsided grin and his eyes radiated appreciation. "You are an extraordinary woman, Winona. After I have slain Grizzly Killer, I will give much thought to taking you for my wife."

Bestowing a sweet smile on him, Winona said, "I would rather be thrown off a cliff or fed to wolves."

A hearty laugh burst from He Wolf. "I would say this Grizzly Killer has met his match in you. Are all Shoshone women so filled with spirit?"

"I cannot speak for all women. I am as I am."

The war party came to the edge of the snow covered meadow, which encompassed a tract of some four acres. They headed toward the center, several warriors bringing up the rear with their eyes on the forest.

Barely able to contain her anxiety, Winona tried one last appeal. "Would you ride on as fast as you can and forget about fighting my husband if I agree to become your wife?"

He Wolf's astonishment showed as he gazed at her. "You love him that much?"

"Yes."

"No wonder he will stop at nothing to get you back," He Wolf said. "But you can save your words. We will not tuck our tails between our legs and slink away like scared dogs. We will meet him here and be done with it."

Winona fell silent. She had used every argument she could think of, to no avail. The battle was inevitable. Now she must think of a means to help Nate without getting herself killed, if possible. If not, then she would die as a Shoshone woman should die, giving her life so her husband might live.

The war party reached the middle of the meadow and halted. After a brief discussion the five Arapahos aligned themselves in a row, positioning themselves about ten yards apart, their mounts facing the forest where Nate would soon appear. He Wolf occupied the center post, directly in front of Winona and the pack animals.

She stared at the warrior's back, her mind in turmoil. Perhaps, if she darted in front of the Arapahos when Nate appeared, it would so distract them that Nate would be able to shoot a couple of them before they could charge. Even so, there would be enough left to easily overpower him.

None of the Arapahos spoke, none displayed the slightest fear. They sat proudly, their spines rigid, ready to acquit themselves honorably. They each held a bow, an arrow nocked to the string.

Winona had never been so nervous. She scanned the treeline, eager to see Nate but dreading what would ensue. If anything happened to him, if he was killed, she wouldn't want to go on. In the time they had been together, sharing every aspect of their lives and an intimacy that touched the depths of her inner spirit, she had grown to care for him with an affection that eclipsed all else. It was an affection that surprised her in its intensity and depth of passion. She had never known love could be so profound, so exalting.

As a small girl playing in the Shoshone village she had often imagined what marriage would be like and pictured in her mind the man most likely to win her heart. Always had that fantasy figure been a handsome Shoshone warrior, a man who had counted more coup than all the rest of the tribe combined. Had anyone told her she would one day marry a white man, she would have laughed at their insanity.

Over the years many warriors had shown an interest in her. Quite a few had approached her father about taking her into their lodge, offering horses and robes and weapons, enough to make her father wealthy. Yet her wise father had never accepted any offer without first consulting her, and she'd always declined. Her mother had urged her to accept before she acquired a reputation as too hard to get, rightfully pointing out that some of her suitors were prominent men in the Shoshone nation and that any woman in her right mind would leap at the chance to marry them.

But Winona had remained aloof. Even she had been hard pressed to explain her behavior. She found many of the men attractive, but they failed to stir her heart. Why, she didn't know, until she saw Nathaniel King for the first time. It was as if a tiny barb had punctured her heart and let out all the love stored inside for years.

Somehow, in a mysterious manner she could not comprehend nor resist, she knew from the start that Nate would be the man she married. The knowledge came as automatically as the certainty that the sun would rise each morning and dark clouds from the west brought heavy rain.

Now she fidgeted and strained her eyes to pierce the shadows under the trees.

The time seemed to drag by.

Nothing moved in the woods.

Off to the east a lone hawk soared, seeking prey.

She began to wonder if Nate had been wounded by the other two warriors. Why else was he taking so long? Then she heard a sound that made her heart leap into her throat and she spun her horse around in amazement.

Nate was pushing ahead recklessly, anxious to catch the Arapahos, when he realized his mistake and abruptly reined up. It wouldn't do to blunder in among the war party like a greenhorn. As Shakespeare had often admonished him, those who survived the longest in the savage wilderness were those who used their heads in a crisis. Craftiness counted more in the issue of life and death than mere brawn. So to rescue Winona and come out alive he must become as crafty as an old fox.

He moved out again, only slower this time, peering intently at the forest before him. From the gait indicated by the tracks, he realized the war party had picked up the pace. He tried to outthink them, to anticipate their next move. What would he do if he was in their place? Set up another ambush, only this time do it right? Or find a spot to make a stand and finish the affray for good?

What was that?

Nate stopped again at spying a stretch of white ahead. He glimpsed movement. Holding a rifle in each hand, he slid to the ground and crouched behind a nearby tree. The distance was too great for him to distinguish details, but there appeared to be a number of riders in a field or a meadow beyond the trees. It took no genius to figure out who they were.

He bent at the waist and advanced until he could see clearly. At the sight of Winona he almost cried out her name in relief. He let his gaze linger on her for a minute before paying any attention to the members of the war party. There were five warriors all told, each one carrying bows.

A frown creased his mouth. Five to one were pathetic odds, all the more so since he couldn't hope to shoot all the Arapahos before one of them nailed him. Two, yes. Maybe three. Four if he was incredibly lucky. But never five.

He tried to come up with a plan, some way of defeating the warriors without endangering himself, but there simply wasn't a means of doing so. Oh, he could hide at the edge of the trees and shoot the warriors from concealment, in which case he stood a fair chance of slaying all five. But even then, they would see the smoke from his rifles and know exactly where to send their shafts. He discarded the idea, not because the gunsmoke would give him away, but because he wouldn't stoop so low as to shoot men from ambush. Only a coward would perform such a dastardly deed.

He returned to his horse, pondering furiously. Since he couldn't honorably shoot them from the relative safety of the forest, and since a frontal attack would leave him riddled with arrows, he came up with another way to go about tackling them. Swinging into the saddle, he placed the Kentucky in his lap and rode to the right. Staying far enough back from the meadow that the Indians couldn't possibly see him, he made a wide loop around them.

His plan was simple. He'd come up on the warriors from the rear. By the time they awoke to his presence, he might kill two or three. Then it would be a matter of overcoming the remainder with his knife and tomahawk.

He considered that he might well die but felt no fear. If Winona lived, the sacrifice was worth it. She had brought him the greatest happiness any man could ever know; his gratitude was boundless, his very existence in the palms of her hands. Now he could demonstrate the depth of his love, could repay her for her kindness and compassion. He regretted, though, that he might not live to see his son or daughter grow to adulthood. The notion of being a father greatly appealed to him.

His horse plodded along wearily, the thud of its hooves muffled by the snow. He checked his knife and tomahawk, making sure both weren't wedged too tightly under his belt. Then he rechecked the flint-lock, verifying the pistol was loaded.

By the time he arrived on the north side of the meadow he was beginning to feel edgy. He licked his lips and halted at the treeline. Neither the Arapahos nor Winona had moved.

Nate raised the Hawken, about to charge, then paused. If he shot those warriors in the back, it would be the same as shooting them from ambush. He might as well paint a yellow stripe down his back. No man worthy of his name would do such a thing.

He grinned at his foolishness, lowered the rifle, and rode from the forest, going slowly, amazed none of the Arapahos had awakened to his presence yet. Not even Winona, whose intuition was superb, had realized he was there. When only ten feet from the pack animals, he stopped, took a deep breath, and asked in a loud, clear voice: "Are you looking for someone?"

Chapter Nineteen

The startled expressions on the Arapahos as they wheeled their mounts struck Nate as so comical that he almost laughed. He had time for just a quick glance at Winona, whose face lit up with affection and hope, and then he concentrated on his five adversaries, all of whom were regarding him in commingled disbelief and fascination.

"You are Grizzly Killer," stated the warrior in the middle of the line, speaking in perfect Shoshone. "We have heard much about you."

"I have come for my wife and our horses," Nate said. "I have no wish to fight you unless you force it on me."

The warrior translated for the benefit of his companions. None of the others spoke. They were staring at Nate, at his guns.

Winona moved her horse over next to her husband's. The Arapahos made no move to interfere. She leaned toward him and said softly, "My heart is happy at seeing you again."

"As is mine," Nate replied.

She pointed at the crates. "They contain dozens of rifles and ammunition. Kennedy and the trappers planned to trade them to Two Owls for beaver furs."

Nate felt a sinking sensation in the pit of his stomach. Now there was no way he could simply ride off with Winona and let the matter drop. Those guns could be used to kill mountaineers. At the very least they would make the Arapahos the most powerful nation west of the Mississippi River, enabling them to conquer all the other tribes.

"I am He Wolf," the warrior who knew the Shoshone tongue declared. "We have heard that you are very brave."

"A man does what he must."

"True. And we must kill you," He Wolf said matter-of-factly. He extended his bow and smiled. "I see you have three guns. You might be able to shoot three of us before we slay you, but we will slay you in the end."

Nate didn't doubt it. He wondered where his own flintlocks were, the pair Newton and Lambert had taken from the cabin. Perhaps they were packed with the supplies or the rifles. If he had five guns, he just might prevail. But he didn't, and all the wishing in the world wouldn't help him one bit.

"It would be too easy for us to kill you with arrows," He Wolf was saying. "There is no honor in that, no challenge. I propose to fight you man on man, one at a time, so that the warrior who finally takes your hair can claim the highest coup. What do you say, Grizzly Killer?"

"None of you will use your bows and I'm not supposed to use my guns?"

"Those are the terms."

"I mean no insult, but how do I know I can trust you?" Nate responded.

He Wolf addressed his fellows and all five of them tossed their bows to the ground. The warrior pointed at the Hawken with one hand while drawing a knife with the other. "What about you, Grizzly Killer? Are you truly as brave as they say, or are the words told about you around campfires nothing but lies?"

For an answer Nate gave his rifles to Winona. She frowned as she took them. "If anything happens to me; ride off," he advised.

"If anything happens to you, I do not care if I live or die."

Nate slid the flintlock from under his belt and motioned for her to take the pistol. "You owe it to our unborn child to live. Promise me you will try if I die."

With evident reluctance Winona answered, "I will do as you want, husband. But the rest of my days will be spent in misery." She placed the flintlock in her lap, her shoulders slumping.

Suppressing an urge to take her into his arms, Nate drew his tomahawk and rode a dozen feet to the left. He eyed the Arapahos and hefted the weapon. "I am ready when you are, He Wolf. Prove to me that Arapaho warriors deserve to be called men."

"Even the Blackfeet fear us," He Wolf bragged, and spoke to his fellow tribesmen in his own tongue.

Suddenly the warrior on the far left of the line, the youngest of the bunch, vented a piercing whoop and charged, waving a war club overhead.

Nate wasn't about to sit there and let them bring the fight to him. To win he must take the offensive, must keep them off their guard. Consequently he goaded his horse into motion, galloping to meet his first adversary head-on, the tomahawk firmly clasped in his right hand. He bent low over the saddle, his gaze glued to the oncoming warrior's club.

The young Arapaho was too eager for his own good. He leaned out to the side, trying to increase his reach but exposing his torso in the process.

Hoping that Lambert's horse was well trained, Nate waited until he was only eight feet from the warrior before wrenching on the reins and cutting the animal sharply to the right. Almost simultaneously he reined up, stopping on the head of a pin, as it were. Unable to compensate, the young Arapaho lunged outward even further and swung his club. Nate knew the swing would miss before the warrior executed it. He whipped his body to the right, turning almost completely around in the saddle, using a backhand strike, and sank the gleaming edge of his tomahawk into the hapless Arapaho's neck as the man went racing past. The edge bit deep, severing veins and arteries, causing blood to spray like a fountain.

Swaying wildly, the warrior rode another ten yards before he pitched from his mount and landed face down in the snow. He tried to rise, his arms quivering, but collapsed in shock with his lifeblood spurting over the white blanket embracing his form.

Nate faced the rest of the band. They were staring grimly at their fallen companion. Spurned into action, the next warrior on the left shrieked and galloped to the attack, a tomahawk in his right hand, his features contorted in rage. Nate rode forward, keeping his own dripping tomahawk close to his side. This next warrior was older, more battle seasoned, and would be harder to dispatch. He girded his body for his next tactic, and when the two horses were almost abreast he swung to the off side, clinging to his animal with just his left leg and left arm.

The warrior cleaved the air as he went past, narrowly missing the exposed leg.

Drawing back on the reins as he straightened, Nate

turned his horse around and closed. The Arapaho was turning his stallion, or trying to, because his animal shied at the sight of Nate's horse bearing rapidly down. Struggling to get the stallion to obey, the warrior lifted his tomahawk in a defensive gesture.

Nate aimed a terrific swipe at the Arapaho's head, knowing full well the man would deflect it. Their weapons clashed and his slid off to the right. Almost in the same motion he reversed direction, lancing his tomahawk into the warrior's side a few inches below the ribs.

The Arapaho stiffened and gasped, then goaded the stallion to the right, losing all interest in the conflict. He clutched at the wound, his fingers becoming slick with blood.

Nate didn't bother to go after him. Instead he urged his horse straight toward He Wolf, his mouth set in a grim line. He couldn't afford to slack off a bit; he must keep attacking until he triumphed or died.

He Wolf was staring at the injured warrior. His gaze shifted to Nate and he smiled enigmatically. Then he lifted his knife and brought his own horse up to top speed, snow showering in all directions from its driving legs.

Nate had about used up his bag of tricks. If he was any judge of character, then He Wolf was a veteran of many encounters who wouldn't be fooled by clever horsemanship. He must do something totally unexpected, something that would take He Wolf completely unawares. Only one idea occurred to him and he mentally balked at trying it. Such madness could well result in his own death.

But what choice did he have?

He made as if to pass He Wolf on the right, waving his tomahawk all the while to convince the warrior he fully intended to use it. Then, when their horses were almost a yard apart, he turned his animal to the left, into Two Wolf's path, deliberately plowing his horse into the Arapaho's.

The animals collided with shattering impact. Nate had angled his horse just right, catching the warrior's mount on the point of its left shoulder. He Wolf's animal went down, but the warrior sprang clear before he could be pinned underneath.

Still astride his horse, Nate launched himself into the air, diving onto He Wolf as the man straightened and they both went down in a swirl of limbs. They separated and rose to their feet with their weapons at the ready.

There was a fierce gleam in He Wolf's eyes. "You are all they say you are," he said, and speared his knife at Grizzly Killer's throat.

Nate back-pedaled, his movements slightly restricted by the snow. The blade nicked his right wrist, drawing blood. He slashed with the tomahawk but He Wolf nimbly evaded the blow.

The Arapaho unleashed a flurry of stabbing and cutting strokes, pressing relentlessly, seemingly determined to end their fight quickly.

It took every vestige of energy Nate possessed to save himself from being ripped open. He blocked, countered, and thrust, his limbs a blur, sweat caking his skin, but he could do little better than hold his own. The sustained combat began to take its toll. On top of all he had previously been through, the injuries sustained, the long pursuit, and the series of fights, this final battle was proving almost too much for his battered, aching body to endure.

He was weakening fast, and from the smug smirk that creased He Wolf's lips, he suspected the warrior guessed it. In desperation he summoned his remaining strength and flailed away, seeking to batter the knife from the Arapaho's grip. But He Wolf danced rearward, staying just out of range.

Nate tripped. One moment he was swinging the

tomahawk for all he was worth, the next his left moccasin gave way on the slick snow and he fell to his knee.

Instantly He Wolf pounced, sweeping his knife down at the white man's upturned face.

Frantically Nate brought the tomahawk up and managed to deflect the blade. In a burst of inspiration he perceived that he was employing the wrong strategy. Instead of concentrating on warding off the knife, he should be trying to get the man *wielding* the knife. So as the Arapaho elevated the blade for yet another stab, Nate sank the tomahawk into the man's left leg.

He Wolf arched his spine and involuntarily cried out, then staggered backwards.

Nate yanked the tomahawk out and rose. He had the upper hand and wasn't about to relinquish it. His arm whipping right and left, he drove the warrior farther and farther backwards. So engrossed was he in trying to defeat He Wolf that he failed to register the drumming sound of hooves until the horse making the noise was almost upon him. Then he glanced around in alarm to find the warrior he had cut below the ribs bearing down on him.

He Wolf shouted something in Arapaho.

Throwing himself to the right, Nate escaped being crushed beneath the animal's powerful legs. He landed on his side, then swept erect, his left hand closing around his knife. If they were going to come at him two at a time in violation of their agreement, then he would face them with every weapon at his disposal.

The mounted warrior checked his charge and turned his horse. His hand was pressed over his wound. Blood coated his skin all the way down to his toes.

Waving his arms, He Wolf yelled at the warrior, apparently trying to stop the man from attacking, but his words were wasted.

Leaning to the right, then the left, barely able to grip the reins, the wounded Arapaho goaded his horse forward once again.

Nate tensed and crouched, prepared to leap either way to evade those pounding hooves. To his astonishment, He Wolf suddenly stepped between the onrushing warrior and himself and faced the animal.

The other Arapahos were shouting and converging at a gallop.

Confused, Nate saw He Wolf raise an arm in an effort to signal the young brave to stop. But the gesture was futile. The galloping horse bore down on He Wolf, who attempted to dodge to the left; his injured thigh caused him to stumble instead, and a heartbeat later the horse slammed into He Wolf and flattened him under its driving hooves. Nate heard a crackling and a crunching sound and blood spurted from He Wolf's mouth.

"Nate! Behind you!" Winona cried.

He whirled, and there were the two remaining warriors bearing down on him, one with a tomahawk, another with a war club. There was fury in their eyes and neither gave any indication of stopping.

A rifle boomed. The Arapaho holding the tomahawk stiffened and fell.

Nate knew Winona had fired. He drew back his knife arm, and when the last warrior came close enough he hurled the weapon with all the strength left in his body. He didn't expect to score, merely to force the warrior to turn aside, but to his astonishment the blade sped true and buried itself to the hilt in the Arapaho's chest. The warrior let go of his reins, clutched at the hilt, and toppled soundlessly.

Inhaling raggedly, Nate surveyed the battlefield.

The badly wounded warrior had stopped fifteen feet away. He sagged, his eyelids fluttering, then vented a groan and fell. After twitching for a moment, he was still.

None of the other Arapahos were moving.

Suddenly he heard footsteps behind him and spun, thinking one of the warriors had somehow revived and was attacking him. Instead, Winona was a yard away, the smoking Hawken in her right hand. She threw herself into his arms and they embraced, her robe parting as they pressed together, enabling him to feel her heart beating wildly. "Husband," she said tenderly. "Husband."

Nate simply held her, his face nestled in her flowing hair, and fought to prevent a flood of tears from overflowing his eyes. A lump formed in his throat. He tried to speak but couldn't. She was safe and in his arms and nothing else mattered.

For the longest time they stood there, immobile, glued to one another, as one in the midst of the vast wilderness, their bodies bathed in the golden sunshine.

Epilogue

Nate and Winona rode side by side on their own horses, winding down into their valley, their cabin beckoning to the east. He held the lead to the pack animals in his left hand. Cradled in his right arm was the Hawken.

Winona held a Kentucky rifle in her arms. She frequently glanced at her mate when he wasn't looking and grinned. "What will you do with all the guns?" she asked at one point.

"I don't rightly know," Nate replied thoughtfully. "We'll bury the crates near the cabin for the time being. They should keep for a while. I'll ask Shakespeare's advice the next time we see him."

"Just so we get rid of them. They are bad medicine."

They came to a clear stretch and a doe bounded from their path.

"Our baby is well despite all we have been through," Winona commented. "In three moons we will have a new addition to our family."

"I can hardly wait."

Winona gazed toward the cabin and glimpsed the horse pen. The sight made her chuckle.

"What's so funny?" Nate asked.

"I was thinking of the four hundred and twenty-two beaver pelts you have buried under the ground in the pen."

"What about them?" Nate inquired. With all that had been going on, he'd forgotten about the furs he'd collected during the last trapping season. As did most trappers, he'd cached his catch until the next rendezvous at which time he would pack them to the annual get-together and sell them for a hefty profit.

"Isaac Kennedy would have given anything to know about them."

"Kennedy was a fool. He never should have ventured out here. Some people have no business being in the wild," Nate said. After a bit he added, "I guess that old saying is true."

"What saying?"

"A man should always know his limitations."

ATTENTION PREFERRED CUSTOMERS!

SPECIAL TOLL-FREE NUMBER
1-800-481-9191

*Call Monday through Friday
12 noon to 10 p.m.
Eastern Time*
*Get a free catalogue;
Order books using your Visa,
MasterCard, or Discover;*
Join the book club!

Leisure
Books

Love
Spell